Lucia

The Mistress of Monteforte

by *Barbara Guarino Kruk*

LA FAMIGLIA

THE HOUSE OF RIZZO

MARIA (Salvatore)RIZZO- SUCRETTI

No children

LUCIA CIOFFI and MATEO RIZZO

The only living children from the union of Lucia and Mateo Rizzo

Luigi Rizzo – *Clergy (no children)*

Helena (Giuseppe) Puglise

Children of Helena and Giuseppe Jerome- no children

Giuseppe, deceased no children

Filomenia, deceased no children

Maria (Michael) CORDELLA

Michael

Joseph

Rosetta

Rafaela (Donato) BANFI

Antonio (1686)

Andrea (1689)

Genaro (1691)

Francisco (1693)

Antoinetta (1696)

Lucia (June 13, 1698)

Table of Contents

BOOK ONE

PADRINO A TRANSFORMATION

Preface

This book has been a labor of love for me. I have laughed and cried, but throughout it all, I found joy in the physical writing and mental telling of the story. I discovered the ability to put in print my most personal thoughts and desires. The characters depicted are purely fictional, but in some rudimentary way, they represent characters from my own family. My beloved paternal grandmother was Lucia Cioffi who married Mateo.

The locations described throughout the book are from my own travels across Europe. While the destinations are real, the persons described are historical figures whom I have used out of their own time in history.

I would like to thank so many people who have painfully sat through hundreds of pages of this manuscript and have given me hope, support, and love. I would like to thank my mother, Josephine, for listening to me dribble on and on about the story, then offer sound criticism for improvement. To my niece, Suzanne Olszewski, for squeezing me into her very busy life, and who has been there for me from word one. To my dear husband Connie for missing me most evenings while I worked. To my friends, Mike and Gae LaSalle, whose expertise with the Italian language was a great help; to Doug Carabe and Ed Graziano; Mickey Pace and Annalisa Poio and a special thank you to my daughters Kelly and Aya Kruk, who helped with editing. Last, but never least, to my son Matthew Kruk for spending hours trying to find the perfect graphic for my cover. I love you all.

Yet, most of all, I would like to thank my beautiful grandmother Lucia who was the inspiration for this novel. She was not only physically beautiful but she exuded an inner beauty and strength as well.

As of this printing, the adventures continue for our intrepid young heiress in the second book in this series entitled **The Ruby Heiress**. In the last and final book in the Lucia series will be **Lucia and the Gypsy's Prophecy**.

Read my non-fiction novel entitled **Connie's Story, a Triumph of Love.**

Write me at MistressLucia@yahoo.com, I would love to hear your comments and suggestions.

PROLOGUE

In a land, where the sun meets the sea, and the inhabitants live in the shadow of the fire mountain, comes the tale of a redheaded enchantress who will one day become the heir of a great empire. Born of a curse, her legendary beauty bares the stain of the blood on her hands. This is an epic tale of a young woman who learns she cannot escape her destiny. You will embark on a journey filled with adventures so vast; forbidden love; lust and intrigue. A priceless cache of ancient manuscripts so important and far reaching their discovery could topple the Catholic Church. Come; follow, as we set forth on an odyssey wrought with mysterious places, and fascinating characters, whose lives are woven into a tapestry of remarkable physical and spiritual beauty.

THE EARLY YEARS

THE BLUSH OF LUCIA

*M*ateo Rizzo was well educated and came from an influential family who owned an ancient domain, whose wealth was not only measured in gold, jewels and the trappings of aristocracy, but in power. The House of Rizzo was one of the most influential families of the Kingdom of Naples. They were decedents of Kings and Doges, with all the history and wealth that came with the title. Spoiled by overbearing parents, Mateo, the heir apparent of the Rizzo fortune, was used to getting his way. One day, while he was strolling in the village, he spotted a redheaded maiden in the marketplace, smitten by her beauty; he made some inquiries and learned of her parentage. Lucia, *sua bellezza era mozzafiato*, with her blazing red hair, alabaster skin, and azure blue eyes, was a prize Mateo had to possess. Luckily, for him, his mother knew Lucia's family, and soon, they married. Mateo was six years older than the fair young Lucia, but that did not matter. Her parents, poor and aging, were delighted that their beauty should find a suitable husband. Of course, the fact that Mateo's family contributed a rather handsome sum to their meager purse certainly sweetened the deal.

Against the wishes of his parents, who had signed a marriage contract upon Mateo's birth for the daughter of the House of Brunellchi of Umbria, a union that would have fortified their holdings in northern Italy, but he would have no part of her. Mateo rejected the homely heiress for the supple young peasant girl. The dissolution of the contract cost the family a king's ransom.

Lucia, then only fourteen years old, was swept off her feet by the mere presence of Mateo Rizzo. He was twenty, educated, had traveled extensively, charming, and debonair. Tall and muscular with an aristocratic nose and strong angular jaw, Mateo looked like a Roman god. His eyes were the color of seasoned olives with an intensity to match their dark hue. Composed and wealthy, everyone assured Lucia that this marriage was a match made in Heaven, and for the first seven years, she would have to agree.

Memories of a gentle lover, a kind, and generous husband, who in the beginning had eyes only for his "*belles dai capelli rossi*" and how he introduced her to the joys of intimacy with love. His joy when she bore his first child, an heir, his son Jerome. Lucia loved Mateo more than life itself. Slowly, patiently, he had molded her into a woman. Mateo taught his young bride how to please him. He instructed her in the art of satisfying a man. He would say, "That mouth of yours is like a serpent's tongue. When you lick me my flesh turns to liquid." Lucia wanted to make her husband happy, but Mateo also wanted her to find her own satisfaction in their lovemaking. He showed her how to pleasure herself, and he would watch as she stroked herself, while he suckled her hard nipples. They enjoyed sex and learned the intimacy of each other's bodies. All Mateo would have to do was look at Lucia a certain way and she could be wet at the thought of his touch.

Her heart ached at the thought of those magical days. Then she remembered very well the hatred of his barren sister Maria Sucretti and the envy of her brother-in-law Salvatore, when one after another she bore more children. Maria hated her, and shortly after the death of both her parents, she assumed management of Monteforte. With the death of his parents, Mateo lost all interest in his legacy, as well as in his life. Lovemaking became sexual release; intimate excitement and love were gone.

His parents, who died of the plague, within weeks of each other, while traveling in France, triggered an emotional breakdown that threw Mateo into a free fall of grief. Slotted to become the master of his ancestral estate and ensuing empire was too much for the twenty-eight year old to face. He began to fight daily with his sister Maria Sucretti and her husband Salvatore.

Salvatore, the Caporegime of the local Camorra, encouraged Mateo's behavior in the hopes of destroying his brother-in-law and capturing the Rizzo family fortune. He would bring him to brothels and gambling houses to squander his inheritance and ruin his marriage.

Maria pleaded with Mateo to get control of his life. He was in a perpetual state of drunken stupor. Maria knew that Mateo would meet with a tragic end if he did not come to his senses. She loved her brother but knew that he was on the path of self-destruction. Her parents had always dreamed that their beloved son Mateo would continue the fortune they had inherited through the House of Rizzo. The responsibility of running Monteforte was overwhelming for Mateo. One night, after years of living under this sibling tension, he had an ugly battle with his sister, which prompted him to gather his family and leave Monteforte vowing never to return. Armed only with the skill of breeding and training horses, Mateo and Lucia, and their children, relocated to Naples.

At first, Lucia was happy to be out from under the possessive and oppressive eye of Maria Sucretti who hated Lucia and made continuous trouble between her and Mateo. The thought of Mateo and her living on their own seemed encouraging and Lucia prayed that their marriage would improve once they were out on their own away from Monteforte. Maybe they could rekindle the love they once shared, and start life anew.

Life with Mateo Rizzo was very difficult for Lucia he was always drunk and vicious to the children, whom he often beat with his riding crop. Her dreams of renewing their once solid marriage, destroyed. The tavern that Mateo now owned was on the main rialto from the docks of the Bay of Naples. The docks were home to colorful and seasoned inhabitants. Mateo, an ardent gambler, had actually won title to this establishment in a card game. He, being a horse trainer, knew nothing of operating such a business, but, given his intelligence, he soon became a successful proprietor. His downfall was the availability of liquor and whores. Soon he became his own best customer for both the drink and the women. He began to spend less and less time tending to his financial concerns and more time gambling, drinking, and whoring. Almost at the point of losing his business, he was deeply in debt to his suppliers, and only able to stay afloat from his occasional winnings at the gambling tables.

Lucia, who lived with the children above the tavern, would watch and listen, learning who to trust and who to be wary. The suppliers all knew her, and she had a keen mind and eagerness to become acquainted with the business. She could not let Mateo know what she was up to because he would have made sure she never set foot in the tavern again. Lucia was a magnet just by her mere appearance, men were mesmerized by her stunning beauty, and attracted by her flaming red tresses. Mateo beat more than one man almost to death for just looking a little too long at his wife. He was jealous of any man having lustful desires on his wife. She was his property alone. Once, she attempted to flee with the children, but could not find refuge with her family or friends, for they all feared Mateo, who had a vicious and violent temper. He had bitten off the ear of one of his gambling companions because he thought that he had cheated him at cards. Life was almost unbearable after her attempted escape, for Mateo watched her every move, and would not let her visit anyone or have anyone come to the house. Lucia and her children were in exile, and Mateo became even more abusive toward her and the children.

The taverns of this international seaside city were strewn with fishermen, sailors, and prostitutes. The sea was the heart and soul of Naples, with its rich harvest, but those who made their living from its bounty were rugged and wild. Neapolitans have always been notorious for being rebellious and unique. The history of Naples is a testament to its people. Once, the most powerful of all Italian ports, Naples flourished as a center for trade, shipbuilding, and fishing.

Naples, which is the capital of the Region of Campania, is a rich tapestry of many cultures, which integrated into its own special blend by those who migrated to its shores. Naples is divided into a Mezzagiorna, which is a north and south. Founded by the Greeks in the eighth century and at various times ruled by Spain, Austria, and the Bourbons, it was this savory mix of different peoples who have stamped this region with its charismatic tongue and tastes. Neapolitans have their own language, and while the city is rich in history and architecture, it is also plagued by pervasive and shocking poverty and filth. Naples has always been a Mecca for foreigners, and those wishing to exploit her riches. It was into this environment that Lucia, *una bellezza dai capelli rossi*, a beautiful young widow, was thrust.

Lucia's shrewdness for business, until Mateo's death, had been a well-kept secret. Lucia had been learning and watching the operation of the business, from both her husband and his workers. She would never express interest or knowledge, because she knew only too well, that he would immediately banish her from any involvement. Lucia, after Mateo's death, raised her children in that tavern, and ran the most successful and managed bar in all of Napoli.

xiv

A TURNING POINT FOR LUCIA

Mateo Rizzo met his death from the knife of a fellow gambler. He was only forty- two years old when he died. By all accounts, the custom at that time was that she would lose her home and her children. If they could not be placed with relatives they would surely be taken to the orphanage.

Lucia would never forget the day she came to know of her husband's death. The memory of it haunted her until the day she too died.

She had been dreading Mateo's return from the gambling house, where he lately spent most of his time and money. He had been gone all day, and now given the lateness of the hour, she retired to bed, with the tension of his anticipated drunken return. Lucia lay in the bed waiting for his return, which was always fearful, for when Mateo had lost at cards, and then drowned his anger in alcohol; the results were disastrous for her and the children. She prayed that he would not come home, and just sleep off his drunken stupor at one of the local bordellos.

She dozed lightly, her body tense, waiting for him to slam through the door, yelling and cursing and ready for a fight. Nothing happened. Lucia realized that he was not coming home and finally fell into a light sleep. By dawn she heard a loud bang at the door, in that split

xv

second she sensed that something terrible had happened. Quickly, she threw on her dressing robe, smooth down her unruly locks, and ran to the door. Opening the door just a crack to see who would be calling at this early hour. Standing in front of her was two poliziotto. "Signora Rizzo?" Lucia nodded, opening the door wider, but suddenly she could not find her voice. "We regret to tell you that your husband, Mateo Rizzo, is dead. He was killed at one of the gambling houses last night. Are you alright?" Lucia felt the floor moving from under her feet, and she was having trouble breathing. She knew they were speaking to her, but the noise in her head, prevented her from hearing what they were saying. Lucia could not see, her vision was blackened by something, but she could not figure out what was happening to her. After what seemed like a long time, she came back to herself and found that she was sitting on the settee in her parlor with a cold, wet rag on her forehead. Opening her eyes, she stared back into a dozen pairs of frightened eyes. The two polizitto were still there, as were her children. Her daughter Anna was wiping her brow and offering her a glass of some amber colored liquid, which she placed under Lucia's nose. She could smell the pungent odor of the alcohol and took a sip. Sitting up straight, Lucia brought herself under control, took the proffered glass, and threw back her head to finish off its contents. "Where is my husband now?" she asked as steadily as she could manage. "Lui e`al Obitorio. Siamo spiacenti signora Rizzo. Ce` nulla di piu` che possiamo fare?" Lucia shook her mane of wild red hair, wiped her nose on her sleeve, and thanked them for their kindness. She would need to go to the city morgue to identify her husband's body.

The day was hot and humid and the hair that framed her beautiful face was stuck to her forehead and cheeks. The sweat traversed the valley between her ample breasts and trickled down her belly. It was a long way to get to the morgue, which was located on the other side of the Bay of Naples. Her oldest son Jerome, who insisted that he must go with his mother, accompanied Lucia. This was an unsafe part of the city, although, it probably was safer than the docks where Lucia maintained her tavern, but at least there, she was in her element and knew most everyone. Finally, the carriage, which they had hired for the long ride, arrived and Jerome stepped down and extended a hand to his mother. Jerome was a tall handsome young man in his early twenties with his mother's coloring and his father's eyes. The combination was very attractive. He told the driver to wait and handed him a few coins to insure that he would wait for the rest of the fare.

There was no mistaking the purpose of this building; it reeked of death. The fetid smell of death permeated through the brick façade, even the area surrounding was devoid of life. The only sign of any human activity was the undertaker's covered wagon waiting to load a body for preparation. They steadied themselves for what was to come, made the sign of the cross, to protect themselves from any evil spirits, and entered the building. A decrepit looking man, who did not look any better than the corpses he was in charge of, asked them the nature of their visit. Lucia almost spat out the answer, thinking to herself, why in the Holy Virgin's name, would I be in this hellish place if I did not have business to be here. She caught herself and told him that she had come to identify her husband's body. He sat at a battered old wooden desk adorned with nothing but a glass bottle of ink, a quill that was worn down, a candle and tattered leather bound journal. The book was open, and there were scratched names on the page with dates after the entries. "What is the name Signora?" At that moment Jerome, seeing the color drain from his mother's face answered *"Mateo Rizzo"*. A weathered finger found the entry for Mateo Rizzo, taking up the quill he asked Lucia for her name and relationship. He then scratched the information on the line beside Mateo's name. "Lucia Rizzo, wife." The wizened attendant, clad in a worn leather apron, led them to the back of the building where the bodies were stored.

The smell of death, with its putrid odor of decay and feces, was so overwhelming that both Lucia and Jerome were gagging. The bile had reached the back of Lucia's throat, when the sheet covering Mateo was lifted. The once handsome face was ashen grey, the eyes, always sharp and ready for a fight, were but black orbs peering from under slack lids. His mouth was agape and his tongue swollen within. The fatal wound, administered by an irate gambling companion, had caused Mateo to bleed to death. Lucia, her hands trembling, could not resist reaching out her hand to stroke his thick curly black hair. It felt sticky and greasy but familiar. This simple touch brought back memories of their early life together, before his parents had died, when life for them was good. Lucia remembered with longing, running her fingers through his hair while he caressed her womanhood. He was a great teacher, and she an ardent student. There was a discrete cough of annoyance from the morgue attendant, who came from behind to replace the sheet. Jerome put his arm around his mother to steady her, and dipped his head to place a tender kiss on her tear-streaked face. He too did not mask his sadness for the loss of his father. Now, anxious to remove themselves from this horrid place, they followed at the heels of the old man back to the outer chamber.

The man in charge asked if that was Mateo Rizzo and they nodded assent. They signed some papers and arrangements ordered to bring Mateo home to Monteforte, the place of his birth. It was only fitting that Mateo should be entombed with his parents, they loved him so much, it was his rightful place. He should have lived to be the Master of Monteforte, but with the death of his parents, his spirit died along with them. Word was sent to Maria Sucretti, his sister, current Mistress of Monteforte that Mateo's body was being transported to Monteforte, and that Lucia and his children would be accompanying his remains. All was in order.

The day Mateo died was a bittersweet day for Lucia and her children. She embarked on her new life, with the love and support of her children. It would be hard, but she had learned many things. Lucia prayed that she would have the strength and courage to make a better life for herself and her family. She had to make it work.

The Neapolitan waterfront was not a place for a meek woman, but Lucia soon became equal to any man, in mind and business acumen. Lucia had surrounded herself with loyal and trustworthy workers. The one she depended upon more than anyone was Augusto, a huge brute of a man, actually he was still in his teens, who was dim witted, but powerfully built and truly dedicated to Lucia and her children.

Augusto lived in the cellar of the tavern. His prostitute mother, who knew he was mentally slow, had abandoned him at birth. There would be no place in her life for a child with a *deformita`*. His mother's handler would kill the child, surely thinking it would be a bad omen for his business. She placed the infant on the steps of the church and ran. Augusto, raised in an orphanage until he was thirteen, and then put out to the streets. Life for someone with his mental challenges was very difficult, but fortunately, his size and strength kept him from being killed by thugs and villains. Shortly after Mateo died, Augusto came to live and work at the tavern. He adored Lucia for her kindness. He vowed to lay down his life for her or the children. He opened the tavern in the morning and closed it at night. Lucia slept well knowing that Augusto was there to protect her.

MATEO'S FUNERAL

Lucia often thought of killing Mateo herself, especially when he would come home after one of his drunken nights of debauchery, having gambled all the food money, only to wake the children with his loud cursing and yelling. After he woke them, and they started to cry in fear, he would then take out his crop, which he carried with him always, and whip them into silence. As Lucia protested these acts of abuse, she too would become his victim, and he would beat her in front of her children, then drag her crying to their bed, and proceed to rape her, with such force and hatred that she often prayed for death to come to him. Now that he was actually dead, she rekindled the lost memories of their early days of marriage, which she had stored away so long ago.

It was the day of Mateo's funeral. Lucia's heart was heavy with sorrow. He was cruel and abusive in the latter years of their marriage, yet when they were first married, their life was like a storybook dream. He was so handsome and strong. She was but a child of only fourteen and had no experience in the ways of womanhood. Thoughts of her wedding night had filled her with fear and anxiety, but he had been patient and attentive to her body. "We shall go slow mi bellezza dai capelli rossi." Mateo was by this time well versed in the seduction of women. He knew that Lucia was a virgin, and delicately introduced her to the art of lovemaking. She was but putty in his hands, and she gave into his every desire. Lucia found that she too enjoyed the carnal pleasures of Mateo's skilled touch. Her youthful enthusiasm and eagerness was not only to please her handsome husband, but also to relish the sensual urges within her newly discovered body. Mateo was an attentive lover, Lucia was an enthusiastic student, and together they explored and devoured each other in a mixture of sexual rapture. Lucia, still only a young teen, quickly matured into a beautiful young woman under the watchful eye of the Rizzo family. She was taught the proper way to handle staff and manage an estate like Monteforte. Understanding that the new Mistress of Monteforte would need to meld into high society, Lucia, with the aide of several tutors was instructed in the basics of educated society. Lucia, never having been formally educated, was quick to learn and highly intelligent. It did not take long before Mateo's parents grew to love the beautiful peasant girl.

Standing there in the cemetery that was part of the family estate, she would never forget the smell of the crypt when the vault of the mausoleum was opened. Mateo would be entombed in the crypt with his mother and father. The dank and malodorous stench of death and decay filled her nostrils and her heart. Lucia felt *un brivido corse la sua spina dorsale* and shook the wave of fear from herself. She still loved him, and would always remember their early life at Monteforte. The day was as dark as the crypt, and the children, mostly grown, and old enough to understand the proceedings, and how the death of their father would affect their own lives, were somber and sorrowful. Only a few people attended; it was a private ceremony. Maria Sucretti looked Lucia in the eyes and again she felt a cold shiver cruise down her spine. Maria, his only surviving sibling, loved her brother and helped raise him. She knew that her brother truly loved Lucia and their children. Maria was so jealous of Lucia because she had children and she did not. Looking now at how her children gathered to her side in support, with love and comfort, while she stood alone with only her misery, she hated Lucia even more.

After the crypt was resealed, Maria invited Lucia and her family back to the palazzo to have some refreshment. Lucia did not want to go, but her children were tired and hungry, and she did not want to push them too hard, so she graciously accepted the invitation. The staff, who all loved Lucia from her days spent there with Mateo, greeted her with hugs and expressions of sympathy. A lavish spread was laid in the dining room, and the children politely indulged themselves, and talked to the servants, who all were amazed at how much they had grown. Lucia quietly looked around the magnificent room then walked out to the adjoining terrace. She had taken a glass of wine and was savoring its smooth, fruity, taste. She was dreaming of the beginning of her relationship with Mateo, and while his parents initially were upset that their son did not marry a girl more suited to their social status, they did in time come to love Lucia. They saw in her the makings of an heiress, but, more importantly, they saw the fruitfulness of an heir-maker. Lucia, fertile as a rabbit, would give them the grandchildren they so desperately wanted. Maria and Salvatore were childless, and there was no love for the social climbing Salvatore, who the Rizzo's truly did not like. No, it was Lucia, the baby maker, who had found a place in their hearts.

"Lucia" the voice was soft and low but strong, it startled her from her daydream. Lucia turned to see

Maria standing just inches from her, with a glass of wine in her hand. The two were in such contrast, yet so much alike, both beautiful, but, in completely opposing terms. Lucia, the younger of the two women, was alabaster in complexion with blue eyes and a soft voluptuous body with full hips. Maria, mature and olive skinned with penetrating almond colored eyes was thin and well sculpted. The one thing they both had in common was their beautiful, thick, wavy, red hair. Lucia's was strawberry blonde, with curls reaching her waist. Maria, *L'amante del castello*, ever the mistress of the manse, wore her darker auburn locks neatly plaited into a reserve bun. Lucia was facing her sister-in-law, waiting for her to speak. "Lucia, I am truly sorry about Mateo. I loved him so much, but I just could not stop him from destroying himself. We have never been close, maybe that's my fault, maybe not, but I want you to come live here at Monteforte, with the children". Lucia, stunned, tried to comprehend this most unexpected moment of kindness, or was it just Maria's way to manipulate her once again. She took a moment to look out into the expanse of the manicured gardens, which dropped to the sea, with the mountains rising in the background. The sight was stupendous, the sky had cleared, and the warmth and brilliance of the sun was on her face. The perfume from the abundant display of flora was filling her senses. A light breeze from the sea wafted across her face, and carried the salty scent of the water. She adjusted her gaze to focus more clearly on Maria Sucretti's face, and tried to delve into those eyes that were the color of cognac. "Why, after all the misery and hardship that I have endured, all the pain that I, no, let me correct that, that his children have endured, why now do you want to help us? Where were you when your brother beat us, gambled the food money, and slept with every whore in Naples? Where were you when I begged you for help? No, I think I will take my children home with me and we will make our own way without your help. It is much too late. Mateo is gone and God rest his soul. He was tormented after your parents died, but there is no place for me or my children here any longer."

Maria, who secretly had anticipated this response, but had hoped Lucia would accept her offer, became suddenly belligerent. Still maintaining her composure, Maria looked away from Lucia, and turned to lean against the terrace knee wall. She was facing the dining room where the children of her beloved brother were quietly talking amongst themselves, enjoying the treats from the repast that was laid before them. The sounds of their youthful banter reached Maria's ears and her eyes welled up, yet, she would not let the tears fall from them. Without turning back, to look at Lucia she addressed her sister-in-law. "You would deny your children their rightful place here at Monteforte? This is not about you Lucia this is about their legacy. The life I could give them here would be so superior to anything you could ever do for them. I would educate them in all the ways that your husband and I were taught. They would live here forever, without any financial worries. Do not be an ignorant fool. You have nothing, unless I desire to give it to you, which I will not give you, even one coin, if you refuse my offer to come live here at Monteforte". Lucia seizing the moment to steady herself rounded on Maria with such vehemence. "How dare you speak to me like that? Do you think for one second that I would allow you to take my children and mold them into your image and likeness? You have hated me since the day I bore my first baby. You are a hateful, jealous, evil woman. It is no wonder God has left you bitter and barren. You go rot in hell!"

As quietly, and composed as she could muster, Lucia, clenched her trembling hands into fists and breathe deeply through her nose. Her eyes were so inflamed with anger she could hardly focus them. She drew herself to her full height, straightened her head, and walked toward the dining room. As she was withdrawing, she felt more than heard Maria hissing to her back. "I will destroy you, and then I will bring my brother's children, heirs of Monteforte, back to me!" Lucia did not answer, but set her shoulders, and doggedly walked into the dining room and gathered her children to leave. That was the last time she ever saw Maria Sucretti or Monteforte.

With the help of her oldest children, she managed to stay afloat. Even though Mateo's family was quite wealthy, they would not assist Lucia, not that she would ever ask for anything because she was too proud. Maria Sucretti, true to her word, did attempt to take the children away from Lucia, by telling the local magistrate that she was an unfit mother, raising her children in a den of sin and alcohol. An investigation was launched without Lucia's knowledge. State officials watched Lucia, and the children, day and night. They found that Lucia sent all the children to school and at midday break the oldest ones would ride their horses, at full gallop to come home to help Lucia serve the main meal to her customers. They would then eat, wash up, rest for a while and return to school. Their life, although physically harder, was now more loving and tension free without their father, who always beat them.

Lucia committed an act that she regretted all her life, which she confessed to her granddaughter Rafaela, only on her deathbed. It was after one of his violent rape episodes that Lucia found she was with child, having already bore six children and barely able to feed them, she went to a house in the city. A young woman, of her own age, took the child from within her. She wept uncontrollably that God would surely judge her harshly for this terrible act. When Lucia's oldest son Jerome, a healthy, handsome, young man, died of the plague, she swore his death was God's wrath. His death was retribution for the one she had aborted.

MARIA and SALVATORE SUCRETTI

Maria Sucretti had been a true beauty, and would have been the prize for any man. She married Salvatore Sucretti, under a contract, entered into by her parents, before she was born. As was the custom of wealthy families, marriages were prearranged from birth without the mutual consent of the parties involved. Marriage united families for social status or financial gain. This was the case of Maria and Salvatore. These were two powerful families, one from Naples, the other Sicily, joined to create an empire on two coasts. It would have been perfect, until greed and lust ruined everything.

Theirs had been a fairytale wedding, even though their marriage. Yet, unlike many of these unions, Maria and Salvatore, in the beginning, did love each other, the fact that their families approved, and this marriage enriched all interested parties, was good for both sides. Maria, a tall and stunning beauty, and Salvatore, handsome with a quick wit, made an attractive couple. For the most part, they were happy. After a few years of trying to conceive a child, but with no success, Salvatore grew weary waiting for Maria to conceive. It was almost painful to attend family functions, with everyone whispering about his lack of virility, and her barren womb.

It did not take long before Maria saw the gradual change in her husband, who started to focus his attentions at first to his business, then to his pleasures. This personal conflict was further complicated by the marriage of Mateo to Lucia. The young beauty, Lucia, was very fertile and bore a son, Jerome, after the first year of marriage and Mateo's parents were elated. As if the pressure to produce an heir was not evident enough, the younger brother and his child bride had trumped, Maria and Salvatore. They hated Lucia for her fertility. It was shortly after the birth of Mateo's second child that the Sucretti marriage disintegrated. Thereafter, Maria was on a personal crusade to destroy Lucia.

Maria's life was filled with riches and extravagant parties, jewels, and a fabulous estate. The only thing missing in Maria's life were children. She could not, or would not, bare any fruit from this loveless union. Soon Salvatore looked for someone who could give him a son, an heir, to carry on his name. That search went on for years in all the nightspots and back street bordellos of Naples. Her heart and her pride were broken. She wanted children. After the death of Mateo, she did everything, short of kidnapping, to gain custody of her brother's children. She especially hated Lucia who represented the woman she could never become.

Salvatore Sucretti, Maria's husband, was smart and cunning, wealthy in his own right; he knew how to manipulate men and money. He had become the leader of a vigilante group of local landowners and merchants, who out of desperation, had banded together to protect themselves against marauding gangs of thieves. Under his strong-arm leadership, the other landowners and merchants, now lived in relative peace from those who would descend upon their land or shop and take whatever they wanted. Salvatore had trained and outfitted a band of men, who he handpicked from the compliment of workers from his own estate, to act as private security for those who would pay him for this protection. It was a very amicable contract for all those involved. Those who subscribed to his consortium were afforded protection, while his coffers were growing fat and fruitful. Thus, the birth of the Camorra was formed under his leadership.

This would have been the ideal arrangement for all concerned, but, like most powerful men, Salvatore Sucretti became greedy. His fees for continued protection became more and more outrageous. If you did not pay, the consequences were disastrous. What started out as a relationship based on respect, quickly turned into one of fear. Sucretti's henchmen would enforce the ever-growing tithe for protection, extracting not only the monthly stipend for their security services, but a percentage of their income. He was hated and feared.

This power and financial enrichment made many business associates, as well as many enemies. After several failed attempts on his life, he decided that he would engage the services of a highly skilled bodyguard. Thereafter, Salvatore Sucretti was always under the watchful eye of his personal bodyguard Giovanni the Roman. His was a kingdom of influence and money, which was fostered by absolute loyalty and savage brutality. Salvatore was a despicable human being with a lust for pleasure. Power corrupts absolutely, and Salvatore Sucretti was power in its most base form. He was cruel and calculating, and his reach was never ending.

Salvatore consorted with wealthy landowners, as well as merchants and traders. His business savvy was well known, and thus, his reputation for increasing profits, while keeping a death grip on any one who crossed him, was notorious. This type of power is all-encompassing, and within a short time, had invaded his personal life. Married to the wealthy, aristocratic, and beautiful Maria Sucretti, an elegant and refined woman, intelligent and well bred, was not enough for his wonton tastes. The one thing Sucretti wanted, the one thing he needed to insure his continued success, was an heir. Maria Sucretti would not give him a child. While she did not divorce him, because of her devotion to her religious beliefs, Maria loathe him for his pandering, which had become notorious. Maria learned that it was not her who possessed the barren womb. Salvatore, because of his sexual preferences, he was a constant fixture of the whorehouses, and thus had contracted venereal disease. There was no way that Maria would even allow Salvatore to be intimate with her, even on the rare occasions when he came to her bed. Maria prayed that he would soon die, consumed by this wretched disease. She could already see the toll it was taking on his once well-sculpted body. The slack skin and pus filled lesions that tattooed his flesh. The former brilliance behind those menacing eyes was dull and black, like his soul. His face bore the disease he carried within him. Death, she prayed, would come soon, for both their sakes. Maria would look at Salvatore, with eyes filled with hate, not only for what he had done to himself, but to her *"se muore come l'animale sone"*.

Salvatore Sucretti made many enemies, especially among those who would become victims of his ever-broadening network of thugs, who enforced his edicts with fervor. Soon they feared more than the thieves they were hired to give protection against. After several nearly successful attempts on his life, he enlisted a personal bodyguard; a man who would one day become the cornerstone of Maria's world.

GIOVANNI THE ROMAN

The bodyguard, Giovanni the Roman, was well suited for his occupation. When asked what his last name was, the answer was simply, that he did not have one, or, he did not want it known. They called him Giovanni the Roman, because he came from Rome. Maria started to call him Giovanni Romano. He did not object to the name, and so everyone began calling him Giovanni Romano. Lean and wiry with sharp features, and deep set dark eyes, which twitched continuously, as they followed every movement. He was stealth and nervous, always on the watch for some misdeed or unexpected surprise. Always impeccably dressed in his signature black waistcoat, Giovanni the Roman made an impressive silhouette. He seldom spoke, but was ever present and privy to all family and business transactions. He became invisible. Giovanni was invisible to everyone but Maria.

Maria, whose interaction with Giovanni was very limited, yet, she felt a special connection with him, and he treated her with the utmost respect. On those rare occasions, when she needed to ask him a question, he would answer when spoken to directly. His voice was deep and he spoke intelligently. Maria would watch the silent man from a distance, soon became obsessed with him. Whenever she was around him, she was self-conscious of his presence. Aroused at the sight of him, she would think of excuses to ask him to escort her to the herb garden, or the vineyard.

It was about a year after Giovanni the Roman arrived at Monteforte, that Maria asked him to come with her to the wine cellar, with the excuse she needed to select a special vintage, and therefore would require help to carry up the bottles. "Giovanni, would you please help me bring up some bottles from the wine cellar?" She had no doubt that he would accommodate her request, but was surprised when he said, "Fernando can do that for you Mistress." With a sharp tone, she replied, "Yes, I know that he can, but I want to make the selection myself."

The cellars were at the farthest end of the castle, and they had to go down many steps to get there. It was dark and cold, which was all the better for the fermentation of the wine. Giovanni had taken a torch with them to light the way. "Be cautious Mistress, the steps are steep and coated with moisture, you could fall. Here hold on to my arm for safety." Maria took hold of his arm, and felt his muscles and straightaway a tension rose between them. She knew that there could never be a relationship between them, for Salvatore would kill them both, yet her heart was racing, and there was a tingling in her womb.

They reached the place where she knew the special vintages were stored. She beckoned Giovanni to come closer with the torch. "Come here Giovanni so that I may see which ones I want to take back with us." Giovanni came closer. He could smell the familiar fragrance she always wore. Maria was tall and her head came close to his. Giovanni had always desired Maria, but remembered a story his father had told him when he was a small boy. It was the story of a fisherman, who sought a prized fish. The fish was beautiful and delicate, and it was said that the flesh of this particular fish was like no other in the world, but to capture this fish meant certain death. A giant eel with teeth like sharpened steel protected the tiny sea urchin. The lure of the delicate creature, and the lust for its perfect flesh, drove the fisherman to dive into the sea and attempt to capture it. Alas, he did not see the eel hiding inside a coral reef. When the fisherman was just about to snatch the fish, the eel, rushed from its hiding place, and killed him.

Coquettishly, Maria asked Giovanni to bring over the small barrel they used as a stepping block to reach the higher shelves. "Giovanni, will you hold me while I reach up for that bottle?" Giovanni was happy to have his hands on his Mistress. "Yes, but please be careful." Giovanni came around to her back, and with his long fingered hands, placed them on either side of her slender hips. It was there, they both felt it, the attraction was undeniable. He squeezed her small waist and she gasped with desire. She lost her footing, and fell into him. He spun her around and kissed her deeply on the mouth.

For a moment, the world stood still, neither one of them was breathing. Giovanni came to his senses. "Mistress, please, I beg you to forgive me. Will you tell Master Sucretti of my indiscretion? I will not apologize, for I love you, yet, we both know it cannot be. There is no hope for it." Maria was stunned, aroused, and scared. "No I will not tell my husband for we would both be killed. We shall act as if nothing has happened. Understand?" Giovanni was scared too, but he shook his head in agreement. They retrieved the wine and left. Neither one ever spoke of the incident again.

Giovanni was there in their home, in their lives, watching, waiting, and always present. Maria had strong emotions about Giovanni the Roman, but she knew that when and where her husband might, so would Giovanni be there as well.

Maria was used to the ever-present servant for her personal maid, Natalie, was constantly by her side, or within a whispers call from her. Natalie was the daughter of Gaetano and Vivian, two of the oldest and most beloved servants Maria ever had. They were born at Monteforte, lived, and worked there all their lives. Natalie, their only child, was also born at the estate. Maria's parents had promised Gaetano and Vivian, for all their years of faithful service, they would raise and educate Natalie like their own. Therefore, when Maria, who was slightly older, was receiving instruction so was Natalie. Both girls learned several languages, mathematics, and, the arts. Natalie, a quick learner, soon became a worthy companion for Maria. The two became friends, but, always, Natalie knew her status within the infrastructure of Monteforte. Maria would always be her mistress, and she would always be her servant, but they loved and respected each other while maintaining their own boundaries. Natalie's place within Monteforte gave her privileges beyond even the most valued servants. She was Maria's personal secretary, her confidante, and her friend. She, like Giovanni the Roman, was ever-present within the lives of Salvatore and Maria.

On more than one occasion, Maria saw Giovanni and Natalia whispering in the dark corners of a room, while stealing a touch or a kiss. While they were invisible, their sense of presence was always there. After a while, encouraged by Maria, they showed affection for each other, but never displaying anything more than a touch or a nod while within eye or ear shot of their respective master or mistress. They were both born, breed, and groomed in the art of their positions. It was common for servants in their position to seek physical comforts from within the household staff, since they never left without being with the heads of the house. Thereafter, Natalie and Giovanni asked Salvatore and Maria if they could wed, and it was granted. The transformation of Giovanni Romano was amazing, even his facial features became softer and more attractive. Natalie was happy and it showed on his pretty face. When together, you could see their love for each other and a twinge of jealousy coursed through Maria at the sight of them. She knew it was a good match.

Natalie and Giovanni were happy and soon that happiness was all the greater for Natalie became with child. The love they shared had mellowed Giovanni, and his demeanor, while still professional, he became somewhat relaxed, and at times, even jovial. The whole household delighted in their joy. It had been many years since there had been a baby at Monteforte. Maria was also enthralled in the anticipation of this new life. It seemed that Natalie's round belly grew every day. Maria would watch her, and the pang of desire to know what it was like to be a mother, would leave her with a heavy heart. She remembered all too well, with longing, her brother Mateo's children. Their tiny presence filled the cold castle with warmth, and echoed the sounds of joy and laughter. She hated Lucia, her sister-in-law, not only because she was the mother she would never become, but also, because she had refused to live at Monteforte after Mateo was killed in that terrible fight at the gambling house. Yet, in her heart, she knew she could never bring a child into this world with her husband Salvatore, and, now it was already too late, for her body was already in the years of change.

BOOK ONE

CHAPTER ONE

THE BIRTH

Torre del Greco
June 13, 1698

$\mathcal{I}$t was already two weeks since they had laid Lucia Rizzo to rest. Rafaela, her beloved granddaughter, decided she would visit the grave today. She had been very close with Lucia, being the first grandchild, but she dreaded going to the cemetery. Odd, she felt compelled to go this day. It was a hot, humid day, but she was thankful, the clouds covered the sun, which gave some relief to the oppressive heat. Rafaela was in her eighth month of pregnancy, this being her sixth child, she carried her extra weight like a yoke.

She trudged up the hill to the grave. The ground was raw and angry, and the flowers that she had left on the day of burial had withered and died. As she made her way slowly, now feeling the full burden of her big belly, she saw that an elderly woman was kneeling at the grave. The woman was waif thin, and her garments were dirty and thread bare. Her head, covered in a black scarf tied around her neck, even though it was stifling in the humidity. The old woman's knurled fingers clutched a small dagger and she appeared to be digging. Apparently, she did not see or hear Rafaela approaching, and continued about her work. Curious as to what she was doing, Rafaela stayed back, and watched, as the old woman labored to dig a small hole with the dagger.

The ground was dry and hard, for it had not rained in many days, and the sun had baked the earth inflexible. A small cloud of dust rose with each penetrating swipe at the encrusted dirt. Rafaela could see that the woman was working hard. Finally, when she was satisfied with the depth of the hole she had dug, she reached into a tattered pouch, which had been sitting next to her. Reaching in, the woman extracted several small objects. Rafaela was straining to see, but did not want to alert the woman to her presence.

The woman moved to adjust herself, and then yelped, as her boney knee struck a rock. This move allowed Rafaela to see what she had in her possession. It looked like small bones, a scarf of black silk, a polished rock, and a clay pot. The woman began placing each item into the hole; and with each placement was chanting and swaying back and forth. Finally, when she had carefully laid each item in its place, she reached for the pot and began pouring some kind of black liquid into the hole. Again, more chanting and swaying. She then spit into the hole and began laughing, not a joyous laughter, but the vilest sound Rafaela ever heard. It made her shiver.

Rafaela could take it no longer, and ran to the grave to confront the old woman. "What are you doing?" The woman looked up and the sight of her made Rafaela again shiver. Her eyes were the color of sunbaked parchment; her skin was slack and sagging and covered in pustules. "Ah the granddaughter, well I am happy you came, I was calling for you." Rafaela was confused "Calling for me? I do not know who you are. I demand to know what matter of malice you have done to desecrate my grandmother's grave."

The old woman lay on her side, apparently she was tired, and needed to rest. "Oh to be sure you are here because I called for you. I needed a witness to what I have done to Lucia Rizzo." She was now relaxed, and when she smiled, the few teeth she had were decayed and blackened. "Witness for what?" At first, the old woman seemed to be conflicted as to whether she wanted to answer, and then thought better of her decision.

"It is a long story, but I have all the time in the world. Many, many, years ago, when la bella testa rossa came to me to take her baby, I warned her that she was already too far gone, and it would be dangerous, but she was half crazed out of her mind, and begged me to rid her of the child. In fact, she paid me two times what I usually got. I took the child, which was already several months, from her womb and killed it. I was young and beautiful also, but I knew how to make a baby go away. I too had done the deed before. I was a whore, who was much sort after.

Five years had passed when la bella testa rossa came to seek me out, but this time it was not to get rid of a baby. She told me that I was the devil and a witch, for when I took her child all those years ago, Jesus and all the Saints had wept, and they were angry. In their anger, they had taken her eldest child, in its place. She was not to be consoled. She placed a curse on me that my womb would never make a healthy baby.

I took no heed to the ranting's of this mad woman, she was consumed by her guilt, and her grief. Little did I know that at that moment I was with child. When I found out, I decided to carry the child to term, and so did not dispose of it, as I had done in the past. When it was time for the birthing, I labored hard it was a big baby that was stuck inside me. The midwife, worked for many hours, the head, finally came to the mouth of my womb, but it was huge, and so she cut me, to let the big head pass. I fainted. The baby was born. When I awoke, I screamed at the sight of my only child. Era un mostro. He was deformed, with the head of a pig, and a twisted body. I could not keep this deformed animal. I took it to the church, and left it at the feet of the statue of Jesus. "If You want him, keep him." I shouted at the statue. I was heartbroken."

The woman stopped her storytelling for the first time. She was panting and fighting to grasp her breath. The long stored memory was heavy on her heart. Rafaela had not said one word, but she knew of the story of how her grandmother had gotten rid of the baby, for Lucia confessed it to her on her deathbed. She had not mentioned any of the details involving this mad woman. It was such a wild story but the telling intrigued Rafaela.

Not waiting for any response, the old hag continued. "To my disbelief, that redheaded witch found my son in the street, and took him into her home. She raised him like her own, and he cherished the ground she walked on. By now, I was already well past my prime, and so too were my days of satisfying my male customers. I came to Lucia Rizzo, one mother to another, and begged her for food and money. She refused, and told me to get away from her, and never to return. She cursed the day I was born, and blamed me for the tragic death of two of her children. She even had the faccia di una cagna to lie, and tell me, she did not know that the deformed monster she housed was my own son. In the end, it was my own son, who tried to kill me to protect that wicked bitch."

Rafaela, overcome by grief, grabbed the ragged old woman, and pulled her to her feet. "What have you put in my grandmother's grave?" The old woman began to laugh, which was not a laugh, but a howling. Rafaela was angry, and slapped the woman hard across the face, which caused her to lose her balance, and she fell down. "Tell me, what is the meaning of this? Tell me now!" The old wretch staggered to her feet, "It is the bones of a diseased rooster, a black scarf so she cannot see her way and a stone from the grave of her dead son, and finally, the blood of a wild boar. Together, they will haunt her wicked soul for all eternity, never giving her a moment's rest. As for you, I called you here, knowing you were with child, to witness this curse." She stared deep into Rafaela's eyes, and now stood so close, that the putrid odor of her decaying breath, was making her want to vomit. In a blink of an eye, the woman raised the hand that held the dagger; it was covered with the black liquid, and slashed it across Rafaela's bulging belly.

Rafaela was shocked, and then instantly felt the sting of the blade, as it sliced through her skin. A dark red stain had come to the surface of her gown. She felt faint at the sight of it. The old woman stepped back, and watched, as the stain grew bigger "You will bring a baby girl into this world with the curse of Lucia Rizzo upon her head. Mark my words." She was backing up, and laughing, that strange and haunting laugh.

Rafaela awoke from her dream soaking wet and trembling in fear. Donato was snoring loudly beside her. She labored out of bed and walked with heavy steps to the table, which held a jug of water. She filled the bowl and splashed water on her face. Since her grandmother died, she kept having the same terrifying dream. The baby leapt in her womb. Rafaela made the sign of the cross and prayed that this baby would be born healthy. It was just a dream she told herself. Just a dream!

The day was already hot and humid and her back ached from the extra weight she was carrying. She had stayed up not wanting to disturb Donato and started to prepare breakfast trying to rid herself of the dream;

that same dream that had been plaguing her night after night. She struggled to carry the bucket of water she had just filled from the well. An intense pain stabbed at her and she felt the warm liquid run down her leg. It was time.

Donato heard her cry for help and jumped with a start from the bed. Rushing out of the room, he found Rafaela doubled over in pain a small puddle of water at her feet. He went to her and scooped her into his strong arms "Cara, it is time; I will go get Olympia and bring her back. On my way, I will stop at Maria's and tell her to prepare. Don't worry, it will be good." Donato was fighting to hide his fears for he too had ill feelings about this child. Silently he prayed for the safety of his wife and child.

"*Gesu il dolore e` insopportabile!*" The pain was unbearable. She closed her eyes and silently invoked help from Jesus and all the saints. The breaths came harder and faster, she lay in a puddle of sweat, the bed sheets clinging to her sodden body like a shroud covered in blood, urine, and bodily fluids. "*Non desperate che sara` solo un po'piu` a lungo.*" "Just a few more pushes, the head is almost out". This news was of little comfort to Rafaela as she gathered every ounce of energy within herself to continue. She had been in hard labor for more than twelve hours and she instinctively knew that at this point anything could go wrong. This birth was like none of the others, all the five other babies came quickly, but this one was different from the start. She could feel the walls of her womb tearing from the strain of pushing. Her entire pregnancy clouded with an uneasy feeling beginning with the death of her grandmother she carried an ominous feeling about this child and now her sense of urgency to relieve herself of this burden weighed on her profoundly.

Rafaela Banfi was in her early thirties but still her youthful beauty was unmarred by years of hard toil and childbearing. She was a strong, intelligent woman and

6

bore some formal education. Taught by the nuns to read and write in her both native Italian as well as classical Latin. Her education was overseen by her beloved uncle, Luigi Rizzo, who a religious cleric. Rafaela, much like the rest of her lineage was olive in complexion with amber colored eyes. She possessed features that at first glance were not extraordinary, but when taken as a whole completed a beautiful picture. By all standards for the times and nationality she was tall, slender and shapely. Donato, her devoted husband, would often tell her that he married her for her body, which was lithe and voluptuous in all the right places. Full lips, breasts like ripe fruit and a well-endowed rounded bottom, yes, by all measures Rafaela was a stunning woman. The life of a fisherman's wife was not an easy one, but her strength of will, and love of her husband Donato, carried her through the hard times.

Rafaela's earliest memories of her childhood were filled with happiness, and times spent with her grandmother Lucia Rizzo. Lucia was a renowned *la bellezza dai capelli rosso,* a redheaded beauty, with the mind and will of ten men. When her grandfather, Mateo Rizzo, died he left her grandmother with a tavern, two horses, and plenty of debts. Although the concept of a woman not only owning such an establishment, but also, running one herself was unheard of during those times, Lucia learned quickly that it was her survival. Rafaela never met her grandfather, he had died before she was born, but knew him in her heart from the grand stories told to her by her Nona Lucia.

The love of Lucia's life was her cherished little Rafaela her first granddaughter. This special relationship fostered a unique bond between the two. Lucia would always tell Rafaela stories of the old days and about life at the palatial ancestral home of her grandfather at Monteforte. As a beautiful young girl, and of her marriage to Mateo Rizzo, the handsome horse trainer who had an eye for the women and a taste for the tables at the local gambling houses. She would describe in vivid detail the riches and architecture of Monteforte, which was the House of Rizzo a castle that was, perched high upon the cliffs overlooking the sea. From her grandmother's vivid descriptions, she could imagine the great palazzo with its ancient structure, acres of land and manicured lawns. Rafaela dreamed of one day going there to see it herself.

Another incredibly sharp pain reached Rafaela grabbing her from her subconscious thoughts and thrusting her back to reality. Why was this birth so difficult? Something was wrong, she felt as if she would die before the baby came. Tears, not from the pain, but from the thought of not seeing her children grow clouded her mind. Who would care for her family if she died? Rafaela was at the point of complete exhaustion the thought of further punishment to her already beaten body was invading her will to continue with the labor. The midwife, experienced and capable, knew only too well that if Rafaela did not give birth soon that she would lose both mother and child and she was damn well not going to let that happen. "Rafaela, my sweet girl, you must be strong and keep your mind to your work. Non desperate che sara' solo un po'piu' a lungo." The midwife spoke softly but reassuringly into Rafaela's ear and stroked the wet hair back from her forehead.

Olympia Mascarnes was delivering babies for four decades and considered more proficient than any doctor. She was already in her late sixties, but her body and appearance definitely did not reek of old age. Brunette hair, tied back into a bun, showed silver streaks at the temples and sides. Her eyes were a rich cocoa color and filled with warmth that held a keen sharpness. She had a cheerful but brisk personality. Olympia knew everyone and his or her most intimate secrets yet she was discrete and never gossiped. She had seen all that there was to see but was never jaded by the wonder of new life held in her hands. She was a deeply religious woman and believed that she was the vehicle for God and the Saints to bring forth new life into this world. She took her vocation very seriously. The business of midwife was not only very important in areas where there were no hospitals or physicians but physically demanding. Olympia widowed at a young age, with three of her own children. Like her mother before her, Olympia had been schooled in the art of birthing infants. This was a time honored profession and much respected. A good midwife was much sought after and well compensated for her work. The lives of both mother and child rested in the ability of the midwife.

It was already eighteen hours that Rafaela was in hard labor and there was always the fear that something could go wrong with mother or child in difficult cases like this. Donato was afraid for his wife and wearily watched over the youngsters, yet, in his mind, he had prepared the cart and horse, which he had borrowed from a friend, ready to speed to the hospital, which was many miles away. Not for the first time, and certainly not for the last, Olympia was afraid for Rafaela and was growing anxious. Olympia had in fact delivered Rafaela into the world and, as with all her babies, held a personal affection for her and now a terrible concern for her wellbeing hung like a dense fog over the scene. Olympia knew Rafaela needed to rest between contractions or she would never have the strength to bring the baby for the final push. She let her doze a moment while she mopped the sweat from her brow and trickled drops of water into her swollen mouth. For this moment, Rafaela was safe until the next pain came. Olympia too was feeling the strain on her old muscles. Her back was sore but it was her fear that made her muscles tense. *Egregio Signore,* she implored the Lord, she could not lose this girl and her child. She prayed for her to deliver this baby and save both mother and child. Olympia sat back in the chair next to the bed and she too closed her eyes for a while. Her mind and heart heavy with fear and burdened with prayer sent her into a restless doze.

Rafaela seemed to be floating in a state of semi consciousness. She was in pain from the top of head to her toes and every muscle was poised for the onslaught of pain. She was dreaming once again of her grandmother, and all the stories she had been told, and she drifted lazily in her mind back to her Nona's beckoning voice, recalling one of her favorite stories. For now, she was safe...

A sharp pain filled Rafaela's womb and the contractions were only two or three seconds apart, she yelled out in pain and Donato flung open the bedroom door and rushed in to see if she was all right. "Sei cara tutto bene?" Olympia, who has been dozing, startled by this outburst, jumped from her chair, took the opportunity to admonish Donato for the interruption, pushed him out the door, and bolted it from the inside. "Out! Get out! She will be fine. If I need you I will call!" The last thing she needed to deal with was Donato. Her focus now was the wellbeing of Rafaela and her child, he could deal with his own fears, she had far greater concerns. Olympia was examining Rafaela and could now see the soft tissue of the head of the baby peeking out of the uterus. It was nearly time. She opened the door and bellowed for Maria, Rafaela's sister, to come and bring the boiling water with her.

Maria Cordella, lived close by, as did all of the family. The two sisters separated by only twelve months, born on the same day April 5th, but one year apart, were very close and shared a deep affection for each other and their extended families. Maria, once she delivered the water as instructed by Olympia, quickly left the bedroom to check on the children and get them ready for bed. The sun had set about an hour ago and the night air was cool and crisp for early June. It had been an endless day and she feared for her sister, something was wrong. She gathered the younger ones, bathe and dressed them, then put them down for the night. Maria finished up with the older boys, who laughed and giggled for about an hour, and then Donato went in with the strap in hand and dealt out a few lashes. After a few minutes of sniffling, all was quiet.

Torre del Greco was a colorful mixture of ancient conquests and assimilation from the melding of the predominant ruling class. It was into this city center, which was no more than a large fishing village, where Rafaela had been born, and would raise her family. All the richness and the brininess of the sea were mixed with her blood, and that of her beloved Donato.

Fishing villages seem to produce more soothsayers than their mountain counterparts. Once, Rafaela asked her grandmother about this very phenomena and Lucia told her that the men who long ago journeyed from distant lands brought back tales of strange and exotic places and people. Sometimes they would conquer these lands and bring back slaves. It was said, that these fortunetellers were descendants from those enslaved souls and that their misery and knowledge of distant lands gave them the power to see the future. Another common myth was that the souls of the people who lost their lives in the ashes of the hot lava from Vesuvius would come back in the form of local townspeople to exact revenge for their misfortune. Like all small villages in any country in the world, everyone knew everybody or were in some way related to everyone in the town. Privacy was an unheard of treasure. Gossip is news, and there are many reporters, some form of truth underlies every story, but most of the time, the details have been so fabricated that the original content has become quite a different story. There is also the pervasive use of myth and superstition, which add zest to all rumors. Torre del Greco had no shortage of their share of local fortunetellers. Although firmly steeped in Catholicism no local was above belief in the supernatural. These simple God-fearing people needed answers to the sometimes-mysterious occurrences in their otherwise mundane lives.

Rafaela continued to labor, the breaths coming harder and faster. For a moment, her mind drifted from her present task and she thought she smelled lilacs and roses, the scent of her grandmother, and a cool breeze floated over her exhausted body. The next sound she heard was Maria gently shaking her shoulder and calling her name, she had fainted and was coming out of it as her sister placed a cold cloth on her feverish brow. "Here take this strap and bite down hard. It will help with the pain." Rafaela tasted the bitter tannin from the leather but knew that she needed to bear the pain or surely, her and her baby would die.

The baby's head was through and she needed to push down one more time to release the child's shoulders. She mustered all the strength she could find, closed her eyes, biting hard into the strap and pushed until there was nothing left within her soul. Once again Olympia prayed "Caro Dio mi aiuti a realizzare questo bambino e sua madre in modo sicuro nelle vostre mani." With the fetid odor of female sweat, mixed with feces, urine, and afterbirth, the baby entered into the world. Olympia moved with deft skill to cut off the cord and work on the infant.

The baby, covered in blood and mucous, yet even that could not hide the child's magnificent little face and body. It was a strong and sturdy body and when Olympia slapped its bottom, it gave a resounding staccato. Maria began washing and changing her sister and while she did that Olympia worked on the infant. Rafaela was too exhausted to move and laid there in a wounded state, whimpering like a beaten animal. Maria moved her gently and started to strip the bed linens and replace them with clean fresh covers. She washed Rafaela thoroughly, combed her hair, and powdered her limp body with talc with the scent of lilacs and roses.

Olympia had removed the infant to another corner of the room where a cradle and table had been set up. These items, passed from child to child and from family to family. All of Rafaela's other five children had been bathe, dressed on that table, and had slept in that same cradle. A special bath of boiled water and a few drops of virgin olive oil and rosemary had been prepared for the bathing of the infant.

Dawn was just arriving over the rise and a light filled the window near the dressing table. The new sunlight filled the room and the scent of summer and fresh ocean breezes filled the stagnant air with new life. As Olympia placed the child in the soothing water and started to wash the afterbirth from the child the baby started to coo. Olympia anointed the infant's eyes with olive oil to remove the mucous and cleaned the nose and mouth. She was smitten with the beauty of this small creature but then she stopped her ministrations upon seeing something that immediately required further inspection. There, just under the left breast was a mark. Olympia knew, from years of experience exactly what the mark was even though she had only seen it twice before but the curse was etched on her face. La maledizione e` stato inciso sulla sua faccia. She made the sign of the cross, said a silent prayer, and took the olive oil and inscribed the sign of the cross on the baby's forehead intoning the protection of Jesus. Caro Gesù, proteggere questo bambino da tutti i mali, she prayed. Olympia quickly finished bathing the baby. She wanted the child dressed before the others came to inspect her. With fastidiousness, she went about her task until she had accomplished the deed. Before she presented the baby to the waiting crowd, she braced herself, drew in a deep breath, and fixed her face into a pleasant smile.

When she was finished, she asked Maria if she was done cleaning and dressing Rafaela. Maria was in fact finished and she prepared her sister to receive her new daughter. Both mother and child were strikingly beautiful. Even after her tremendous ordeal, Rafaela looked calm and contented with her child at her side the two looked like a Botticelli fresco. Maria and Olympia, who had labored hard next to the mother to make this such a blessed event, were worn and haggard. Olympia seemed anxious and tired and her face wore an expression of melancholy. Anyone seeing her would attribute her anxious face to the efforts of her labors.

Before she announced the delivery and everyone rushed to see the baby her last official duty was the filling out of the birth document. She would later record it in the Hall of Records with the local magistrate and subsequently an official sealed copy sent to Naples, the next largest city, then recorded in the Book of Births for Torre del Greco. *It was Sunday, 13 June at 5:45 a.m. witnessed by Olympia Mascarnes, Midwife and Maria Cordella. The Family name – Banfi and given name was blank. Padre – Donato Banfi, Madre – Rafaela nee, Pugliese, Banfi. Born in the village of Torre del Greco in the Year of Our Lord, 1698.* Olympia asked Rafaela what was to be the child's name and she replied that she would like to discuss the matter with Donato. "I want to talk to Donato first. I really would like to name her after my grandmother Lucia, but I want to make sure he agrees. I will send word of our decision." Rafaela hesitated for just a moment overcome by her emotions and reached out for Olympia's hand. "Thank you for all your love and support for surely me and my baby would be dead already." She kissed the hand she was holding and Olympia bent down stroked her hair and kissed her with such love and emotion that she had to hold back her tears. "È il lavoro del Signore che faccio. Thanks to Him you are both safe. I love you Rafaela. Take care not to over exert yourself.

Maria is here to help."

Before she left, the room Olympia came to Rafaela's bedside, brushed an errant curl from her pretty face, and kissed her gently on the forehead. She then laid her hand on her head and said a silent prayer of thanksgiving. A single tear cascaded down her worn face and she fought back the rest. Olympia took a deep breath, straightened herself, and gathered her bag to leave. Rafaela reached out her hand and stopped her, "Caro amico, è qualcosa di sbagliato, ti sembra triste?" Rafaela could sense that something was wrong but did not know what it was. "No, Bella, everything is fine. I am just getting old." With that, she bent once more, embraced Rafaela, and proceeded out of the room. Rafaela took such a chill that she shivered from head to toe and then brushed it off to exhaustion.

Rafaela wanted so much for her daughter to be named Lucia not only for her grandmother but for the saint as well. Since she was very little her Uncle Luigi, the Monsignor, would read her stories of the lives of the saints especially the ones with family names. She mentally recorded the stories of her name and that of her grandmother.

Legend states that hundreds of years ago, a young girl named Lucia, who was born in Sicily to noble parents, and who, as a young child, offered her virginity to God in a vow, which she kept secret. Lucia's mother urged her to marry a young pagan. The matter was resolved in a way that was to mean glory both to Lucia and for God. Lucia's mother became very ill and as a result became blind. Lucia, who was just a child, encouraged her to go to the tomb of Saint Agatha and pray for help. They made the pilgrimage and their prayers for a cure were answered. Lucia then told her mother of her desire to give herself and all that she possessed to God, in gratitude for the favor recently granted, her mother agreed. When Lucia's promised fiancée` heard of what she had done he accused her before the magistrate of being a Christian. The Romans, under the persecution of Diocletian, attempted to shake her resolution of virginity and tried to burn her at the stake, but their efforts were thwarted by divine intervention and the girl was saved. Finally, Lucia was put to death by the sword in 304. December 13th celebrates the feast of Saint Lucia. She is venerated as a patron of those afflicted with any eye disease. The poet Dante prayed to Saint Lucia for the relief of an eye ailment, and in his *Divine Comedy,* he gave this saint one of the most honored places in heaven, next to that of Saint Giovanni the Baptist.

Her job completed, Olympia moved to the door of the bedroom and greeted the small crowd of family that had held vigil during the night giving Donato encouragement. These births were always a cause for both joy and fear. Many times village women died in childbirth or the baby died, either way, until the midwife triumphantly emerged, all concerned parties held their joy. Gathered in the kitchen of the small stucco house, which faced the only street on the wharf, were Rafaela's family and they were all speaking in hushed tones. Donato's parents were dead and his remaining brothers and sisters were scattered all over Italy. He enjoyed a special place within Rafaela's family. When they saw Olympia, drained of color, exhausted but smiling, they let out a resounding cheer and each in turn embraced the much-loved midwife. The youngsters were starting to stir with all the noise and excitement.

Donato was the first to enter the bedroom and as he approached the bed, the sunlight was streaming through the open window and the sounds of a new day were serenading the room's inhabitants. He gingerly walked to the side of the bed and tenderly kissed Rafaela's forehead. Donato never stopped being in awe at the first sight of his newborns, each one was a miracle and testament to all that is good with the world. He was a complex man with deep desires and strong faith. Donato was five years Rafaela's senior but his rugged good looks and muscular body from years of working on the fishing boats gave his chiseled features their manly sexuality. His touch was soft but firm and he looked admiration at both his beautiful wife and their lovely new daughter. "This was a hard one for you my sweetheart" Donato stroked the errant curls from his wife's face. She was bone tired but took his hand in hers and kissed it. "She is beautiful isn't she? Already she looks just like Nona" and the tears left her eyes but she was still smiling. "Yes, she is very beautiful, but, look at her mother, she would have to be so" he kissed her lips and brushed away the tears from her cheek. "You rest; I will bring our little angel to meet her adoring family. Rafaela, I love you and thank you for making my life so wonderful" he too had tears in his eyes. "But first we must give her a name." Donato had laughter in his eyes. Until this moment neither one had discussed names for the child as was their custom. Now standing there beside her bed Donato knew in his heart that Rafaela would want to name the child after her beloved grandmother. Lucia Rizzo was a wonderful woman whose strength as matriarch had held this huge family together for two generations. The whole village, but especially her favorite granddaughter, Rafaela, mourned her death. Secretly, in her heart she knew that if she bore a female child she would name her Lucia in honor of her grandmother. Donato knew his wife's feelings for her grandmother and willingly told Rafaela that he thought it would only be fitting if they were to name the child Lucia. "Cara, I think we should name the baby Lucia after Nona. Do you agree?" Rafaela knew that her husband loved her grandmother but he loved his wife more and for that, she was so thankful. "Yes my darling, I would love to name her after Nona." Donato with the burden of this anticipated birth was exhausted both mentally and physically. The thought of losing his beloved wife was inconceivable.

This giant of a man gently bent down and retrieved his new daughter from her mother's side and once again, the baby cooed. She looked at her father with huge azure blue eyes and pouting mouth and he melted. He proudly cradled his precious prize in his muscular arm and with his head high and his back straight walked to the front room where all had gathered in anticipation of this moment. Without exception, everyone sighed and gasped at the sight of this lovely creature. Lucia's expression was so peaceful and angelic that her perfectly molded little face struck everyone, which was cherub-like in its roundness with peaches and cream complexion. Olympia had weighed the child in at ten pounds four ounces, the largest of all Rafaela's births. Donato felt someone tugging at his pant leg. When he looked down he saw tiny little Antoinetta, his three year old daughter, struggling to see her new baby sister and playmate. He lowered to his knees and let the two sisters make contact for the first time. Antoinetta impulsively took the baby's hand and kissed it, and once again, Lucia cooed contentedly. Antoinetta in a sleepy voice said "Papa, lei è così bella. Lei è il mio bambino e sarà prendersi cura di lei." The older sister was extremely gentle and told her father how pretty her new baby was and how she was going to take good care of her. Donato then raised himself and brought Lucia to see her big brothers. There was the oldest, Antonio who was now twelve, Andrea who was nine and a half, Genaro who was seven, Francesco who was five and little Antoinetta now three. It was quite a troop but they were some of the best-behaved children in the family, perhaps in the entire village. Donato and Rafaela were good parents but strong disciplinarians. All the children had little jobs and the ones that did not go to school were to help their mother about the house and garden. Their mother kept an immaculate house and all those fortunate enough to have eaten it raved about her cooking. Donato was always playing with the boys or taking them out on his small boat to go fishing or swimming in the Bay of Naples. Donato and Rafaela lived a charmed life in a picturesque village surrounded by their loving children. Life was wonderful and God was certainly good to them. Grandmother and grandfather, both so proud and stoic, that these were the descendants of their seed. In Italian families, the oldest of the clan feel that their fertility and that of their ancestors were gifts from the Creator. Helena and Giuseppe were particularly blessed that their line had not been besmirched by any malformation in their offspring and subsequent lineage. Simple country people could be cruel and unmerciful to a child born with a handicap or deformity. Beauty of body and mind were to be venerated and praised.

Already word was being sent throughout the village of Donato and Rafaela's good fortune. There were many jealous hearts that day in Torre del Greco. It was not possible that one family should have such good luck.

The village women were preparing meals in their kitchens to deliver with their blessings to the family of Donato Banfi. Helena would this very night send word to her brother the Monsignor of The Basilica of St. Theresa the Little Flower to arrange for the Christening, to be held in two weeks. As was the custom, Rafaela, with the new babe, would be confined to the house until the Christening to ensure that no evil spirits could invade the vulnerable body of the newborn. Uncle Luigi the Monsignor would officiate at the ceremony to be held at the local church of St. Francis of Assisi. Father Palumbo, the pastor of St. Francis, was always happy to see Uncle Luigi, as they were friends from their youth. Uncle Luigi came somewhat frequently to Donato and Rafaela's home and had in fact baptized all of their children, which was truly an honor to their family.

It was almost seven in the morning and Donato gave back his prize to his wife and kissed her goodbye. He was on his way to work. As he exited the house, the neighbors were already waving their handkerchiefs and biding him *"Bono Salute!"* on the birth of his latest child. Male virility was an asset to be treasured and Donato Banfi had certainly proven his masculinity by the number of strong, healthy offspring. He stood even taller than his six feet and thanked them as he cockily strode down the strada, which led to the public dock and to his waiting boat. Donato was greeted by his fellow fishermen, who had waited to put to sea, to extend their heartfelt congratulations with hardy pats on the back and some bawdry remarks as to his male parts, but all in good humor. They then presented Donato with a fine cigar. Jokes about them hoping his catch for the day was as big as his own whale. He handily assured them that he had the biggest whale on the sea. To that they all laughed and cheered and said they felt sorry for poor little Rafaela. Donato assured them that she was very pleased with his whale. With that, they all climbed aboard their boats and cast out to the sea. There would be much merriment in the Banfi household this evening. Donato looked out upon the magnificent Bay of Naples with Mt. Vesuvius in the background and sucked in all the pride and wonderment of what had happened during the night. He felt the joy and sorrow of his responsibility to Rafaela and his children. His eyes filled with tears and his heart ached with happiness. He was a lucky man. This was a joyous day in the Banfi family.

CHAPTER TWO

THE CHRISTENING

Torre del Greco

June 28, 1698

Rafaela closed her eyes and fell into a deep peaceful sleep with her newborn daughter at her side. Both mother and child slept for several hours until Rafaela was awakened by the sound of Lucia softly fussing and crying to be nursed. Rafaela took her swollen breast from under her nightgown, laid the baby on her side, and placed her nipple in the baby's mouth. Immediately she began to suckle and her fussing stopped.

Maria went home to get some rest and check on her family. Helena now took over the task of preparing the family meal and tending to the other children. Her son-in-law would definitely be hungry and tired when he came in from the sea that night and a special meal was certainly the order of the day. Helena loved Donato as if he were her own son. She loved him for his kindness to her and Giuseppe and because he honored and respected their Rafaela and their children. He was a hardworking man and a good provider. After Helena had finished preparing the meal and had sent Giuseppe and the other children to the market, she checked in on her daughter and the baby. It was almost noon and the infant needed to be changed. She picked Lucia up from Rafaela's side and brought her over to the old battered table, which had been dressed with a lace trimmed linen cloth and was set up in the corner of the bedroom. She had reserved all her attention for his moment of bonding with her newest grandchild and remembered with longing when her own children were infants. Lucia did not cry or fuss, and the older woman, just stared at her with love. She was so pleased that Rafaela and Donato had decided to name her after her mother. It was really quite an honor.

She saw Lucia for the first time in the full brightness of the glowing June sun and was smitten by her beauty. The roundness of her head, the full head of hair, the blue of her eyes and the pouting little mouth, her chubby little body with the folds of skin and fat little thighs that longed to be kissed and nuzzled. This child was so different from fragile, petite Antoinetta, whose features were sharper, and who had her father's olive complexion. She was certainly going to be a beautiful woman, but in a decidedly different way. Her hair was the color of freshly roasted chestnuts, her eyes were almond shaped and hazel in color, and the richness of her olive complexion was exotic. She would probably grow up to be very petite and slight of built. She had a mild temperament and was beloved by her four big brothers who treated her like a china doll. Antoinetta knew from the first time she saw her little sister Lucia that she liked her face and that they were going to be very good friends.

Helena embraced Lucia with such love and warmth that the child snuggled in her arms. She thought of her beautiful mother, and the hard life she had, and only wished that she had been there to witness this birth from the granddaughter she loved so very much, and to know how they honored her by giving the child her name. But then a tinge of hatred crossed Helena's heart as she fought the repressed memory of her beloved son who her mother had sent to Sardinia to be educated by her uncle the famous cleric, Abbot Lorenzo Cioffi. He was but a mere boy when Lucia Rizzo insisted that he be sent to the mysterious and forbidden island. Her mother had promised that Jerome was meant for greatness, and thus required special training by the infamous master. While she loved her mother, Helena never truly forgave her for taking her boy away.

She tried to brush the pain of her son away, but the moment she laid eyes on Lucia, she saw Jerome's face. Helena wept for the love of her boy.

As she changed Lucia, she noticed the *medicina voglia*, a birthmark of such significance it filled her with fear. An ominous feeling came over her and her heart was sorrowful. She crossed herself, then made the sign of the cross on the baby's forehead, and said a prayer to the Blessed Mother to protect her granddaughter from any evil. She would mention this birthmark to her brother Luigi the Monsignor, and have him give a special blessing over the child. She dressed Lucia and placed her back at Rafaela's side. Helena would not discuss this matter with her daughter until she was feeling better, in a day or two, and then she would tell her of the significance of the omen. However, for now, she must go about her business and continue to prepare for tonight's celebration. Helena was a naive woman who believed, like most of the peasant people, in *sostantivo superstizione*. This was how they could answer all those mysterious events in their lives. Superstition, driven by fear and ignorance, countered by religion, put together they were deadly weapons.

There was much merriment in the Banfi household that evening, and the best wine was brought up from the vat in the cellar. Helena had outdone herself with the feast she had prepared. The children were all playing with their cousins and friends in the backyard, while the adults sat under the arbor, which was covered with lilacs and the sweet pungent odor filled the air. The evening was intoxicating, and Donato carried Rafaela to a chair under the arbor, while the babe, was carried out in her cradle. It was so refreshing to be out in the cool air with a mixture of sea breeze, lilacs, and the perfume from the glorious flower garden, which Rafaela took great pride in, with its statue of the Virgin perched on a platform overlooking the wonders nature had created.

Helena sent Giuseppe home because the small house was already bursting at the seams with people. She slept with Antoinetta in a small bed in the attic. The little girl was so thrilled at the thought of her grandmother sleeping with her she could hardly contain herself. It took the child a long time to fall asleep; she kept asking when she could play with her new sister. Finally, after several stories she fell fast asleep. Helena, drained from the ordeal of the past two days, looked in on Rafaela, and prepared Lucia for the night, or at least the next several hours although she did seem to be a very good and contented baby.

By the third day, life in the Banfi household was returning to normal. Rafaela was again on her feet and the children were busy in the garden. Donato was out to sea and Helena and Rafaela and the baby were finally alone for a peaceful afternoon under the arbor. As they sat, three generations, there was an unsettling silence. Helena knew her daughter sensed that something was wrong, and the older woman realized that this was the best moment to tell her of the baby's birthmark. Hesitantly, Helena opened the conversation about the beauty of Lucia and what a good baby she was and how happy she seemed, and how the other children especially Antoinetta loved her. The conversation was all very animated, yet Rafaela knew there was more to come. Her mother was a woman of few words and of even fewer compliments. Rafaela always knew her mother thought she was beautiful, but Helena was not one to shower you with glowing compliments.

Rafaela helped her mother by coming directly to the point and asked Helena to tell her what was the matter. She thought that perhaps her father had been drinking too much or that her mother was ill. Many thoughts ran through her head. "Mamma what is wrong? You seem very unsettled. Did someone say something to you? Are you ill?" Helena started to speak very softly, Rafaela was straining to hear what she had to say, and then, Helena's facial expression suddenly became very grave and sullen. Rafaela listened intently to her mother and the discovery of the birthmark on the infant's torso. At first Rafaela was somewhat perplexed by Helen's reaction "non c'e' motivo di preoccuparisi, Mamma. So what, everyone has some kind of a birthmark." It was at this point that Helena reached into the cradle and picked up Lucia and unwrapped her from the linen blanket that she was swaddled in. She lifted the baby's nightshirt and exposed the birthmark. This was the first time that Rafaela had seen the baby's body. The cherry red mark was no larger than a small seed and was located under the baby's left breast. Rafaela came very close and examined the *macchia*; it was a few moments before she realized what it actually was-a *capezzolo*. Rafaela saw the tiny nipple and drew in a deep painful breath. While she was not ignorant, or generally superstitious, she still harbored the nuances of her ancient background.

Rafaela asked her mother what was the meaning of this birthmark, and Helena ever so softly, almost whispering, related a story.

"Thousands of years ago, Agothe, God of Mars, impregnated a Roman vestal virgin whose name was Engracia. Naturally, when the high priest discovered her with child he assumed that she had engaged in sex with a man, so he banished her to Vesuvius where she was to be cast into the raging flames of the volcano as a sacrifice to the Gods for her indiscretion. Although she

begged and pleaded, swearing that a human being had not violated her, the high priest did not believe Engracia's story that she was the love slave of the God of Mars. By divine intervention, she was saved by Mars and brought to the mountains. There in the mountains she gave birth to three offspring of the God of Mars. These children were half human and half God. Because they needed to be suckled so, Mars gave Engracia a third nipple. One day she left her offspring in the woods alone and escaped to the nearest village. While she was gone, a lion devoured one of the babes. Mars was so angry and sad, that in his rage, he decreed as a punishment for her disloyalty, a curse was placed upon Engracia. From that day forward, any man who looked upon her magnificent face would fall in love with her, but she would be incapable of loving him back, because the nipple Mars had given her to suckle his beloved child, who Engracia had abandoned and who had died, would make her desire only sex not love or commitment. Engracia, and all her descendants, would pray for a loving relationship, but would have a life filled with animal desire and loveless affairs".

Rafaela's first reaction was total denial. It was not another nipple on her baby's body but just an ordinary birthmark, her mind would not, could not accept this fact. What seemed like an eternity but, in realty, were only a few moments, she sat there and tears started to well up in her eyes. How could this horrible fate come upon her child, what matter of evil had she committed to warrant such a punishment from God. Helena said that perhaps one of the villagers had placed the evil eye, *mal locua*, upon her while she was ready to conceive. The deed was done and the only thing they could do now was to have Uncle Luigi perform a special blessing upon the child and have novenas said regularly for her spiritual wellbeing.

It was decided that Helena would go home that night so that Rafaela and Donato could have privacy to discuss this horrible thing that had befallen their blessed baby. When Donato arrived home after a long day of hauling fish, he was tired and hungry. As usual, he washed, ate and played a little while with his boys, spent some time with Antoinetta and then sent everyone to bed. Since it was hot and close in the small house, Rafaela asked Donato to join her under the arbor. She brought out two glasses of Chianti and a bowl of fruit. They sat down and were just talking of the day's events and Donato told her of the bountiful catch he had and was able to sell the whole boatload to someone from Naples. It was a good day.

Donato sensed that Rafaela wanted to tell him something, so he asked her "Cara, cosa c'e'?" Rafaela, with tears in her eyes, could hardly form words. Frightened, Donato sprang from his chair to come kneel by her side. "What, what is it?" the urgency in his voice prompted Rafaela to blurt out her response. "Lucia, she has a mark, a medicina voglia, a birthmark. But no, not just a simple mark, it is a capezzola". Donato seemed confused, "of course she has a nipple she is a female", he said with a dazed expression. "Donato, do you not understand, she has tre!" His mouth opened to say something but he could not find the words. Finally, he spoke "Come può essere? È pericoloso? Qual è il problema?" a confusion of thoughts were running rampart through his head. Rafaela had no true explanation for his questions, the only thing she knew was that physically it was not dangerous, but in the world of superstition, it might be later on in life. Choking back her tears, Rafaela retold the story her mother had shared earlier in the day. Donato was stunned and sat quietly for a long time before he answered. "This means nothing. It is only an old moglie storia. Put it from your mind, but, if you must find peace with it, speak with Uncle Luigi to bring you comfort. I am sure he will tell you not to put any stock in such tales of fancy. Mars, ugh, what sciocchezze! Lucia is healthy and perfect." Donato, the practical fisherman, a man of nature, always saw the reality before the supernatural and thank God, because the moment he said it she immediately felt better. He came around to where she was seated, brought his chair close to hers, and grabbed her hand with perhaps a little more force than he intended. "Rafaela, Cara, only man can put harm on someone; and, Jesus would not make such a perfect creature only to bring her harm. Non c'e'preoccupare di." He picked up her hand and kissed it then caressed it within his huge powerful gripe. His outward bravado did nothing to squelch the feeling of foreboding he held in his own heart. He too had been born to the same tales and superstitions as his wife. He would pray for the wellbeing of his baby girl.

The two weeks passed quickly yet there was much preparation for the house and garden for the christening of a child was a sacred ceremony in their religion. As promised, Uncle Luigi would officiate over the baptism. Helena had met with her brother several days before the event was to be held, and told him of the birthmark. Luigi was a learned man and a devout man of God. Although he knew there was no factual evidence to any of these old wives tales, his upbringing was steeped in mythological tradition. He knew it would not be prudent to minimize his sister's concern for her granddaughter, but wanted to reassure her and Rafaela, that he would perform a special blessing over Lucia, and that the Blessed Mother would protect her from any evil.

Several days before the christening was to take place, Uncle Luigi came for a visit to Rafaela's house. It was the first time he would see the new baby. He was dazzled by her beauty and cherubic face. Something so innocent and made in the image of God could not, would not, be wrong. He embraced Lucia with such unabashed love that tears welled up in his eyes and he prayed fervently that her life would see blessings beyond all imagining. Monsignor Luigi Rizzo was a prominent cleric in the Roman Catholic Church for southern Italy. He was a man who commanded respect and authority. At this moment, he felt small and inadequate, as he felt the vibrations traversing through the infant he held so dearly in his arms course through his own body. This child was special, he did not know what it was, but she would grow to be famous. With a heart heavy with anticipation, he prayed with all the fervor of his rock solid faith that Lucia's fate would be blessed with grace. He saw that Rafaela sensed a change in his demeanor and she shuttered, for his part, he tried to brush the feeling of uncertainty from his mind and heart. Lucia was special just like his mother. He could not help but see the face of Jerome, his nephew, in this innocent child. His sister Helena was never the same after his mother sent Jerome to Sardinia to be educated in the dark and mysterious ways of his reclusive uncle Lorenzo Cioffi. The resemblance was both frightening and exciting. Was baby Lucia the kindred spirit of his long lost nephew?

"Rafaela, your mother has told me of the macchia on Lucia. The ways of the Lord hold many mysteries. It is not for us to question what He does. My sister and I grew up fearing things that people could not explain. When something bad happened, or when someone was born malformed, right away it was the devil's work. No. This is not true. You must banish any of those thoughts from that pretty head." Luigi brought his two massive hands up to Rafaela's face and cradled her head in his hands. He looked unwavering into those amber eyes and spoke from his heart. "My sweet niece, you were my mother's favorite. She was an exceptional woman with strength and beauty beyond anyone I have ever known. This child will grow in her image with love and strength. You need not fear for Our Blessed Lady together with Nona Lucia, will watch over her." Still holding her head, he bent over to kiss her forehead, and, each cheek. Even as he spoke the words, hoping that his voice did not betray the feeling he was harboring, he prayed.

Uncle Luigi went to pick up Lucia once again. He continued to hold the baby and she nuzzled in his arms as he sat in the garden and gazed upon the child. He explained to his niece that her mother, his sister Helena, was raised under the veil of superstitions, and that although her stories were amusing, they had very little factual basis. He had been fortunate enough to find the calling of God, and was sent to the seminary to be educated in the arts and sciences before such fanciful tales could influence him. Yet, he also knew that for there to be true good there would always be true evil. He had witnessed many acts of the devil and shuddered at the thought. Instinctively he made the sign of the cross on Lucia's forehead, and then crossed himself.

Luigi Rizzo was a huge, powerful man, who would easily pass for a burly laborer rather than a highly educated theologian and scholar. He had in fact written and published several ecclesiastical papers and wrote regularly for the Vatican. His face was ruggedly handsome, and his graying temples gave him a distinguished air, although the fashion of the day was to wear a powdered wig Luigi refused such ornamentation except when officiating at official Vatican ceremonies. His hands were massive and often sported calluses from his hobby of gardening. The Basilica of St. Theresa the Little Flower had the most gorgeous rose garden Rafaela had ever seen. Uncle Luigi claimed his roses grew so well because he watered them with holy water. Luigi's voice with resonant and when he sang his incantations during the mass the congregation was inspired. Although extremely intelligent, he could converse easily with even the lowliest peasant or the

Pope in four different languages. He had graduated at the top of his class in the seminary and was quickly advanced through the ranks. It was even rumored that he was being considered for Archbishop of Naples.

Rafaela was so confident in what her uncle had told her, and believed so fervently in his spiritual power, that she buried all thoughts of any misfortune coming to her child that psychologically she would eventually cease to see the birthmark on Lucia's body. Faith is a powerful tool in the control of the mind, and Rafaela's faith was unwavering, more so in her uncle than perhaps her religion.

Monsignor Luigi Rizzo performed the baptism of Lucia Banfi with all the pomp and ceremony of royalty. The choir was singing and the whole family turned out for the event. The small church was filled with the family and friends of Rafaela and Donato Banfi. The church, resplendent in its Gothic architecture, which family and friends had decorated with flowers, was a mixture of sights, sounds, and scents. The church of St. Francis of Assisi was a place of solace and peace for all the inhabitants of Torre del Greco. Its congregants were baptized, received the sacraments of Holy Communion, Confirmation and Holy Matrimony and ultimately the Last Rites. It held memories of great joy, but, at times of sickness or death, it was also a refuge for those in pain. Donato and Rafaela were both baptized, confirmed, and married in this church and each of their children had come into grace from its font. Someday their bodies will be blessed for the last time from its altar. The organ bellowed out the songs so familiar to Rafaela, the melodies of which she often chanted while doing her gardening or sewing. The combination of floral scents and the exotic smoke from the incense filled her nostrils with the smell of faith and love for Jesus. The first several pews were filled with the chatting and smiling faces of her family and a few friends. Most of the celebration would happen back at her home where half the village and all her relatives were anxiously anticipating a grand party to commemorate this blessed event.

Uncle Luigi, for his part, always the showman, dressed in the riches of his position, did not fail to entertain the audience. With his robust voice pronounced each Latin word of the prayer that would cleanse baby Lucia from the stain of original sin. Reaching into the marble font, he drew the holy water into the silver cup and began to pour the water over Lucia's head. She winced at the temperature of the water but did not cry. "In the nome of the Padre, the Figlio, and the Santo, I baptize you, Lucia Helena Banfi". He sang in his rich baritone the incantations of their faith. The sunlight dappled through the magnificent stained glass windows scattering prisms of colored light across the pale stucco walls. It was comfortably warm with a mild fragrant whisper of a breeze coming from the open doors. This huge man, clad in all his regalia, stood tall and proud, a symbol of his faith and in his out stretched hands he adoringly held Lucia. Her beautiful face beaming with pleasure at the sights and sounds surrounding her, and he, with child in hand, offered her up to the Lord, and at that instant, as if on cue, a shaft of brilliant light came from one of the stained glass windows. Lucia turned her cherubic face toward the light and smiled. Luigi, the man and the priest, ever so gently kissed her upturned face and presented the newest member of the Holy Catholic Church to her adoring family.

The weather was perfect, and after the services, everyone was invited back to the house for the gala celebration. There were delicacies of every shape, taste, and description. Helena, Rafaela, Maria and several older aunts had been cooking for two days preparing this elaborate feast. Giuseppe had brought several gallons of his own select Chianti wine. Even Olympia had managed to steal a few hours to join the merriment. While Olympia knew that Rafaela and her immediate family were well aware of the mark that clouded the child, she did not refer to its existence nor did they. For now, Lucia was happy, healthy, and safe and she would always keep her in her prayers, but, today, she would have a good time and relax. It was a most splendid party and the proud parents were honored that so many were able to join them on this special day.

The afternoon was balmy with the ever present breezes from the Bay of Naples. It was a time for celebration with family and friends. These hard working people received great joy from these types of gatherings. The women sat under the shade of the grappa vines chatting about the latest news from Naples and Roma. Since Rafaela was such an accomplished seamstress, they sought advice on their own sewing projects. Zia Nunziatta had made a few extra stops by the wine bowl and was slurring her words and making snorting sounds. Nona Helena was exhausted and dozed off while pretending to be part of the conversation. Maria was shepherding the youngest family members to an area where she could safely monitor their activity.

The men were sitting around sharing stories from their many fishing trips. Donato was retelling for the hundredth time the story of when his younger brother-in-law Carmine was out on one of the fishing boats and was teasing the seagulls. Tempting the sea birds with fish bait, playfully throwing pieces into the air but making sure they landed back in the bucket. Carmine was laughing so heartily with his head thrown back and his mouth wide open. Suddenly one of his victims swooped down from out of the sky and bombarded Carmine's face with all his droppings. Men were laughing uncontrollably at poor Carmine, but it was all done in good humor. They sat there smoking their cigars and drinking their wine, making small talk while others were playing cards or bocce ball. As the day drew long, and the sun set over the bay, the sounds of contentment filled the air. Life was good, for today.

CHAPTER THREE

LIFE IN THE VILLAGE

TORRE del GRECO

Life in Torre del Greco continued in much the same easy way that it had always been. The town of Torre del Greco, a sleepy waterfront village on the Bay of Naples at the foot of Vesuvius, dove si incontrano il mare e` la terra, where the sea meets the land, is approximately twenty kilometers from Naples. The name means "Tower of Greek". During ancient times, its location to both the sea and the formidable presence of the volcano made it the perfect site for the construction of a coastal watchtower. This tower became inhabited by a Greek hermit hence the name.

Torre del Greco was a small fishing village that lived in the shadow of the great mountain. This was where Donato and Rafaela made their home. Vesuvius, the only active volcano on the mainland of Europe, the name means "the unextinguished" fucco negli occi, it had destroyed the ancient city of Pompeii. While the dread of the volcano was always present, the locals made their peace with the fire monster.

According to legend, the citizens of Torre del Greco bought back their village from the Marquis of Monteforte, an ancestor of the current inhabitants of Casa Monteforte, and thenceforth, the city flourished as a maritime trading and fishing port. The history of this region is an intricate tapestry of many different countries and peoples who brought the threads of their cultures to the region. It was into this rich past that Lucia Banfi was born.

The small stucco houses were painted in the colors of a traditional Mediterranean scheme, with pale yellow, soft orange, petal pink and azure blue. Flower boxes hung like jewelry from the windows and balconies. The small shops had their shingles hanging out over the doorways announcing their goods or services. Several merchants serviced the town. There was the butcher, the linen and fabric shop, the bakery, two trattorias, a barber shop whose proprietor was also a sometimes surgeon, the general store where one could purchase household items and the apothecary that sold medicinal herbs and charms. The air was clean and crisp. The inhabitants of Torre del Greco were very fortunate people. They enjoyed the benefits of the sea and the beauty of the mountains. The torrid Mediterranean sun warmed their days with salty breezes from the sea and Vesuvius cooled their nights. It was an idyllic place steeped in beauty and folklore. The rich soil produced some of the most delicious vines while the abundance from the sea brought forth sustainable food and the prized red coral. Eventually, Torre del Greco became known for its legendary cameos and coral jewelry.

The Banfi family lived in peaceful harmony and all was well with them and their loved ones. The boys were getting so big and strong like Donato and they were all doing well. Antonio, who struggled through his studies, but loved the freedom of being on the sea, would more than likely assume his father's role as a fisherman.

Andrea, the most serious of the Banfi boys, was a brilliant mathematician. Now at sixteen years old he would be going off to Padua to study at the university thanks to Uncle Luigi who had found a sponsor for his talented nephew. Genaro, even at fourteen, showed a great aptitude for art and was becoming a favorite of the local patrons. His latest accomplishment was a fresco commissioned by the Pastor of Saint Frances of Assisi. This was so special because it was his family parish and everyone in the village knew that he was the artist. The family was so proud.

Francesco, only twelve, seemed to have the call to the ministry of the Lord, and that pleased Rafaela and Donato very much. This coming summer during school recess Uncle Luigi was going to let him stay at the seminary for three months to see if he truly felt the vocation. Francesco would have to make his first commitment to the religious life by his fourteenth birthday. He was so excited at the prospect of spending time with Uncle Luigi. Everyone knew since he was a tiny boy that he had the calling.

Little Antoinetta, a very mature ten, was an aspiring musician and big sister to Lucia now seven. The two girls loved each other very much and grew closer every day. Antoinetta adored her sister and Lucia depended on her big sister. Oddly enough, Lucia at seven was bigger than Antoinetta. Life was good and God had given them many blessings.

CHAPTER FOUR

THE BIRTHDAY PARTY

Monteforte
April 13, 1692

Sparrows were singing and the honeybees were swarming around their hive. Maria was so happy to be in her blooming garden. With hands covered to her wrists in the rich Mediterranean soil, she happily hummed her favorite tune. She stepped back to drink in the fragrant aroma of the pungent earth and brushed a fly from her face leaving a smudge across the bridge of her nose. It was hot. The sun was high and beads of sweat ran down her sun-kissed face. With her burnt sienna hair, now streaked with silver and gold, she did not betray her age. Today, her birthday, Maria Sucretti would reach forty years of age. For these times, she was considered an old woman, but she neither looked, nor acted, like the numbers of her years. While Maria had been born to wealth and never truly had to toil and labor, she had kept herself in prime physical condition. Her toned and supple body was accustomed to walking up and down the steep cliffs from the palazzo to the sea, which Maria did every day to keep her youthful figure. Her tall lean body looked like that of a woman twenty years younger. The only disloyalty to her years was the silver threads that wove through her beautiful auburn tresses, yet, when Natalie, her personal servant, would fix her hair, she would always manage to hide those menacing strands in the most conspiratorial way. With good straight teeth and a near flawless complexion, Maria Sucretti was still beautiful even in her maturing.

"Mistress, it is nearly time for you to get ready for the party. Come, we must get you bathe and dressed for the guests will be arriving before you are even prepared." Natalie was anxious to get Maria ready for the party her husband Salvatore was giving her in honor of her birthday. He rarely, if ever, showed much interest in Maria anymore, but every year on her birthday, he always invited guests to help celebrate her special day. This party would be extra special since it marked a milestone, for few people reached forty years of age. Life was filled with hard labor and childbirth, famine and disease. Surprising, even to her, was the fact that Salvatore was still living. She had thought that if someone had not yet assassinated him, by now the syphilis would have killed him for sure. Sadly, he still lived. By comparison, to his wife Salvatore looked worn and haggard. His body hung like wet laundry from its frame, and his skin, which once was muscular and tawny, now was slack and grey. Pus filled nodules dotted his face and neck. His once strong and sculpted body was slightly hunched making him appear as if he had shrunk. The eyes were deep set and dark, almost black. He had lost most of his teeth from the disease and so he sported a thick mustache to cover most of his mouth. If it were not for his magnificently tailored clothing, he would have passed for a vagabond. His appearance was in such stark contrast to his power. Let there be no mistake, regardless of his physical attributes, Salvatore Sucretti, was the leader of a criminal network so powerful that no one would cross the invisible line to usurp his authority. His was the last word and there was no debate. A disubbidire a lui doveva morire.

Maria was dreading the coming hours. She hated these affairs since she knew that everyone laughed at her husband's charade of affection. Salvatore, in addition to being a ruthless criminal mastermind, was a notorious whoremaster. His pandering caused him to contract his deadly disease. She stood there trying to will the day to be over. Maria was a proud woman, but, because of her devout faith, she did not seek to dissolve their loveless and barren marriage. Looking around she breathe in the beauty that was Monteforte, her ancestral home, the sights and sounds of its timeless fortitude. She knew her obligation, closed her eyes, prayed for the strength to get through the evening, and followed Natalie to her rooms.

The house was ablaze with activity. Fernando the matri di casa, now clad in his powdered wig and finest waistcoat, was busy giving instructions to the house staff. He oversaw a vast network of staff from the housekeeping to the stables. Fernando, who had been with the Rizzo family since he was born, as were his parents before him, was known as the General. Everyone took orders either directly from him or from his assigned delegates. While there were minions in different areas, such as food preparation, gardening, animals, laundry, he, Fernando, was the person in charge of Monteforte. No one questioned him, or his power to reward or punish. Those who disobeyed his orders were dealt with swiftly, with no recourse. Nevertheless, he was a fair and honorable man, and while the staff feared him, they loved and respected him. He was like a father to all of them. Both Maria and Salvatore knew that Fernando controlled Monteforte; yet, they also knew he would never do anything contrary to what his position dictated. Fernando was now inwardly anxious, although his outward appearance never belied his true feelings. Everything needed to be perfect, not only as a tribute to his master and mistress, but to uphold his own reputation for perfection.

The cook was barking orders to his subordinates to fetch this or that. The heat generating from the summer kitchen was intolerable. Marcello, who was the son of the former chef, was very young to hold the position as the Master Chef. He was irritable from the heat. He was a rotund man and felt like he was being poached. He had discussed the menu for the party first with Fernando, then with the Mistress. It was an ambitious assortment of hot and cold appetizers, a pasta entrée, meats being roasted in an open pit near the stables to keep the smoke from filling the terrace, but the rich aroma of roasting lamb was delicate and mouthwatering. Marcello was a genius with food and could transform even the simplest of fare into something extraordinary. He loved to show off his skills at parties like this, but the insufferable heat was putting a strain on his corpulent body. Much like Fernando, he had been raised at Monteforte, but had been sent to Rome and Paris to learn the finer art of cooking. Sometimes, given their knowledge and status within the estate, their opinions clashed, and Maria, as the Mistress of the Manse, would have to intercede to make peace. She loved them both, as she did all her staff, and treated them like family. There were serving girls, grooms, footmen, all afoot scurrying about with assorted tasks like drone bees flitting around their hive. Tables were laden with exotic fruits and cheeses just brought in from France, an array of meats and fish prepared in several different styles to showcase Marcello's vast knowledge of food preparation. Even Fernando was impressed with the range of favors and presentation of the various dishes.

The table had been set with vases of beautiful roses, which they had picked from Maria's garden. The musicians, were just now arriving, these were several of the prodigy from the recently established Neapolitan School of Music in Naples. Maria Sucretti was an ardent patron of the arts, and had been one of the first to support this wonderful establishment. The candles were reflecting a warm, soft glow from the sparkling Venetian crystal chandeliers and wall sconces. An entire stuffed roasted boar was the centerpiece of the meat table. Breads woven into thick braids, some filled with eggs, prosciutto, and cheese, looked too beautiful to eat. Pastries of every type were piled on silver platters. Mounds of fruit, rings of imported cheeses and salamis, nuts and figs grown right on the grounds of Monteforte were displayed in a most tantalizing manner. It was all very marvelous.

Salvatore had invited nearly a hundred guests. Maria knew that few, if any, were actually coming because it was her birthday, but, because of who he was, once invited, it was an insult not to accept. She dreaded the endless notes of thanks she and Natalie would have to write for the gifts people would bring; gifts from the most extravagant to the most God awful piece of jewelry. She hated this, but knew she could never stop it. No one wanted to insult Salvatore Sucretti. Everything was set for what was going to be a wonderful celebration in honor of Maria's fortieth birthday.

If only Maria would have been happier at the prospect of meeting her invited guests. Natalie had all to do to get her Mistress ready. "Come, you will be late to your own party. What a tribute to reach forty years of age and to look like a twenty-year-old woman. You look lovely." Natalie, who had just finished putting the jeweled combs in her mistress' hair reached for the looking glass so that Maria could see herself and the finished results. She took the proffered mirror and walked to the doors that led to her balcony where the light was still strong even though the day was growing long. A shaft of light was caught on the reflecting glass, which bathed her face with a soft warm glow, which gave her skin a radiant hue. Maria Sucretti, tall, thin, and aristocratic, was a handsome woman. Her gown for this evening was the color of copper with seed pearls encrusted along the plunging neckline. A lace bodice was trimmed with matching pearls and caressed her full décolletage. Her full bosom, made even more outstanding by the bone stays that Natalie had so ingeniously sewn into the bodice of her gown, and the tight laces from her chemise were designed to emphasize her shapely torso. She was stepping into her petticoats with their bone hooping which she hated. She smoothed down the voluminous layers of copper silk, which shimmered in the light. Natalie had out done herself with adorning Maria's wavy hair with jeweled combs and tiny roses. The jewels she wore were family heirlooms. She touched the diamond pendant at her neck and felt it sit warmly in the hollow of her throat, and remembered her mother telling her that someday it would be hers, and a feeling of loss filled her heart with an unexpected ache. She knew she was alone in this world, and that all her family was dead. It was a sense of fear that infiltrated her dreams and brought great sadness. Looking over the balcony terrace, she could see the whole expanse of Monteforte and often asked herself "Who will come to be master of Monteforte?" The question was never answered.

Natalie came over to inspect her mistress. "You truly look like a queen. That color brings out your lovely skin and the dress is perfect for that tiny waist. I am so jealous." Maria ever so graciously took Natalie's hand and kissed it. "If it were not for you to attend to me I would look like a stable hand. I love how you fixed my hair so all those nasty silver strands are invisible. Thank you. Now, you get dressed so you can come to the party. Now, go." Maria loved Natalie, not just as a competent maid but also as a lifelong friend.

Maria was pleased with the way she looked, but there was no joy in her eyes. She would have to pretend that this birthday celebration was such a loving gift from Salvatore whom she despised. Ever the fraud, Salvatore, gave the public appearance of a faithful husband, while, behind their fans and smoke rings all knew it was a farce. "Bugie, la sua vita era niente ma si trova? Gesu, why don't you let him die and leave me in peace?"

Maria, born of aristocracy, was a social icon, married to the head of the Camorra, knew her place. She stood, set her slender shoulders, and brought herself to her full height. She inhaled, taking a deep breath to calm her temper, and walked down to meet her guests. Waiting at the foot of the massive staircase was Fernando. He looked appraisingly at his Mistress and nodded at her beauty. Extending his arm, he stood tall and proudly escorted her into the room. As she emerged into the grand ballroom of Monteforte, all eyes were focused on Maria. She could hear the audible whispers and saw the faked smiles. Then from the back of the room Salvatore came forward with an appreciative smile, he extended his hand to her, she accepted it courteously, and he drew her to the center of the room. They stood, side by side, painting such a contrasting image. Maria was beautiful, elegant, and the picture of radiant health, while Salvatore, dressed in the finest brocade waistcoat with ruffled collar and cuffs, his silk breeches contouring his lower body to the knee and met by his silk stockings and handmade leather shoes with gold buckles, could not erase the disease that had infested his once powerful body. His fashionable powdered wig, in sharp contrast to his dark mustache, his wrinkled skin, and slight hunch gave him the look of an old man, even though he was only a year older than Maria. He took a glass of wine from a tray being passed by a serving maid and lifted his glass. "A mia moglie bella su questo suo quarantesimo compleanno. Lei può vedere molte più in buona salute. Salute!" and the crowd roared with good cheer and tipped their glasses in response. Salvatore then grabbed her close to himself, and planted a hard wet kiss on her mouth. He whispered in her ear, "Tonight you and I will make love." She brushed him away as nonchalantly as she could without acting upset, and turned and smiled to the guests, while raising her own glass in thanks for their well wishes. The thought of sharing her body with this pig of a husband was so revolting that she felt the bile rise in the back of her throat.

Maria, ever the lady, worked her way through the crowd sharing bits and piece of conversation and gossip, receiving kisses and well wishes. When she finally found a moment alone, she shuddered at the prospect of being intimate with Salvatore. If he thought for one moment she would allow him to come even within her bedchamber, never the less her body, he was sadly mistaken. Then she comforted herself with the thought that he will be so drunk by then he would be lucky to be standing.

The evening went off like a well-planned script. There were tables set with embroidered table coverings and crystal candelabras heaped with huge platters of food expertly prepared by Marcello and his staff. The whole roasted lambs were brought in from the spits with the aroma wafting throughout the room with the sizzle still hissing. An entire table was set with sweetmeats, breads, and pastries of all sizes, shapes, and colors. Wine and liquor was flowing free and everyone was enjoying himself or herself. At the end of the long room were the musicians. They were wearing their finest coats and wigs all set up with violin, cello, and harp. Fernando had moved the grand piano to the corner where they were to be placed and left enough room for an ample dance floor. Everything was resplendent as she looked around and saw that her staff had seen to even the smallest detail. The screens, so discreetly arranged in the farthest corner of the grand ballroom, near the doors to the terrace that were used as toilets. There was one on the left for men and one on the right for women. Each side had its own attendant to see to the needs of the guests. She was very proud of all of her staff. The guests complimented Salvatore and Maria on the quality and quantity of the food and drink.

Fernando had truly accomplished a grand level of hospitality. Once everyone had left, Maria thanked him and all the staff for their efforts. Fernando, ever the faithful servant, came over to his Mistress. "May I give you a birthday kiss Mistress?" she was not surprised by this intimacy and accepted it for the love it held. "Of course Fernando, thank you." He reached up with both hands, cupped her face, and landed a soft kiss on each cheek. "Dio vi benedica Mistress. Tutti ti amiamo." Maria was so touched a tear came to the back of her eyes. "Now Mistress, you must get your beauty rest and we must clean up. I will serve breakfast to you in a few hours. Good night." Fernando, bowed deeply and left to begin orchestrating the cleanup efforts, even though it was very late, she knew by the time she came down to breakfast it would be as pristine as if no one had ever been there. "Good night Fernando. Thank you."

Exhausted, Maria made her way to her bedchamber. Waiting, or at least dozing, on the settee was Natalie. Natalie was herself thirty-seven years old, and she too looked much younger than her years. Upon hearing her Mistress enter the bedroom, she roused herself to greet her with congratulations. "I had come down for a while and everyone was talking about how beautiful you looked. They were complimenting the lavishness of the party and Monteforte. It was a wonderful party and tomorrow we will begin the task of opening the presents and writing the thank you notes. But, for now, I must get you to bed, before you start to look your age." Maria laughed and welcomed the good humor and help of her old friend and faithful companion. Natalie undid the laces of her bodice and carefully helped Maria step out of her gown then untied her corset.

Maria was so tired but she went to the toilet to wash before going to her bed. Natalie had laid out her nightgown, and was turning down the spread from the elegantly carved four-poster bed, which had been a family heirloom. After washing her face and body with rose water, she came to sit down by her vanity. Maria slipped on her nightgown. Natalie was taking out the combs and pins in her hair, and started brushing out her long luxurious tresses, when the door to the bedchamber swung open and a drunken Salvatore was standing in the doorway. His laugh was both repulsive and terrifying at the same time. "Ci sono, mia cara moglie, vengo a darti il tuo regalo di compleanno". The mere suggestion of intimacy with him made her stomach jump into her throat. Maria felt Natalie shudder. He advanced toward them. "Leave" he growled to Natalie but Maria held her wrist and told her to stay. Natalie, a look of dread on her face, was frozen to the spot. Salvatore then grabbed Natalie and jerked her away. The maid protested and tried to escape. "Salvatore, don't you dear come closer!" Salvatore was furious; he had Natalie in a death grip that the maid was wincing from the pressure on her wrist. He suddenly raised his other hand and landed and audible slap across Natalie's stunned face. "Bitch, when I give you an order you obey me. Maybe you need a lesson in respect for your Master." Natalie, had never before been treated with such abuse, was scared and shocked. Salvatore spun her toward the bed and threw her down. "Lay across the bed and lift up you gown. I am going to teach you once and for all who the Master of Monteforte truly is." He had taken off his belt and was lifting her gown to expose her bare ass. She squirmed and he held her down. The thwack of the leather meeting flesh resounded in the large room, and again another blow found its mark. Natalie was by this time screaming for him to stop. Maria was pulling at his arm but she could not control his maddening violence. He was pounding the leather strap against Natalie's bare bottom and she was welting up. Maria let go, ran to her dressing table, and picked up the only object she could find to use as a weapon. She had the long, sharp, pin she used to secure her hat in her hand; she raised her hand above her head, and thrust the pin into his neck. Salvatore released Natalie with a surprised look on his face, reached up to his neck, and in one quick movement ejected the pin from his bleeding neck. Dazed, he roiled with fury at Maria, grabbed her by her long thick hair, and threw her to the floor. Maria landed with a thud and she immediately felt the sensation that something had cracked in her ribcage, Salvatore reached her in two leaps and was cursing. The last thing she saw was the leather strap coming toward her face. She was semiconscious but could hear more screaming in the back of her head. She could not tell if she was screaming, or if it was Natalie. Her first thought was to save Natalie. Maria raised herself, or at least tried, to get up, but the entire world was spinning out of control. Her face was stinging so bad she could not see, and then she realized that her right eye was now completely closed.

Giovanni Romano had been going through the palazzo, securing all windows and doors and making sure that there were no guests remaining in the house. Sometimes, these parties, with the free flowing wine, would have people passing out from a drunken stupor. He felt confident that all was in order and was looking for Fernando to let him know that all was secure, and that he would be going up to his rooms for the night. He found Fernando supervising the cleaning of the grand ballroom. "Ah, there you are, I want to let you know that all is in order, everyone is gone, and I locked up all windows and doors. By the way, you did a very good job, my congratulations. Good night old friend." Fernando liked Giovanni, he knew the man was a bodyguard and trained assassin, but respected him for the work he did, and his loyalty and sense of honor. "Much thanks Giovanni. Good evening." Giovanni was about to take his leave, when they both heard the terrified screams coming from upstairs. Giovanni took the stairs two at a time and reached the top in seconds. He paused to hear what he could not see. His years of training for moments like this brought his mind and body to sharp attention. There was another scream, which was coming from his Mistress's rooms. Giovanni took the only weapon he had at hand, which was the knife he always carried on his belt. Because there were so many people at the party that evening, Giovanni thought it wise to put his pistol away so as not to frighten some of the ladies. Everyone knew he was Salvatore's bodyguard but he hated to look the part of a Camorra.

Stealthily, he looked up and down the hall, to see if anyone was hiding in the long shadows of the hall. Seeing no one, Giovanni crept toward the open door of the Mistress's bedchamber, sounds of struggle and screaming were coming from within. Silently he cursed himself for his vanity that he did not have his pistol on him. He was trying to determine how the thieves got in and how many there were. His mind was racing, trying to settle a plan when he heard Natalie's voice pleading with her assailant to stop beating her. In that split second, he abandoned all sense of personal safety and charged into the room. There, to his horror, he saw that Salvatore had been beating his wife Natalie, was splayed across the bed, with her bottom raw and bloody, and Mistress Sucretti was crouched in a heap on the floor. Both woman were badly beaten, blood covered their faces. Salvatore was pounding Maria with his leather belt, cursing with such intensity that the spittle was foaming from his mouth, giving him the appearance of a mangy rabid dog. Natalie was screaming for help. The scene seemed too unreal to be truly happening. Never in his life did he think that his master would perpetrate such an atrocity upon these two special women. He knew the man was a cruel beast, having witnessed some of the heinous abuses he had inflicted upon unwitting persons, but this was beyond anything he would ever have imagined.

Giovanni was trying to make some decision as to how to stop this mayhem. He ran to abort the next blow from finding its target when Salvatore turned on him, and landed the intended lash against Giovanni's neck. Infuriated, Giovanni handily disarmed him of the belt. Salvatore went insane with fury, and rounded on Giovanni, who was built like a warrior. They struggled for the knife that Giovanni already had in his hand, anticipating finding bandits, but instead, only to find his master beating both his wife and his mistress.

Salvatore, in the second it took Giovanni to recover from the blow, managed to snatch the knife away from him. Giovanni, now recovered, was trying to dislodge the knife from Salvatore's grip, but he was in such a state of madness, he could not be reasoned with, or controlled. Giovanni was surprised at the strength of the wizened man, but had seen this behavior in people who have lost all sense of reality. The dance of death continued for a few moments, when suddenly the body of Salvatore jerked violently, then went completely limp. Giovanni suddenly found himself holding tightly to the limp body of Salvatore, with his eyes bulging and the death gurgle coming from his mouth. Giovanni was dazed at what had happened and shook his head to reconcile the situation. The knife, still clenched in his hand, had not made contact with Salvatore's body, yet he was gasping for breath. Up to this point, all Giovanni's concentration had been centered on the struggle at hand. He had obliterated the distracting sounds of the room. Now, unexpectedly, he became aware in his surroundings.

Standing just behind Salvatore, he suddenly noticed Fernando with his hands on the hilt of a large kitchen knife, which he had thrust into his master's back. Giovanni, still holding the inert body of Salvatore shifted him to the floor. Salvatore was wheezing for breath, with his mouth urgently opening and closing trying to grab what air he could. His eyes were bulging and black as coal; his skin was growing pale and turning cold. Giovanni turned him slightly on his side, and reached behind the prone body and seized the protruding knife. There was a small quaffing sound and whoosh of air as it came out of the lungs. Blood was now flowing rapidly over the body, and on to the floor.

Fernando was in a state of disbelief, with his eyes dark and red as fire. He was trembling and looking faint. Giovanni moved from the body knowing that in a few seconds his master would be dead, and truly not caring to give comfort to this monster, but more urgently trying to help Fernando. Seeing the state of Fernando, he grabbed him under the arms, and dragged him to a chair. He was mumbling incoherently, with a mixture of sweat and tears running freely down his cheeks. Giovanni knew the signs of shock, and went to fetch the basin of water. He got a linen towel and wiped the older man's face. There was a decanter of brandy on the side table, and poured him a few ounces of liquor. Fernando held the glass with the brandy; it shook so badly that Giovanni was sure none of the alcohol would reach the man's mouth. "Please Fernando you must drink this to calm your nerves. Go on, take a drink". For the first time, in all the years that Giovanni Romano had lived at Monteforte, did he now notice the true age of this man. The lines of his years, were now etched in his distressed face, he looked frail and not the controlled matri` di casa, the Generale` as all the staff referred to him as. Fernando looked frightened and old. He seemed more weary than scared. "I am sorry not for what I have done, but, only that I had not done it years ago. Signore` Sucretti had done many things to the younger maids and even some of the young boys, but, I always turned a blind eye. When I saw my Mistress lying there on the floor, all I could think of was how to save her." He turned his face toward Maria, who was still lying in a bundle, and wept. Fernando was in love with her, since the day she was born, there was nothing, even, murder; he would not do to keep her safe.

It now occurred to Maria that everything was quiet. The screaming had stopped and someone was lifting her off the floor. Her mouth went dry, and for a second she had the impression of floating in air. *Am I dead? I cannot be dead, I am breathing.* Slowly, hands were touching her, and a deep soft voice, a familiar voice, was speaking to her, while another voice was asking her something. A cold, wet, rag was placed over her swollen eye. Well, surely I am not dead, for the pain is still there. She tried to shake the fog from her head but the movement caused her to wince from the pain. "Mistress, please speak to me, are you all right?" It was the sobbing voice of her maid Natalie, but even though she tried to answer, something was holding back her voice.

She knew she was lying in her bed, when, finally, she was able to open her left eye. It was difficult to focus, but after a few minutes, she was able to see quite clearly. Gingerly, she reached up to the right side of her face, and felt the bulge where her right eye should be. Her face prickled with pain, and her neck and throat ached. These slight motions were caught by a figure sitting in the chair near her bed. With the sunlight as a backdrop, the tall figure approaching her was not immediately recognizable. She realized it was Giovanni Romano whose impressive figure loomed over her. Maria felt small and weak. "Mistress, how are you? Can you open your right eye?" Maria tried to speak but the sound did not come to the surface. She panicked, and then she tried to open both of her eyes, but could not. A flood of fear came over her, and her body started to tremble. "Do not fear Mistress, you were beaten, and nearly strangled to death. Your voice will come back in time. Your eye is badly swollen and we have been putting cold rags to keep the swelling down. I have sent for Doctore` Migliani to tend to your injuries." There was both fear and sadness in his soft voice. He saw the question in the expression on her face, and then Giovanni spoke gently, but matter of fact. "Mistress, Signore` Sucretti is dead." Maria took a moment to digest what Giovanni had just said. To let him know she understood, she squeezed, as tight as she could, his hand, which had been caressing her own. "Rest for now Mistress, you are badly bruised and need to heal. Someone is with you always." For the first time in the twenty plus years, she had known Giovanni the Roman he bent and kissed her cheek and forehead. She was moved by the sense of security and comfort it gave her. She settled herself to find a comfortable position and soon feel off to sleep.

Fernando, appeared at her side, upon seeing her he gasped and tears fell down his unshaven cheek. Maria had never seen him with an unshaven face. He reached up to stroke her head, and said simply "I am so sorry Mistress. Doctore` Migliani is on his way, but in the meantime drink some broth to gain your strength." He held a cup of warm broth in his hands, and with the help of Giovanni, they gently lifted her to a semi-seated position. The warm liquid felt so good going down her aching throat. She closed her left eye and drank sips of the welcoming elixir. She was already starting to feel better from the ministrations of all concerned parties. They gently returned her to her resting position and she fell into a state of unconsciousness.

Panic reached Maria in a wave of unrestrained emotions while she was dreaming of what had happened. All she could feel were long boney fingers clenching tightly around her throat and the inability to breathe. She thought to herself, this is what drowning must be like. Maria suddenly jerked herself from her sleep. She needed to think; how they would rid themselves of Salvatore's body so that no one would suspect that Giovanni had killed him. Surely, there would be an inquiry. She must think quickly. The urgency of the situation must have been written all over her face. Opening her left eye she saw Fernando, who was visibly shaken, yet seemed to shake himself into reality. It would be at least two hours before the doctor arrived, time enough to contrive a plausible story. He was fluttering around the room, cleaning and putting things back in order. Maria tried to speak but still her voice would not leave her throat. Her head was pounding and her face felt numb. The pain was palpable. She was trying desperately to come back to the surface of reality, but while she could hear the frantic movements around her, she could not bring herself to move. She succumbed to the fog that engulfed her body and heard no more sounds.

After a while, she didn't know how long, she felt hands probing her, someone had lifted her right eye, a searing pain went through the back of her head, and they were turning her head from side to side examining her. She wanted to scream 'stop' but nothing came out. "Mistress Sucretti, Mistress, Maria, can you hear me? Open your eyes." Maria knew the voice of Doctore` Migliani and tried to respond to his questions. He was probing her body, and she winced when he reached her torso, she had broken at least two ribs when she fell after Salvatore had struck her. The fall probably accounted for the sizeable lump on the side of her head, which was throbbing. "Maria", he said, addressing her casually, more out of sympathy, than to merely address his patient in a formal manner. "Maria, you must rest, you have gone through a great shock, and I have given instruction to Fernando as to how I want them to care for your injuries. I will come again tomorrow. If you should need me send word and I will come immediately".

Doctore` Migliani had been caring for Maria Sucretti all her life. He was an ancient man but kind and well respected. Maria, upon hearing his voice, opened her left eye, and begrudgingly attempted to open her right eye, but to no avail. She looked at the old man who was upset at her appearance and reached for his hand. He found hers in his own and gave her a gentle squeeze. "Non preoccuparti mio caro sarà meglio presto". He bent down to kiss her forehead. Maria felt like a child and the tears welled up in her eyes and tumbled down her face. He reached over and wiped the tears from her swollen and distorted face. She saw that he too was crying.

The doctor wiped his face with his handkerchief, blew his nose, and stood up. He had been sitting on the side of Maria's bed. His old body was nearly bent from both age and probably dampness in the bones. Fernando came by his side immediately to assist him and the two old men faced each other. "Fernando, you must prepare a poultice to draw out the inflammation in her right eye, which must be changed every few hours. Have the cook prepare a salve of pig grease, rosemary, and anise, and rubbed gently on her neck and throat. You did well by giving her the warm broth, you are to continue that, but be sure it is not too hot. I have bound her ribs. When she is washed, do not have them remove the bindings, which must stay until I am sure the ribs have reset. Do you understand?" Fernando, exhausted, and worried for his mistress answered in the affirmative. "One last thing, get some rest yourself, you look as poorly as Mistress and Natalie." With that, the doctor took his leave to the carriage that had been waiting for his departure.

It was just the two of them in the room, Maria and Fernando; she grabbed for his hand and opened her left eye to find his face. He knew what she wanted and so he sat gently on the side of the bed. "Do not worry Mistress; all has been taken care of. We..er..we have taken Signore` Sucretti's body away. We have told the staff that someone had entered from the balcony trying to steal your jewels and encountered you and Signore`. There was a struggle, and the thief, after stabbing Signore` Sucretti, beat and robbed you. Natalie, hearing the sounds of struggle came in and was caught in the fight. Giovanni who was tending to the securing of the house was not at hand to rescue his master. We will wait until you have recovered enough to have a funeral and the burial will be in the crypt." Maria painfully tried to speak but only a hoarse whisper came instead *"Natalie?"* Fernando answered as softly as he could, "Natalie is shaken, bruised, and scared, but she will heal. Doctore` Migliani has tended her wounds and left instructions. I put her to bed and little Sofia will see to her needs. She fears for you, but, I have assured her that she need not worry." Maria attempted to smile but felt her face grimace more than smile. "Mistress, you really must rest. I will have Natalie come to see you when she feels better, but for now, I must insist that you try to sleep. Doctore` Migliani has given me strict orders that you must rest." Maria closed her eye and nodded slightly. Fernando brushed her cheek with the lightest touch and bent to kiss her forehead before he left.

She could not remember how long she had slept, an hour, a day, maybe forever. In her dreams, she saw Salvatore leering at her, cursing and taunting her with those black, soulless eyes.

Maria felt someone in the room. She opened her eye and saw Giovanni Romano standing over her. A look of profound sorrow etched on his homely handsome face. He touched her hand and she let him embrace it. "Mistress, please forgive us, we did not mean to…" She saw the cup with the broth on the table and tried to reach for it, he saw what she wanted and brought it to her lips. She sipped its contents and wiped her mouth on her sleeve. "Giovanni" she whispered. He came closer to hear her muted voice. "Si lo so. Mi hai salvato da quell'animale." "How is my Natalie, is she hurt?" Giovanni's expression suddenly turned to anger, but, he controlled himself, and merely shrugged his shoulders, "She is hurt, but, she will heal, at least physically. She is very worried for you." Maria nodded, but even that small movement made her head throb. The last thing she heard was Giovanni leaning over her saying "I am sorry."

She did not know what time it was, but knew she had slept for a while. The room was dark. They had not opened the shudders to the balcony. Only slivers of sunlight sneaked through the thin spaces of the slatted wood. The door to her room opened and Fernando was escorting Doctore` Migliani into the room. The poor soul looked worse than she did, but he was neatly attired in his morning coat, with his trimmed mustache and his powdered wig, which was only slightly askew. Fernando was followed by a small procession of maids, each maid laden down with either a bucket of water, linen towels, or a tray of food and a vase of fresh flowers. One of the little uniformed girls rushed to open the shutters, and threw open the doors to the balcony. It was a beautiful sunny day and the breeze from the sea filled the room with scents from the garden below. Maria felt better just at the smell.

"Buongiornio Mistress. Come ti senti?" the doctor was jovial in spite of his decrepit features. "I have taken the liberty to instruct your maids to freshen you as well as your bed. But first I must check you to see that all is healing." He examined her face. The swelling was much improved, and the area around the eye, while still tender, was starting to turn various shades of purple, blue, and yellow. It was painful to keep her eye open, but at least now, she could manage to see fairly well when it was. He poked and prodded her head and neck. The salve, which Marcello had prepared, had been applied faithfully every few hours, as was the poultice that had been placed on her damaged right eye. "Mistress, I am going to take off the bindings around your ribs, it può causare qualche disagio." She nodded and the doctor proceeded to enlist the aid of one of the maids to hold Maria upright while he unbound her ribs. Maria let out a difficult gasp, as the bindings were undone. She was happy to be set free of the constricting wrapping but flinched when the doctor gently pushed on her side. "It will be sore for a while but it is mending beautifully. After they wash and change your gown, I want you slowly to get up, with assistance, and go and sit on the terrace for a little while. Then come back to your bed and rest. Later, you may repeat this process but do not do too much. I will come back at the end of the week." Maria whispered her thanks and once he left, the maids, like a swarm of drone bees around their Queen, got her stripped, washed, and dressed in no time. Maria asked for Natalie and was told that her personal maid was feeling ill. "Have Doctore` Migliani tend to her!" "He already has Mistress. She must rest but will come to see you later. Is that all right?" Maria was so sorry that Natalie had been so abusi da parte di suo marito ormai morto that her heart was filled with pain, but, she just nodded.

With the help of one of the maids plus Fernando, they moved Maria to the terrace. It was a magnificent day, with the sun coming over the mountains and the breeze gently blowing from the sea, she sat there, turned her face toward the rising sun, and basked in its warmth. Her eyes were closed against the glare of the sun when she felt a shadow cross her face. She opened her eyes to see Natalie standing over her. Natalie's lovely face was bruised and swollen. Her lip was cut, her nose swollen and a black and purple ring circled her eye. She was walking with considerable distress. "Oh Cara, io sono sono veramente dispiaciuto per quello che ha fatto Salvatore a voi." Natalie reached with both her hands and lovingly embraced her mistress' face and looked into her eyes with such deep compassion, "This is not your fault. Now it is finally over. He is dead." The two victims, who had shared so much during their lives, now also shared their common pain. They haltingly embraced each other careful of their bruises and wept. Marie, even though she knew it was a sin, was actually happy that Salvatore of dead. He had shamed not only himself but her for so many years. She had prayed that God would take him, but now he was gone and she would be rid of the monster he had become.

"How are you doing?" she asked in a horse voice. Never one to burden her mistress, Natalie answered truthfully. "I will not lie to you my beloved Mistress. I am in a great deal of pain. Never in my life have I been so abused, but that is not so much what pains me. I am heartbroken at the sight of you and while they all reassure me that you will heal perfectly I am still fearful for your health."

"Do not fear for me my dear sweet friend. In time we shall both heal."

CHAPTER FIVE

THE INQUISITION

Monteforte
April 23, 1712

Already ten days had passed since the party and all the confusion surrounding the death of Salvatore Sucretti. The Magistrate had been called to make a formal inquiry regarding the circumstances surrounding the murder. When the Magistrate arrived with his assistants, Fernando, looking so pale and elderly, but, impeccably clad in his uniform and powdered wig, greeted them formally and escorted them into the solarium. Capitano Buscemi was formally introduced "Mistress Sucretti, I am Capitano Buscemi, Magistrate for the City of Naples. I have come to make the investigation of the circumstances of the death of your late husband Signore Salvatore Sucretti." Capitano Buscemi seemed rather impressed with himself, and almost forgot to introduce his two assistants, then realizing his blunder, after he saw the stares and polite coughs, made the formal introductions. "I am assisted by Sergeant Corelli and Private Assante". At this point all three, like trained animals, bowed deeply from the waist. The Capitano, was a stout middle-aged man, with a bulbous nose and thinning hair, which could be glimpsed from the inexpensive wig he wore that seemed too small for his rather large head, and he generally sported a pompous attitude. His uniform coat, while clean, was frayed around the worn cuffs, and at least two sizes too small. He was a short man, and smelled of onions and bad breath. His two minions, stood off to the side, and listened intently to the description of the circumstances that had brought them to Monteforte. The private, had asked Fernando for the use of a small table, paper, ink and quill, which he dispatched with great speed. Once he was seated at a small table, which was now supplied with paper, a fresh bowl of ink and a new quill, the young man removed a pair of spectacles from his pocket and placed them precariously on the bridge of his long, hooked, nose. He was a homely, but studious looking fellow, in his late twenties. Thin as a waif, his coat was new but his stockings and shoes had seen better days.

"Now Mistress Sucretti, I realize this is very painful to speak about, but, in your own words please describe for me the circumstances surrounding the death of your late husband Salvatore Sucretti. Maria swallowed hard trying to make her voice heard "It was late, all the guests had left, and Fernando and his staff were cleaning. I said good night and came up to prepare for bed. I was exhausted from all the festivities of the party." The capitano interrupted her "where was Natalia at this time?" Maria resumed her story "Natalie had come up early in the evening to look in on Rosalie, her daughter, who had not been feeling well. I knew she would be waiting for me in my bedchamber, which is next to her rooms, to assist me to get ready for bed. I arrived and we were talking about the party and some of the guests. She was undoing my hair and was going to prepare my bath when Master Sucretti came into the room." Again, the capitano interrupted her by asking, "Did your husband share this bedchamber with you Mistress?" Maria was getting uncomfortable by these questions and her throat was aching "No. He, my husband, kept odd hours, and because of his illness was up and down all hours of the night. We had agreed years ago to have separate bedrooms so as not to disturb my sleep." The capitano just nodded and then asked, "So why was he in your room that night?" At this question, Maria Sucretti blushed a deep crimson, she replied in almost a whisper "he wanted to make love to me for my birthday."The capitano, coughed to cover his embarrassment. "Please continue." "Salvatore was here in the room talking to me and Natalie. I was sitting at my dressing table and Natalie was undoing my hair when my husband came over to give me a kiss. At that point, Natalie realized that he was going to stay, and was getting ready to leave the room. It was then that we first saw the intruder. Everything happened so quickly after that I am not even sure what exactly happened."

The young Private Assante was taking down every word trying to capture the fast moving conversation. Several times, he meekly interrupted the proceedings to have a statement repeated; this action added much to the annoyance of Capitano Buscemi. "Ah, I understand Mistress but please try, it is most important." Maria was getting tired and the fear of giving the wrong story was making her even wearier. "Fernando please bring me some water my throat is very painful." It was at this request that Doctore` Migilani came over to her side. "Are you able to continue Mistress?" there was concern on the physicians face. Maria meekly nodded "I will try, but I am not sure how much more I can stand." The physician gave the capitano a stern look and narrowed his eyes. "Take as long as you need," said the capitano. "We were just talking when we saw a man come through the doors leading from the balcony. He ran over to my husband, knocked him down, and then he grabbed me and threw me to the floor. Natalie tried to run for help and started to scream. He then grabbed her and started to beat her. My husband got up and there was a struggle. The man pulled out, or had in his hands, a dagger, I don't know, it happened so fast and then he stabbed Salvatore." Maria who was now sobbing took the glass of water and was trying to drink but then started to choke. The doctor, who was sitting next to her, was hitting her back and she gasped, but finally caught her breath. "Capitano, I must insist that you put an end to this interrogation. You can see that Mistress Sucretti is hurt."

Sergeant Corelli was silently absorbing the details of the story that they had contrived, which was plausible, even though there was now a manhunt for the alleged thief and murderer. He had an intelligent face and keen eyes. He was in his thirties, tall with an athletic build, he could be considered very attractive. He wore no wig, his black wavy hair was tied with a leather strap into a neat queue, and he sported a thin mustache. His coat was tailored to a well-proportioned body. He started moving catlike around the room, as if trying to piece together the scene being described by the victims. All eyes had shifted toward the sergeant, much to the dismay of Capitano Buscemi.

Sergeant Corelli moved to the tall windowed doors leading to the balcony, opened the shutters, and walked out. He leaned over the railing, calculating the distance from the ground below to the rail, and then turned to look into the room. He was making mental notes, without thought, he started to brush his mustache with his finger, and his eyes were darting back and forth. He was not satisfied with his mental adjustments, as compared to the testimony given. A wave of fear was starting to penetrate the atmosphere of the room. "I calculate the distance from the garden to this balcony to be well over twenty or more feet in height. Would you agree Capitano?" Capitano Buscemi was watching his subordinate with fascination. "Yes I would have to agree to that estimate." Apparently, this was a normal ritual performed by the Sergeant; even the mousey Private Assante had stopped his furious note taking to observe the ministrations of his superior. Everyone was focused on Corelli who was approaching Maria. "Excuse me Mistress Sucretti, but, can you describe what this assailant looked like? Was he tall or short, fat or thin?" Maria stared at him as if he were speaking a foreign language. Her face, still badly bruised and her right eye was not completely opened. She gave the appearance of almost winking at him. Her mind was moving quickly, much like her outward appearance, her larynx had been terribly bruised when Salvatore tried to strangle her, and so her usual clear voice was muffled, and it pained her both mentally and physically to speak. "Mistress did you not hear my question?" he asked in a harsh tone and then waited for her response. Maria was dumbfounded and did not speak. "Let me ask the same question of you Natalie." The sergeant sauntered over to the trembling servant. "Can you describe the man who killed your Master? What was his height, his weight, his facial appearance, anything that will help us capture him?" By now, the muscular form of the Sergeant was looming over the frightened Natalie. "Answer me woman" he demanded and grabbed her arm in a tight grip. At that moment, from the corner of his eye, the Sergeant saw the movement of Giovanni Romano. "I don't know." Natalie started to shake and was crying; his face was so close to hers that she could feel his warm breath on her cheek. "You mean to tell me that neither you, nor your Mistress, can describe the man who beat you both almost to death and then killed your Master? I find that very difficult to believe." The

Sargent was furious, and his face was flushed with agitation. "Perhaps he was as tall as me, or maybe as tall as your husband? Was he fat or of average size? Give me something." By now the tone and volume of his voice and mannerism was threatening.

Natalie, who had never been exposed to such interrogation, was scared not for herself but for her beloved husband. She knew that the Sergeant was considering him as the prime suspect for the murder. She needed to pull herself together before Giovanni would attack the Sergeant. Sobbing she said in a soft voice "I told you he was wearing a mask. A mask! I told you we did not see his face." She then brought her hands up to her face and started to weep.

Giovanni Romano who had walked to his wife's side and had caught the attention of Capitano Buscemi who said "Signore Romano, please step back." Giovanni, who had lost all color from his face, narrowed his eyes, and replied, "Ask your Sergeant to remove his hands from my wife. Now." The capitano was not a stupid man, and wisely gave a look to his subordinate to unhand the woman, which he did. Giovanni stepped back slightly but let his presence be a warning to the sergeant. The tension in the room was so thick it was almost visible. Maria was truly fearful that Giovanni might do something foolish.

Giovanni was watching Fernando whose pallor was grey. The old man with his powdered wig and impeccable uniform was shaking. Giovanni feared that the old man might come forward with the announcement that he had killed the sadistic Camorra Caporione to protect his beloved Mistress. Giovanni could not, would not, allow that to happen.

Doctore` Migliani who now jumped into the conversation and instructed the Sargent that neither of the women were in any condition to be speaking. He explained that Mistress Sucretti's vocal chords were severely damaged, and unnecessary speaking could create permanent loss. "Doctore` Migliani, I do apologize, but, do you Doctore' not think the death of a prominent man such as Signore Sucretti is not important enough to ask a few questions of someone who was witness to this terrible act?" His tone, while respectful, was also authoritative, but the doctor would not back down. The doctor, now obviously annoyed, turned directly toward the senior member of this trio and addressed the capitano in a somewhat threatening tone. "Capitano Buscemi, I must insist that Mistress Sucretti, as well as her personal maid Natalie, both of whom have sustained extensive injuries, be left to rest now. You may come back in a week or two, after she has had a chance to recover. Certainly, we do not want to cause permanent damage to the Mistress. Signore Sucretti's death, while unfortunate, will keep."

Doctore` Migliani, ancient as he was, was both educated and known throughout the area, his imperative, plus the obvious fact that the dead Salvatore Sucretti wasn't going anywhere, was enough to put a halt to the proceedings. Everyone, even the Capitano, breathe a sigh of relief. The only one who was not satisfied was Sergeant Corelli.

Maria was both physically and emotionally exhausted. The color had drained completely from her face and she started to sway in her chair. Seeing the obvious tax this investigation was placing on her the Capitano, a seasoned bureaucrat, thought better than to cross the doctor and risk hurting the Mistress Sucretti, word of which would be passed to his superiors. Sergeant Corelli was not pleased, and his actions spoke more than his nonverbal sentiments. All three gathered themselves to leave.

"Mistress Sucretti, please accept my condolences on the loss of your husband and for the pain you and your maid have endured, however, before I can close this matter I must ascertain further details about that evening. We will be back to complete our inquisition. I will send word when we will return. I would ask that none of you leave Naples. Thank you and good day." As he was leaving, Sargent Corelli gave a menacing eye to Giovanni Romano. It was not done yet.

Throughout the proceedings, Corelli was eyeing Giovanni Romano. It was not a secret that the infamous Camorra boss hired Giovanni as his bodyguard. He was also smart enough to know that there was something wrong with the story they had told, and that everyone seemed anxious including Giovanni the Roman. He was trying to figure out how the thief got from the ground to the top of the balcony, which had to be a good twenty feet since the lawn slopped down toward the formal gardens at that spot. It was possible that he disguised himself as either a guest or a servant, worked his way upstairs, and was caught in the act. There were far too many unanswered questions, and just by years of experience, Sergeant Corelli knew a rat when he smelled one. The sergeant had made diligent inquiries, with his entire known underworld contacts, for the alleged identity of this would be murderer, and so far, no one was either willing, or able to give him a name.

It was possible that Salvatore Sucretti was marked for assassination and the attempted theft was just a cover for his murder. On that front, Corelli had any number of people who would want Sucretti dead. Everything the two women had told him about the attack seemed to hold some grain of truth, except how the attacker got into the room, and how he left, without anyone noticing him. Rationally, he could understand the shock experienced by both Mistress Sucretti having been severely beaten, and now left widowed, as well as her personal servant who had sustained serious injury. Yet, there was no weapon, and the fact that the assailant left the two women alive to be able to identify him was suspect in itself. However, they did say he wore a mask. This whole scenario was smelling more, and more, like a professional assassination, disguised to look like a robbery gone wrong. God knows it was not the first time someone tried to kill Salvatore Sucretti. Salvatore was not only the head of a powerful international criminal network, which made a fortune in trade, both legal and illegal, but he was a cruel and demented enforcer. Sergeant Corelli thought it would be interesting to see the power play for Sucretti's position. Who would be the next Caporegime?

Corelli also knew that wherever Sucretti was, Giovanni the Roman would surely have been close at hand. The answer to that question was answered with the underlying truth that Giovanni was securing the villa, just as he did every night. When the mayhem was in progress, and given the size of the palazzo, it would have taken a little while to check to see that all the invited, as well as uninvited, guests had departed. While he knew that they were all lying, he also knew that there was some measure of truth at the basis of this story, and that he, Sergeant Mario Corelli, police officer for the City of Naples, was glad to see that Salvatore Sucretti, the wicked crime leader was dead. His only regrets in this case, were that two women were damaged, and that he would now have to deal with the next upstart Camorra boss. Dio aiuti tutti. It was agreed between Capitano Buscemi and Sergeant Corelli that they would close the Sucretti investigation since they were relatively sure it was a rival Camorra Caporegime who had ordered the hit on Salvatore Sucretti. Of course, the official record for public consumption would be that a 'would be thief was caught in the act and in the struggle had beaten the Mistress Sucretti within an inch of her life, as well as her maid Natalie Romano, and then killed Signore` Sucretti as he was defending the two women'. Therefore, the file was complete and the case was closed. Unofficially, Sergeant Corelli was bitter, because he knew there was something wrong with this whole story, but, a very bad man was now dead, at least he could find comfort to ease his mind in that resolution to the matter.

CHAPTER SIX

THE CRYPT

Monteforte

May 5th, 1712

The injuries to both the widow and her maid were documented and Doctore` Migliani's account of the events of that evening were recorded. It seemed that all the legal issues had been properly disposed of, and thus the funeral arrangements could be made as soon as possible.

Since the word got out that Salvatore Sucretti had been murdered, and the near fatal injuries to Mistress Sucretti, a profusion of gifts, food and flowers had been delivered daily to Monteforte. Letters of condolence were stacked in piles on Maria's desk. All visitors were refused based on the orders of Doctore` Migliani. Maria was in no condition to see anyone. She never thought that she would mourn Salvatore, but in her heart, she knew she once loved him very much. She wept more for the knowledge that she was truly alone in this world, with the deaths of both her parents, her only sibling Mateo, and now her husband. She started thinking about Mateo's family, and remembered the last time she had seen them was at the burial of her beloved brother. She must try to make peace with Mateo's children they were the legacy of Monteforte.

Maria woke the morning of the burial having had a night filled with violent dreams. She was still sore and aching, but the physical damage to her face was gone.

Natalie was in her room and was just now opening the shutters and doors to the balcony. Early morning mist, which was seeping into the room, carried the scent of the sea. In a few hours, the sun would burn it off and the sky would be vibrant. "Good morning Mistress. I have your breakfast. Do you want to eat inside, or on the balcony?" Natalie was trying to be normal, but her voice betrayed her. She too had prayed along with her Mistress that Salvatore would soon die, but, now that he was, she felt a slight grip in her stomach. She fussed around the room not making eye contact with Maria. When she came near her bed, Maria grabbed Natalie's arm and held her close. They looked at each other and the tears were running down their faces, and then they hugged each other swaying back and forth. It was real. "I am so sorry. He had no choice. Salvatore would have killed you." Maria gently pushed Natalie away so that she could look at her directly. "I do not blame Giovanni. He did what he had to do to protect us." For a second Maria saw a dazed look fall upon Natalie's face. *"What is it?"* Natalie seemed stunned and unsure. "Natalie, tell me." Maria had known Natalie all her life, they were as close as any sisters could be, and she knew something was wrong. "I thought you knew." "Knew what?" Natalie, eyes hooded, answered. "It was not Giovanni who killed Salvatore, it was Fernando.*"* For a moment, Maria just stared at Natalie with a blank face, her mind racing through the scenes of that terrifying night. She remembered seeing Giovanni and Salvatore fighting. Giovanni had his knife. They were wrestling for possession of the knife. Then she passed into unconsciousness. "Fernando killed Salvatore?" It was meant as a statement of fact, but came out as a question. "Yes. When he came into the room after Giovanni arrived, he saw that they were fighting. He looked at you on the floor, all bloody and unconscious, and thought you were dead. He had picked up the large carving knife from the food table, and had come up as quick as he could. Without any hesitation he drove the knife into Salvatore's back." Maria was dumbfounded.

She had worn a simple black silk gown, her black lace veil covering most of her face. She chose to wear no jewelry and pulled her hair back into a simple bun. She insisted that Salvatore's burial would be private. Six of her servants, all dressed in their finest coats, carried the solid cypress casket, up the steep hill to the family crypt. Baskets of flowers lined the path and adorned the opening of the crypt. The entire staff, together with Doctore` Migliani and a few very close friends, were in attendance. It was a small gathering for such a powerful man. Maria did not want a spectacle. Father Marconi, a family friend who conducted Sunday services in the Chapel at Monteforte, had said the Mass of the Resurrection, for the repose of Salvatore's soul. He had made his way up to the crypt and was now throwing holy water on the casket and praying. "Signore noi affido l'anima di Salvatore Sucretti nelle tue mani. Amen." Giovanni and Fernando slid open the heavy steel door of the crypt. The last time Maria had been up to the crypt was for the burial many years past of her beloved brother Mateo Rizzo. The loss of her family, now so real, and so heavy upon her heart, made Maria weep. Natalie, who was standing next to her, gathered her to herself, and together they cried.

The smell of death and decay crept out of the unsealed tomb like the whisper of ghosts long forgotten. Two grooms with lit torches ventured inside to light the space. Even though it was hot outside the damp, dankness was stagnant within. The marble bier was vacant and waiting for Salvatore's casket. The six pallbearers who had been standing at attention during the priest's final prayer with a nod from Fernando once again lifted their burden, marched into the crypt, and placed the casket upon the stone bier. Father Marconi followed behind, saying prayers, and dousing the casket with holy water. The small procession led by Maria and Natalie reached the mouth of the tomb. Giovanni and Fernando were already inside. Only Maria and Natalie proceeded in. Once inside, Father Marconi placed a carved, gilded cross on top of the lid, while Fernando placed the plaque with Salvatore's name, date of birth and date of death, inscribed upon it on the casket. He took a silver hammer from a small shelf that was on the south side of the tomb and withdrew four nails. He drove the first nail into the finely polished wood of the casket, each bang of the hammer echoing into the confined space. Maria jumped with each penetrating thud. When it was done, Father Marconi, came to the foot of the casket, "Nelle tue mani affido l'anima del nostro fratello Salvatore. Riposa in pace." One more sprinkle of holy water and he stepped back. Maria placed a single red rose upon the lid, and softly, almost to herself, said, "I hope you find peace, for once I loved you." Tears cascaded down her grief stricken face. She turned to leave, but first she went to each casket laying her hand upon its lid, and said a silent prayer for her father, mother, and brother.

Maria knew that the remaining stone bier was hers.

CHAPTER SEVEN

THE DAY THE MOUNTAIN ROARED

Torre del Greco

It had been a very difficult year and it was not even half over. Donato was starting to feel the effects of the hardships of the sea, the scars of hard work and exposure to the elements, were slowly making their mark on that chiseled face and body. Still strong and powerful, yet he moved just a little slower, and the eyes gave away the pain in his body and soul. This was one of the hardest years Donato ever recalled. The nets came back empty many days, because the waters were so rough, that the fish stayed closer to the bottom. The whole village was feeling the pressure of the loss of income. Donato prayed that the weather would change and change quickly. The Banfi's had managed to save a meager amount, which would tide them over for the next couple of months, but they feared that if something happened to Donato they would be in terrible financial straits.

Rafaela, while Lucia and Antoinetta went to school with their older brothers Genaro and Francesco to watch over them, began doing custom sewing for the wealthy women who lived in the country villas outside of Naples. The hours were long and the ride by mule was arduous and tiresome, but she knew that she had to help her husband and bring in some extra money to the household. Donato at first put up a fight, but realized that they must work together in order to keep their family well fed, and their children in school. Antonio, already a fine example of a man, was going to the boats everyday with Donato. While Donato wished for an easier life for his eldest son he knew that the young man, unlike his siblings, loved the sea and nature, and although he was smart in the ways of nature, he was not meant for the classroom. Rafaela for her part knew that Antonio was happy with his life and would work hard, have a family, and be a good father to his children, just like her husband.

They struggled for the next couple of months, but all was going well once again, and they were all looking forward to the spring ahead. The day started like every other day in the sleepy village. It was very dark this morning when Donato rose from his bed and looked out the window. He silently cursed to himself, that if the weather were going to rain, he would be soaked all day out on the water. He came back to bed and Rafaela stirred, and Donato kissed her neck, his big hand followed the line of her hip, she instinctively moved to his touch. He reached her full breasts and started to rub his thumb over her nipples, which responded in the affirmative. She opened one eye and gave a half smile, rolled on to her back and spread her legs. Donato loved to touch her body she was always so ready. He began hiking up her nightshirt and reached the curly wet mound he was seeking. Slowly he caressed her, slipping into her wetness, and was tickling her with his sizeable finger. He took out his finger, reached up and put his finger in her mouth, and she sucked it until it was wet with her saliva, then he took it and inserted it into her waiting sex. Rafaela was moving in time to his strokes, with a soft moaning, almost a purr. Donato was at full attention by now. He rolled on top of her, wiggled down to the foot of the bed, with his long legs dangling over the end of the bed; his mouth found what he was pursuing. He darted his tongue in, around, and around her musky lips. Rafaela, already on the brink of eruption, grabbed his thick wavy hair, and pushed his face down into her hot vagina. At the same time, Donato was rigorously rolling her rock hard nipples between his big thumb and index finger, the calluses causing friction. With his expert touch, Rafaela came in very little time. He used his knee to spread her almost to the breaking, his fingers still working their magic, suddenly her back arched and she shuddered, in one swift motion he put his full erection into her waiting sex. Donato was a very well endowed man, and even though Rafaela had given birth to six children, she still winced when he entered her. At first he slowly inserted himself, moving in small circles, in and out, in and out, working very hard to control himself from ramming her. She could feel his full weight and his stiff erection. "Ah, Cara, you feel so hot and wet. I want to come very quickly, but, I also want to linger to give you pleasure." His mouth found hers and she tasted the musky salt of her sex on his tongue. They found their rhythm, which was so familiar in seconds, two bodies in one motion. For his part Donato controlled his urge to climax, at least for a little while, then when he could tell that Rafaela was ready to offer up her womb, he began a steady tattoo, banging her deep and hard, until they both came at the same time.

Their bodies were drenched with sweat and exhaustion. Panting, but satisfied, Donato slipped off her throbbing body, slick with the scent of his seed. For a fleeting moment, Donato thought that if it rained maybe he would stay home and make love to his wife all day. "Dite stare a casa oggi e posso farti fare le fusa come un gatto addestrato tutto il giorno?" With a sly smile of appreciation, Rafaela answered, "While the thought of making love to you all day would be wickedly delightful, sadly, I must go to work." Donato pouted his bottom lip, squeezed her lovely rounded ass, gave it a smart slap, and grunted. She informed him that she must go to work today; it was the final fitting on Rosalie Belmonte's wedding gown, and that the wedding was this Saturday. Disappointed but resigned, Donato, slinked out of bed, his rock hard body was glistening from the exertion of their lovemaking. Rafaela got on her elbows and watched him saunter across the room to get his clothes. She never got tired of looking at his body. His ass was especially high and taut with muscles that complimented the broad expanse of his shoulders and narrow waist. He turned, and she could see that his thoughts of a casual day of sex were still clinging to his manhood. "Ah, you see that He is not so willing to dismiss my proposal of the day's activities. La poveretta è già solitaria." Rafaela made some sympathetic sounds and said "Oh mio povero bambino così solitario. He will just have to wait until tonight when Mommy comes home to play with Him." With head down, and lips pouted, Donato resigned himself to a celibate day, and got dressed and sulked to the kitchen to start the coffee. That was his sole household duty in the morning was the making of the coffee. Rafaela reached down to stroke herself, feeling the sticky wetness of her lover, her clit ached from his hammering, but she was contented with the soreness of her body. Her nipples were a deep rose and still hard. She pinched them and felt a slight twinge lurch in her womb. She stretched wishing she could stay in their bed with the warmth and scent of fresh sex, the taste of her own musk on her lips, but duty called. The entire household was beginning to take life and everyone went about their normal morning routine to prepare for work or school. There started a terrible thundering the ground was trembling under his feet. Donato instinctively went into the yard to check the weather. It was too warm and too soon in the year for thunderstorms. Above the horizon, a thick cloud cover was sweeping over the land from above the mountain backdrop. The thundering became louder, the cloud cover more dense and the temperature of the air was rising rapidly. He stood there, trying to comprehend the situation. His shirt was already wet with humidity with his hair matted to his head. Perspiration was dripping from his face and body. The only other time Donato had this feeling, was during a fierce storm while he was out to sea many years ago and his trawler almost capsized into the water. He had prayed then that he would never know that feeling again, but it was back once more to seize him.

Rafaela was by now up and dressed, as were the children, everyone was proceeding with their morning routine as if nothing were wrong. Donato made a half turn looking back into the doorway of the kitchen and the scene was so normal, so real, and then, as if in slow motion, he turned back and saw what was beginning to look like a wall of clouds quickly rolling down from the mountain. The ground was starting to quiver under his bare feet, and tiny flakes were gently falling from the sky. Lucia came running out to see what was going on, she had read about snow, but, of course, living that far south had never physically seen a snowflake. She extended her hand in front of her to catch the flakes; she called to her father to show him her prize "Papa, look, snowflakes! Did you ever see snowflakes?" Donato was suddenly roused from his deep thoughts, and although never having lived through a volcanic eruption, he was raised on many fables of the infamous

Vesuvius' wrath. He pulled his youngest child to himself and said in a voice, the depth of which was filled with fear, "It is not snow. The fire mountain is erupting. Hurry, go and gather your things, we must leave. Hurry now!" Lucia was never witness to her father's fears; she shuddered at the thought of what could make him so scared.

As if ignited with energy, the head of the house began to formulate a plan of escape. Donato ran into the house and told Rafaela in as stern, and as calm, a voice that he could muster, to take all their valuables. "Cara, the volcano is erupting. We need to leave now. Get the most important things and ready the children. Hurry there is little time!" Donato instructed each child to get a small bag with two or three changes of clothing. "You must gather your things quickly. We have so time; you may take whatever is the most important little item you can personally carry." They were to assemble in the front yard in less than five minutes. With military precision, the mission was accomplished. There were no questions or any sounds except for a few sniffles. Rafaela wanted to be strong not only for her children's sake but for Donato. They had both grown up with stories of the horrible aftermath of these eruptions, and were both now in the grip of fear, but they had to put their own fears aside for the safety of their children. Since Antonio was the oldest, he joined with Donato in organizing a plan of escape.

The air was getting thicker with the rapidly falling flakes of ash, and the town looked like it was a winter wonderland. All the rooftops and trees were covered in a layer of white ash, except for the constant thundering and the quivering of the ground, the scene was so surreal that they almost forgot the severity of the situation. The air hung with the pungent odor of sulfur, and after a little while, it became nauseating. People started to gather in the square, and panic was starting to take hold of the town. The fire bell was ringing, and since it was early morning, most people were home. The magistrate, along with a few of the younger men, were going from house to house, banging on doors to warn every one of the impending disaster. Pandemonium was beginning to set in, as the crowds grew larger. People were running in all directions, mothers were holding on to their young children. Men were shouting and cursing. The animals were confused, dazed, and terrified, most people had the presence of mind to set their livestock free, and they too panicked in the chaos. A plan of evacuation had to be set in motion as quickly as possible.

Donato was evolving a plan in his mind. He excitedly conversed with several other men in the square, and a plan was developed. Quickly they caught up with the magistrate and his men. Donato explained the basics of the plan he had formulated. "All those who can fit will be loaded on to any floating vessel. The women and children will be first, with the youngest males from each family to board. Since there are many boats, large and small, docked at the pier, this should work. We will make our way to Naples, and warn all those villages along the route." The magistrate agreed that it was a simple but workable plan. They knew that they could not out run Vesuvius on land her reach was too long and too vicious. Their only hope was to take to the sea, and make way for the nearest port, which was Naples, about sixteen kilometers, due north. Any boats they came across on the sea from neighboring villages were enlisted to help in the rescue effort. A call of warning was sent out to other nearby towns. Like ants, the fishermen loaded their boats and started a flotilla. Donato Banfi collected his family, which consisted of Antonio, Andrea, Genaro, Francesco, Antoinetta, Lucia, and Rafaela, and loaded them into his small fishing boat. He decided that since it was his plan, he would be the last to leave, insuring that all the others were safely out to sea. When they were aboard, they waited to see if there were any lone stragglers remaining on the pier. The mass exodus had been executed remarkably quick, and with such precision, it was almost military in style. As they were about to shove off Lucia cried out that there was a man running down the cobblestone street to the dock. "There, over there, an old man is running. Papa, we need to wait for him." He was tall and lean, actually skin and bones. Donato recognized him as one of the old fishermen, whose name was Giovanni Romano. He instructed Antonio to go get him and bring him onboard. "Antonio, go help old Giovanni, he will come with us." They were the last to leave. The sky was growing ominously black with smoke billowing from Vesuvius' mouth; the stench in the air was suffocating, thick and putrid. They, along with every surface, were covered with a film of ash.

Donato told them to shift their positions in the boat to make way for the old man. When Rafaela realized who it was, she told Donato softly, that she did not want the old man to come into the boat with them. "No, let him go with some else." Her voice sounded urgent. Donato knew she was scared, and, so was he. He seemed agitated and questioned her reasoning for such a cruel thing. "There is no one else. We are the last. What is wrong with you?" She told him that she got scared whenever she saw him in the market, or on the street, because he had the evil eye. Donato for the first time in many years, truly got angry with his wife, and roughly shoved her to one side of the boat, she attempted to plead her case, but he would not even consider such stupidity. "Caporegimena tranquilla. Avrebbe lasciato un vecchio morire?" "Can we leave an old man here to die?" Rafaela was surprised at the tone her husband was using. This was not a joy ride; this was a matter of life and death, in the face of extreme disaster. "Donato, please, this man will bring us bad luck?" She pleaded to have him go with someone else, but by this time all the boats were overflowing with people and making their way to the open sea and safety. Francesco reached for his mother's arm, and gently, but persuasively, guided Rafaela toward the front of the craft, and whispered in her ear "Mama, Dio ci proteggerà non possiamo lasciarlo morire nella lava calda."

Of course, God would protect them, and she knew she would not leave him to die in the boiling lava. Rafaela suddenly felt small and ashamed, that her young son had to remind her of the kindness of God, and that she should be exercising that virtue to all of God's creatures. She never really knew how wise and good Francesco was until that very moment, and then she thanked the Blessed Mother for him. She knew that they would be safe, but the road to recovery would be long and hard. Rafaela made the sign of the cross, and said a fervent prayer for her family and this stranger.

Antonio, always obedient to his parents, was evolving into a strong and wholesome young man. His muscular frame was filling out and he had grown to almost six feet tall. Even his voice had taken on the baritone of a robust young buck. The toil of many hours a day at sea, hauling in the heavy nets, had given him not only a powerful body, but also a maturity beyond his years. The sun had bleached his curly hair to a warm, golden pecan color, and his skin was a rich bronze, which set off his deep-set hazel eyes. Expertly jumping off the boat, and racing toward the figure on the shore, his parents swelled with a sense of pride for their son.

Antonio ran with great speed toward the older man, and practically carried him to the waiting boat. "Come with me to our boat. We will bring you with us to Naples." The old stranger was gaunt, but still stood tall, his large hands reached to Donato's outstretched hand that pulled him into the boat. He stumbled into the boat in Donato's hast to set sail. The only seat open was next to Lucia. She sat close to the old man, and when the boat started it lurched forward, and the old man almost fell over. The little girl gently leaned into him to keep him steady. He looked at her with such gratitude and appreciation, the child immediately formed a bond to the old man. "Don't worry my Papa will bring us to safety. My name is Lucia Banfi. What is your name?" The stranger, his voice filled with sad and ancient memories of a little girl of the same age replied, "My name is Giovanni Romano. Thank you for helping me." Lucia slipped her hand into his until they reached the Port of Naples.

Giovanni Romano had grown up in Rome. He came from a military family whose exploits were legendary. As a small boy he was sent to the home of a wealthy merchant as a groom. There he came to the attention of the master of the house who saw potential in the boy. He was given instruction in language and the art of the sword. Giovanni was smart and learned quickly. In no time, he excelled with the sword and soon found that he desired to seek adventure. When he reached eighteen years old, he asked his master to release him so that he could become a soldier. He left his position and became a soldier for hire. He traveled to France and became a mercenary. It was during his time in France that Giovanni earned a reputation for his ability with a sword. After a few years of fighting in France, he became homesick. Finding that he longed for his home,

Giovanni made his way back to Rome. One day he was sharing a glass of wine in one of the taverns when a band of men came in search of him. The leader of the group, a swarthy man in his thirties, asked the tavern owner if he knew of a man named Giovanni the Roman. "Who is asking?" replied the burly owner. He knew Giovanni well but would not give him up without explanation. The stranger looking around at all those sitting in the dark room belted out his reply "I have heard of this Giovanni the Roman by reputation. His skill with a sword is well known, and I have come with the purse of my master to offer him a position." Giovanni hearing this proclamation eyed the band of men and its leader. They were all strong and well groomed. He needed work and so he stood up. "I am Giovanni the Roman. Who is it that seeks me?" The leader came over to him and looked at him appraisingly up and down. "My name is Bernardo. I am the Chief Guard at the palazzo of Monteforte in Sorrento." Giovanni, who was a tall, lanky man with a taut muscular frame, looked down at the stranger. Bernardo looked the young gaunt soldier up and down. "With that face you had better be good with a sword," everyone laughed including Giovanni. A wealthy man named Salvatore Sucretti from Sorrento employed them. He was the Master of Monteforte and head of an enormous estate. Giovanni had heard of Monteforte and of Sucretti. Of course, Bernardo neglected to mention that his employer was a Camorra lord. Giovanni who was down to his last cent was very eager to find work but he was cautious. Bernardo sensing his apprehension lifted the pouch from his belt and hefted it in his hand. "Are you interested?" asked Bernardo. There were many coins in that pouch and Giovanni was ready for yet a new adventure. "Well Signore` as soon as you hand over that purse I will be ready to ride." Bernardo tossed the purse to Giovanni with a solid slap on his back, turned to the tavern owner, and said "A round of your best wine for everyone." Turning to look Giovanni in the eye he lowered his voice and spoke directly "Si farà bene il mio giovane amico per diffidare del tuo nuovo padrone. Non attraversare lo."Giovanni, warned by Bernardo to be wary of his new master, had an impending sense of dread, but he needed to work. Therefore, Giovanni the Roman, who was in his late twenties when he became the personal bodyguard for a famous Camorra boss, came to live at Monteforte. The work was easy, the food was good, and he enjoyed all the benefits of living and working for a famous Camorra lord, at least in the beginning.

After the death of Salvatore Sucretti, Giovanni Romano left Monteforte, his master was dead, and he wanted to start a new life for himself and his family, so he came to settle in Torre del Greco. Now, a middle-aged man with a wife and child to support, he realized that his talents with a sword would be no use to him. He, like all those who lived in Torre del Greco, took to the sea and became a fisherman. It was hard work, and he was away from his family for long periods at a time. He had been on a merchant spice ship on route to Africa and had been gone eighteen months. When he returned, he learned that his family had died of a terrible plague, which had swept through Naples and the surrounding towns with such devastating effects that it had wiped out whole villages. He never married again, and went to sea for long voyages at a time. During a whaling expedition off the coast of Sardinia, a fellow mate while attempting to harpoon a whale accidentally blinded him. He was a rugged, craggy old man who kept to himself, and lived in a shanty at the end of the village. Only a few of the men ever talked to him, and the locals had created stories to go with the house and his looks. Without his eye and his unkempt appearance, he did look somewhat hideous. On top of all that was physically wrong with him the fact that he kept to himself and had no family, added to the illusion of his mysterious past.

The first of a series of thunderous roars came from the mouth of Vesuvius, as pieces of the crater spewing violently from the top of the giant mountain, reaching the land below with such force as to create holes upon impact. A roiling stream of hot molten lava was flowing from the top, and sweeping the trees and foliage in its path like so much dust. It was both a terrifying and magnificent scene unfolding before them. Everyone was awestruck and afraid. To think that several hours ago they were fast asleep in their beds, and now as they looked from their boats all that they owned now destroyed. It was a very helpless feeling, and a silence so palpable, pervaded the regatta, as they hoisted their sails to seek the safety of the sea. The sea was the mother of these humble people. She provided food to feed their families, a livelihood for their men, and with the residual products, she gave birth to several cottage trades. Shell jewelry was crafted and brought to the larger inland cities. Conch shells were fashioned into cameos, and then brought to merchants in neighboring villages and larger towns, and sold to the wealthy. Even the kelp or seaweed was sold to be used in making face powders, and for medicinal uses. Their first instinct in the face of disaster was to embrace the safety and comfort of the sea.

Donato knew he had to put as much distance between their small boat and the shore. His massive arms, toned from a lifetime at sea, deafly moved the oars with great speed. Antonio taking his rhythm from his father moved in harmony, giving them a head start to avoid the impending deposit of molten lava. Together, father and son, rowed with great intensity and purpose. Andrea and Genaro jumped in and helped while Francesco prayed and comforted the girls and his mother.

Suddenly, a deafening explosion succeeded by yet another shattered the silence, even louder than the first. Large and small pieces of debris from the mountain were falling like rain from the sky. All the people in the boats were covering their heads for protection from the flying objects. The boats were some distance from the shore, when a final devastating thrust, burst the volcano wide open, and a river of molten lava heaved from her belly. The lava was flowing with such force and speed that it would soon reach the shore. When the molten lava reached the water, the intense heat created steam, and made the water bubble. The shore was blanketed with the cooling lava, and where the water was shallowest, the lava was piling up and making small mounds. It was a ghastly and terrifying sight. There was no wind, and the air hung thick and hot, an almost nightmarish silence, save the roaring of this volcanic demon, which convulsed and coughed and spat its evil across the village, while racing toward the next unsuspecting town to devour everything in its path. They knew that once it had reached the water it would eventually simmer until it stopped. The speed and ferocity of its power was astonishing. The bubbling water surrounding their shore was steaming and the fish were boiling in its wake.

Having momentarily stopped rowing to witness the action, Donato , Antonio, Andrea and Genaro, silently took up their oars, and once again began laboriously rowing the tiny craft, ever northward to Naples. Although she said nothing, Rafaela sat there covered with soot from the ash, and looked older than Lucia had ever thought her beautiful mother could look. Her father's face was weary and filled with anxiety. For the first time in her young life, Lucia felt genuine fear. The idea that the two most important people in her life were so worried was a cause for great apprehension in the child. She studied the faces of the others aboard the boat, and went from one to another. Her brother Francesco, had his eyes closed, and she noticed his hands working the beads on his rosary, even covered with soot, his gentle face had a fervent and holy expression that filled her with hope and courage. Antoinetta sat there scared and quivering, she seemed smaller than usual, her delicate features, were marred by a mixture of sweat and tears. Lucia turned toward the old man next to her, and on his face, he wore the pain and sorrow of all his long life. His hideous outward appearance could not hide from Lucia the kindness and gentleness within his very soul. Instead of being repulsed by him, Lucia was attracted to the strange man that now looked worse than ever, being masked by the covering of volcanic ash. Their eyes met and a single tear welled up in his good eye, the other hidden by a homemade patch. She reached over and touched his shriveled hand, and he responded by taking it into his and gently squeezing. Moving her gaze to her two big brothers Andrea and Genaro, she saw the look of mature concern on their handsome faces, and thought how different they were. Andrea was probably trying to mathematically calculate the number of rows it would take to reach Naples, while Genaro the artist, was painting a picture of the devastation in his mind.

Donato silently prayed, as did all the boat's inhabitants, clearly they knew that their lives would be altered forever. Torre del Greco, the town of their birth, their home, would never be the same for them, at least not the way it had been before. They were scared and apprehensive. Donato and Rafaela, although not one word passed between them, knew secretly that life would not be easy starting all over again, but they were young enough and strong enough to make it work, they had to for their family.

When they were far enough beyond the shoreline, Donato and Antonio stopped rowing, and the boat gently rolled in the waves, the noise was deafening. Vesuvius was still violently heaving debris and lava from her mouth. Where the lava had spilled over into the sea the dead fish were beginning to rise to the surface, it was an eerie sight. The sky was almost black as night even though it was early morning. They started to pick up some wind and their boat moved along steadily as they caught up with the makeshift entourage as they proceeded to converge on Naples.

The convoy finally reached the Port of Naples. Upon entering the harbor, the lead boat already informed the Harbor Master of what they had escaped. The news spread like wildfire, and people from all the nearby streets came to see if they could assist. The local churches and school, as well as the hospital, were turned into shelters for the homeless,. they were given places to wash the encrusted soot from their bodies and clothing, they were given a hot meal, and pallets were set up for the night. Tomorrow, the process of rebuilding their lives would occupy the rest of their days. For now, they were safe, alive and fed.

The next day, all the churches offered masses of thanksgiving that God had saved so many, and for the hope that all those who were presently unaccounted for were somewhere safe, and would be able to get word to their loved ones.

The black billowing clouds could be seen as far away as Naples, and the ash was falling, as the wind would shift. The air, was filled with the scent of charred debris. The few animals that did escape were dazed and confused. Thousands of dead fish washed upon the shore. The sights and sounds of death and chaos were everywhere. Vesuvius purged her bowels for several days without mercy. The small towns of San Sebastino, Arcolo, Massa di Somma, and others were also engulfed in the mass destruction. There were thousands of displaced people, and the local officials feared that disease, from unsanitary conditions, would spread throughout the makeshift housing clusters. Those who were fortunate enough to seek shelter in surrounding villages with family or friends were the lucky ones.

After three months of living in one of the temporary shelters of a local church, Donato and Rafaela Banfi received word that Maria Sucretti, Rafaela's great aunt who was her grandfather's sister, was still alive, and had a castle in Sorrento. They had already arranged to have Francesco go to stay with Uncle Luigi and possibly start the seminary a little early. His school record was so good, and he was so worthy, that Uncle Luigi had suggested the idea, especially in light of the present circumstances. That lifted the burden slightly for the Banfi's at least for the present.

Antonio would continue to work with Donato on the fishing boats, but the two girls needed to go to school, and they were picking up all sorts of ideas from being lumped in with strange children. As fate would have it, they were burdened with the old man Giovanni Romano, who stayed close. The old man tried to get work here and there, but with all the young able-bodied men, no one wanted a crippled, half-blind old man. He volunteered his time at the church and did odd jobs, and tended the parish garden. For his trouble, he received a hot meal and a clean cot to sleep on. The days passed and Giovanni Romano's work in the garden became almost artistic. He pruned and shaped the shrubbery into beautiful designs of a cross, a dove, and a fish. In time, he would create a lasting memory of his presence in this place. His talents were unknown to Donato and Rafaela, until one day the Pastor thanked them for bringing to his parish such a talented master of the garden. They were both stunned at the news of his work and upon seeing these living pieces of art were even more puzzled by the strange man who kept to himself. He gave them his love and concern. Only Lucia knew of his work, for he had taken her to the parish garden many times in recent weeks. They had developed a strong bond between them, a kindred spirit of mutual love and respect.

Rafaela, even as a small girl, remembered the stories from her grandmother Lucia, about how Maria Sucretti, her sister-in-law, always made trouble between her grandmother and grandfather. She remembered distinctly, the stories of how Maria tried to take Lucia's children away, after Mateo was killed. That she was very wealthy, and knew that Lucia and her children were practically starving, but would not help them. She confided her fears to Donato, who by now knew the stories, and they pondered a solution to their problems. In the meantime, Donato and Antonio had to go to sea and make a living, or surely, they would remain not only homeless vagabonds, but starving ones as well. Rafaela's talents as a dressmaker were in such demand in the large city of Naples that finding work was easy. Her problem was where to leave the girls while she, Donato, and the boys were all at work. The schools were overflowing, and there would be no openings for quite some time. Several of the nuns at the shelter where they were staying gave them their religious instruction, but she knew that would not be enough.

With Genaro and Andrea, it was easier. Uncle Luigi had arranged to have both boys sent to the Universita` di Florenze. Where the money for their admission came from was a secret that Monsignor Rizzo was keeping to himself. He had told Donato and Rafaela that they were not to worry about the finances. Uncle Luigi was like a religious Camorra Caporegime, and they knew better than to press him for any details. The boys were genuinely excited to be at the university and were doing well. They wrote often telling of their progress. Dio benedica lo zio Luigi. So far, four of her children were settled, at least for now. Rafaela's main concern was for Antoinetta and Lucia; they needed to be in school. They needed to be safe, while she, Donato, and Antonio were at work. Che cosa hanno a che fare sono stati? Rafaela asked herself a thousand times a day what she should do about her girls. She never found a good answer. Both Donato and Rafaela were feeling the strain of finding a good solution for their daughters. Pregano per la beata madre per l'orientamento e le risposte. Rafaela hoped her prayers would be quickly answered; she knew that nothing good could come of them being alone for ten or more hours a day. God help them! Blessed Mother send me an answer to my prayers.

CHAPTER EIGHT

SIGNORE` PAGLIMENTI

Naples

The decision of the future placement for Antoinetta and Lucia, came sooner than the Banfi's had ever dreamed. In an effort to help their parents, Antoinetta and Lucia found a job in a dress shop. Their parents were very angry with them at first, but as time went on, they realized that in order to make enough money to move back to Torre del Greco and build a new home they needed money. The girls argued that since they could not go to school just now, that it was better for them to be useful then to stay around the shelter and be bored. Their parents finally agreed. The two sisters felt so grown up, and knew that although the work was hard and the pay was poor, that they were helping their parents, and soon they could go back to their beautiful little town. They all hated Naples, the streets were filled with carts, vendors barking their wares and people who were generally nasty. There was trash and filth everywhere. It was especially bad now that the city was deluged with all these displaced people. People were begging for work, food, and shelter, the streets were littered with humanity. The conditions were breeding grounds for disease and crime. Robbery and rape were a daily occurrence.

No one was truly safe.

And so it was that the girls went to work, in one of the many dress fabbrica in the city. These were rundown buildings, in the worse part of the city, with little or no ventilation, and many hazards. They left at seven in the morning, and did not return home until seven in the evening. Rafaela always fixed them a lunch pail, which they sometimes lost to hungry ruffians on their way to work. Although they were very hungry by the time they returned in the evening, they were more fearful to tell their father or brother, because of the threats of future reprisals. After a short time, they realized that if they hid their food in their petticoat, they could escape attack. There were many menaces along the route to and from work. On the day, they got their pay; they took a different route home.

Because Antoinetta was older, and had apparently inherited her mother's talent for sewing, she was given a better position. She could cut the pattern and actually sew garments. Lucia was relegated to cleaning threads from the finished products, or cleaning up the floor of the sewing room but Lucia was watching and learning. Now and then, when they were short-handed for help, Lucia would step in. It was not too long before the talents and intelligence of the two girls made its way to the eye of the proprietor. Their swift little fingers could do twice as many pieces in the hour, which only prompted curses and evil stares from their coworkers. The two sisters kept to themselves, and ate their lunch in a corner of the sewing room floor. Sometimes they were afraid of the older women, who would heckle them for pushing so hard, and for trying to impress the proprietor. "Ehi tu poco streghe meglio non spingere così difficile. Voi potreste trovare in un incidente." Threats were made to Lucia and Antoinetta.

Once, one of the women made a hot iron fall from its hook near the hearth that almost scalded Lucia. They were sure these were not idle threats being made against them. There were however, one or two, who stuck up for them, but for the most part they were in constant fear inside the work place and out.

The owner of the factory was a middle-aged obese man, named Signore` Paglimenti. He always wore a white waistcoat trimmed in brocade. His general appearance looked clean, until he came near, and his body odor reeked of stale onions and tobacco. He had a comical mustache, which was black that curled at the ends, and contrasted with his powdered wig. He had a shiny gold watch that peeked out from a small pocket in his coat. On the bridge of his nose hung half glass spectacles that he always had to look over to talk to someone. There was something sinister about him, and the way he looked at Antoinetta made her skin crawl. Signore` Paglimenti knew the girls were fascinated by the watch. Never having seen such an object they were thrilled when he showed it to them. "Vieni qui ragazze. Vuoi vedere il mio orologio abbastanza?" They laughed and giggled when he would show them the shiny object. The other women would warn them "Be careful young ones. He is a dangerous man. Signore' ama le ragazze giovani." Antoinetta and Lucia just thought they were being jealous, because Signore` Paglimenti was kind to them and noticed their good work. Sometimes Signore` would bring the girls sugar treats. He even gave Antoinetta a small cameo pin. The day he gave it to her, he called her into his back office, opened the box, and walked over to pin it to her dress. Antoinetta recoiled at this intimacy. He stopped and just handed it to her with a lustful stare. "It is a small gift for such a beautiful young woman. Ti piace?" Antoinetta looked at the lovely cameo and was shocked at such a gift. "Oh yes, it is beautiful Signore' Paglimenti, but, I cannot accept such an expensive gift." "Do you mean to insult me?" he pouted. She never expected him to respond in that way. "No, of course, it is just so very generous." Paglimenti came a little too close, and she could smell the putrid mixture of alcohol and decaying teeth. "I will think of a way you can repay me?" he whispered and touched her arm. Antoinetta recoiled and lowered her lids in a sheltered expression. She wore the cameo at work, to the jeers of her fellow workers, but quickly took it off when they left. She did not know if her parents would want her to accept gifts from a man. This banter between the proprietor and the two sisters went on for several months. While they had relaxed their opinion of the big, smelly man, yet were mindful of their co-workers warnings. Signore' Paglimenti's attentions went on in the same banal manner for months. He was always respectful, but there was that underlying look of lustful appetite. The girls were getting more suspicious of his desires, and more alert, to his mannerisms. As time went on, the older women grew more accustomed to their presence and became friendlier.

One evening, when they had been exceptionally busy, the girls had stayed a little later to finish their work. "Girls, don't be too long, it is getting dark," shouted Carmella, one of the nicer women with whom they had become close. Everyone was leaving, having finished their work, and since it was Friday, they had all been talking about their plans for the weekend. Antoinetta and Lucia were envious that they had nowhere to go. "Have a good weekend Carmella, we shall see you on Monday" waved Lucia. The sisters were busy finishing their work. Antoinetta had but one more piece to sew, and Lucia was sweeping up all the debris from the tables and floor. The only candles still burning were the ones by the door, where Antoinetta was working, and several in the back office; otherwise it was dark in the building.

Signore` Paglimenti was in his office, which was all the way to the back of the sewing floor. They were just about finished when Signore `Paglimenti's appearance near their table startled them. He was so huge, that he almost completely blocked the light from the candle that hung from the wall behind him, and cast an ominous shadow. The two girls were frightened by the big man and quickly started to pack up the last of their day's work. "Ah Signore` you scared us" quipped Lucia. "There is nothing to be scared of I just want to talk to you both." As they were getting ready to leave Signore` Paglimenti went over to the door and threw the bolt, which found its mark with a clang. The girls jumped from the sound. "What do you want to talk to us about at this hour? It is getting late, and our parents will be worried if we do not come home soon." Their hearts were pumping so violently, they were afraid that it would certainly jump out of their mouths. A little bead of perspiration started to form on Lucia's forehead. They told Signore` Paglimenti that they were now finished, and could he please open the big door so they could go home, because their parents would be angry if they came home too late. He started to laugh so loud and sinisterly, that it echoed throughout the large room and penetrated the girl's ears. "It is early. Do not worry. Antoinetta come over here I want to show you something". He had pulled the gold watch from his pocket and lured her to his side. She gingerly came forward but stayed at arm's length. "Come closer, how can you see from there? It is dim in here." He held the watch close to himself. Antoinetta was conflicted. She wanted to see the time, but was nervous to come closer. She was very near by now, and Signore` Paglimenti brought the timepiece down near his waist. As she was looking, he grabbed her hand and threw back his waistcoat. Her eyes grew huge as she saw that his cock was exposed, and standing straight out. He brushed it against her hand and she jumped back. "Hold him," he barked. Antoinetta stood paralyzed for a moment, then realized that she needed to get Lucia, and escape.

Suddenly, he lunged toward Antoinetta, and his powerful grip engulfed her slender arm as he yanked her off her feet. She struggled and started to scream. Lucia, who, up to this point, had been going about her business of cleaning up, in the hopes of getting out before it was pitch dark, heard the sounds of struggling. Lucia hearing her sister scream reacted instantly. Lucia armed with the broom she was sweeping the floor with, wielded it like a sword. The broom found its mark and stunned Paglimenti. He grabbed the stick in his powerful hand, and used it to pull Lucia toward him. Caught off balance she nearly fell on top of him, then with his one free hand, he landed a solid smack across her face and she tumbled head over heels backward. Temporarily dazed, and crying from the stinging pain in her face, she retreated to a dark corner. In her numbness, she heard her sister struggling with her assailant. The tiny Antoinetta was no match for this brut, who had by now overpowered her completely. As Antoinetta lay whimpering on the floor, like a wounded animal, Paglimenti was quickly making short work of hiking up her petticoat. His fat, ugly body was smothering the petite frame of her sister. Antoinetta's valiant attempts to ward him off were becoming a losing battle. Her womanhood was now exposed, and Paglimenti was making lascivious grunts and gasping to catch his breath. "Taci. Se avete il coraggio di dire a nessuno che ti invierà per gli zingari." His raspy voice told her to be silent, and if she even dared to tell anyone, she and the other brat, would be beaten some dark night on their way home and their bodies given to the Gypsies, to be sold as sex slaves in Turkey.

The fat pig was fumbling with the ties on his breeches. Succeeding in undoing them, his breeches falling to the floor, his fully erect penis now totally exposed. "Look how big he is, and I am going to stick all of it into that pretty little slit of yours. He likes when it's the first time, nice and tight." He leaned over and licked Antoinetta's face with his tobacco stained tongue, and she gagged at the smell of his breath. Antoinetta did not say one word, but her eyes were on fire, and her teeth were clenched. She was thrashing about trying to get free, but the effort was too much. Lucia could see that her strength, under the weight of Paglimenti, was draining her. Lucia started yelling for him to let her go. "Non essere geloso rosso, sarà il tuo turno successivo. Ottengo due al prezzo di uno, un affare molto buono. Ah, don't be jealous, I will take care of you next little one." Lucia was horrified at the thought of being next. She must act quickly.

Lucia could not stomach to see her sister like this any longer, she mustered every ounce of courage she had, and was about to just run over and start beating Paglimenti. She reached up to a nearby sewing table to steady herself, and regain her balance. Her left eye was almost swollen shut from where that beast had struck her face. Her hand brushed against something cold and hard. In the darkness, she felt the cold steel of a large pair of cutting shears. In her drunken fear, she grabbed the shears with both hands, and ran toward the hulking figure, with the blade fully extended in front of her. The steel found its intended target, and she practically fell upon the shears that sliced through the layers of fat like churned butter. The long shaft of the steel shears punctured Paglimenti's upper shoulder, and blood began to spurt from the incised area. "Cos`e`?" he roared. He was confused and disorientated, and his mind did not register for a few seconds what was causing this excruciating pain.

Paglimenti rolled his bulk off Antoinetta, as he was trying to reach the scissor to pull it from his shoulder. His fat arm could not reach around far enough to extract it. Lucia in that second of confusion reached down and pulled Antoinetta to her feet. She staggered but managed to stay upright. Their every muscle charged them into action, and they raced toward the bolted door. With strength they never knew existed within them, they managed to disengage the bolt and open the door. "Cagne. Puttane. Ucciderò entrambi." Paglimenti was screaming, "You bitches! Whores! I will get you," He was crying out obscenities at the top of his lungs. They ran out, never looking back, and kept running into the darkness. Blindly, Lucia half dragging her sister through the streets not even knowing where she was going, but running.

Their route took them past the church and the rectory garden. It was very dark, and well past the time when they should have been back to the shelter. As they rounded the corner of the rectory garden, they collided into Giovanni Romano, who was by now beginning to search for them along with Donato, Rafaela, and Antonio, each one taking a different route to find their whereabouts. The old man grabbed their arms, and was about to scold them for being so late, but then saw their faces, and their disheveled appearance and stopped. The girls were gasping for breath, and sweating in spite of the cool night air. Antoinetta was sobbing and trembling, her clothing was torn, and her long hair, which she always wore in a braid piled atop her head, was down and loose about her face. Lucia's eye was completely shut, and a bluish purple ring surrounded the area. Her nose was swollen and a large red mark sat on her upper cheek.

Immediately, Giovanni took them into the courtyard of the rectory garden and sat them down, near a statute of the Blessed Mother, in a grotto of granite surrounded by beautiful yellow roses. "Chi ha fatto questa cosa a voi?" He demanded to know who did this terrible thing to them. They refused to answer. They were trembling and shaking their heads. Finally, Lucia spoke up in a choked quivering voice "Signore` Paglimenti from where we work. He tried to do something very bad to Antoinetta, and I stabbed him with the scissors. We cannot tell Papa or our brothers; they will kill him then be hanged. What are we going to do? Please help us, we are so scared." Lucia, who was in a state of shock, was rambling, and speaking so rapidly that Giovanni could hardly understand what she was saying. He assured them that whatever they told him would be kept a secret, and he solemnly swore this oath on the grave of his dead child. The girls knew no one would ever swear on the dead, especially such a religious old man, if they did not mean to keep the oath. Antoinetta was too embarrassed to tell the story so Lucia recounted the events of what happened earlier.

"Now tell me what happened...slowly" the old man was trying to be calm, but he had a hard time looking at them without being upset. They looked at each other, Antoinetta was ashamed, and Lucia was furious, but scared of what will happen to them. Softly, Giovanni Romano took her hand in his. She could feel the calluses on the bony fingers but somehow felt safe. "Come inside and tell me the whole story."

If their parents found out, they would be so upset, because they had told the girls not to go to work in the first place. Giovanni Romano was a patient and wise old man, and he immediately devised a story to help the girls work this out with their parents. He took Antoinetta and Lucia into the cellar of the rectory where he slept. "Go in there; I have a basin and water. There is a clean linen towel, and above the shelf is some soap and a comb." He told Antoinetta to go into the room and clean herself up, and straighten out her clothing and comb her hair. Next, he examined Lucia's eye and cheek, and cleansed the area with a wet rag. As he was wiping the dry blood from her face and the tear stained cheeks, Giovanni Romano suddenly and without any words began to cry. He remembered so well his own child, and the love of his wife, and all that had been lost so many years ago. He loved all the Banfis, but he truly loved Lucia, because her goodness had shown through from the first moment they met. The pain he felt in his heart for his own loss was far less than the anger that was welling up inside him for the abuse these two sweet girls had to endure at the hands of that pig. Lucia saw that he was overcome with emotion; she reached up and wiped the tears that were falling from his good eye. "Padrino, do not cry, I am fine. I worry about my sister. What will happen to us? I am very scared." Giovanni Romano knew that he must remain strong for their sake. He choked back his tears, and in as calm and as firm a voice he could manage, he assured them for the third time, that he would work it out. "Bella, don't worry, I will see that all it taken care of."

Once Antoinetta emerged from the room she looked neat and put together, but her eyes were different. She saw an ugliness tonight that she never knew existed. Giovanni Romano saw her pain, and coughed back the bile that reached the back of his throat. He delicately asked her if the man had violated her womanhood, "Cara, did Signore` Paglimenti touch you down there? Did he penetrate you?" Antoinetta was humiliated, yet, she answered calmly, "No Padrino, my sister stopped him before he put..." with her head bent, and her voice so strained, she stopped speaking. There was a sigh of joy from the old man. He was happy but confused about how Lucia had stopped him just in time. Once again, they made him promise, on his oath, not to tell anyone of these events, for surely Lucia would go to jail, and Antoinetta would be sent to a convent. No one would ever believe that they were innocent, and had not provoked the incident. Next, they told, as best they could, the entire story, including the attack on Paglimenti by Lucia.

Lucia, always the leader, drew in a deep breath. She closed her eyes as if reliving the events of earlier that evening. In a soft voice, barely audible, she commenced her story. "We were just finishing our work. Antoinetta was putting the last stitches on the piece, and I was cleaning up with the broom. Signore` Paglimenti came from the back. All the others had gone home, and it was just the three of us. He threw the bolt of the big door and came toward us. He tried to trick Antoinetta into seeing what time it was from his watch. Then he grabbed her toward him and started to touch her breasts. When I heard her screaming I had the broom and came over to hit him with it, but that fat pig was too strong, and he slapped me so hard across my face that I fell down." Lucia was panting from the recollection of the events. Giovanni, seeing how upset she was, told her to go slow but to continue. "*Calma, non ti agritate*! It is over and you are both safe."

Again, Lucia took a deep breath, in an attempt to cleanse her mind, she began, this time a little stronger. She reached out to grab her sister's hand, which was clenched into a tight fist. When Lucia touched her, she immediately engulfed Lucia's hand. "I could see that the beast was exposed, and was now on top of my sister.

She was fighting so hard to throw him off, but it was impossible. He was pulling her skirts up." At this point in the story, Antoinetta started to cry, little sobs of pain and embarrassment. Lucia was trying, very delicately, to go around the more graphic parts. "I was trying to steady myself because my head was pounding from the pain in my eye. I was feeling for something to hold on to. It was dark in the back of the room. I reached up to a sewing table near where I fell to balance myself. My hand felt the cold steel of the shears. I got up took the shears into both my hands and ran to where they were." At this point Lucia was sweating and her hands were trembling. Giovanni Romano had seen this reaction to shock many times. Luckily, he had in his small room a bottle of brandy that he used when his old bones ached from the dampness. He went to the shelf and uncorked the bottle, and poured some into the wooden cup that sat next to it. He handed it first to Antoinetta and then to Lucia. Fortified from the brace of the liquid Lucia continued her tale. "I thrust the shears into his shoulder and he squealed like the fat pig that he is. He was cursing then got off my sister. I pulled her to her feet and we threw the bolt of the big door. Then we ran and ran until we met you." With that final statement Lucia collapsed on the bed, her eyes closed, the rag covering her left eye and the tears rolling down her face. Antoinetta was still sobbing, but sat stock still on the edge of the small cot.

Giovanni Romano listened intently, and then said to them that they must not tell their parents what had happened, that it would cause them all plenty of trouble. Signore` Paglimenti, was, after all, a very wealthy and influential man and knew all the magistrates. "You must listen to me, both of you. You cannot tell your mother and father what happened. Surely, your father and Antonio will go there and tear his heart from his fat body. We must devise a story that will keep everyone safe. You understand?" Both girls nodded. They knew what would happen if their father and brother found out what Signore` Paglimenti had done to them.

If Donato found out he would surely kill him, and then be hung for his trouble. The story they were to tell their parents was that on the way home the street hoodlums thought they had money and tried to rob them, and they ran away to avoid getting beaten or killed, and in their flight from the robbers Lucia fell to the ground and hit her face on the stone walkway. That they were both too frightened to go back, especially since it was already dark, and they would have to walk home along the route where these tyrants lurked waiting for their next victim. So, they went the long way around, for safety. This, they all agreed, was a believable story. "Ah, but what if Signore` Paglimenti goes to the Polizia?" Lucia asked with a quivering tone. "Don't worry Bella, I will go talk to him, and suggest that would be a poor idea, since your father and brother will surely kill him once they find out what he tried to do to you." Giovanni Romano assured them that he would go see him right now to straighten things out, and to secure Paglimenti's silence. All was agreed.

Giovanni Romano promised to meet them later at the shelter, but not to tell their parents that they had met up with him, and to go directly back to the shelter. He was going to talk to Paglimenti, and that they must stay to the story. Once the girls were calmed down, the old man set them on their way toward the shelter, which was only a short block away in the basement of the main church. Sister Margarita, one of the nuns who helped the displaced families with their needs, greeted them. Sister Margarita knew that the Banfi's were out looking for the two girls. "Ah, Dear Virgin, what happened to the two of you? Are you all right?" Lucia, always the talker, now for the first time, told the story they had contrived with the help of Giovanni Romano. "Oh my Sweet Jesus, thanks be to God, they did not kill you both, or worst kidnap you. I am so sorry. Come, I will get you some supper, you poor girls." Lucia and Antoinetta were holding hands, and Lucia gave her a reassuring squeeze. It had worked this time. Everyone had already had their supper, but the girls related their story to the sister in charge of the kitchen, and she gasped in terror for their plight. She took them, hand in hand into the convent, and gave them some leftover soup and a piece of bread with some hard cheese. When they were finished, she gave them each a cube of sugar, but told them not to tell the other children they got it, because she did not have enough to go around, but it was a special treat in view of their troubles. As they were going back to their designated area in the shelter, their frantic parents came running over to them, and taking one look at Lucia's face, started to interrogate their whereabouts. They related the story now for the third time, and felt more confident with its content this time.

Donato, as expected, was angry, and wanted them to point out these little animals so he could beat them to death. They stammered for a second, then Lucia quickly interjected that they wore kerchiefs over their faces. Their father was very angry and cursed loudly, but was quickly admonished by Rafaela, who reminded him that he was in church. He bit his lip, but his eyes were on fire, and his muscles were tight and bulging under his shirt. He swore that if he ever caught those bastards, they would regret the day their wretched mother gave birth to them. This was no life for his family.

Antonio, Andrea, Genaro and Francesco were more or less settled into their new lives and so the burden of caring for them was now gone. Tomorrow he would devise a plan to leave Naples. That was the end of the discussion, until Antonio, their big brother, came in and the girls repeated the story for the fifth time, with one or two more details for interest. He too cursed these street urchins, whom he knew lurked in every dark alley throughout the city, he too, having been accosted on more than one occasion.

Some time had passed before Giovanni Romano entered, and seemed genuinely pleased to see that the girls had arrived back unharmed, and they once again retold their story that the three had concocted earlier that evening, for the sake of appearances. Their performances were noteworthy. They tried to find out what Giovanni had said to Signore` Paglimenti, but the opportunity did not make itself available. It had been a long and terrifying day, and so they said good night to all, and gave kisses all around. It was agreed that the very next day the Banfi family would search for a home in the nearby outskirts of Naples, and that the girls would have to be placed in some sort of school, perhaps Uncle Luigi could get them into a convent school, at least until they could get settled.

The next day proved to be a turning point in the lives of Lucia and Antoinetta. There was much commotion and conversation about the streets. Everyone was talking about the awful fire last night, and that a man was killed in the blaze. The girls were curious and started to pay attention to what was being said. They soon learned that the dress shop owned by Signore` Paglimenti had burned to the ground last night, and it appeared that Signore` Paglimenti, who was working late, was burned to death in the horrible fire. Those who had gathered near the site were commenting on the fact that the building was one of the worst firetraps in the city. They were also talking about Signore' Paglimenti and that with all his money how cheap he had been to his workers and family. One woman said that it was rumored that he had affairs with some of the girls, and that his poor wife worked like a dog, while he was fooling around. "Pig that he was he got what he deserved. I worked in that hell pot for a while. Disgusting man, that Signore' Paglimenti, he was always trying to squeeze the flesh from the young ones. I hope he rots in hell." Another older woman, then spit on the ground to mock his behavior. A younger woman said that the old, fat pig got what was coming to him, she only felt bad for the wife and children. Apparently, Signore' Paglimenti was not very well liked, and his passing did not bring one tear to anyone. The only true concerns for his passing were the workers who had to find new jobs, and that some of them were owed back wages by this filthy slob.

The girls ran blindly toward the rectory garden where they found who they were seeking. There they found Giovanni Romano working quietly on his beautiful flowers; he was kneeling before a life size crucifix with the corpus of Jesus so real the girls were afraid to gaze fully upon its form. It was a strange sight to see the old man tending his flowers, and wondering if he had set fire to the shop with Signore' Paglimenti still in the building. They could not imagine that he was capable of such a demonic act, but it was too coincidental that this turn of events should occur after the incidents of the evening before. What really happened would remain a mystery forever in the hearts and minds of Antoinetta and Lucia. Yet they knew that Giovanni Romano had killed the one person who could have destroyed them and their family. Why had he risked his own life and freedom for people he hardly knew? On his face there was an expression of sorrow that matched the expression on the face of Christ on the statue that stood in the garden. They knew. They were relieved that this nightmare was behind them, and that they owed it all to this old man. Not a word passed between the three of them in that garden, but they all kneeled before the powerful image of Christ on his cross and prayed for God's forgiveness, and the secret they would all carry to their graves. Giovanni Romano had become their Padrino, their godfather.

Giovanni Romano knew that he must find a way to get those girls away from Naples. They were prime targets for the thugs that roamed the city. He had sent a note to his former employer, Maria Sucretti, at Monteforte, that her great nieces were in danger, and explained briefly the situation. His only hope was that she would send word that the girls were welcomed at Monteforte under her protection.

True to his word, Donato Banfi went to search for a new home for his family. Rafaela went to her assigned appointments and Antonio took to the boats to earn money for the family. Antoinetta and Lucia stayed and helped Giovanni in his garden. It was a wonderful day for the two girls. That evening, they all gathered to share a bowl of soup and a loaf of bread at the shelter, Donato recounted his day's journey into the countryside in search of a new home. He was tired and disappointed, the next town outside of the city was many miles away from the seaport, and there was no school. He told the family that tomorrow he would go with Antonio, in their small boat, back to Torre del Greco, to see if they could start building another home where they used to live, or try to find one along the coast not too far away. They all agreed that it was a good plan. Later in the evening Donato confided to Rafaela that the children were not getting the proper nourishment, and that they needed a home. Rafaela knew that Donato was thinking of sending the girls to a convent for a while until they could start a new life. She also knew it would be the best thing for them, but in her heart, she was scared to let them go. "Cara, we must sacrifice ourselves here in this hell pot, but, you see what happened. Next time we may not be so lucky. We must get them away from here." Rafaela knew that her husband was right, but the thought of them being away was too much to bear.

CHAPTER NINE

THE DECISION

Monteforte

Two weeks later the note from Giovanni Romano reached its destination. When Isabella brought Maria Sucretti the missive, she stared at the handwriting. It was somehow familiar. A hand she remembered from long ago. It was sealed with a simple glob of wax and no insignia. She turned it over in her hand and held off her curiosity for just a moment trying to fix the script in her mind.

Maria thanked Isabella and took the note to the terrace. She sat down with the note and felt something strange pass over her. With a slightly hesitant hand, she undid the seal.

Dear Mistress Sucretti,

It has been so long since I last saw you. Our parting was with great sadness. I am sure by now you have heard of the destruction of Torre del Greco. The family of your brother's granddaughter, Rafaela Banfi, has befriended me. She has two young daughters, Lucia and Antoinetta, who must be placed somewhere. The thugs that roam Naples have abused them. Their parents fear for the lives.

Mistress, they do not know of my connection to you or Monteforte. I am writing this without their knowledge in the hopes that you will be able to help. I am staying at Our Lady of Lourdes Church in Naples. They are also here as refugees.
I am your devoted servant,
Giovanni Romano

Maria read the note with such intensity that she felt herself tremble. After all these years, she thought that Giovanni Romano was surely dead. The words plunging like a dagger into her heart. She closed her eyes, the breeze from the sea surrounding her now as she sat upon the terrace. The day Giovanni Romano left with his wife and child was one that Maria had never forgotten. It was several months after the death of her husband Salvatore Sucretti. While the official inquest had been completed, Sergeant Corelli was still sniffing around Monteforte, asking questions of the servants, interviewing the guests that had attended her birthday celebration, and interrogating her, and all those connected to the events of that fateful evening. Sergeant Corelli was like a dog on the scent of a juicy bone. Maria Sucretti had lodged a formal complaint with his superiors, but since the case was never resolved, it was still an ongoing investigation. Corelli was threading softly, but would not let it go. Giovanni Romano was the only likely candidate for the death of Salvatore Sucretti. Fernando, pleaded with Maria to turn himself over to Corelli, but after a long discussion with Giovanni Romano it was decided that Giovanni, Natalie and Rosalie their daughter, would leave Monteforte to put a stop to Corelli's investigation. Maria knew that Fernando, elderly and frail, would never survive a trial and imprisonment. Giovanni assured her that he would take good care of Natalie and Rosalie. Maria had no doubt that Giovanni loved them both, and would do all that he could to give them a good life.

When all plans were finalized Giovanni Romano packed up his family. It was the morning of the day of their departure, the whole house was sober, for Giovanni, Natalie, and Rosalie were beloved. Maria was still in her bedchamber, she could not bear to see them leave. Natalie was not just her servant, but also, her lifelong friend, who grew up together and had lived like sisters all their lives. When Rosalie was born, it was as if new life had been infused into the stone walls of Monteforte. Now, not only would she lose her best friend, but, the joy of this child as well.

"Mistress, I will miss you so much. My heart is broken at the thought of leaving you. Rosalie cried all night, she cannot even come to say goodbye." The tears were cascading down Natalie's lovely face. Maria embraced her so that the two meshed as one, and together they sobbed. Maria knew that unless Giovanni died, she would never see her dear friend again. Finding some composure Maria gently held Natalie at arm's length and looked into her eyes "I have loved you as a sister and a dear friend. If ever I can assist you or Rosalie you must let me know. It is because of Salvatore, who, even in death haunts me that you must leave. I will go to my grave cursing his soul. Dio aiuti tutti noi." There was a sudden rush of noise and bounding into the room was little Rosalie. She was a lovely little girl, with her mother's complexion, and her father's intense dark eyes. She was smart and had a jovial personality. She ran to Maria and hugged her so tight she could hardly breathe. "Mistress Zia, I love you and I will miss you always." The little girl was tall and strong for her ten years, and Maria bent to plant kisses all over her face. "Bella mia, I will miss you too. You must be strong and listen to your parents. If ever you need anything come to Zia and I will help you. I love you."

In the doorway stood Giovanni Romano, his dark, slim, silhouette indicating it was time to go. "It is time. We must leave. Rosalie, go see Isabella, she wants to tell you something. Natalie, help her with her things, the boat is waiting, and the tide is ready. I will be there in a moment." Maria gave them each a final hug and kiss, brushed the tears from her own eyes and stood there waiting for Giovanni. He patted the little girl's head, kissed his wife, and came into the room. "Giovanni, I am so sorry" but he stopped her from speaking. "Mistress, this is not your fault. If Fernando had not killed Salvatore, surely, I would have. He was out of control. It breaks my heart to leave you here, but we have no choice. Corelli will not let this go away, he is out for blood, and I cannot let them take Fernando, he has been like a father to me. This is what we must do. If I may be so bold, I would like to tell you that I too love you." He came to her, and with great gentleness embraced her, and she felt the wetness on her cheek. When he stepped back, she walked to her desk and retrieved an envelope. Handing it to him, she told him of its contents. "I have made arrangements to have an account set up in Natalie's name in the Bank of Naples. There will be sufficient funds in it to help you all get started. I have also set up a dowry for Rosalie. It is the least I can do." Giovanni knew better than to protest this generosity. "It is under the name of Giovanni and Natalie Verdi and Rosalie Verdi. I had Signore` Mendecino, my avvocato, secure new documents for the three of you. Everything you need is in this purse. "How can I ever repay this generosity? Sei stato così gentile a noi tutti questi anni. God bless and protect you always." With that, they were gone.

So long ago, and yet the pain of their leaving was fresh on her heart. They were her family. When Maria got word that Natalie and Rosalie had died of the plague, she was inconsolable for days. She wept until there were no more tears. She knew that Giovanni was devastated, and tried to send word for him to come back to Monteforte, now so many years later the scandal of Salvatore Sucretti's death had long since passed. Nobody cared that the Camorra Caporegime was dead. Giovanni sent word that there were too many memories at Monteforte and he thanked her for her kindness. Maria was left once more to carry her sorrow to herself. Taking the note to her desk, she sat down, drew a piece of her special parchment from the drawer, and reached for the quill. What shall I say to this ghost from the past? Maria thought that she spent so many years trying to convince her sister-in-law Lucia, after the death of her brother Mateo, to come and live at Monteforte, only to be rejected. She was not sure she wanted anyone connected with Lucia to be part of her life. She put the note from Giovanni Romano in the drawer and decided to think on the matter before she responded. This was not an easy decision.

After a restless night, filled with dreams of the past, Maria Sucretti resolved that she would send a messenger to Naples in search of the Banfi family. She took out the note and read it again. Two young girls, now that might be interesting. She took the paper and quill and began writing, not even sure what she was going to say.

Dear Giovanni,

Your letter came as a shock after all these years. I am pleased to see that you are alive. I have given your request great thought and have decided to let the two girls come to Monteforte.

I am sending my footman, Nicko, with this note and he will bring the girls back to Monteforte. I am sending a letter of introduction for their parents regarding his identity.
Be well old friend. God bless you.
Maria Frances Sucretti, Mistress of Monteforte

One week later the note reached Giovanni Romano. One of the sisters came with the note for him and told him there was a young man waiting for instruction. Giovanni Romano came to the front vestibule of the rectory where a handsome man in his early twenties greeted him. Well groomed, tall, and slim, he wore a footman's uniform and he bowed to the old man. "Good day Signore`. I am Nicko and have been sent to find you by Mistress Maria Sucretti of Monteforte." Giovanni nodded then escorted him, without preamble, into the rectory garden.

It was only then that Giovanni broke the familiar seal of the Casa Monteforte. Before he opened the note, he felt the richness of the paper, which was scented, and admired the bold script on the face, which bore his name.

Giovanni Romano

She had given him that name. His mind drifted back to an earlier time, when he was a young swordsman, fresh from being a mercenary in France, and was introduced to his new master, Salvatore Sucretti. He was dumbstruck by the opulence of the castle and forbearance of the man before him. Then he saw her, elegant and slim, sitting on the terrace, a ray of sunlight highlighted her auburn hair. She turned to see who the new stranger was and her eyes glazed over him. She only nodded and then turned back to look at something in the garden. Maria Sucretti was a beautiful woman.

It took all the courage Giovanni had to read the note. It was short, Maria was not a frivolous woman, but addressed his concerns. He now realized why the young man, who was waiting patiently, had brought the missive in person. He was to bring back Lucia and Antoinetta to Monteforte. Giovanni, now that he had secured their admission to Monteforte, needed to convince Donato and Rafaela that it was the only sensible solution to their current problem. However, how was he going to do this?

"I am Giovanni Romano," he said. "Your servant Signoreˋ Romano, my Mistress holds you in great esteem, and said that I must abide by whatever you say." The young man bowed courteously. "I have been instructed by Mistress Sucretti to wait until you make arrangements, then I am to escort two young girls back to Monteforte." Giovanni needed time to think, to make a plan. "I will need a day or two to make the necessary arrangements. Can you find an inn until I have completed all that is required?" Smiling, Nicko replied "There is no need for that Signoreˋ Romano, I have a sister who lives not far from here, I will stay with her until the matter is resolved. I will give you her name and how to send for me when it is time." Giovanni was relieved that he now had some time to formulate a plan. Nicko, a friendly fellow, wrote down the information for Giovanni and was on his way.

CHAPTER TEN

A PLAN

Naples

Giovanni's plan was simple, or at least on its face, it appeared to be straightforward. He would tell Donato and Rafaela, that having heard of the disaster with Vesuvius, and that Torre del Greco was destroyed, their aunt, Maria Sucretti of Monteforte, had sent a messenger to find them. After making many inquiries, the messenger came to the church because he was told that a family fitting their description was sheltered there. Sister Bernadetta came to get him and he spoke with the messenger who told him of Mistress Sucretti's desire to be of help. Giovanni rehearsed that story several times and it sounded true even to his own ears. Now the test would be to tell it to the family without any hesitation. For the first time in years, Giovanni Romano was happy. He was happy at the thought that his piccolo cappelli rosa Lucia would be safe.

Giovanni Romano who always shared his evening meal with the Banfi family, told his story about how Maria Sucretti heard of the disaster at Torre del Greco, and of the servant she sent to see if any of the family was still alive. Rafaela looked to Donato and they seemed amazed. Could this be the answer to their prayers?

Maria Sucretti was Rafaela's great aunt, and sister of her late grandfather Mateo Rizzo. She had grown up with stories of Monteforte and Maria Sucretti. Her aunt had the means to care for the girls and she was alone in that big villa. "Why does she want us to come to Monteforte?" it was more a statement than a question. "We might consider the offer. It would be good for the girls. I am afraid if something like what happened last week should come again that I would hunt down the animals who did that and kill them. I am fearful for my daughters. For that matter I am fearful for you too Rafaela. Maybe you should go with them to Monteforte, at least for a while." Antonio who was absorbing the conversation now joined in his father's sentiments "Mama, I see what goes on in the streets, it is no place for my sisters. Papa is right, if they come after them again we must find them and do harm to them. You know we will. Please think about it." Antonio was a quiet young man, who loved being on the sea, his wants were modest, but under that mild exterior was an honorable warrior. There was no doubt in Rafaela's mind that her son, and her husband, would find and kill anyone who laid hands on those girls. Rafaela, faced with this daunting reality, was very afraid.

Donato reminded her that she had sent her servant all the way here to search for them to extend this generous invitation. "Cara, she even sent her servant to find us, so she must be sincere in her offer. You know Antonio and I cannot come with you. We must make a living so that someday we can have our lives back, and then be gone from this retched place. If you are not comfortable with sending them alone, you can go with them, and I will come as often as I can. We must do something before we all perish." Donato's voice quivered because he knew that it was only a matter of time before his worst nightmares would come true. She said she would think on the matter for a few days and give her answer after she discussed it with the girls. "I will pray to the Blessed Mother for guidance. I know this is a dangerous place for two young girls. We must work, so we can once again live a normal life, in our own home. Give me a day or so to think." Rafaela choked back the tears, but in her heart, she knew that something had to be done. At this point, Giovanni Romano, who had been silent all this time, entered into the conversation. "Donato you know I love your family as if it were my own. I serve no purpose, I have no job, I will gladly go with Antoinetta and Lucia to Monteforte, to watch over them and protect them. It is the least I can do. I am an old man with no other use to my life." At this point Lucia and Antoinetta, who had been silently listening to everything, got up and went to Giovanni Romano hugged and kissed him. Lucia, always willing to express her feelings said, "We love you Padrino you are not useless." Both girls, holding hands told their parents that they were scared and wanted to go somewhere, anywhere, away from Naples.

The next day, Donato and Antonio set sail for Torre del Greco, in hopes of finding the town they knew and loved, and their old homestead. What they found was complete devastation and destruction. The wrath of Vesuvius had altered the shape of the mountainside, and caused all the vegetation surrounding it burned. The ground covered in charred lava with the dock and village were in rubbles, the beach littered with thousands of dead fish and sea creatures. It was a horrific site, and tears flowed from their eyes. Everything they ever had, or knew, was gone, and the possibility of rebuilding their lives in this wasteland destroyed. It would be many, many years before Torre del Greco, and its surrounding neighbors, would be able to call this place home. Dio aiuti tutti. Antonio, sensing the despair in his father, placed his big-callused hand around his shoulder, and together they stood shoulder to shoulder, two strong men, with tears rolling down their faces. "Don't despair Papa, we will be a family once again. Soon!" Donato turned to face his son and kissed him on each cheek "I pray for that day my son." They turned their boat around, and headed toward Naples, once more in utter silence and despair. Donato felt tired and weak, and a veil of hopelessness covered his soul, he cursed, and cried, and prayed for renewed strength for himself and his family. Antonio, who was wise beyond his years, sensed that his parents needed him more than ever to deliver them to a new hope for their future as a family. He silently swore to make them proud of him, and to help them start to find a proper home. He would work twice as hard to earn more money for the building of a new house, two men, father, and son, with one dream.

It was very sad that evening when Donato and Antonio came back with the reports of Torre del Greco, and what they saw, and everyone gathered and prayed for guidance. Rafaela had spoken to the girls before Donato came home, and had explained to them that it would be a temporary move for them, and that their lives would be much better with their great-aunt Maria in Sorrento. She told them that they would be doing their parents a great favor by going there, so that they could work later and harder, without the fear of someone hurting them while they were at work. After much discussion, and promises of a short duration at Monteforte, the two girls agreed that if their parents thought it was a good move, at least temporarily, it would also get them away from the shattering events of recent memory. "We have made a decision," announced Rafaela in a timid voice. "Antoinetta and Lucia have agreed that they can no longer be safe here while we are at work, and there is no school available, for them. If you are willing Giovanni, you will escort them to my aunt and maybe she will let you stay with my daughters." She had a death grip on Donato's hand with tears in her eyes. Giovanni Romano, head bent, "I would be honored to go with them. Thank you."

Giovanni Romano was relieved, for he knew that this would be the best move for his beloved girls. He sent word to Nicko, that it would be a couple of days until the girls were prepared, and that he would send notice when they were ready.

The next few days were busy ones for Rafaela and the girls. Both mother, and daughters, worked feverishly to put together some dresses and petticoats to take on their journey. It was an anxious time for all of them. Donato continued his daily quest to find new lodgings. Rafaela was always amazed at the strength of her beloved Donato. He managed to squeeze time between his working hours to look for new living accommodations. Of course, together with Antonio, they would soon be making enough money to afford to rent rooms in the poorer district of the city. Two days before their scheduled departure, Rafaela once again made inquiry at the local school for placement of the girls, but the situation had not changed. There would be no openings until the next year, which were still several months away. Satisfied that she had done all she could at present, she accepted that the girls would be better off with their great-aunt until they could establish some permanent roots.

Life for the Banfi family was changing rapidly. Francesco wrote faithfully every week to his parents and every two weeks to his sisters. He knew that God had called him to this life and he was happy. As for Andrea and Genaro, they were off to pursue their studies. Uncle Luigi was such a driving force in all their lives Rafaela and Donato could never repay him for all he had done for their family. Andrea was on his own and in the next few years have completed his studies from the university at Padua, where he was now working as a professor's apprentice, and supporting himself on his meager stipend. Andrea's goal was someday be a professor of mathematics. A lofty goal, but his current instructors had great hopes for his advanced intellect. Unlike the others, Andrea was not a romantic; he would become a practical man of numbers. He did not have the time or inclination to write to his parents and rarely came home. It was not that he did not love his family, but he had always been so engrossed in his studies from his earliest days. Andrea showed the most potential for book learning. He would spend hours working on some equation even forgetting to eat, needing to be called several times to the supper table.

Genaro on the other hand, was a true romantic, and showed an aptitude for drawing and painting. These brothers were complete opposite. Genaro would spend hours drawing from nature or sketches of his brothers and sisters. He especially loved to draw birds and small animals. Locally his talent was well known, and his drawings were on display at the school, and even at church. Another sad thought for Rafaela was that all the beautiful pieces of art that Genaro had created had destroyed in the aftermath of the destruction. Genaro had assured his mother that he would create more and better art. Father Vincenzo told Rafaela and Donato that Genaro had a God given talent that must be nurtured. As little gifts, he would paint landscapes or floral designs for his family and friends. Genaro, artistically gifted, as well as a very bright youngster, was quickly developing into a brilliant young man. He soon became a person of interest to a very wealthy patron of the arts, Signore` Trocchio. Signore` Trocchio was an arts and antiquities dealer, and a dear friend of Monsignor Luigi. With a little maneuvering, Uncle Luigi persuaded Signore` Trocchio to be the benefactor of this artistic prodigy. Uncle Luigi's sphere of influence was far reaching, the wealthy always want to be in the good graces of the church, and so the goal was to have Genaro attend the Accademia Di Belle Arti Firenze in Florence.

When Uncle Luigi came to ask permission to send Genaro to the Accademia he gave Rafaela and Donato a brief history of the place. In his robust eloquence, Uncle Luigi read aloud "It was founded in 1561 with high patronage of the Medici. At first, the academy met in the cloisters of the Church of the Santissima Annunziata. Pietro Leopoldo, Grand Duke of Tuscany, decreed in 1784, that all the schools of drawing in Florence be combined under one roof, under the direction of the Accademia, now renamed Accademia di Belle Arti Firenze, and that it was to contain a gallery of paintings by old masters, to influence the studies of the young artists. The Accademia, and the adjoining Gallery still occupy the lands that were assigned in via Ricasoli, a former convent and hospice." Pleased with his performance he continued, "So you see it would be a great honor for Genaro to attend this fine establishment." Rafaela and Donato trusted their uncle, and knew that if he went through all this trouble to get their son into this wonderful school, he must have talent. In the meantime, Genaro was pacing back and forth, waiting for this parent's consent. The boy knew very well the reputation of this venerable institution of art and learning. For Genaro it would be a dream come true. Rafaela was the first to speak "Uncle Luigi we trust you in all matters. If you think this is a good opportunity for our son we will agree."

Genaro started his life at this most prestigious institute, which at first was a rocky road; he was struggling with the social life of one of the most cosmopolitan cities in the world. There was a definite social class, and Genaro did not fit in with the young aristocrats that practically ran the accademia. His clothes, his speech, his entire social demeanor was different, and they never let the peasant boy forget who he was and how he came to be in this place. It was only when creating his art that Genaro was in his element, and only then, that he felt in control. The professors were somewhat mixed about his place at the school, some were very hard on him, while others enjoyed the interest his work was receiving from some very influential patrons. He worked extremely hard, and wrote to his parents very often, giving them news of his progress, and seeking their advice. Rafaela and Donato were bursting with pride, yet were somewhat apprehensive about the effects of all this recognition on their country-bred child.

Rafaela would often think of each of her children and recall the words of her beloved grandmother, "Each child is different and special, like the fingers on your hand, each one has a function, but separately, they cannot work outside the main body of the hand". All her beloved children were special in their own right, and she was proud and adored them. Donato was proud also, but he was a man of practical wisdom. He would often struggle with the fact that Genaro might not get the recognition he deserved as the talented artist he truly was because of his social status, but, luckily, at least for now, he did have the patrons or connections he needed to succeed. He was both humbled and skeptical about Francesco becoming a priest, and when he thought of how smart and handsome his son was, he would feel a twinge of regret, but would quickly recover by thinking of Uncle Luigi and the good life he was enjoying as a cleric. Francesco enjoyed his time at the seminary so much that he was truly convinced that the priesthood was his calling, continued to pray for his vocation, and spent many hours at church. He was such a soft spoken and gentile boy. Lucia truly loved Francesco the best of all her brothers. Lucia once told her mother that Francesco wore the face of a saint. His beautiful eyes were filled with hope and kindness. Being the youngest of the Banfi boys was not easy for the meek and slightly built child. Their rough and tumble play was more than Francesco could compete with, but they in turn were gentle with this special boy. He was not a sissy or coward, he just did not want to hit, punch, or tackle like lion cubs learning to survive. Every night, since he learned his first prayer, Francesco gave the grace at the supper table. Francesco delighted and encouraged his baby sisters with stories of the Blessed Virgin and all the saints. Of course, with great piety came the jokes and ridicule of his peers. Luckily, for Francesco, his big brothers would often spare him from too much abuse at the hands of the town ruffians.

CHAPTER ELEVEN

THE ARRIVAL

Monteforte

The days flew by so quickly and their preparations were finally complete. The morning arrived for their journey to begin. Nicko, clad in his sharp uniform, looking handsome and dashing, arrived early with the carriage he had hired for the journey. His black wavy hair not covered by powder or wig and pulled back in a tight queue. He obediently bowed to Donato and Rafaela. "Good morning Signore` Banfi" then bowed deeply to Rafaela "Mistress. I am Nicko, footman for Mistress Sucretti of Monteforte. I have been instructed by my Mistress to take exceptional care of these two young ladies." Antoinetta and Lucia were blushing and excited, not only by the anticipation of the trip, but at the looks of their escort. Donato, ever the protective father, addressed Nicko, in a voice more abrasive than he actually intended "Guard my daughters with your life. I am sending their godfather, Signore` Romano to accompany them on the trip." Nicko, who was also tall and well built, stood even with Donato and Antonio, and responded, "I vow to care for them as if they were my own sisters. Please do not worry Signore` Banfi." Nicko bowed deeply and placed a reassuring hand on Donato's arm.

While the driver loaded their bags into the back of the carriage there was an air of understated sorrow. The driver wore a bright blue waistcoat. He was an older man, stout and short. He had a wide brimmed hat that shielded his eyes and a trimmed white beard. He climbed down from his seat and bowed respectfully to Donato. Removing his hat, he introduced himself. "My name is Gaetano Zanga, your servant signore`." Donato acknowledged the driver and asked, "How long will it take to get to Monteforte?" Gaetano Zanga, a man who had been driving coaches for many years was well versed in the local terrain. "It is approximately twenty kilometers, but the road is rough and all uphill. We will need to stop at least once. It is good weather today and we are getting an early start. I believe we should be there before sun set." Donato was confident in this man's ability and thanked him with a plea to take good care of his girls. Gaetano reassured him that it was a safe route mostly through farmland. "Signore` on my return if there are any messages I will stop by here to tell you."

Antonio was the first to approach his sisters. "Now, you two stay out of trouble and be good for Zia Maria. If you need anything, or find you do not like it there, just send word and Papa and I will come right away to get you. I love you both." They hung about their big brothers muscular neck like barnacles to the bottom of a boat. Next came Donato "I want you girls to behave. You must be respectful and helpful. If you need me just send word I will be on my way in no time. Watch over each other and be mindful of Signore` Romano. Ti amo mio bellezze." Their powerfully built father seemed to have shrunk under the weight of their departure, and he had tears in his eyes but held them back for the sake of his family. Lastly, Rafaela, who could not mask the pain of their leaving came to them "Entrambi ti amo così tanto.

If there were any other way, we would not be sending you away. We will come soon with news that we have a new home where we can once again be a family. Be good, be careful, and always be there for each other. Make us proud that you are respectful to your aunt." There were hugs, kisses, tears, and promises to write. There was a tremendous sense of loss from their parents, but somehow they felt more at ease knowing Giovanni Romano was going with them. "Giovanni take good care of my babies" implored Rafaela. "Don't worry I will be with them always." As he was about to board the carriage, Rafaela handed him a letter addressed to her aunt. "Please Giovanni give this to my aunt." Giovanni Romano hugged and kissed Rafaela, Donato, and Antonio then climbed into the carriage. They boarded the carriage and waved from the window, until they could only remember where their parents and brother had been standing. This was to be the beginning of many new and wonderful, yet sometimes frightening adventures for the threesome.

BOOK TWO

CHAPTER ONE

THE ADVENTURE BEGINS

Monteforte

Their journey was pleasant and uneventful. The hours passed by rather quickly, but the road was rugged and uphill, yet the scenery was beautiful and breathtaking. The carriage, lushly upholstered inside, could do little to buffer them from the jolting bumps from the rugged terrain. Nicko called down into the coach "We will be stopping soon for food and refreshment. There is an abbey along the way." Half way to their destination, they stopped at an ancient Abbey, to take a break and refresh themselves. One of the monks who was gaunt and tall greeted them cordially. His robe, worn and frayed about the wrist and hemline, and his beard was long and scraggly. At first glance, he appeared older, but upon closer inspection, he was probably in his early twenties. Nicko arranged to have fresh bread, wine and some ham brought to one of the crude wooden tables under the arbor at the rear of the abbey grounds. It was cool and pleasant. The monk that first greeted them introduced himself as Brother Vittorio Fermelli.

Nicko sensing that the girls needed to relieve themselves after having endured several hours on the road asked the monk if there were any facilities for them to do so. "Please mistresses come with me." Brother Vittorio took long strides and a quick pace led the way. They were heading away from the arbor and toward the Abbey. It was an ancient structure cast of stone in a classical gothic design. They came to a loggia that ran the length of the back of the building. It was cool and their footfalls made patting sounds on the stone floor. Every few feet in niches against the back wall were statues of various saintly deities. They reached a timeworn wooden door, which the monk opened. It was dark and somber in the chapel, the only illumination coming from the tall stained glass windows, and several lanterns that were strategically placed along the walls. The familiar smell of incense and candlewax perfumed the air. Lucia was looking all around, a feeling of comfort descending upon her tense young body. She would have loved to linger with the comfort of its protection, but Antoinetta was pulling at her sleeve to continue. Finally, he led them down a dim narrow hall to a small room. The girls entered into the tiny cubicle with its only embellishments consisting of a large carved crucifix nailed to the stucco wall, a battered wooden table upon which sat a chamber pot, pitcher of water, bowl, and linen towels. Brother Vittorio said, "I will be just out in the chapel. When you are done please meet me there. Take as long as you need." He then bowed closing the door behind him. A few minutes later, the sisters emerged from their toilet, refreshed and starving. They saw the monk on his knees facing the altar praying. He had not heard their approach and Antoinetta made a soft courteous cough. "Ah, there you are. Feeling better?" They assured the friendly monk that they did in fact feel better and were starving. He smiled warmly and led them back to the arbor. "I'll be back with some refreshments." Off he went, his long, slim, brown silhouette recessing into the back of the abbey.

Nicko and Giovanni Romano went to the well out back and washed themselves. They had asked the driver Gaetano to join them but he declined, stating that he needed to water and feed the horses, and that he would get something when he was finished.

Rafaela had packed the girls a basket with bread, cheese, and fruit, which they shared with the men. The arbor was fragrant and gave good shade from the hot sun. The girls were already tired from the hours of riding but were somewhat refreshed from having washed themselves. They munched on the goodies but were too excited to enjoy either the trip or the food; their thoughts being consumed with meeting their aunt.

Nicko, a jovial young man, was making conversation with Giovanni Romano. They sat in companionable conversation for a while. Brother Vittorio came back with a tray laden with some fresh figs and a dish of olives in oil. Lucia, always with a curious mind, asked him if he knew of Monteforte "Excuse me, but, do you know where Monteforte is?" she asked shyly. The monk surprised by the question, eased himself on to the opposite bench, and looked at the girls. The men were quietly talking to each other and absorbed in their own conversation. "Why do you want to know?" Lucia, who was not usually shy, but was not accustomed to casual conversation with strangers. "My sister, Antoinetta and I, are going there to stay with our aunt. My name is Lucia. We used to live in Torre del Greco, and then the volcano came and destroyed our home. We had to go to Naples, but it was very bad there, and our parents did not want us to stay any longer. We are going to live with our aunt Mistress Sucretti of Monteforte." Lucia was rambling so fast that it was difficult to keep up with the whole story.

Fortunately, Brother Vittorio was able to follow the tale. "Oh, I am sorry for your trouble. I heard many people died, and many more lost all their possessions and their homes. I am very happy to see that you both seem fine in spite of your hardship." He had warm grey eyes that were set deep into tanned skin. His hands were large and callused from hard work. He was not very handsome, but he exuded an air of quiet compassion. His full lips peeked out from under his scruffy mustache and he had a nice smile with straight white teeth. Brother Vittorio's voice was soft and soothing. "Yes, I have been to Monteforte on several occasions. Mistress Sucretti is a most generous woman; she gives alms and food for the many poor that we assist from this Abbey. I am sure you will be happy there."

With his last sentence completed, the bells of the Abbey rang. "I must leave now it is time for adoration of the Blessed Sacrament. Take care of yourselves. I will remember you and your family in my prayers. God bless you." Brother Vittorio had reached out and placed a hand on each of their heads, and closed his eyes for just a second. Lucia felt the vibe of his blessing course through her body. He immediately got up with no further society and removed himself quickly to the Abbey. Using the monk's exit as a signal Giovanni Romano and Nicko also stood and said it was time to leave. The girls packed up their basket and made their way back to the carriage. Lucia settled herself into the coach and looked back to see if the monk was there. She knew that someday she would meet him again.

The carriage lurched forward, shoving her into Giovanni Romano, who caught her in time to prevent her from crashing into the door. They rode for a long time in silence, each person contemplating the days ahead.

The air was crisp and clean and the sun was shining brilliantly on the lush foliage. The trek was difficult over the rocks and small vegetation that lined the road but Gaetano was an experienced driver. Nicko was having a bawdy conversation with him regarding the best brothels in Naples. Apparently, they were frequent customers of one or more of these favorite establishments.

Some of the finer points of their comparisons of the various charms of the women were discussed in lower voices. For sure, they were in complete agreement on one particular whore, whose talents were far superior to the rest. They were talking and laughing heartily. After a while, they both settled into mundane conversations, and Lucia lost interest in trying to hear what they were saying. She too tried to free her mind of the possibilities of what would be her future, at least, for a little while.

The scenery was spectacular with the mountains forming a natural barrier on their left and steep cliffs that dropped many kilometers to the water to their right. Along the route, they came upon rows and rows of lemon trees, which imbued the air with the scent of citrus. Groves of olive trees littered the intermittent patches of level ground while small farms were nestled into the mountainside. More than once, they had to stop for a passing herd of goats. Giovanni Romano had settled into a comfortable position inside the coach and occasionally nodded off for a catnap. The sisters had never truly travelled outside of Torre del Greco except for their recent move to Naples. Their experience in a large city like Naples had been damaging and they hated the city.

Naples was always crowded and dirty, and filled with lots of people you never really know. They were very fearful of what they were going to encounter. This place was so different from Torre del Greco, which was where the land met the sea. There it was flat and they could walk straight out to the sea. Now they were reaching for the heavens way up into the mountains with the sea at its feet. Everything was so strange and beautiful.

Lucia and Antoinetta sat dazed by the scenery unfolding before them. Ladies lowered their heads and men tipped their cap, even the children stopped their play to watch the carriage pass. Visitors were rare and those who could afford such a fine carriage must be wealthy. There was a cart pulled by a mule, which was blocking the roadway, and Nicko gave a loud call to the farmer, who waived and called back. Both girls giggled and waved at the farmer. The older man driving the cart waved, and slowly moved out of the way, then tipped his cap as they passed. It was an extraordinary feeling to see the reaction of the locals to the passing carriage. The sights, sounds and even the smell of this area of the country were so very different from Naples and of their beloved Torre del Greco.

Their journey continued for quite some time, and as they drove, they noticed the people were getting fewer. The mountains were rising as they were climbing into an ever-higher elevation. It was picturesque like one of Genaro's paintings. The colors of the trees and the plants and flowers were deep hued and intense. The bright yellows from the lemon trees were in stark contrast with the muted tones of the olive branches. Yet, the very nature of this contrast of colors created a stunning pallet. With the wind blowing into the open windows, they could smell the clean fragrant aromas of the surrounding countryside. So much had happened to them in the many months since the volcano erupted, so many new people, some of them, had touched their lives in such a good way, like their Padrino, Giovanni Romano, and some horrible people like Signore` Paglimenti. They felt the separation from their family, but realized that it would be easier for their parents, and Antonio, if they did not have to worry about them.

As they neared the foothills and getting further away from Naples, they became more anxious and woke Giovanni. He too was quite nervous. Giovanni Romano had been dreaming of Mistress Sucretti. It had been nearly twenty years since last he saw her. Her beauty and intelligence were formidable. She possessed vast wealth but had become a recluse, and rarely left the confines of her stately castle. Her holdings were many and diversified. Her business savvy was known throughout Europe. Her empire included holdings in America, as well as several African cities. Yet with all this wealth and power, her life was miserable and lonely. She had been married to the ruthless Camorra Caporegime Salvatore Sucretti. Maria and Salvatore had never been able to have children. His mind harked back to the day he and his beloved Natalie and their darling daughter Rosalie left Maria Sucretti and Monteforte. It was a difficult parting and hearts were broken. Mistress Sucretti's generosity had assisted them to make a new life, to buy a home and to start over. The dowry that she had established for his beloved Rosalie, sadly, had been used for a lavish burial for her and his wife.

The stain of the murder of Salvatore Sucretti was forever imprinted on Monteforte, and on all those involved. So many lives had been ruined, and the pangs of sorrow pulled at his heart at the thought of his deceased wife and daughter. Would they still be alive if not for the death of Salvatore Sucretti? Giovanni Romano dreaded coming back to the place that had filled his heart for so many years with both love and hatred. Would he be able to stay? He must stay for as long as Antoinetta and Lucia were to be here, after all, he had given his word of honor to their parents.

The carriage continued to climb, but by now, the sun was slowly coming over the sea for its evening rest. Crimson strokes were painting the trees and ragged patches of short vegetation. The air too was growing cooler, and the scent of lemons, mixed intoxicatingly with sea breezes. In spite of the fact, that all three inhabitants of the coach were tense with anticipation, they could not help but feel the wash of tranquility cruise over their exhausted bodies. The girls were fighting to stay awake.

Soon they came to an elaborate iron gate, flanked on both sides by a high stone wall, which extended as far as the eye could see on both sides. There were two men dressed much like Nicko on either side of the gate. The carriage came to a stop and Nicko jumped down instructing Gaetano to wait. He embraced both men and they spoke for a few moments before they opened the huge gate to allow them passage.

Giant cypress trees lined both sides of a long winding path. There were poles with lanterns spaced so many feet apart. It was steep, and the horses were straining to make the climb. Gradually, the path started to become level, and the cypress trees gave way to a lush green grass lawn. The lanterns were now glowing brightly, casting a soft warm light over the expansive carpet of green. They were coming closer and now, for the first time, could see the looming edifice of the castle unfolding before them. It was imposing but elegant. Constructed of local limestone and granite it was a pale grey. The turreted roof was black slate with copper cupolas. It was so large and extended so far pass the pathway, that their line of vision could not encompass the entire structure. With the sun nearly set, an aura of russet gold backlighted the castle and made the stone glow a subtle shade of rose. It was overwhelming, beautiful, and breathtaking all at once. The closer they came to the structure; it seemed to be growing taller and more impressive.

Monteforte's location, for centuries, made it much sought after as a prize, in the battle of acquisition of power of the ruling classes. From its highest elevation a panoramic view of the neighboring mountains, approaching ships from the sea, and an impenetrable fortress, which was perched atop an unnavigable cliff, was the ideal retreat for any ruling lord. This location, unfortunately, also lent itself, due to its remoteness, to become prey to privates and marauding bandits. It was difficult for the reigning lord to protect the small villages and merchants, who were always being threatened and victimized by these unsavory elements. Salvatore Sucretti, then sitting Master of Monteforte, decided to form a consortium of likeminded landowners and merchants to ban together to ward off repression, and so the Camorra was formed as a rudimentary vigilante group. Many would argue that the price the Italians, and ultimately the world, would come to pay for the formation of this Camorra society, would be far too reaching. Those at the top of the Camorra food chain were richly rewarded, while those who were victims of their greed, lust, and extortion, were offered up as sacrificial lambs. Respect, obedience, and trust were the key words for this group, which had its tentacles in every country of the world. The Camorra's vast fortunes, as well as all of their holdings, were divided by territory with a Caporegime heading each "family" for a designated region. The constant struggle to maintain your position of power within the structure of the "family" was a daily life and death battle. The richer, the more powerful, the territory of one Caporegime over another became a power struggle for dominance. It was into this world of the Camorra that the young Giovanni the Roman entered. He was absorbed into its society and became a trusted servant and bodyguard of Salvatore Sucretti. Monteforte was the crown jewel of the Camorra network, its vast riches of land, location, and all coveted priceless antiquities.

When the carriage finally fell into the dark shadow of Monteforte the girls, eyes wide with wonder, the thrill and fear, vibrated throughout their supple young limbs. They never knew they had such a wealthy relative. The only person they ever knew that lived in a place like this was Uncle Luigi but that was a church and he did not own it.

As if someone had rung a hidden bell, several servants immediately emerged from behind stone walls to greet the new arrivals. Nicko jumped down and began talking familiarly to two of the female servants. Coming on the scene were three young grooms, all parties were formally dressed in their uniforms even given that the hour was already late. Gaetano also came down from his bench, but held the reins, for the horses were a little jumpy, given all the activity that was happening around them. He walked to the back of the coach and started unloading their bags. One of the female servants instructed two of the grooms to take the bags to a certain room in the south wing. The third young man was engaged in conversation with Gaetano as to where the stables were located, and that he would accompany him to settle the horses, and to get him some food and a place to sleep. Nicko joined them in this conversation and he slapped the driver on the back with words of thanks for a safe journey. "Ah, Gaetano, I will see you in the morning at breakfast. My little friend Marco will get you some food and a clean pallet. I am sure Mistress Sucretti will want to see you before you leave. Good night sir."

With their bags off to an unknown location, the driver and carriage heading to the stables, the threesome were left standing in front of the castle in a stupor of anticipation.

Giovanni Romano was left standing there with his hat in his hand, and was at once happy and sad for his coming back to Monteforte, bile was reaching the back of his throat, and his heart was pounding in his ears. So far, he knew none of the servants, of course, twenty years was a lifetime for most people. Nicko was now talking with the two female servants. They were young, pretty, and slightly flirtatious with him. He was, after all, quite handsome and very friendly. Antoinetta found that she was a little jealous and then stopped herself with a mental slap, but noted the atmosphere and attitudes never the less. Nicko now came to them, and with a grand bow, "Welcome to Monteforte. Please follow me, I have been told that Mistress Sucretti awaits your arrival." As if one cue the two female servants stepped toward them. Nicko smiling widely "May I introduce Marianna and Sophia. They will be your personal servants while you are here at Monteforte. If there is anything you need or desire, just let them know, and they will assist you." The two women, both perhaps in their early twenties, were perfectly neat in their uniforms. They wore simple homespun cotton gowns in a dark grey trimmed with white lace. Their hair pulled back and plaited then wound into buns. They wore no cap. The girls were not sure who was who, and for their part, the servants were smiling warmly from ear to ear. "Come Mistresses you are expected." Bowing very deeply they lead the way into the daunting edifice of Monteforte. Lucia was holding her breath, and Antoinetta was squeezing her hand with all her might. Giovanni Romano silently followed, head bent, trying desperately to hold back his tears. Everything was just as he remembered it. Even the smell of the place was exactly the same, candlewax and polish. An overwhelming desire to run to his room and see his wife and daughter washed over him. He felt Lucia tugged at his sleeve to follow.

They found themselves being lead through a series of staircases and hallways, until they finally stopped in front of a large double door at the end of a rather long hallway. They came to a stop in front of two enormous solid carved wood doors. One of the maids, Lucia was sure if it was Marianna, knocked softly, and waited for a response. "Enter." She then pushed open the doors and entered the room. It was huge with large windows that reached from the floor to the ceiling. The ceiling, which had to be twenty feet high was decorated with wide wooden beams that had intricately detailed carvings. The room smelled of old books, and the scent of drying paper, leather, and flowers. There was a luminous candle glow and an undertone scent, which was a pleasant mixture of candlewax and polish. The focal point of the room was a massive stone hearth that was burning slowly and cast a playful dance of shadows upon the ceiling. Its mantle ornately carved of limestone, and above it was a life size painting of a beautiful young woman, with olive complexion and deep rust colored hair. She had a serene beauty and inward confidence. Lucia, always curious, was looking all around, up and down. Lucia's eyes glowed with delight at the sight of shelf, after shelf of leather bound books.

She loved to read and knew she would spend many hours of her day in this room. Then, like a hawk, focusing on its prey she spotted the woman in the chair. Sitting regally in one of the two chairs flanking the fireplace was an elegant looking older woman whom they naturally presumed was their aunt. The more aggressive maid, probably Marianna, motioned for them to approach the woman. She was clad in a rich tapestry gown with jewel tones of red, emerald, and sapphire. Her hair, which was long, was plaited into a thick braid and studded with pearls. It was the color of autumn leaves mixed with silver and gold strands. She sat straight and a long swanlike neck supported her head. Given her age, her skin was still tight and lightly burnished. The eyes caught Lucia's attention. They were the color of amber liquor, like the kind her grandfather would take out of the special cupboard on Christmas Eve. The light flickering from the fire glinted golden sparks in their depths. They were eyes that were at first cold then warm, changing in an instant. Her mouth was set in a cordial smile, welcoming, but reserve. All, in all, the general appearance was that of a queen upon her throne. The hands, one sat casually upon her lap, the other was holding steady to a leather bound book. "Come here by the light so that I can best see you." Her voice was low and earthy, the words clear and well spoken. Her diction ringed with breeding and education. The girls, holding sweaty hands, approached, not too close, but near enough for the light from the fire to illuminate their faces. Antoinetta, the first to speak announced, "It is an honor to meet you Mistress Sucretti. I am Antoinetta and this is my sister Lucia." As if by mental will, the girls came closer and bowed deeply. A wide smile that showed straight white teeth emerged across Maria Sucretti's face.

She looked at them for what seemed a long time before she spoke. They were so different these two sisters. Antoinetta was petite just like her mother, the same coloring, and mouth. She thought the girl was shy but intelligent. Lucia, the name alone conjured up the image of her sister-in-law. This one was tall and sturdy, with skin like fine porcelain, the trademark red hair, and azure blue eyes of her namesake. It was uncanny how close a resemblance she bore to her brother's wife. Maria was both thrilled and frightened to bring these two into her home and her heart. Time would be the best prophecy of whether she had made a wise decision. She resolved to take one day at a time.

"I am very pleased you have come to Monteforte, this is the ancestral home of your great grandfather, Mateo Rizzo, who was my brother. I hope you enjoy your stay here. It is late and you must be very wary from your long journey, I have planned a light supper. Marianna and Sophia will be your personal servants, whatever you need they can get for you. Go now, and they will show you to your room, then we will dine." Once again, Marianna, Lucia was pleased that she had guessed which one was she, turned, and was leading them out of the room. Lucia stopped abruptly, turned on her heels, and blurted out "Thank you Zia." Then Lucia, not waiting for a reply, rushed to catch up with the small party.

Giovanni Romano was lurking in the shadows of the room. Once the little parade of women had left, he stepped into the light, but kept his distance. Maria saw him for the first time. These many years had not been too kind to the man before her. She would have recognized him anywhere but here at Monteforte, twenty years later, he had changed. She had changed. Life had changed. Giovanni bowed deeply "Your servant

Mistress. The years have graced you with much kindness; you are as beautiful as the day I left here twenty years past." She beckoned him to come closer, "Ah, Giovanni you have suffered much, I wish you had come after Natalie and Rosalie died, we both needed to find comfort in their passing. I have mourned their deaths every day since first I heard." Tears were creeping down her elegant face, but she did not wipe them away. "Giovanni you are welcomed to stay here for as long as you wish. Please take up your old room and I will have someone bring your bags. I am so happy you are here. You must join us for supper and then tomorrow we will catch up on so many lost years." Giovanni who was unaccustomed to such familiarity was uncomfortable. Finding his voice, he said, "Mistress I cannot take up my old room, I am no longer in the position that I once enjoyed. I am but an old man, with nothing but a few years and strong hands left." His head bent as if in supplication.

Maria Sucretti, knowing that Giovanni Romano would accompany her new wards, had thought about the awkwardness of having him here at Monteforte, and yet in her heart she knew she wanted him more than ever. "Giovanni, you are no longer my servant, you are the guardian of my nieces, and therefore must be shown the respect that position demands. I can only imagine the pain you must be in just to be here with all the memories that these walls hold for you. The memories, good and bad, that they hold for me as well." Maria got up from the chair and slowly, thoughtfully, unfolded her long, lean, body like a butterfly emerging from its cocoon she stood with all the presence of royalty and squared her shoulders. She stretched out her hand in an invitation for Giovanni to take it. He seized her proffered hand and delicately brought it to his dry lips. "Ringrazio il mio amante. I thank you

Mistress, but, no matter what title I am given I will always be your servant." With that, he fell upon one knee and once again lovingly kissed her hand.

Maria pulled him to his feet and looking him in the eye said, "This is the least I could do for my sister's husband. I loved Natalie as my sister and Rosalie as my niece. They are gone, you are still here, and I must care for you as they would have cared for you. Welcome home vecchio amico." She gently laid a peck on his cheek. "Now, please go get ready for supper, I am starved, and, I am sure those girls must be hungry." Giovanni was mortified to think he did not have any proper clothes. His embarrassment was on his face, which had flushed his gaunt cheeks. "What is troubling you Giovanni?" He was biting the inside of his lip, his head down, he told her haltingly "Mistress, I am ashamed but I do not own a proper coat for supper. I will eat with the servants in the kitchen." Maria was not surprised given the general condition of his present appearance. "That is nonsense, I will have Giorgio find you a proper coat for now, and then tomorrow I will have the tailor make you some new clothes. You must set a good example for my nieces. The matter is closed. Hurry, I am too old to eat so late." He gave a halfhearted laugh then said "Me too." After a moment's hesitation, he asked, "Fernando, he has passed?" In that split second Maria's face adopted an expression of deep pain. "Ah, I am sorry, of course you wouldn't know. Yes, three years past, he died from the flux. I wish he had known that you were alive. He often spoke of you; you were the son he never had. When news of Natalie and Rosalie arrived, he was heartbroken. As we all were. Sadly, all the other staff, except for Marcello, who is also getting up in years, have passed. Giorgio, who was born here, has replaced Fernando. He is younger and learning but doing a fine job. Maybe you can take him under your wing." With that, he bowed deeply; turned and headed for the door, when he reached the doorway he turned "Mistress, è bene essere casa." Yes, Maria thought to herself, it is good that you are home. She smiled sincerely and gave him a nod.

CHAPTER TWO

PADRINO A TRANSFORMATION

Monteforte

Marianna and Sophia shuffled off Antoinetta and Lucia quickly. It was a long walk upstairs, down hallways and then finally to their destination. They would share a room, at least for now, until they were more comfortable with the castle. Both girls gasped when Sophia, she was the younger of the two maids, opened the door. A dim light cast a soft glow throughout the cavernous room. They stepped in on tiptoe, as if afraid that if they threaded too heavily the dream would be shattered. Both servants stood back and let the girls absorb the grandeur of their new accommodations.

In the middle of the room stood two beds made of mahogany that had canopies of yards and yards of cream-colored silk that billowed to the floor. The bed was covered in a matching cream-colored bedspread with embroidered stitching and scalloped edges. The mattress must surely be goose down because it was so thick and high. On an opposite wall were two tables with washstands and two free standing mirrors. On another wall was a doorway and flanking it were two sets of closed doors. The one excited maid, Sophia, rambled on and on with such pitch and speed rendering her message almost impossible to understand. She practically flew over to the other side where the doorway, which led to a hall, then flung open the two sets of doors to reveal a matching set of spacious wardrobes. Through the doorway she went and

148

beckoned them to follow, she could hardly contain her enthusiasm. They were bewildered but dutifully followed her, and to their utter amazement, they found themselves in the most beautiful toilet they had ever seen, even in the most extravagant book they had ever read could not compare to what they were looking at this very moment. Cream porcelain tile inlaid with bars of gold covered the walls. The floor was laid in a matching cream marble with gold veining. Golden mirrors were hung from the wall over the washbasin. There was a tub sunk into the floor, and surrounded by potted flowering plants, and jars filled with oils and lotions. A giant window that went from floor to ceiling that framed the mountains and vineyard and the adjoining gardens, it was so breathtaking that even in the setting darkness they could see the splendor.

The younger servant, Sophia, was waiting for them to speak but the two girls stood awestruck. Their silence used as a vehicle for trying to soak in all that they had just witnessed. The servants started to giggle and that broke the ice. The girl introduced herself as Sophia and started her excited speaking. "Mistresses I am Sophia and this is Marianna, you will come to know us much better. Mistress Sucretti instructed us to be at your service. Now it is getting late and you must get ready for supper." Marianna, the more mature of the twin maids, hurriedly moving around the room added, "Mistress Sucretti does not enjoy when her supper is late. So please hurry and get ready. Sophia and I will be back in a short time to bring you to dinner." With the warning laid down to them the servants left leaving them to get ready.

In their modest cottage by the sea in Torre del Greco, Rafaela had decorated their outhouse with pretty plants and curtains but it was still an outhouse. The two girls were not quite sure how all this worked – but they were fascinated to learn.

Standing there in the middle of the room that was as big as a house, the two girls turned to each other, grabbed their hands together, and started to dance around the room. When they were exhausted they plopped on the floor lying on their backs, and looking up to the mural on the ceiling then started to cry. They were not sure why they were crying, but they knew they felt guilty that they should be living in this castle, and the family who loved them was left behind to struggle. Always the big sister, Antoinetta pushed a wayward red curl from her sister's face "I feel sorry for Mama, Papa and Antonio, too, but, while we are here they will be free to do what is necessary for us to have a home, and one day, soon, to be together again. For now, we will do what we are told and try to learn as much as we can, so that we will be able to help when it is our time." She kissed her sister, got to her feet, and put out a hand for Lucia to hold on. Both of them got up and raced for the toilet, which was amazing to them. There were baskets filled with fragrant soaps, and on the vanity where bottles of creamy lotion that smelled so good. There was fresh water in the lavish wash bowels that were set into a marble stand. They each chose a scented soap, which was such a luxury. Soap, except for the kind their mother made, was very expensive, and now there were bars and bars lying in a basket. "Mama would love this, don't you agree sister?" Antoinetta was intent upon washing her face and hands and brushing the dust of their journey from her gown. "Oh yes she would be in heaven. We must write to her tomorrow and tell her all about it. But for now would you please get ready." "Here, let me help you get ready. Sit down I'll brush your hair." Antoinetta brushed a wayward curl from Lucia's cherub like face, and looked deep into those mesmerizing azure orbs. She could not help but think how beautiful her sister was, and what a stunning woman she would soon become. "There! Now you look civilized," they both laughed. "Now, let me get myself ready. Sophia and Marianna will be here soon." Lucia watched as her sister combed out her own long, thick tresses, which were wavy, not curly like hers, and a silken texture the color of onyx. Her skin was a rich olive with chestnut eyes. She was petite but shapely. Overall, she was exotic and sensual. Lucia admired her sister, and was sometimes a little jealous of her beauty, which was in such stark contrast to her own. Lucia was tall and sturdy, not fat, but curvaceous. Her hair was a mass of curly red ringlets that were generally unmanageable. Her skin was white as marble. The only feature that Lucia really liked about herself were her eyes, which her mother always told her were the same as her great grandmother for whom she had been named. Lucia always felt awkward about her height and body, especially when she was next to Antoinetta, who looked like a delicate flower. They both put themselves together as quickly and efficiently as possible. They looked good, overall, and they were starving.

A subtle knock at the door and then it gingerly opened and Marianna, the older and more subdued of the two maids, entered into the room to collect them for their audience with their aunt. She eyed them appraisingly and then gestured with her thumb and index finger to her cheek in the national sign of approval. All was well. Her counterpart, Sophia, the younger and more energetic of the two, appeared on the threshold of the door, out of breath from running, caught sight of the two girls, and proclaimed loudly, "Bella, bella, bella!" Each one grabbed a girl and off they galloped through the long corridors and down a long, steep, staircase that lead to the main dining room. When they reached the massive mahogany doors that were closed, the older of the two maids knocked tentatively and waited for the response to come.

"Come" was the return. They entered the room one at a time and stood near the doorway until summoned to enter completely. The room was magnificently decorated, like pictures from fairy tales that their mother had read to them many times. The long table was dressed with the finest china and candelabras flickered soft lights from their glowing tapers. The crystal glasses shimmered in the basking glow from the tapers. Adorning the soaring ceiling was a massive Venetian crystal chandelier. It was so large it covered half the ceiling. The light from its many arms cast a warm yellow glow over the entire room. At the head of the table sat their aunt, she was clothed in a rich royal blue silk gown that was encrusted with tiny seed pearls. The sheer elegance of the garment spoke volumes about her sense of style and grace. She was clearly a woman of great taste, and her calm and confident demeanor only reiterated her self-esteem. She was a woman who had learned early on, what her place was in this world, and did whatever was necessary to maintain that level of power over all she possessed including human beings.

Their aunt was engrossed in reading something, but once she caught a glimpse of the two girls she immediately stopped what she was doing and addressed them, "*Come my dears, sit down near me so that we may dine in comfort and conversation. I want to know all about you and your family. Your grandmother was very special to me, her and her family used to live here at Monteforte. Come, please sit, and we shall have our first meal as a family.*" Their assigned escorts seated them one on her left and one on her right.

Once they were settled into their big, overstuffed chairs, they looked at each other across the table and a little giggle escaped from Lucia's mouth. Antoinetta shot her a look that would have stopped a train. Lucia instantly lowered her eyes and bit her bottom lip to stop herself from being giddy. Mistress Sucretti suddenly burst out into joyful laughter at the interplay of the two sisters. As if by spontaneous combustion, all three of them were laughing almost hysterically. The ice had been broken. Their aunt for the first time in countless years was truly happy and filled with joy.

In the midst of all this merriment came Giovanni Romano. Lucia's eyes grew wide when she saw him and a little gasp left her mouth, which was gapping. He was wearing a dark blue waistcoat and his linen shirt was crisp and clean. He had on white linen breeches and silk stockings, the only thing that betrayed him were his shoes, which were old and worn, but he had made a valiant attempt to shine. He seemed to be standing taller and his face was relaxed. He had a black silk patch over his damaged eye, which he had never worn before. His hair combed and tied into a neat queue. The transformation was nothing short of miraculous.

"Ah, Giovanni, please come join us" the catch in her voice matched Maria Sucretti's expression which was not lost on any of those at the table. She was appraising her newly arrived guest with warmth and perhaps admiration. Maria saw before her not the old man with the damaged eye, gaunt and sullen in a borrowed coat, but the visions of a swarthy young soldier who had come long ago to Monteforte, tall and sinewy and full of piss and vinegar. Maria Sucretti licked her lips, which had gone suddenly dry and tilted her head. Giovanni, who for the moment seemed confident of himself, bowed deeply and found his seat at the table. "Good evening mistresses. Tutti sembrano così belli." His candid express of their beauty was so out of character that Lucia was wondering who this new man truly was, and what had they done with her Padrino, yet, she liked this new person. They had never heard their Padrino speak in such a manner, it was amazing.

To the girls directly he inquired, "Are you both finding your way. I am sure your maids will help you with anything you need. Of course, I need not tell you that Io sono qui per voi in qualsiasi momento." For the first time they could see a genuine smile light his face. Lucia thought he looked handsome and not so old and decrepit. "Padrino, si guarda molto bello" Lucia, so overcome by his appearance, blurted out how handsome he looked. The second the words left her mouth she regretted it, but then was pleased that she told him, for she could see its reaction on him. As a hint of pink, painted Giovanni Romano's weathered cheeks, at this remark he smirked. "Why thank you Mistress Lucia." Giovanni Romano had never addressed them formally as 'mistress' and it sounded strange to their ears. Antoinetta was just absorbing the situation and nodded in agreement. Amused and delighted Maria Sucretti was observing this small drama unfold and her heart was filled with joy. She too agreed with her niece's assessment that Giovanni Romano did look handsome.

From a hidden side door, a man carrying a tray of food emerged. "Antoinetta, Lucia, this is Giorgio. He is the maître d' casa of Monteforte. If you have any special requests please let him know and he will try to have whatever you desire prepared. Giorgio, let me formally introduce, Signore` Giovanni Romano, whom you have already met, Mistress Antoinetta and Mistress Lucia, they will be our guests for as long as they wish, please make them feel that Monteforte is now their home." With that instruction given, Giorgio made a low bow to his two new mistresses and the gentleman, then turned toward his Mistress and did the same.

Giorgio had been just a boy when Giovanni Romano lived at Monteforte, and was well aware of the reason for his departure. Stories of Salvatore Sucretti were notorious, as were the circumstances surrounding his death. The infamous Giovanni Romano was legendary. Giorgio had heard stories for years about the exploits of Salvatore Sucretti and his Camorra connections.

Giorgio had a warm, but austere face, and had been raised on the estate and had been schooled in the art of his position. He held much power and exercised it dutifully. A rather short but slim figure, he was meticulously dressed in a black linen waistcoat and white linen shirt, and wore his brown hair combed back and tied with a black ribbon. He stood with perfect posture, which made him appear taller than his actual height; he possessed an air of assurance of his status within the manor of Monteforte. Their aunt went on to tell them that Giorgio had been born on the estate and so had his father before him. For four generations they had been in the employ of the Sucretti family. Giorgio, his wife Carmela, and his two sons, Alfonso and Enrico, all work and live on the estate. "Anything you want to know about Monteforte, just ask Giorgio and he will tell you." Giorgio rendering a grand footed bow went about his duties of serving the first course of the meal.

A bowl of steaming soup was ladled into the bone china bowls its aroma was mouthwatering. Once Giorgio left to prepare for the next course, the conversation started. *"So my dear nieces tell me everything about your family and where you had lived and all the news of the family. I have been isolated here at Monteforte for so many years that sadly I have lost touch with everyone."* She sensed the hesitation of the girls, but then slowly saw that they wanted to talk about their parents and siblings. Lucia started about her parents and then about her brothers. How she missed her brothers and she told of what they were doing. She was very animated and spoke non-stop. Their aunt listened attentively and asked appropriate questions to show she was involved in the conversation. Throughout,

Antoinetta just sat quietly and nodded from time to time. "Antoinetta, would you like to say something? You are very quiet." " Oh no Mistress, I am just listening to my sister. She has said everything just as if it were my own thoughts. I, no, we, are so grateful that you asked our Mother and Father if we could come here. Naples was a horrible place and we were very scared to live there. Our parents were frightened to leave us for a minute. I only miss not being able to go to school. Will Lucia and I be able to attend school?" " I am sorry Antoinetta, but, there are no schools near Monteforte, the only school is in Sorrento, which is many kilometers away. However, do not be sad. I anticipated that we should have your education continue, so I have arranged to have you taught right here at Monteforte. Starting next Monday, you will have several tutors in all the major disciplines of education. This is the way I was taught, and so it will be for the two of you, but, for now rest for the next several days, we will get to know each other, and you two can explore the grounds. I caution you not to go beyond the property line. There are many wild animals and bandits on the roads and in the surrounding woods. If you want to go to Sorrento, Nicko will take you in the carriage."

Giorgio was serving the main course, which was some kind of white fish that had been prepared over an open fire. The smell of the wood was still fresh on the skin of the fish. There were fresh vegetable, olives, and hot, crusty bread. When they had consumed more food than they had seen in their lives, the two girls surrendered to the last course. Once again, Giorgio soundlessly appeared with trays of boundless food. This time he had gelato, which is a creamy flavorful delight, set in glass goblets and decorated with cherries, blueberries and slices of oranges. How could they resist, they had never before in their life tasted such delicious food, each course presented with care and sophistication. They were all stuffed and satisfied. It had been a very long day for all of them.

When they had all finished, Mistress Sucretti rang the tiny crystal bell that was always at her side. From behind walls several servants, all dressed in crisp uniforms, appeared, bowed, and methodically began removing all traces of the fabulous feast that had been laid before them. The table cleared, Aunt Maria rose from her seat at the head of the table. *"Ladies, Giovanni, please join me in the library, to relax a little before we retire for the evening"* and without an acknowledgement of their consent, she glided out of the dining room, and proceeded down a long, wide hallway. The two girls rose quickly and followed without as much as a peep. Lucia was walking with her head up admiring all the beautiful paintings that lined the walls to the library. She thought to herself that someday her brother Genaro's paintings might be hanging on the walls of a great castle or even a famous museum. Suddenly, without any forethought she caught up with her aunt who was several yards in front of her. Reaching her side Lucia grabbed her hand. The old woman stopped abruptly and stared at the anxious girl. "What is it child?" Lucia blurted out "I just wanted you to know that my brother Genaro is a great artist like the ones who have pictures on your walls." Her aunt looked mildly amused and then said in a gentle and commanding voice "Well, if he is as good as you say Lucia, then we must see some of his work."

Lucia, pleased with herself for having promoted her brother, slid her hand into Maria Sucretti's and continued walking to the library. Her aunt accepted the invitation and strode the few more steps to a set of polished mahogany doors. Antoinetta was watching this whole scene with wonder; she was always astounded by the actions of her younger sister. Maria Sucretti grasped the ornate gold knob and pushed open the heavy carved door. Upon entering the room Lucia squeezed the hand that was in her grip ever so slightly, and a huge smile came upon her glowing face. This was where she first laid eyes on Maria Sucretti. Sarebbe sempre essere un posto speciale non solo per il loro incontro, ma perché amava i libri. Truly, Lucia would always cherish this special room, not only for her love of books, but she was sure, of her relationship with this intriguing woman.

The room smelled of leather, velum, and polish. Lucia breathe in deeply the aroma of its contents, as if to infuse the knowledge within into her very soul. They stepped on to a thick carpet that was embellished with exotic designs, never had she seen such patterns and colors, and quite spontaneously, kicked off her shoes, and wiggled her toes in its plush pile. Antoinetta looked horrified at this display of behavior but said nothing. There were animals, birds, fish, flowers and fruits all woven into a plush rug that covered ninety percent of this huge room. There were stacks and stacks of books bedecking the walls. On those walls without stacks of books were paintings and sculptures, and in the center of this room was a large round table with leather chairs around it. Books piled high on top of it in no particular order. It almost looked like someone had been researching something, and had left the books right there so that they could come back for more. Who would have been this mysterious investigator? It was such a huge room but it seemed so intimate and warm. At the rear was a stone fireplace, whose fire was kept burning in anticipation of their return, and was casting a warm glow over the room. In front of the hearth were two tapestry covered antique chairs. Lucia who was twirling around the room was positively in her glory. Antoinetta, who was trying to ignore the antics of her sister, looked all around with a sense of dignified pleasure. All of the Banfi children had grown up with a love of books and enjoyed reading. Rafaela made sure that her children would be exposed to a wealth of learning. They had very little, but she always found an extra lira for a good book.

Maria Sucretti was beaming at the sight of happiness this room brought to her two charges. She mindfully made her way to one of the chairs by the fire. A small table was perched on the side of her chair and she rang the ever-present bell. As if anticipating her every desire Giorgio appeared with a silver tray upon which was a silver coffee urn, cups and several small jars and dishes. Antoinetta went to Lucia and gave her a kiss. "Che cosa è che per?" a little surprised, Lucia asked what that was about. "That is for remembering our dear brother Genaro. He will be a famous artist someday. I just know it."

"Come here girls. Come sit by me. Giovanni please join us. Would you care for some espresso or some cognac?" Giovanni Romano came and sat in the chair opposite Mistress Sucretti. His long thin body enfolded by the plush chair. It was not a command but an invitation. Maria Sucretti's voice was soft and her eyes were warm. "Now that you are here we must find out more about each other. I must address your needs. In the letter, your mother sent with you she spoke of your education and how she would so much want you to continue. Unfortunately, there are not schools for many, many, miles from here. Therefore, I have contacted a dear friend of mine, he was a Professor at the Universita` of Florence, who has left his position, and he has agreed to meet with both of you to see what type of instruction you will require. He will be arriving a week from today. I understand that you will also need some clothes, and have arranged to have my dressmaker come tomorrow after breakfast to take your measurements." Lucia and Antoinetta just sat there huddled on the large overstuffed settee which was directly facing the fireplace, with their mouths open, holding on to every word their aunt of saying. *"May I take a book back to my room?"* asked Lucia sheepishly. Antoinetta pinched her arm, before the aunt could answer. Antoinetta jumped in saying, *"I'm so sorry for my sister's forward behavior. Please do not take her bluntness for bad upbringing."* With a stifled chuckle, Maria Sucretti seeing the tension between the two sisters replied. *"I am so happy that Lucia wants to read. Please feel free to take, do, see, and try anything you want, both of you. This will be your home and you must be comfortable here. There is only one place you will be forbidden to go."* Maria Sucretti's tone had suddenly become sharp and cold and her expression was intense. *"You must never go into the catacombs that lie in the subbasement of the castle. It is too dangerous.* Mai! Capisci? Rispondere a me?" her voice had taken on a granite tone, her eyes grew dark and cold. Maria Sucretti, her demeanor had instantly changed and she was demanding an answer, she wanted to be sure that they understood the imperative of never going down to the catacombs. "Sì Mistress non ci vado" they said in frightened unison. As quickly as her mood came that is as quickly as it left. Once again she was back to the kind old dowager she was only moments earlier. The two sisters shocked by the transformation, sat in silence until the aunt opened the conversation on a much lighter note. She offered them cappuccino, which they had never had before, and placed a small dollop of whipped cream on the top of each. The steam made the cream swim in the cup. Sipping with delight, they were offered biscotti. After a while of sitting there talking and enjoying their drink the sound of a grand case clock started to chime. Lucia jumped off the chair to see where the sound was coming from, and located it at the far end of the room. Gleefully, she ran towards it to examine it. It was magnificent. Looking up at the timepiece, she was struck by the intricacy of the design, with its gold faceplate and pendulums. It was nine o'clock. This was truly a place of rare beauty with objects of art, books, and history. She promised herself to explore this place in depth tomorrow. She sensed she was being watched, turning she saw her aunt and her sister standing behind her. "Ti piace che orologio Lucia?" asked her aunt. "Oh yes Mistress. I love this room; it makes me feel happy and safe. May I come here tomorrow?" " Yes, of course you may, but only after the dressmaker is finished with the both of you. Now, it is time for all of us to go to bed. I am sure you are very weary from your long journey." Then, as if by magic, their two assigned servant girls appeared at the door of the library to whisk them off to their bedroom.

Before leaving, Lucia, unable to control her emotions, started to cry. Her aunt quickly came to her side and asked what was troubling her. "I'm sorry Mistress everything has been so wonderful like a dream, but, I am sad for my Momma and Papa and my brother who are working very hard while we are living like princesses. You have been so kind and generous to us. Thank you." With that, Antoinetta started to tear up, and she too thanked her aunt for her kindness and hospitality. "You are both very welcomed. I am so happy you are here. Do not worry, your parents will be fine, and soon they will come to Monteforte to visit you. I promise. Now, off with the both of you, before you make me cry." They both ran to her and gave her hugs and kisses then went with their maids to get ready for bed. Before they left, they both went to Giovanni Romano hugging and kissing him with great love. "Good night my two bellas, sleep well, until we see each other tomorrow." It was obvious to Maria that Giovanni loved these girls like a father. Lucia acting impulsively, quickly came back and rushing over to her aunt whispered into her ear "May I call you Zia?" Maria not sure how to respond, but touched by this intimate request said "I wish you would. Thank you." She held Lucia to herself for a moment and gave her a kiss on her forehead. "Good night Lucia."

Maria Sucretti sat there gazing into the embers of the fire and felt a pang of sorrow within herself. She had longed for children her whole life, and now finally, she had two darling girls that she would raise as if they were her own flesh. She tried to deny it, but she could not help but claim special kindred to Lucia. The girl was brilliant and impetuous. Her beauty was flawless. She saw herself in the eyes of this child, but saw also her sister-in-law the girl's namesake, comfortably nestled behind those penetrating eyes. As for Antoinetta, she bore a remarkable likeness to her own mother, who had died while traveling in France so many years past. Maria could see the seriousness and blooming womanhood of her sullen beauty. So different were these two sisters, not only physically, but also emotionally. Maria knew she would be challenged by Lucia's honesty and straight forwardness, while Antoinetta would always be guarded with her feelings. For the first time in so many years, she was anticipating tomorrow, and the days to come, with great joy and expectation. These two had breathe life into this musty old castle and into the heart of this old woman.

Giovanni Romano was still sitting in the chair, watching the flames licking the logs of the crackling wood. The warmth of the flames mirrored the love in his heart. He broke the silence "Mistress, what will you have me do while I am here?" Maria shaken from her own reverie looked at him with such passion and longing "I want you to be my friend, my companion, and help me raise these two girls. Will you?" Giovanni was speechless, never in his wildest dreams would he have thought that he would return to Monteforte and, if he did, he would still be a servant. "I can my Mistress and

I will." Maria needed to rest and was certain that her old friend needed rest as well. "Good. Then I must retire for I fear these two little girls will be keeping us busy. I shall say good night." She rose and he followed, "Mistress, you have made so many people happy, especially myself. Thank you." Giovanni went down on one knee and kissed her hand. Marie held it and helped him up, "Welcome home Giovanni, I am so happy you are here. Buono sera."

Maria was exhausted, but the excitement of her newly arrived guests left her unable to sleep. She decided that she would write a note to Rafaela and Donato to let them know that their girls had arrived safely.

Dear Rafaela and Donato,

Antoinetta, Lucia, and Giovanni Romano arrived at Monteforte safe; a little weary from the journey, but in good spirits. You have raised two wonderful girls who have not stopped speaking about you and their brothers. I will do all that I can to make them happy here. Next week their tutors will come so that they can continue their education, which I know, is very important. You are welcomed at Monteforte whenever you wish to come.

Grazie per aver portato gioia a una Caporegimena anziana.

Maria Sucretti, Mistress of Monteforte

Maria having written the note felt relaxed and happy. She would send it back with Gaetano the driver to be delivered upon his return to Naples. Maria climbed into her bed and felt a warmth spread over her tired body. Fino a domani...

CHAPTER THREE

THE WOMAN WITHIN

Monteforte

Antoinetta and Lucia were eager to see Monteforte in the daylight. This was day two of their adventures and it was already promising to be good. The day was filled with brilliant sun light and soft ocean breezes that were coming through the open balcony doors. The song of birds carried on the wisps of air that filtered through the open windows. They were busy getting washed and dressed for breakfast and their meeting with the seamstress. They had slept with dreams of the future dancing through their heads.

Lucia asked her sister "Is it always so beautiful and sunny in this place?" Antoinetta, sitting at the vanity gazing at her image in the mirror replied, "Well, little one, we shall see." Lucia, with her full lips pouting responded, "Don't call me little. After all I am much taller than you." "Yes, but I am more beautiful and smarter than you will ever be! Besides, I am a woman now and you my little pet are still a child!" Lucia was outraged and was just about to bounce on Antoinetta when the two maids burst into the room to collect them for breakfast. Steaming with anger, Lucia mentally noted her revenge.

They were brought to the breakfast room, which was in the solarium. This room was basked in bright sunlight and surrounded by walls of windows all facing the ocean. Every window was open and since the room was round, there were breezes on all sides making the space light and airy. Huge potted plants occupied all corners of this giant room. Their colors and perfume added to the magic of the atmosphere. The furnishings were simple and made out cedar wood with brightly colored fabrics. All together the room was enchanting. Lucia was filled with a fun playful feeling. Aunt Maria was seated at the large distressed wooden table reading and drinking her espresso. When she heard them enter, she immediately welcomed them to sit at the table. There was an assortment of sweet rolls, fresh sliced fruits, dates, figs and nuts. In front of each of them was set a plate with an egg in a holder that Lucia had never seen before. "Zia Maria what is this egg in the shell?" Maria Sucretti liked the way Lucia addressed her but it felt foreign to her. "That my dear is a soft boiled egg. Watch me and I shall show you both how it is prepared." With the demeanor of a skilled surgeon, she took up her knife, aimed it at the crown of the egg and sliced through, carefully removed the top of the egg and set it down. She then took the small spoon that was lying on the table next to her plate and slowly, carefully, began to mix up the inside of the egg while adding a pinch of salt and pepper. "Now you can both try." They were fascinated by this display of culinary mastery.

Lucia was excited to try this technique. She eagerly attacked the egg and split the shell. "Oh Zia Maria I broke the shell" she cried. "Don't worry we shall get you a new one. It takes patience and practice." That was a hint for Giorgio, who was ever in the wings, to dash back down to the kitchen and retrieve another egg. In the meantime, Antoinetta with her delicate fingers and endless patience, ever so lightly removed the top of the shell with perfect precision. Her smug expression only added to Lucia's earlier frustration with her sister. "Well done Antoinetta, you have a light touch. Now enjoy." Antoinetta, a quiet protagonist, snickered at Lucia. Lucia squinted her eyes and barred her teeth at her sister, but to no avail, Antoinetta just put up her nose at the chaffing of her younger sister.

In a few moments, another egg appeared in front of Lucia. She swore to herself that this time her sister would not out do her. With determination, she picked up the sharp little knife in her strong hand, and with deep concentration, she executed the removal of the eggshell. It was perfect! "You see Lucia, when you take your time and think about what you are doing, you can accomplish anything; very well done. Now you can enjoy your hard work." Her aunt looked at her with great satisfaction, and thinking of herself and how, when she was younger, she rushed into many situations, only to regret it afterwards. This child will learn, but first she will face many trials, but in the end, she will be the stronger for it. Lucia took her first spoonful of this delightful egg, and smiled broadly at the taste of this little delicacy. It was soft, creamy, and deliciously rich. She thought she should have this every day for breakfast. Lucia shot her sister a look of triumph, which sadly held no punch. Lucia could never get the best of Antoinetta, who would never relent or apologize, even when she was wrong, it made Lucia insane with anger.

Maria looked at both of her wards and realized for the first time that they were not children. Antoinetta was almost fourteen, which by most standards, she would be called a woman. Her petite frame and slender body could not hide the supple bosom and tiny waist. She was fully mature and sensually beautiful. Antoinetta carried herself with confidence and maturity. Lucia was eleven and very tall, not only for her age but also for her gender. Her body was developing nicely, with full breasts and a high rounded bottom, which sat upon long shapely legs, Lucia built like a female warrior, tall, lean, and beautiful, with striking features Lucia looked like a goddess. It was truly amazing to see the two sisters side by side, and wonder if they came from the same parents. Antoinetta looked like Angelina Rizzo who was Maria's deceased mother, and former matriarch of Monteforte. Not only were their physical attributes so similar but so were their personalities. Antoinetta was quiet and sullen; it was hard to know what was truly going on behind those simmering amber eyes. Like her great grandparents, Antoinetta was a mirror of the Rizzo family. Lucia, who was the picture of her great grandmother and namesake, wore her emotions on that lovely face, with those penetrating blue eyes. Those eyes that could turn from playful to fearsome in a moment never left doubt about her feelings. Lucia was identical in looks and personality to her brother's wife.

It was determined in that split second that Maria Sucretti, Mistress of Monteforte, knew who the heir to her ancestral home and vast fortune would be. How ironic that the one woman she both loved and hated, the one woman she wanted to destroy, the one person who she so wanted to be like, was now standing before her. It was fate that brought Lucia to Monteforte but it would be Maria Sucretti who would make her its Mistress.

They were introduced to the seamstress Laura, who was accompanied by three young girls and a rather sturdy young man. They carried baskets filled with sewing notions and the young man, who was eyeing Antoinetta, pushed a small cart filled with bolts of fabric. Aunt Maria was rapidly giving the seamstress instructions on the style of dresses both fancy and casual for the girls. She had made all of her selections and then called each of them over for a review. Both Antoinetta and Lucia were familiar with this process having helped their mother on many of her projects. Antoinetta was very impressed with the quality of the fabric. She had only seen such material when the wealthy families in Sorrento had commissioned her mother. To think that she would be wearing such expensive clothing was overwhelming. Their aunt then showed them some designs that the dressmaker had brought and asked if it pleased them. Then the woman produced a pedestal for each to stand upon and started taking measurements. At this point, the young man, Pietro, was asked to remove himself from the room and to close the solarium doors behind him, and to wait in the courtyard until he was needed to bring out the cart. As he was leaving, he caught Antoinetta's eye and gave her a wink. She looked stunned, and summarily dismissed him with a reproachful look. Appearing wounded Pietro slinked off to his designated waiting area.

The dressmaker enlisted the aid of two of her assistants and the third did the recording of the measurements. They measured for dresses, and also for petticoats. The whole process took several hours. It was only after they had finished with Antoinetta did Laura and her little drones begin with Lucia. "Ah, you are very tall Mistress Lucia, come down from the box. I see we will need to allow for more growth in the bust." She was speaking to her assistants but Lucia felt like they were sizing up a cow. "We shall put full boning in the bodice, and laces in the waist. Allow for a longer hemline she will grow sooner." Lucia was mortified with herself. Maria seeing this little play between the seamstress and her niece came over and said "Laura, make sure you emphasize the tiny waist of Lucia." Maria then pinched her niece's cheek, which was burning red with color, and Lucia smiled with satisfaction. "Oh yes Mistress. They are both quite beautiful, and I shall make them even more so in their new gowns." When the seamstress was finished, they were released and told to relax and go out to the garden until lunch.

The Garden

Once they reached the garden, the two girls chatted merrily amongst themselves, they were filled with excitement regarding their new wardrobe. "I will write to Mama tonight and share with her all that has happened to us," Antoinetta announced. Lucia was prancing around the rich and colorful flower garden, her attention drifting from what her sister was saying. She was absorbing the splendor of her surroundings, exploring the different types of flowers, the statuary embedded into the plantings, and observing the various creatures within this magical place. Butterflies of varying colors and sizes, bees and hummingbirds were all buzzing about in organized chaos. Unaware that she had abandoned her sister, Lucia continued to explore the grounds, having left the flower garden she was moving toward the vegetable garden, and from there she could see that the landscape dramatically inclined toward the sea. She ventured on so that she was perched at the top of a steep embankment, which led directly to the water some distance from where she was standing. To her left she saw a chiseled pattern in the cliff side of the embankment. Her curiosity was now peaked and she decided to explore where this led.

Moving slowly she made her way to the area where there was a pronounced declivity in the cliff face and stopped. It was almost undistinguishable from her present view, and looked to be just overgrown vegetation from where she had been standing, but now, given her vantage position it was much more defined. Cautiously, she made her way through the tangle of briars that were hiding the opening to the place she had spied. The undergrowth was thick and pinching at her legs but still she moved forward. She needed to find out where this path led. With much effort, Lucia made her way through the thicket, the small pinchers on the undergrowth biting at her legs. She could see that a few trickles of blood were creeping down the sides of her stockings. It was hot in the mid-day sun, and she was sweating with the effort of fighting through the bushes. Finally, Lucia made her way through the maze of brush. Stepping into the blazing sunlight and seeing the Mediterranean Sea beyond was almost too irresistible. Lucia felt her heart beating faster. Right there at her feet were the makings of an ancient stairwell. The time worn slabs of coral that originally were carved into the side of the cliff, wound their way to the bottom of the embankment, and down into the sea, were now only a fragment of what must have been the entrance to some passageway. Over time, perhaps decades, these were all that remained of the original entrance. There were no handrails and the steps looked jagged and narrow. A film of lichen and algae left a glistening coat on their surface. Lucia, having grown up by the sea, knew very well that they would be slippery. Too frightened to step down from the top, Lucia laid down on the ground with her head extended over the side past the first step, which dropped sharply to the steps below. Following the path with her eyes, the color of which matched the azure waters of the sea beyond. Lucia spotted swallows flying overhead and then disappearing into the cliff. She was intrigued as to where they went. Inching herself even further over the side of the cliff, she caught a glimpse of a darker spot on the face side of the rock formation. From here, she could just make out the outline of an opening at the bottom of the cliff. The last step licked by the salty waters, which was clear even in the dim light. She could hardly contain her excitement, and almost missed the sound of her sister and Sophia calling her name. Lucia knew that she would be in trouble for venturing out by herself, but she would keep this special place a secret for herself, and vowed to come back some day to see where the mysterious steps would lead.

Quickly, she gathered herself together, and fought her way back through the briars. She emerged, with her hair matted to her face; she was covered with sweat and dirt. She ran to the vegetable garden, and knelt down, pretending to have fallen. She cried out to the oncoming voices, and let them fix her location. When Sophia saw her lying down in the dirt, she ran to her to see what had happened. The excitable young maid was so distressed at the sight of her, that she was ranting so rapidly that Lucia, and now with the arrival of Antoinetta, could hardly understand what she was saying. "Dio mio che cosa è accaduto. Sono male?" Frantically, she asked if Lucia was hurt. "I am fine. I just tripped and fell" Lucia replied. Sophia knew that this would mean trouble for her since Lucia was her charge. She started patting down Lucia making sure nothing was broken or terribly damaged. Lucia brushed her hands away and stood up. Antoinetta seeing that her sister was not injured broke into a tirade. "What in God's Holy Name are you doing? Sophia and I have been looking all over for you. Dove sei andato?" Lucia bit her lip, trying to conceal the lie she was about to tell. "I went nowhere. You see where I am. I tripped. That is all." Antoinetta and Sophia were so upset that Lucia almost shared her little adventure with them, but then thought better of it. "I was just looking around and came here in the garden. I was going to surprise everyone and pick some vegetables for supper, but then I was startled by a swarm of bees. I began running away, and fell. Dispiace che volevo sconvolgere chiunque." Lucia's contrition was so convincing that Antoinetta immediately softened, and they both hugged and kissed her, and started to fix her hair, and Sophia withdrew a white linen hanky from her apron and wiped her sweaty dust encrusted face.

"Let us hurry, you must get washed and dressed for supper. Now hurry, *avanti*." Lucia for the first time realized why they were so frantic at her absence. She had been gone for several hours, she had not even thought about being hungry until her belly started to growl. The three swiftly moved over the path to the main house. The girls would bathe and dress for supper. Lucia, so proud of her ruse, and daydreaming of the next chance to make her move, was almost unable to contain her pleasure. Happily, she vowed that this adventure would one day be continued...

Sophia and Marianna were hauling buckets of hot steamy water, which they dumped into the tub for the second time. Lucia, because of the state she was in from her adventures in the garden, had taken her bath first. Marianna, at the initial sight of her had scalded the younger Sophia for her lack of attentiveness. "What if she had been seriously hurt? So many hours passed. You should have called Nicko and me to help find her. Mistress would have killed all of us if she died." Sophia, fighting back tears, just put her head down and did not answer. Lucia was so sorry for the trouble she had caused, but was so thrilled at having found her secret place, that the situation quickly left her mind.

Antoinetta asked the two maids to step out, stripped off her clothes, and stepped into the luxurious tub. She was thrilled to have warm water for her bath. She selected her own soap bar, after carefully smelling each one, and lathered up her beautiful petite body. Her hands traced the curves of her developing frame. She worked the soap into her long thick hair and massaged her head, taking the bucket of clean fresh water that was set on the side of the tub with a large wooden ladle and scooped its contents over her head. It felt so good. She lingered for a moment on her breasts, which were firm and round and she felt the weight of them, then let her hand search for the patch of womanhood that was nestled between her slim thighs. Antoinetta felt a maturity she had never experienced. She knew that it was her duty to protect Lucia and that they must never be separated. It was getting late she must get ready.

Stepping out of the tub, she retrieved the linen towel that Sophia had left for her. Standing with the towel wrapped around her, she caught her own reflection in the gilded mirror that was on the opposite wall. She released the towel that she had wrapped her dripping body in and was pleased with her image. Looking at herself, she realized that she looked so much like her mother. Her full breasts enhanced by her olive skin and petite frame. She was so different in every way from her sister. Antoinetta thought about the tall, sturdy build of her ivory skinned sister, and just for a fleeting second, was jealous of the near perfect features and alabaster skin of her redheaded sibling. Lucia's piercing blue eyes could never hide her feelings. Lucia was genuine and honest but fierce and adventurous.

The warm breeze from the open window whispered over Antoinetta's olive skin like a fine layer of gauze. She saw the jars of perfumed creams and decided she would smooth some on her toned body. She chose a jar that smelled of jasmine, spread a generous amount on her shoulders, and gently covered her taut breasts. As she spread the fragrant cream over her erect nipples, she felt a tingling and shuddered. She gently pinched them and was amazed that she felt a sudden heat in her womb.

She continued down her flat belly slithering down to her inner thighs. When she reached her patch of thick black womanhood she let her fingers enter the inside of her clit. The feeling was at first shocking and her body tensed with the sensation. Instinctively, she wiggled her finger ever so slightly. It felt good and she started to breathe more rapidly, a bead of perspiration rose on her upper lip. Her finger felt the hot wet moisture. It tickled, but in a different way than she had ever known. Her whole body was prickling with sensation, her swollen breasts were full, and her nipples were standing at attention. She wanted more but dared not explore too deeply; at least not today. Antoinetta was satisfied that she had anointed her whole body, and was feeling good about herself. This place was magical and she felt so special and grownup. The banging on the door by her over anxious sister disturbed her magical moment. "Sono mai venuta fuori di lì? È necessario ottenere pronto anche." She shook herself back to reality, and told Lucia to be quiet and get dressed. "Taci. Ho anche fatto." She took one last lingering look at herself and knew she was now a woman, and would learn all the secrets her body would reveal over time, but for now, she must get ready for supper with her family.

CHAPTER FOUR

A MOTHER'S LONGING

Naples

When Maria Sucretti handed the driver Gaetano the note for Rafaela and Donato Banfi she also gave him two purses filled with coins. "Gaetano, I am entrusting you with two very special things, but first I must pay you for the fine job you did in bringing my guests safely to me. Here is a purse with your pay." The driver, who generally only dealt with senior servants, was surprised at the audience with the mistress of the castle. He bowed deeply to show his appreciation. Maria continued in her authoritative, no nonsense manner, "You are to bring this note, together with this second purse to the parents of the young girls you brought here. Rafaela, my niece and her husband Donato. I am sure you will know how to find them. If you are in doubt, you may speak with Signore` Romano and he will give you further instruction."

Gaetano realized immediately that whatever was contained in that letter must be important for Mistress Sucretti to speak with him personally. "Do not worry Mistress, I am your obedient servant and will bring both the note and the purse to their parents. I know very well where they are staying. Thank you for your generosity and confidence in me." With that said, Gaetano, with a formal footed bow, turned to leave, but before he reached the door, Maria called to him. "Yes

Mistress." Maria her voice just slightly choked said "Please let them know that if ever they wish to come to see their daughters they can contact you and I will take care of the cost." Once again, the driver bowed "Of course. Your servant Mistress" and then he was gone.

The next day Gaetano, pleased with the generous amount Maria Sucretti had given him, sought out Rafaela and Donato to deliver his message. He made his inquiries where Giovanni Romano had told him they were staying. Sister Bernadetta told him that the Banfi's work until dark and that he should leave whatever he had and she would give it to them. He assured the nun that it was no trouble to return that evening, for he had specific instructions from his employer to make sure he personally delivered his message.

It was dark by the time Rafaela met up with Donato and Antonio. She had been working all day on a special gown for a very wealthy duchess who was particularly fussy. Her neck ached from sewing all day and her nerves were frayed. Donato and Antonio were not especially happy themselves, their catch for the day was quite meager. So they sat to their supper in the confines of the cellar of the church surrounded by all the other refugees in sullen silence.

They were not quite finished with their simple meal when Sister Bernadetta came to get them. "Rafaela, there is a man who has come to see you and Donato. He came earlier but I told him you were working. I have him waiting in the front vestibule." In that split second a thousand things ran through Rafaela's mind. Has something happen to my girls? Where were the boys? Her children were spread out in many directions. Donato, who could always read her, anchored her by placing his powerful arm around her shoulders. "Come; let us see who this stranger is and what he wants. Antonio you come too." The three of them trudged after the little nun. It was already late and many of the inhabitants of the cellar were fast asleep. They went quietly as not to disturb anyone. Sister Bernadetta, always jovial said, "Donato, when you are finished with your visitor please lock up. I am scheduled for the adoration of the Blessed Sacrament in just a few short hours I need to go to bed." Donato nodded "Of course sister. Do not worry I will see to it. Good night and thank you. Ah, sister, please say a special prayer for all my children, especially my girls." Sister Bernadetta looked him directly in the eye and said, "I have been doing that. Your faith in God will protect you and your family. You are a good man and loving father and your wife is a good mother. Good night." With that, she turned and made her way up to the convent sleeping lofts.

Rafaela and Antonio were waiting for Donato to finish his conversation with the nun. He waved them to come and then opened the heavy door that led to the exterior vestibule. Standing there was the driver Gaetano. Donato remembered him distinctly from the early morning encounter just a few days earlier. His heart dropped to his feet. He could see his wife and son's common reaction. Something must be wrong why this man would make two trips to see them. In a harsher tone than he meant it to be Donato asked, "What has happened? Where are my daughters and the old man?" Gaetano, never expecting this greeting took a step back. "Signore` Banfi, there is nothing wrong. They are perfect." "If all is well than why have you made two separate visits in search of us? Se è soldi aggiuntivi che cercano devo non dare." Donato assured the driver that if he was looking to extort more money from him he was after the wrong man. Silently, Antonio, as tall as and even more muscular than his father, came to stand next to him.

At this point, Rafaela sensing that her two men were itching for trouble stepped in front of them. "Signore` what is the nature of your visit?" The tone and intensity of fear in her voice let the driver's shoulders relax just a hair. "Please, there is nothing wrong I came to bring a message from Mistress Sucretti. Your daughters are well and seem to like Monteforte. The Mistress already looks like she lifted ten years since their arrival." He reached carefully, so as not to excite any response from the two Titans before him, into his coat and brought out the note as well as the purse. Mistress Sucretti instructed me to deliver these to you, and he placed the items as if they were delicate crystal into the open palm of Rafaela. "What is the purse for?" Gaetano, now more relaxed just shrugged his shoulders and said, "That is none of my business. I did as I was told. Now it is up to you to make what you will of it. I must take my leave I have a long trip tomorrow. Good night. Oh, Mistress Sucretti also said that when you want to go to Monteforte you can get in touch with me and I will take you there. She will pay the cost. You can reach me at the carriage house near the Harbor House" He put back his hat, bowed deeply, and then remembering something, added "Ah, Signore `Giovanni Romano, said to tell you that all is well and that he is with the girls always." He then opened the big door to leave but before he got through Rafaela grabbed his arm. He turned to look at her and she said with tears coming down her face "Signore` grazie." She came close and kissed his cheek. He just bowed his head and left.

The three of them were dumbfounded. It was Antonio who suggested they go into the sitting room where there was a lit candle to see what the note said. "Papa, you, and Mama go. I will secure the door and make sure all it locked up tight." His father was grateful and nodded a silent affirmation. He had been tired and depressed from the long day they had, and now the tension of the last few minutes had drained both himself and Rafaela. Antonio was a devoted son and a wonderful young man. Antonio knew it would be him to care for his aging parents. It would not be a burden; he truly loved his parents and knew, as the eldest child, it was his obligation to care for them later on in life.

Donato took his wife by the hand and went into the dim room that was used to receive visitors to the church. He brought a small bench to where the single candle was set into a holder on the wall. Rafaela was holding the note; she could feel the fine vellum of expensive paper and could still smell the faint scent. Her hands were trembling and her heart was beating a tattoo in her ears. Donato's big, callused hand came and rested on her neck, which he massaged with great delicateness. His mere touch sent a wave of desire through her body. It had been so long since they had been intimate. There was no privacy in their present quarters and she longed for, no she needed, the touch of her husband upon her tired body. Donato, ever mindful of her needs as well as his own, bent down and kissed her neck very tenderly, his voice hoarse with desire "Lo so. Sono disperato con il desiderio, ma non non c'è nessun posto qui per tali pensieri. Presto il mio amore. Presto!" Donato confirmed what his wife already knew. His longing for their lovemaking was so real and formidable they could both feel it. He assured her that it would not be much longer. He pressed his body into her back and she could feel his desire, which was now very apparent. He told her it would be soon. It would never be soon enough for either of them.

The entrance of Antonio, who looked slightly embarrassed at the intrusion, interrupted their thoughts. He just stood, head bent, arms folded across his chest waiting. Donato was the first to break the silence. "Please Cara open the letter we cannot wait any longer." Antonio felt relieved that the intimacy between his parents was now gone and they could resume the work at hand.

It was a strong and elegant hand that had written the note. There was a wax seal in blood red with the crest of Monteforte engraved on it. It was a bird of prey, perhaps a falcon, with a sword clutched in his talons. On the outside was written their names. Carefully, so as not to tear the paper, Rafaela broke the wax seal. She unfolded the note and read silently to herself. Donato knew better than to ask her to read it aloud before she had finished it contents herself. They waited patiently until she was finished. An expression of peace came to her features and her body seemed to soften. Tears once again came creeping down those lovely cheeks, which had grown tired and taut from hard work and desperation. Donato's patience could only be contained for so long "Well?" Rafaela, "Oh, I am sorry. I was just thinking of my babies." Antonio, came over to his mother, knelt by her side, and kissed her hand. "Mama, don't worry. They will be fine. Please share the news you have with Papa and me." She loved this son so much he was truly his father's son in every way possible. Rafaela looked at him and thought, lucky the woman who marries my son. "Yes, of course." She coughed slightly and sat more erect. Rafaela began to read aloud the short note.

Dear Rafaela and Donato,

Antoinetta, Lucia, and Giovanni Romano arrived at Monteforte safe; a little weary from the journey, but in good spirits. You have raised two wonderful girls who have not stopped speaking about you and their brothers. I will do all that

I can to make them happy here. Next week their tutors will come so that they can continue their education, which I know, is very important. You are welcomed at Monteforte whenever you wish to come.

Grazie per aver portato gioia a una Caporegimena anziana.

Maria Sucretti, Mistress of Monteforte

It was a short note and to the point, but its message spoke volumes to the grieving family. Rafaela when she finished, carefully refolded the note, kissed it, and tucked it into a hidden pocket in her gown. They were relieved and so distracted that they almost forgot the purse sitting in Rafaela's lap. It was only when she stood to leave that it clanged upon hitting the floor with a noticeable thud. Antonio, who was still on his knees, reached over, and retrieved the heavy leather pouch, he felt its weight and gave a low whistle as to the heft of it. "Papa this is pretty heavy." He then chucked the bag to his father who caught it with ease. Donato, mimicking the actions of his offspring, shifted the bag from hand to hand; trying to calculate how much was in the bulging little sack. They were teasing Rafaela and were enjoying that she was now annoyed. Rafaela was now the one who was impatient. "Well?" All three looked at each other and laughed. It was good to laugh. Laughing was something they had been very short on doing since the day the mountain roared and destroyed their lives.

Donato opened the bag with care. There was a battered but polished table behind them and he spread the contents of the bag upon the table. It was a small fortune in coins. Rafaela gasped clutching her hand to her mouth. Antonio's eyes grew wide and Donato just smiled. "Oh il mio Dio. This is a fortune. Do you both realize what this means for us? We can get our own place. Oh il mio Dio." They stood there staring at the money and knew their lives would once again be changed. Fearing that someone would see, Donato quickly shoved the coins back into the leather bag, and stuffed it into his shirt. Its weight felt foreign, but at the same time, the thought of what it could buy was comforting. "Tomorrow we find a place to call home." Rafaela was trembling with joy and Antonio was smiling broadly. Maybe, just maybe, things would turn out for the better. Rafaela turned to them and said "let us go to the chapel and say a prayer of thanksgiving for the safely of all our loved ones who are not with us, and for Zia Maria Sucretti who has given us a wonderful gift of hope." They agreed without any hesitation, and made their way to the chapel. For the first time in so very long there was a little bounce in their step. "God bless Zia Maria," Rafaela prayed.

That night returning from the chapel making their way in the darkness they found their pallet of straw among the mass of humanity, with the stench of unclean bodies, the snores, the farts and those who, despite the lack of privacy still found sex possible, they embraced each other with renewed passion and hope. It was a wonderful feeling. Donato whispered in his wife's ear, "God knew I would not live much longer if I did not make love to you soon. Il mio cazzo è così forte che ho paura potrebbe caere e poi muoio." Rafaela was vibrating with silent laughter, but she too felt the desire for their intimacy burning fever within her own body. The thought of his rock hard cock, which was boring through her back, made her womb throb with hot desire. A smile in the cover of darkness came to her lips, as she remembered what Donato had said, that his cock would fall off and then he would die, was that even possible? He was just crazy. "I'm not sure God was considering your sexual needs when he let this gift come to us."

Donato, his massive body pressed against his wife's back, his huge callused hand lay upon her belly. He started to nibble her ear lobe and the hand, which had been dormant, was on the move. He reached first for her full swollen breast, it was waiting for his eager touch. Slowly he circled the nipple to tease her, the rough fabric from her night shift scratching the tip to add friction. He continued with his hot mouth on her ear and her neck. His hand, which was creeping down her taut belly, started to hike up her shift until it came to her clit. By now, Rafaela had her face buried into her pillow to stifle her moans. Donato was enjoying this pleasurable punishment. At first, he just moved his hand casually around the inner thigh, but she spread her long legs apart in anticipation. He could feel the heat emanating from her womb. His mouth was dry with passion and he had to keep licking his lips. When she could not take any more, she grabbed the object of her delightful pain, pinched his hand, and brought it to her panting clit. At that point, Donato relented, took her hand in his, and brought her fingers to herself. He was the puppet master moving her fingers in and out. Rafaela's body was sodden with sweat as was his. When he felt that she was at the breaking edge, he pushed her hand aside and with his middle finger thrust it full into her. Deep and penetrating, the long finger found her sweet spot, and she came with such force that he had to put his big heavy leg over her to keep her down. She was gasping into the pillow. Her back arched in agonizing pleasure. Donato, who had found his own pleasure, was sticky and wet with his own desire spilled. Exhausted from their efforts they laid spent and motionless until their breathing became regular. "Cara, I love you. Now we can rest." With satisfied bodies and happy thoughts of house hunting, they fell quickly asleep.

The next morning just as promised the little trio set off to find new lodgings. It was not going to be easy given the fact that so many people had been displaced to Naples because of the volcanic disaster. Rafaela, before leaving, told them that she needed to send a note to her aunt. So, while they were making inquiries, she asked Sister Bernadetta for paper and ink. The friendly nun, always willing to assist, brought her into the convent quarters to the library. It was magnificent and filled her with thoughts of what Monteforte might be like.

The paper, which was of a good quality, felt good in her hands, she had not written anything in a long time. She sat for a moment reflecting and organizing her thoughts.

Dear Zia Maria,

How can I begin to thank you for taking my girls? I am so happy that they will be able to continue their education. Lucia is especially fond of learning. I pray they do not drive you mad. With the very generous gift you sent, we can now look for new rooms in a decent place. There are no words to express our gratitude. Thank you.

When we are settled and back on our feet financially, I will send word, and with your permission, we would love to come see our daughters.

God bless you for your kindness and may He watch over all who dwell at Monteforte.
With love and gratitude,
Rafaela

Having completed her note she reached for the burning taper and deposited a few drops of wax upon the back to seal her missive. She then addressed the front.

Mistress Maria Sucretti, Monteforte, Sorrento

Rafaela, looking down at the note, was pleased with both its appearance and its content. She tucked it into her pocket and went to look for her men. Today, they would begin a new life...

CHAPTER FIVE

A FIRE STARTS

Monteforte

For the last few days, Giovanni Romano was keeping busy trying to acquaint himself once again with his old home. Very little had changed, yet, so much had changed, but, more importantly, Giovanni himself had changed. He found himself looking for ghosts in the dark hallways and empty cavernous rooms, but nowhere could be find Natalie his dead wife nor his beloved daughter.

Giovanni found a friend in Giorgio, who was impressed with the old stories he had been told while growing up on the estate of the former bodyguard. "Signore` Romano, the stories, are they true?" Giovanni smirked and pretended ignorance "What stories did you hear?" Giorgio, looked shy, not wanting to offend his guest, haltingly said "Stories of the old days here on the estate. About Signore` Sucretti and the things he did, even stories about you and about the night he was killed." Giovanni was quiet and sunk his head into his chest. Giorgio was now embarrassed for having asked. "Excuse me Signore` Romano, I did not mean to insult or offend you in any way. You are an honorable man and the Mistress she loves you."

Giovanni took a deep breath, picked up his head with what seemed to be considerable effort and looked at Giorgio with his one good eye, his damaged eye was covered with the black silk patch. For nearly twenty years Giovanni Romano had tried to repress who he had been and the things he had done for Salvatore Sucretti. Surely when he was a young mercenary soldier in France he had seen and done many things, but, that was war and he was a soldier. He had repented and confessed his sins many times, pleading with God for absolution. He begged for forgiveness and mercy for his deeds. He tried to find solace in his heart but none existed. Giovanni Romano felt empty and alone. He had tried desperately to wash his mind of the memories of his beloved wife and daughter because they were far too painful, but being here in this, place, the place where it all started had stirred his mind and his heart. There was no escape, and so he might as well confront his demons head on.

Giovanni gathered his thoughts and simply replied "Yes Giorgio, all those wicked stories are true. Master Sucretti was a vile man who cared for no one. His death was too long in coming. Someone, I, should have killed him long before. Fernando, before I left here so many years ago, had confided in me that he had been aware that the Master was raping both the young girls as well as some of the boys. Fernando, as casa di maître, should have stopped him, but he did nothing. We were all afraid not only of the man but more of his power.

I remember one time there was a man who worked in the shipyard. He was in charge of smuggling spices and other rare items from the Far East. It was a risky business and the government was on to him. The man, his name was Mario, was afraid for his family. If he were caught, they would send him to prison, and his wife and children to the poorhouse or worse. Mario, came to the Master, explained the problem, and said he was going to leave and take his family with him. The Master, said, if that is what you desire go ahead. He was calm and even cordial. When Mario left, he instructed two of his henchmen to go to his house that night and kill all of them, even the youngest child. This would be an example of what happens to those who are disloyal. That is what they did. No questions asked. They just did it. The message rang out, loud and clear, that once you were tied to Camorra Sucretti, death was the only way out. Loyalty and unquestionable obedience were required. Fear, my friend, is a powerful enforcer of men."

Giorgio was in rapt attention to this story. "I am sorry Signore` Romano, I did not know. Yes, I had heard, but, you know how stories, especially in a place like this, grow out of proportion." The overseer was an intelligent man; he would have to be to run an estate the size of Monteforte with such organization. Giovanni thought to himself that Fernando had chosen his successor wisely. Giorgio with compassionate eyes continued. "Fernando, often spoke of you Signore`. He always considered you the son he could never have and longed to know of your condition. I was much younger when the news of the death of your wife and daughter arrived. The whole estate was thrown into mourning. I am sorry, but, I was too young to remember them, yet, between the Mistress, Fernando and the older staff, the stories were wonderful. They must have been so special."

Giovanni Romano, unashamed, did not wipe the tears from his face. The wetness from the tears left the silk patch that covered his damaged eye stained and the fabric clung to the skin. Quietly, with a hoarse voice "They were." Looking over at the man who was seated across the table, Giovanni saw that he too was crying, and did not make to cover his emotion. He then knew that Giorgio would be his friend.

Giovanni loved working in the garden; he had become accustomed to working in the rectory garden at the church where they had found shelter after the volcano erupted. It was peaceful work and calmed his mind. He asked Giorgio to introduce him to the head gardener. "Giorgio, do you think he would mind if I helped in the garden. I need to keep busy and require some physical exercise." Giorgio chuckled, "Signore` have you not seen the size of this place. Of course, he will be delighted that you offer assistance. Come, I will take you to meet him. His name is Ambrose he was born here on the grounds and lives in the cottage with his wife Pepina, and their two sons."

The two men walked in amiable silence for a while then Giovanni spoke. "Giorgio, how has the Mistress been? Does she get many visitors?" He was not sure but Giorgio thought Giovanni Romano was asking if Maria Sucretti had any male companions. He wanted to laugh but thought better of it. "Very few people come to Monteforte to visit socially. Mostly they are the managers of her various business ventures. I do know she has a Professor who comes now and then and he stays for a few days. They are quite friendly." On that last piece of information, Giovanni Romano nodded his head and seemed deep in thought.

"Ah, here we are, I will get Ambrose. Wait here Signore`." Giovanni reached for Giorgio's arm to halt his progress, "Giorgio, please call me Giovanni. I will consider you my friend." Giorgio seemed stunned and then a broad grin came to his jovial face "It would be my honor sir. Are you sure that the Mistress would not object?" Giovanni, pleased that the Mistress held him in such high regard replied, "I am sure."
"Then it shall be Giovanni. Thank you" and with that he went off to find Ambrose.

A few moments later Giorgio reappeared with a short, bone thin man. His skin was so tight and sun tanned that he looked like leather had been stretched over his bones. He gave a wide smile that revealed his toothless gums and bowed deeply. "Ambrose, this is Signore` Romano, he is a special friend of the Mistress. He would like to do a little gardening around the property. Perhaps you could give him some tools and find him some old clothes." Ambrose looked Giovanni Romano up and down, assessing his ability to work with his hands. Giovanni had worn one of the fine waistcoats that the tailor had made for him and he did look rather refined, even with his dampened eye patch, which was quickly drying in the hot sun. "Yes, of course, whatever Signore` wants to do is fine with me. I will get everything you need ready. Tomorrow shall I call for you at the main house around seven in the morning?" Giovanni liked the little man and replied, "Yes that will be fine. Don't worry I have my own garments that will be suitable for my purpose." Ambrose bowed deeply and left for his work. Giorgio said, "Will you walk back to the house with me or do you want to be alone?"

Giovanni Romano needed space and time to collect his thoughts, and find a balance between his heart and his head. "Thank you Giorgio, I will walk around the grounds for a while. I'll be up for supper."

It was still early, Giovanni having set out before sunrise and finding Giorgio, had sought his company for breakfast. He decided to take some exercise; the movement was good for his aching bones. The last few days of such fine and plentiful food had already made his belt tight, but he felt good in many ways. The fog had lifted and the sea breeze was whispering through the trees. Giovanni loved the smell of the sea. He missed the solitude of being in the middle of the water with nothing but sea and sky for companion. It gave a man time to reflect on his life. Now he found himself walking along a steep escarpment, which fell sharply to the water. It was a magnificent sight. There was no sound save that of the conversation of nature. The soft chirping of young birds in nearby trees, tiny swarms of insects disturbed by his presence and the lapping of the waves as they ran to the shore were the only sounds around him. It was not an easy walk, the ground was covered with low bushes, and the exertion was making him sweat. He stopped to remove his coat and throwing it over his shoulder he continued. It was a pleasant hike up the escarpment but he was not used to such physical effort. He was mentally chastising himself for becoming soft and out of condition. In his younger years, he had honed his body to be tight to endure physical pain. The sun, which was now high in the sky, was hot and his mouth was dry. He had worked up quite a sweat. Not wanting to get his new linen shirt smelly with perspiration, he found a stump, sat down, and removed him shirt. Carefully he draped his shirt over a bush to let it air dry. He found a patch of grass, fanned out his coat, and laid down. The sun falling upon the slim torso that retained its muscular form which, given his age, was still in good shape. Giovanni lying back took in a deep breath and thanked God for the respite for his aching body. He started to doze, his body tired both from the exertion of the climb and the warmth of the sun. All of a sudden, he felt a shadow pass over him. Reaching his hand up to shield his good eye from the glare, he was shocked to see Mistress Sucretti standing over him.

He was startled but pleased to see her. She was bent, with her hands on her thighs, and looked as though she had been walking hard. "Mistress, what is wrong? I never expected to see you here." Maria just smiled, recovering her usual poise and said, "I come this way every day to exercise. It gets harder every day." Giovanni chuckled knowing how she felt. He suddenly became conscious that he had removed his shirt, and was quickly trying to recover it from the bush he had left it on to dry. "Don't get up Giovanni. May I join you?" He was embarrassed by his half nakedness. Maria for her part looked admiringly at his body. "Forgive me Mistress I didn't know you would be here. Let me get my shirt." By now, Maria had sat down next to him on his coat and placed her hand on his hot dry arm. "Don't. It has been ages since I have seen the body of a man. Let my old eyes enjoy it for a minute." He smiled and felt the burn of red-hot embers come to his cheeks. Maria too was flushed, was it from the exercise or from the closeness to Giovanni Romano. Her hand was still on his arm and her fingers were fondling the hair that had now begun to prickle. "I confess it has been far too long since I have been touched by a beautiful woman." They were both shocked and pleased with this intimacy but did not quite know how to proceed.

Giovanni thought to himself, do I dare attempt to touch her, to kiss her. Without further thought, driven by desire, he came closer, their faces an inch apart, and then reached for her head and drew her to his lips. It was a soft, tender kiss. His lips were dry, and he feared that his breath was not fresh, so he did not try to place his tongue in her mouth even though that was his longing. At first, she was tense and slightly resistant, but as he was pulling back, she came toward him to stay the kiss. He was pleased. His fingers caressed her hair, which for the first time was loose and flowing about her thin shoulders. He could smell her clean body with its natural perfume and felt the mist of lust upon her cheek. He broke away. "If I have transgressed I am deeply sorry. I could not resist. If you are offended I will leave Monteforte immediately." Maria was aroused, confused, and hesitated to answer. Giovanni, thinking that she was so angry that she could not speak, started to get up but she held him down. "I have always desired to be in this moment such as we are. From the first day, you came to my home to meet with Salvatore I wanted to be with you. I saw you that day and something changed within me. I was sitting on the terrace when you arrived. You were cocky and full of yourself. You stood there and then you saw me. Our eyes met and I knew I wanted you. Then you fell in love with Natalie and I put my desire to rest. After the death of Salvatore, after you left I had nothing. I had no one. You had taken my sister and my niece. You had taken my hidden lover and my desire with you. Now you have come back. We have both lived and lost. We have both loved and lost. It is our time to be together, at last."

Giovanni could not even begin to comprehend what was happening. "Do you mean to say that you desire me?" he could not believe he had the courage to speak so plainly to his former Mistress. He was just a servant, long since out of her employ, and now come back by an odd turn of fate. Not affording her an opportunity to answer he jumped back into his conversation "You cannot even imagine how long, how many days and nights I had dreamt of this day. Long before I found my love of Natalie, I would secretly watch you. Every movement, every word was recorded in my mind and etched on my heart. I knew that to desire you would mean certain death for both of us, and so I too put my love away to spare you from harm at the hands of that monster. Then Natalie found her love for me and I too found her in my heart. The day we left was so hard. After Natalie and my darling Rosalie died, I also died. Who would have dreamed that nature, an act of God, would bring us back together. Natalie knew that I loved you, but she also knew that it could never be for us. She loved us both with all her heart. I am sure between her and God we are here now."

Maria was weeping, as was Giovanni. He brought her to himself and stroked her back, which was erupting with sobs. He felt her pain and her sorrow for the loss of her beloved Natalie, not her servant, not her friend, but, her sister and the child of her womb her darling daughter Rosalie. Maria said a silent prayer. "God watch over them and bring them safely to your Paradise. Thank you for this act of unselfish love."

"How can this be, I am nothing? I have nothing to bring to this relationship. I was your servant." The pain was so deep in his voice he was trembling. Maria pulled herself from his embrace her eyes were on fire. "What does it matter Giovanni. We are old; I have already chosen who will be the next ruler of Monteforte. I know you do not want me for what I can give you, or for my money, we have denied our love for a lifetime, it is our time now. We, I especially, have to answer to no one for my actions and neither do you. Let us enjoy what little time we have left."

"I will treasure your body and offer you what is left of my own. I am forever your obedient servant." Maria was shaking with desire and would have thrown herself upon her new lover but knew that was not how it should be. They had dreamt of their intimacy for nearly forty years and she would make it special. Maria wanted love, not lust, but would not lie to say that she was not wet with passion and she could see that Giovanni was fighting his own inclination. "I will give you all that is mine; body and soul, love and desire, all you have is to ask and it shall be yours." They held each other for what seemed a long time, soaking up the love they felt for each other. Theirs was a love, so long denied, a passion so long stifled that its release, its acknowledgement, had made them exhausted. Maria risolto che lei farebbe loro prima volta insieme qualcosa da ricordare. Maria promised herself that when they were finally together for the first time she would make is memorable...

CHAPTER SIX

A SECRET PLACE

Monteforte

Life at Monteforte under the kind but stern eyes of Mistress Maria Sucretti continued on a whirlwind level. Every day there were many things to do and to learn. Their aunt had engaged the services of some of the most renowned educators in Italy to tutor Antoinetta and Lucia. Their eagerness and natural intelligence made them model students. They were schooled in the fine arts of music, dance, language, and art. They were outstanding in their ability to grasp mathematics, literature, and history. Quickly, Lucia demonstrated her ease with learning. She was growing and thriving, absorbing all that she learned, she was always pushing her own limits.

Lucia loved to learn but she also loved being outside. Maria Sucretti with the help of Gandolfo, the Master of the Horse, had purchased a wonderful horse for her. Lucia had named him Apollo after the Greek God. He was a huge animal, nearly seventeen hands, he was the color of silver, and he had one blue eye and one brown eye. He was an extraordinary animal of great intelligence with an even temper. Lucia went to the stables every day to ride Apollo. She groomed and fed him whenever she could. For his part, Apollo loved Lucia. The instant he caught sight of her he would whinny and stamp in his stall. Lucia never came to him without a lump of sugar, which she would keep in her pocket and he would nudge her until she gave it up; it was a game they played. Gandolfo was waiting for Lucia every morning. He loved Lucia and taught her how to ride and care for Apollo. She was a natural rider. Lucia knew how to soothe the horses; she had an inborn rhythm that the animals understood. She did not fear the horses and they responded to her.

Antoinetta was the complete opposite and wanted no part of the horses. She hated riding and said the animals smelled. Antoinetta occupied her time with domestic things and reading. She was a skilled sewer and did beautiful needlepoint items. She enjoyed going down to the kitchen and watching them prepare the food. Antoinetta wanted a husband and children. That is all she talked about while Lucia wanted her freedom.

This morning Lucia was taking Apollo for their daily run down to the seashore. It was a bright sunny day and the sky was as blue as Apollo's one eye. The smell of the sea was magic for Lucia, and she would breathe deeply inhaling its essence, which filled her with thoughts of her father. She would never forget how, when she was little, she would wait by the dock until her father would bring in his boat. He would call to her on the shore, his deep voice filled with joy at the sight of her. He was a handsome man, big as a house, and strong. He would tie up the boat, hoist the day's catch over on to the dock, and nearly run to his daughter. With nostrils flaring, she caught the scent, the scent of her father. He would scoop her up in those powerful arms and smother her with kisses, his clothes damp with a mixture of manly sweat and sea. Lucia caught the tears at the back of her eyes but smiled at the thought of him. It seemed so long since she had seen her parents and she longed to see them. Even though they wrote back and forth, she missed her family. She would get and send letters to her brothers who were at seminary or university, but it was hard not to see them.

Lucia sent up a silent prayer that they were all well and prospering.

With the wind in her hair, the sun warm upon her face, she let Apollo free rein. The magnificent beast, much like his mistress, was powerful and he loved to run hard and fast. Soon they were just at the border of where the land met the sea. Lucia was happy because there were no lessons today, and so they could spend as long as they liked riding and exploring. Both woman and beast were happy.

As they neared, the edge of the estate on the seaward side of the property Lucia saw that there was a shallow cove. She had never been this far and wanted to explore the area. Getting down from Apollo, she hobbled him, and he contentedly was grazing on a patch of grass. She reached in the bag that she always kept tied to her saddle and plucked out two apples, one for her, and one for Apollo. Lucia, on the request of both Gandolfo and Giovanni Romano always carried her small dagger, which she now used to cut the apple for Apollo. The horse was very pleased with the treat and grunted his appreciation. Lucia, having fed her beloved steed, was eating her own while looking around.

It was very hot and Lucia decided that since no one was around she would go for a swim in the shallow cove. Quickly she removed her riding gown and stripped down to her shift. It felt so good to be free from that hot garment. She took off her stockings, hiked up her hem, and waded into the pleasantly refreshing water. It was clear. Her initial intent was just to wade in but the water was so captivating she could not restrain herself, plunged headfirst into the water, and was swimming in the coved tidal water. She went a little further and came upon a grotto that sprang out of the water. It was obscured from the shore and so she had not seen it until she was in the water. It was shimmering in the reflection of the sun and water. Soon she realized that she could stand in this part of the cove and gingerly walked into the dark coolness of the covered grotto.

She was careful of where she was walking since there were sharp rocks and broken shells. The water was cooler here and she felt the slightest chill creep up her back. Was it the temperature of the water or just a sensation of something odd? The rock shale was luminous inside the cave like interior of the grotto. A blue shimmer was emanating from the rock and casting a beautiful glow like sun drenched crystal on the water that stood motionless at the base of its walls. The walls themselves seemed to be moving or breathing she could not determine which. The sight before her was breathtaking and strange. Lucia had never seen anything like it; she was at once mesmerized and frightened. Tiny fish swam up to her legs and feet, and were nibbling at them and she smiled at the feeling. Her eyes now totally adjusted to the darkness, she realized for the first time that her legs were glowing. Lucia wanted to scream out in fear but knew there was no one to hear her. Her next impulse was to run. Yet some force was holding her there, she felt paralyzed. She could see the bottom even in the darkness that blocked the light from outside. She squinted and rubbed her eyes, she thought there were designs inlaid on the grotto floor. She bent down submerging her face into the water, which to her amazement did not smell or taste of salt. An areola of light surrounded her head and she felt calm and peaceful. With her face in the water and her eyes open, she could clearly make out a pattern covering the floor. It was not a natural formation but manmade of that much she was certain. It was a familiar pattern, perhaps something she saw in a church. It was definitely laid to direct you straight ahead. Where had she seen this? Lucia made a mental picture and hoped she would remember it later.

She ventured a little further into the recesses of the cave, abiding the direction on the floor, and was bewildered that it was getting brighter the further she went. The water level had receded and now only as deep as her ankles. What a wonderful and strange place this was. Lucia, given her height, had to duck her head so as not to hit the ceiling of the cave. She could see that the light was coming from two places. There was a hole in the rock bed on the wall just above the waterline about two meters in diameter. She looked through the hole and gasped at the sight before her. Just beyond the wall that housed the hole was a cavernous opening that glowed brilliantly within the recesses of the dark cave. No longer afraid, Lucia knew she had to go there. The hole was large enough for her to wiggle through. She put her head in first to see what was immediately beyond the wall. It was almost completely dry except for what little moisture was created by the atmosphere within the cave itself. The floor continued into this interior space. Carefully, she tied her shift around her waist to give her freedom of movement. She self-consciously looked around, even though she knew no one was there, because now the entire lower half of her body was exposed, but she did not care. She lifted one long agile leg over the side, while balancing herself on the rock opening, which was wide enough for her to straddle while she got purchase to steady herself. The foot that she had sent through had found solid ground and she felt more secure. There was just enough room so that she could bend her torso to slip over the edge of the opening. She then swung her other leg over and let out her breath, which she had been holding. She was inside the large cave. Her heart was drumming in her head and she was taking rapid breaths. She did not notice at first, but then realized, in this space, she could actually stand her full height, and there was still plenty of room overhead. Being able to stand upright, gave her more confidence she did not feel claustrophobic.

Lucia walked to the center of the space, which was glowing brightly. Where was that light coming from? Lucia could not find the source of the light. Her eyes were darting all around absorbing the sensory images that were forming in her head. It was definitely a natural structure, but one which had been discovered by man long ago, and used with some regularity for some purpose. What could they have used this place for she wondered? Lucia was walking around, her feet sliding on the mosaic tile floor from the algae that had coated its surface. Considering its location in the middle of a body of water two things stood out in her mind. First, it was not salt water, even though a huge body of salt water surrounded it. Second, what could make this light glow, so strange and wondrous in a dark cave? After thinking for a little while a third notion came to her head. Who built this place and why? She was intrigued by the prospects. It was deadly quiet, the only sound was her own breathing, yet she could swear she heard something. All of a sudden, from a cavity that sat near the farthest wall, came a deafening gurgle, instantly followed by a plume of steam and hot air, which vomited from the depths of the earth below. By instinct, she crouched down and covered her head with her hands, to protect herself from any falling debris. The cavity then belched and a short puff of steam rose from its opening. What in God's Holy Name was that? She went as close as she would dare. The mist that lingered was hot and smelled of sulphur; the fetid odor turned her stomach, which made her gag. She had read about natural springs but was sure none existed in the middle of the sea. Her stomach rumbled, and she realized she was hungry, and suddenly thought about Apollo. With a final look around Lucia knew she would be back to find the hidden secrets of this strange place.

Lucia did not want to leave but she knew she could not leave Apollo out there for too long. She made a cursory walk around the large space. She touched the ragged rock walls, which were in stark contrast to the smooth tile floor all of which seemed odd. She deliberately bypassed the mouth of the cavity from where the steam had spouted. She then saw a depression in one side of the wall opposite from where she was standing. Coming closer she saw that it was a passageway with worn steps that had been carved into the rock wall. It was dark, but there was enough illumination from the glowing room to guide her step. After about ten feet, the steps disappeared into what smelled like damp earth. Again, not for the first time, Lucia thought this place was filled with odd things. She tried to dig an opening with her hands, but the dirt was hard and mixed with shell and rock, which was cutting into her fingers. Thinking if only she had some kind of a tool, she could use it like a spade to loosen the dirt. Just about to give up the cause, she thought about her dagger, and then she cursed herself for leaving it in the pocket of her riding gown, which was laying, on the beach. Promising next time to come prepared, Lucia felt that it was time to leave. Without warning, she doubled over in pain. Clutching her lower belly, she felt a sharp stabbing pain, which was traveling down into her womb. She panicked for a moment. She had never experienced such a sensation in her life. Her genitalia were fully exposed and she reached to caress the source of where the pain was emanating. To her absolute horror, even in the dim light, she could see that her hand was covered in blood. She checked to see if she had injured herself but knew she had not. Her mother, even

Antoinetta, had warned her that her time for her courses would soon come. Lucia felt miserable and sore. Her full breasts hurt and the pain in her pelvis was uncomfortable. She dreaded the thought of her monthly courses and all the trouble and inconvenience. Damn! She left in the same manner that she entered, but now the tide had come up, and she was waist deep in the glowing water, which felt amazing on her exposed ass and womanhood. She waded out and began untying her shift. She reached the mouth of the entranceway and realized she must have been in there for a long time. From the position of the sun, it was already midday. She dove back into the salt water and with long rhythmic strokes came back to where she had started in very little time. Grazing peacefully was Apollo right where she left him. Lucia was so relieved that he was all right. Exhausted, she lay upon the grass near Apollo and closed her eyes for a while. When Lucia awoke her shift was dry, but the wind had taken her gown and shifted it to the edge of the water, which was lapping it in its wake, it was a mess. Her hair was matted and tangled, with wild, unmanageable curls, springing from her head. Her clothes were wrinkled and encrusted with sea salt and sand. Her shift was soaked with blood and sand. She devised a plan to avert all inquiry of where she had been.

Returning to the stables, she was fortunate that it was time for the midday meal and all the servants were to their supper. She sneaked around the back, brushed Apollo quickly, with a sincere apology to do a better job tomorrow, and slinked out back before anyone noticed her. When she reached the main house, she was hot, smelly and had a fine layer of sand in her private places that was chafing her. She had wadded up the hem of her shift and stuffed it between her legs to control the flow of blood down her legs.

She needed a bath. She ran through the pantry, hiding like a thief, when the coast was clear she ran full speed to her room. Thankfully, she reached her room and no one saw her, or the condition she was currently in, for surely they would have inquired as to how she got that way. Lucia stripped down naked then pulled the cord for either Marianna or Sophia to come.

Luckily, for Lucia, Sophia came. She could be trusted to keep quiet. Marianna would have scolded her. "What have you done to your riding gown? It smells of something horrid." Lucia could not look her maid in the eye, so she pretended to be doing something with her back toward Sophia. "I was out riding with Apollo and he stumbled over a bush and I lost my hold and fell. Don't worry, I am fine, in much better condition than my gown, but nothing is bruised or broken, except for my pride." The maid picked up the soiled gown with two fingers holding it away from her and grumbling something under her breath about being a *maiale* and quickly went off to retrieve hot water.

When Sophia returned with two of the kitchen girls to fill the tub, she asked if Lucia needed any help. "No I am fine really I am. Thank you. I will take my bath and then dress for dinner. Was anyone asking about my whereabouts earlier?" Lucia wanted to have a valid excuse for missing the midday meal. "The Mistress asked why you were not at supper and Antoinetta told her you took Apollo for a ride. She seemed concerned but not angry. Master Giovanni had volunteered to go find you, but your sister told him you had packed a basket." Sophia who knew very well that Lucia had not packed a basket asked, "Are you starving to death?" Lucia with pouting mouth put her head down and said "Yes. However, it can wait. I must wash first I can't even stand my own odor." The two girls laughed, and Sophia clamped her hand to her nose, waving her hand to dissipate the smell, in a mocked affirmation of the odor. "Oh Sophia there is one more thing. I began my courses today. It is the first time. I will need rags. Can you help me?" With eyes wide, the maid had a smile on her face "Ah Mistress Lucia, today you are a woman. I am very happy and proud for you. Bella, you must be very careful now to protect yourself with men. I will have Marianna talk to you." "No, please don't. I know what to do; my mother and sister have told me. Please." Sophia was hesitant but agreed. "It will be our secret."

Lucia welcomed the hot water on her tense muscles. The cramping in her womb had subsided, but her breasts were full and hurting. With the thought of having to deal with her new situation, she was miserable. She had a long day and was distraught, but consoled herself with thoughts filled with an anticipation of further adventures. She would discover the secrets of that place. Tomorrow she would see if she could find out from the books in her Aunt Maria's vast collection any information on how the water could glow as she had seen. She could hardly contain her excitement.

Having bathe and dressed Lucia felt better. Looking in the mirror, she saw someone new reflected back. She did feel different, older than her years; it was a very strange feeling. Sophia had shown her how to fold and position the rags, which were now waded up between her legs. It felt so cumbersome and she wondered if everyone would know. She decided to tell her sister and her aunt, and be done with it, so that if Sophia slipped, they would not be angry that she had not told them.

Lucia felt as if she was walking with a pillow shoved between her legs and was waddling slightly. Standing straight with her head up, she waltzed into the dining room. Thank God only Zia Maria was there. "Ah, Bella, come sit by me for a little while. I missed you at midday supper. Lucia, you look ravishing this evening, the day of being outside looks good on your face." Lucia was beaming especially at the thought of her secret place. "Zia, I got my courses today." Lucia having made the statement unceremoniously watched her aunt's reaction. "Bella that is wonderful news, I am very happy for you. You know what that means?" without giving Lucia a chance to respond her aunt continued. "Now my sweet girl you must be very careful with your body. Men will be after you like bees to the flower. Come let me give you a kiss. Did you get Sophia to help you?" Lucia came to her aunt who hugged her tightly, reached with both hands on either side of her face and looking at her directly said "Oh mia Bella tempo sta passando così velocemente. You are so beautiful, strong, and smart and someday you will be an important woman. I am so proud of you." Lucia could see the love in her aunt's eyes. "Sophia she showed you what to do?" Lucia nodded "Yes. I feel like a duck with the way I am walking. I already hate this!" her aunt laughed. "I do not know any woman who enjoys it, but it is the natural way. When you get old like me, it goes away. No more babies can come." She squeezed Lucia's hand and they sat companionably until the others arrived.

That night after a delicious meal, Lucia decided to tell Antoinetta her news. "Antoinetta, I just wanted you to know that now I am a WOMAN also." The older sister caught off guard seemed confused for just a moment. "You are bleeding?" she asked in a questioning voice. "Yes. I hate it already." Antoinetta went to her younger sibling and gave her a hug and kiss. "You will get used to it. I hate it too. Now, more than ever you must be careful with your body." Lucia, looking sullen said "I don't have to worry no men even look at me. It is you that they drool after." Antoinetta sat down and grabbed her sister's hand beckoning her to do the same. "Lucia,

I have been jealous of you since the day Papa first brought you to me on the day you were born. You cannot understand that you are different but perfect. Tall, with skin like marble, and those eyes are so beautiful. Yes, I am pretty, but I look like everyone else with my dark complexion and dark eyes. But you, my little WOMAN, are special." For the first time in her life, Lucia did truly feel special and hugged and kissed her sister.

"Thank you Antoinetta."

CHAPTER SEVEN

THE REVELATION

Monteforte

After a long while, Mistress Maria Sucretti who was sat at the head of the dinner table with Giovanni Romano on her right and Lucia and Antoinetta on her left seemed especially contemplative this evening. For some reason Lucia sensed that something was odd, different, the atmosphere was charged and the table, while always perfectly dressed, seemed exceptionally festive this evening with no special occasion announced. There were flowers and all the fine crystal laid out. Aunt Maria looked stunning in a red silk gown that brought a lovely blush to her skin. Her hair had been done up with tiny roses, and she was wearing her favorite cameo broach. Actually, Giovanni Romano looked handsome in a brocade waistcoat, his silver streaked hair neatly plaited into a queue with a black leather thong. Lucia thought to herself that he had undergone an astonishing transformation since coming to Monteforte, maybe it was the good food, and healthy air or the fine clothes but he seemed younger and happy.

Dinner this evening was outstanding. Marcello had prepared a new pasta dish with ham and peas in a cream sauce, followed by medallions of veal surrounded by fresh vegetables. Lucia could not wait to see what was for dessert and while the conversation around the table was of the day's events, there was something in the air. The girls talked of what they had been taught and Antoinetta promised to play a tune she had learned on the harp; the normalcy of the evening was still strained.

Maria Sucretti over dessert, which was a rich blood pudding with a cognac sauce quietly said, "Antoinetta and Lucia, after discussing it with your Padrino, we have decided to tell you a story." Here was what Lucia was waiting for and she could hardly contain herself. Without further hesitation and taking a deep breath, Maria Sucretti the ever-poised mistress of the manse continued, while Giovanni Romano smiled at her warmly. "This story begins nearly forty years ago. A young soldier came here to Monteforte at the behest of my late husband Salvatore Sucretti. We were both young and he was tall and strong and handsome. From the moment our eyes made contact, we knew we loved each other, but there was no help for it. The young man hired to be the bodyguard for my husband who was the head of the Camorra. I am sure by now you both have heard all the terrible stories about him. To his credit, Salvatore and I truly had a loving marriage for the first ten years. Then, when we did not have any children, he became bitter and turned to other things to find his happiness. He became diseased from going to the whorehouses and using opium. Over the years, his faithful bodyguard married my personal maid Natalie and they had a beautiful little girl named Rosalie.

One night after a party, my fortieth birthday party, Salvatore was so drunk he tried to rape me and was abusing my beloved Natalie. Fernando, you heard of him also, he held the position Giorgio now has, saw what Salvatore had done and killed him to protect us. When the magistrate and his officers came to investigate the murder, they assumed that the bodyguard had killed Salvatore. Therefore, the bodyguard had to flee with Natalie and their child, so as not to expose Fernando, who would have been hanged.

I suppose you are wondering why I am telling you this old story. That young soldier was your Padrino, Giovanni Romano." Maria watched as their eyes bulged from their heads and their mouths hung open. Giovanni reached for Maria's hand and gave her a gentle squeeze.

"Zia Maria, what a wonderful story and now you are both together. I am so happy for you both." Lucia stood so quickly that her chair almost tipped over and she bounded over to her aunt and her beloved padrino with kisses and hugs. Tears were coming from all their eyes it was such a singular moment.

"When will you marry? Soon?" Lucia was practically jumping with joy. Giovanni spoke next, "We will not marry. There is no need. We are too old to have children so there is no legal reason for us to marry. We are united in our love for each other. Mistress and I wanted you both to hear the truth from us. I never dreamed, even though I had hoped and prayed that we could ever be together. After my wife Natalie and my daughter Rosalie died, I prayed that I too would die. Then the volcano erupted and I came to find your family. When that matter with Signore` Paglimenti happened I knew I had to do something. I also knew that you were Mateo Rizzo's great granddaughters. So I contacted Mistress, and she graciously said you two could come here. I never expected that she would want me to stay, and, more amazing, that she would want me to be her companion. Now you have the whole story."

Antoinetta for the first time spoke. "I am so happy for you both. It is like the fairytales I have read. True love does find a way no matter what the odds." Lucia thought, "Why didn't I say that." Antoinetta was the romantic in the family.

It was Maria's turn to break the momentary silence. "Giovanni and I will live here at Monteforte as husband and wife. We shall share our bed and our love.

We shall share that love with the both of you. We hope you are comfortable with that arrangement." Almost in unison, both girls answered, "Of course we are. We love you both." The release of tension between Maria and Giovanni was so visual it was obvious. Maria had decided that tonight would be their wedding night since it was already so special.

Antoinetta nudged Lucia and motioned that they should go to their room. Her sister pinched Lucia who wanted to continue asking all kinds of questions about their former relationship. As she was giving them her good night kisses Lucia asked her aunt "Zia, can I now call Padrino, 'uncle'?" Maria had a bright smile on her face and Giovanni Romano was beaming. "Bella, you may call him uncle if you wish, I am sure he would not mind. Would you mind Giovanni?" she asked. Giovanni Romano stood up and grabbed both girls in his arms. "I love you like daughters, I would be so happy and proud if you called me uncle. Thank you for making this so easy for us. I love your Aunt and will do everything in my power to make her happy." All four choked back their tears and the girls said their good night and left.

It was Giovanni who broke the silence after the girls had left. "Thank you Maria for this gift. I am so happy." Maria now stood, she was shorter than Giovanni, looked up to his face, and said, "Shall we make this our wedding night?" Giovanni swallowed hard, Maria could see his Adam's apple move in his thin, muscular neck. "Are you ready, I do not want to rush you?" Giovanni was not sure if it was she he was worried about or himself. It had been a long time since he had been with a woman, and was not sure what Maria's expectations of him might be. "I am ready but I want you to be ready as well." Giovanni with his hands cupping her face and his voice deep and sensual said, "Maria my love, I have dreamed of this night forever. I am afraid I will awaken and find myself alone and abandoned. I desire you more than my life. I am afraid that I might not be the man you had hoped. It has been many years since Natalie died, and I do not want to disappoint you." Maria's eyes were piercing and the deep rich brown sparkled with golden flecks; she placed her hands on top of Giovanni's and with desire, rattling her bones said "I am not worried. It is not lust that I desire, but love. We will find our comfort in any way we can. I love you with no expectation, with no reservation, just love me back." They kissed with such passion and feeling that they both felt a little off balance.

Giovanni then took her hand and they walked out to the terrace. It was a warm evening with a star filled sky. The breeze from the sea was like whispers in the air. Giorgio came out bearing a tray with two glasses and a small dish of confections. He placed the tray on the table, poured them each an after dinner cordial, and addressed both of them "Mistress, Master, will there be anything else you will require this evening." Maria Sucretti had spoken to Giorgio earlier in the day about her decision to live as husband and wife with Giovanni Romano. She made it perfectly clear that while they were not legally married, he was to instruct the entire staff that, Giovanni Romano was the new Master of Monteforte, and that they were to afford him all the honor and respect that they had so faithfully given to her. Giorgio was pleased with this arrangement and told his Mistress so.

It was Giovanni who spoke, "No thank you Giorgio we are set for now. Oh, the dinner this evening was superb, please extend our gratitude to Marcello. Good night." Giorgio smiled warmly and bowed. "Good evening to both of you, Master."

Giovanni Romano, having once been a servant at Monteforte felt strange in this new position, but knew that it would not be proper for him not to share Maria's place. He was more than a little anxious about his

211

feelings regarding tonight. He handed her the glass it was delicious and smooth and calmed his nerves. They sat in companionable silence for a while and then she said, "Giovanni, I am going to our room. I would like to refresh myself before we retire. Do you mind?" Giovanni was almost grateful for the few moments he would allow himself to gather his courage. "No, of course not, please take your time. I shall come along in a while." He extended his hand to Maria who was sitting in her chair, and before she left, he kissed her hand. "I will not be too long."

When Maria arrived in her bedchamber Isabella, her body servant, was waiting for her. She had laid out upon the bed a beautiful ivory silk dressing gown that was embellished with tiny silk roses. "Isabella, would you please make ready my bath." Isabella hurriedly left to retrieve the water. Maria stripped out of her red silk gown and undid her long, thick tresses. Within a few moments, Isabella, accompanied by two of the kitchen girls, filled her tub. Isabella came to brush out her Mistress' hair and plaited it into a loose braid, then pinned it up for her. "Mistress shall I wait until you have finished?" Maria knew that the maid was also anxious about the new arrangement, and having never had a Master of Monteforte to answer to she was unsure of how to act. "That will be all for this evening Isabella. Do not come for me in the morning until I ring for you. Thank you." The young maid loved her mistress and was happy for her. She came to Maria and gave her a kiss and a gentle hug "Sarà meraviglioso amante non abbiate paura!" Maria felt like a young bride on her wedding night. She kissed her back, "It has been a long time since I was with a man. I am very anxious but happy." Isabella pouted then smiled "Enjoy!"

Maria was finally alone with her thoughts. She stepped into the tub and began a methodical cleansing of her body. Her fingers were trembling slightly and her heart was racing. She wanted to wash and be dressed before Giovanni would come up. After thoroughly washing, she stepped out to dry off. She caught her image in the long looking glass. "What will he think of this old body?" She looked from side to side and turned around to glimpse her ass. "Well not too bad for my age." She lifted her full breasts and was pleased that they were still round and the nipples were taut. She spread fragrant oil all over herself, between her legs, and inside her private and her ass. She was not sure what Giovanni would want. Salvatore, when they were still in love liked to make love to her front and back. "Would Giovanni be a good lover?" Having finished her ablations she went and slipped on the silk dressing gown. It glided over her freshly oiled skin and felt sensual against her charged feverish skin.

There was a hesitant rap at the door. "Come." She heard her own voice and was amused at how husky it sounded. Gingerly, Giovanni stepped into the room. This would be their first night together in this room. The last time he had been in Maria's bedchamber was the day he left Monteforte and a chill ran up his spine. "Oh please come in. I am almost finished." She was sitting at the dressing table having just unbraided her hair and was brushing it out. Giovanni who had changed into his dressing robe and came over to where she was seated. His hand took the brush mid-stroke and he began brushing her hair. After a few strokes, he bent down and started kissing her neck and then her earlobes. They were both vibrating with anxious desire. He put the brush on the table, spun her around, and took her hand in his. He was so tall and she lifted her face toward his. "You are as enchanting as the day I first saw you." Then he kissed her gently but with such passion and love. Maria, her knees betraying her, was a mass of emotions. She tried to admonish herself not to cry but there was no help for it. "Sweetheart ciò che è sbagliato?" Giovanni knew what was wrong for he felt it within himself. Would the promise of this night, held for decades, be destroyed, or fulfilled? Would the memory of a beloved wife and a wicked husband come between them? He brought her to sit on the settee by the balcony door.

Her room overlooked the flower garden and the sweet perfume wafted through the open doors. The symphony of night noises filled the silence. She was breathing deeply as if she could not catch her breath. Giovanni stroked her head and brought her to his chest to comfort her. He did not push her and just patiently waited for her to find her composure. When the tension finally eased from her body, he could feel the release. "Giovanni, I am so sorry. I do not know what came over me. Please forgive me." He pushed her chin up toward his face and brushed back an errant curl from her cheek. "We have the rest of our lives to be intimate. There is no rush. I am so happy just to be here next to you. I love you."

Maria, now in control of herself, stood up, pulling Giovanni, urging him to follow her. She made her way to the big-canopied bed. This was her grandparent's bed. She had shared the bed with Salvatore so many years ago. She sat down and patted the space next to her and Giovanni obeyed. Slowly he untied the silk cord at her neckline and the silky fabric lent no resistance. The material slipped off her shoulder exposing her flesh. Giovanni's heart was palpitating, driving the blood to every part of his body. He felt the heat of his desire traveling to his groin. He was breathing rapidly. He reached up and with one finger traced the outline from her earlobe to her shoulder. Maria shuddered. He repeated the process on the other side. She closed her eyes and felt his warm kisses on her neck and shoulders. Ever so slowly and with a delft touch, he

214

pulled the gown down to her waist. Her arms were still attached within the sleeves. He just looked. Nothing was said. No movement. He just looked.

Maria was struck silent. She did not move a muscle. She watched him. Giovanni was crying. She still did not speak afraid of damaging this perfect moment. He took both full rounded breast one in each hand; with each thumb he caressed her swollen nipples. He held up her breast as if in adoration and kissed each in turn. His mouth fell upon the right nipple and he licked, nibbled, then suckled making Maria groan with pleasure. He then paid homage to the left breast repeating the process. A bead of sweat alighted Maria's upper lip and her skin glistened with a mist of lust.

Giovanni was slowly separating Maria from her dressing gown. First one arm was coaxed out of its sleeve then the other. She was now completely naked from the waist up. She did not feel awkward or exposed Giovanni had seen to that. He stood, untied his robe, and let it fall to the floor. His erection was rock hard and the muscles in his abdomen were tight, his body was still strong and sensual. He still had a full patch of black curly pubic hair that haloed his rather generously endowed cock. His testicles were full and hung like pendulums. It was a tantalizing view. Maria could hardly contain her emotions but did not want to appear forward.

He made her stand and her gown fell in a puddle at her feet. Again, he stood back to admire the vision before him. Maria was well preserved for her age. Never having borne children her belly was flat and tight. She had an abundant nest of chestnut hair that sheltered her throbbing womb. Giovanni took a step back to take in the whole picture. Taking her hand, he turned her around so that he could see the back view. Giovanni gasped ever so slightly at the sight of her ass. It was full and round, like her breasts, and sat high atop her thighs. He impulsively fondled each cheek letting his middle finger slip down between the cleft. Maria responded to his touch with a murmur of yearning. Finally in a deep, soft, voice that trembled ever so slightly he spoke, "Mia cara Maria, sei più che persino osato sogno che si sarebbe. You are so much more than I ever could have dreamed. I have no right to have such a beautiful creature. Please may I pleasure you as best I can?" Maria turned and knelt in front of him, she took his manhood in her hot wet mouth, gradually absorbing its firmness into herself. She had forgotten the taste and scent of a man's seed and its recollection caused her to abandon all sense of ladylike behavior. With one hand on his cock, she kneaded his testicles with the other. Giovanni was getting weak with desperate lust.

He got her up and lifted her onto the bed. Spreading her legs he started from her toes kissing and licking her ankles, calves, thighs, slowly approaching her womb with a swift flick of his tongue, just caressing her musky clit, again, and, again. Maria's body was pulsating to his every touch. She was wild with longing. At last, using his fingers to expose the object of his own desire, he took his tongue and tantalizingly licked her clit. So softly, it was almost imperceptible, then more rigorously, the little clit growing with every stroke. When anticipation could no longer be controlled, he thrust his face completely into her, devouring her womb with a hunger that he had not enjoyed in twenty years. Maria erupted, spilling her musky juices all over him, and he happily lapped her with ravenous delight. Giovanni was not done with her yet. He flipped her over on to her belly in one swift motion, and again standing with his body between her legs, he began kneading her ass, planting kisses and licking her cheeks. Maria had lost all sense of embarrassment, her body was his to do as be pleased. She never had remanded her body to Salvatore with such wonton need. Giovanni took his middle finger, which he had in his mouth and lightly slipped it into her cleft. He wiggled it, carefully prodding the anus to accept it and when he felt the muscles give way, he began a rhythmic motion, in and out. Maria was blind with lust. Giovanni was pleased that she was such a willing partner, and continued his ministrations on her beautiful body. Spreading her cheeks just a little more, while still sliding his long finger in and out her anus, he continued to pleasure her. His touch was so delicate, so enticing, that Maria felt herself drift to a height of sexual pleasure she had never experienced.

Giovanni, who was on the verge of coming to his own eruption, nudged her over on to her back. Guiding her body so that he could come on to the bed, she spoke in a raspy voice "I have never felt so much pleasure in all my life." Giovanni was pleased, but now the real test would be if he could make her come when he was inside her. He softly bit her nipples, "harder, Giovanni that feels good." Giovanni obliged by placing her swollen tit in his wet mouth and nibbling her, his hand between her legs, his finger plunging harder and faster into her clit. He could not let her come all the way; he wanted her to climax with him inside.

He got on top of her in one swift movement. His cock was throbbing so much that it was painful. Maria had expected it to be a little difficult since she had been celibate for so long; the thing she never expected was this level of gratification. She got hold of his cock, it was hard and wet, her thumb rubbing the wet little head spreading the sticky essence and guiding it willingly into her clit. She opened her legs as far as she could to accept Giovanni's generous cock. He went slowly, so as not to chafe her unaccustomed womb. It was wet. She was ready. He could contain himself no longer. He drove his cock deep into her willing body; they gasped and groaned with pleasure. He began a cadence so strong that his body was a mass of sheer tension. They were sweating the sweat of longing, lust, and love. The room was scented with a mixture of sex both male and female. They were experiencing a ritualistic dance of animal desire so long denied. Together they were panting and struggling to keep up the pace, until, at last, Giovanni emptied himself as she arched her back to receive his seed. Pushed beyond exhaustion Giovanni slid off her, their bodies soaked with sweat and musky juices. It was fantastic.

Giovanni panting said "Cara che era così meravigliosa. Grazie." Maria was so contented replied, "I did not think sexual intimacy could reach such a point. Grazie."

They held each other, not wanting to let go, for fear that, the dream would end...

CHAPTER EIGHT

THE SHARING

Monteforte

Lucia was spending all her free time in the library at the castle. Her aunt who loved knowledge, and was a highly intelligent woman, had amassed an extensive collection of books, both ancient and contemporary. She would tell Lucia that it was very difficult to be a woman and run an immense empire. She would say, "Listen to me Bella, you must be knowledgeable on all subjects. È necessario essere a volte una civetta, un architetto e un mercante, forse tutti in una volta, ma si deve sempre essere quello di controllo. Capito?" It was so important that Lucia understand her place in the world, of running an empire like Monteforte, with its array of business and political connections, and ultimately to become the Mistress of Monteforte. She grasped the concept that at times she would have to be perceived as a flirtatious young beauty, yet capable of overseeing the construction of a new shipyard or vineyard, or meeting with her various merchants who exported her wares. She knew she must have the knowledge and courage to stand up to the responsibility of being a wealthy woman. To possess the knowledge to be wise and sometimes ruthless, yet to be honest and just, not only for her own sake, but also for all who depended on her ability to lead. The thought of it thrilled and frightened her at the same time.

Professor Umberto Fragoli, like several others, would come daily to give her and Antoinetta lessons. Professor Fragoli was Lucia's favorite. He was a middle aged man, handsome in an academic way. His hair, which he wore in as neat queue, showed a distinguished greying at the temple, and he had a thin mustache. He was tall and thin and had good straight teeth. He was dark with a swarthy complexion. Lucia thought that he could have been an athlete when he was younger. His body was still fit and appeared muscular even under this coat. Overall, he was quite pleasant in both appearance and personality. The thing that made Professor Fragoli stand out from the others was his sense of adventure. He had told them stories of how he had travelled all over the world. He had gone on expeditions to Egypt and the Orient. His next big adventure was to go to America.

Lucia, still filled with the hunger to explore the cave, but, anxious to learn the secret of how it could glow in the dark. in the middle of the sea. After her lesson, when Antoinetta left to get a cooking lesson from Marcello, Lucia stayed back. The professor, sensing that there was a lurking question in her mind inquired, "Mistress is there something you wished to ask?" Lucia took a deep breath as if contemplating whether she wanted to bring the teacher knowledge of her discovery. She knew she needed to acquire information, so she asked, as generally as she could. "Yes, professor, there is something I would like to know. One of Mistress Sucretti's exporters was here not so long ago and he was telling me a story of a place he had been, where there was a cave carved out of the sea that glowed bright as sunlight. I dismissed him as making a fantasy to entertain me, but he swore on his mother's eyes that such a place existed. Do you know of such a place?"

The Professor looked amused at her question, sat down, crossing one long slender leg over the other, and took out a cigar. Carefully, he reached into his pocket, extracted a small sharp knife, and cut the tip of the cigar. Then he took the object and put it into his mouth to moisten the dry outside leaves. He then reached for one of the tapers that were in the stand on the table and slowly he turned the cigar in his mouth, the flame of the candle licking the tip and ever so surely it caught on fire. He removed it from the flame and fanned the smoke while concentrating on keeping it lit. Finally, the tip glowed like hot embers, and he sucked the smoke into his mouth, creating small rings when he exhaled. The ritual completed, he sat back and looked Lucia straight in the eye.

"Yes, it is true. I have been to such a place." Lucia's eyes grew wide and she felt her pulse race. "Where is such a place?" Professor Fragoli was a teaser, but a skilled teacher and avid storyteller. He enjoyed the learning process as much as his students did. He loved Lucia's thirst for learning, and always paid special attention to her interests. He took his time in answering, sitting in his chair making rings with his cigar smoke. Lucia rather enjoyed the smell of the smoke and inhaled deeply. "I was a young student at university, and several of my fellows decided to go fishing. We set off in two small boats. It was a beautiful day and the fish were plentiful. Suddenly, as is the nature of the sea, the weather, with little warning, changed; the sky grew dark and the water rough. We were pretty far out for such tiny boats. My friends in the other boat started to row back to shore. Me, and my friend, were doing so well with our catch, we told them to go ahead, and that we would meet them up later. They warned us not to stay too long. We agreed, but the catch was too enticing, and we needed the money, so we stayed back. After short time, just as quickly as it came, the sea got calm and a brilliant ray of light came over the place where we were; relieved, we lost all sense of fear of the storm. Then, in moments, everything changed. A wave the size of a mountain erupted from the water. All we could see was a wall of water crashing down upon our tiny boat. We knew that if we separated we would die. Quickly, we tied a rope around our waist, joining us together. We managed to stay afloat during the first onslaught of the crashing waves. Our boat, which was barely seaworthy to begin, was threatening to sink. We were scooping water out but there was no help for it." At this point Professor Fragoli stopped to pour himself a glass of wine from the decanter that was on the library table. He poured a half glass for Lucia as well, and offered it to her with a sad smile. Lucia accepted the glass and was happy for it; her mouth was dry with anticipation of the story. She could see that his eyes were bright, but there was a sense of forlorn sadness behind them.

He drank deeply from the glass, and closed his eyes for a second. Lucia thought to herself that he was either trying to recall the story, or, trying to forget what happened. Taking a deep inhale on his cigar, which, had almost gone out, he once again took up the story. "It was only a minute later, when the boat was plucked up by the next wave, and shattered into kindling sticks, and we were thrust into the roiling sea. We kicked and stroked as hard as we could. We could see there was a small outcrop just ahead. We were sure we could make it; after all, we were young and strong, and very good swimmers. The one thing we did not count on was the pulling of the under current. It was dragging us to the bottom. My friend panicked with overwhelming fear; he was thrashing about like a caught fish. His struggling was weighting me down as well. I had my fishing knife in my waist, and gave thanks to Saint Michael that I had not lost it yet. I tried desperately to keep him afloat, but he was insane with fear. He was flailing and kicking with all his remaining strength to fight back the ominous waves. Finally, when he could go no further, he looked at me and said, "Tell my mother I love her" and he ducked his head down under the water. The last thing I saw were his eyes looking blindly at me. He was bigger and heavier than I was, and his now dead body was pulling me down. I had to break free from him, before I too would drown. Franticly I sawed through the rope that bound us together. The knife was wet and slippery, and I almost lost it in the struggle. At last, I managed to sever the rope that attached us. Philipe was already dead, and drifted, as if carried on angel's wings to the bottom. I watched in horror, as he daintily danced down into the blackness of the sea. Panic and sorrow clutched at me. Every muscle, every instinct for survival was telling me to go on. When the waves would recede, I could see the small mass of land, which was my goal. With no strength of body or mind I kept going, pushing myself beyond all endurance, praying to the Blessed Mother for her protection."

A small bead of sweat had formed on Professor Fragoli's forehead and he was breathing rapidly. Lucia so caught in the passion of his telling of the story that she could feel her own body tense, and the air was filled with the scent of anticipation. He took another long swill from the glass, as did Lucia. His cigar had since gone out and he once again placed it to the flame of the candle, and Lucia watched as he carefully, slowly, turned it to have it catch the flame. She could see him trying to take control of himself with the distraction of lighting the cigar. She quietly waited, saying nothing to break his concentration of the telling of the story.

Satisfied that the cigar was ready, he took in a deep drag and filled his mouth with smoke, and slowly exhaled through his mouth and nose. He did not make rings, but she could see that he felt the comfort from the act of smoking. This was serious business and there was no need for frivolity. He resumed the story, watching Lucia's rapt attention, but not receiving any joy in its telling, yet Lucia knew he felt compelled to recount its details.

"I made it to the shore of the little outcropping. I was beat and broken. I had lost my friend and almost my own life. What should have been relief and joy for my own survival was clouded by my deep sorrow for the loss of my best friend. I laid there on the small patch of earth, the sky dark as night and the wind howling in my ears. It started to rain. No, it was more than just rain; it was the sea coming down from the sky. I knew I had to hide, to find some sort of shelter. On hands and knees, I crawled around, desperately trying to find some place to wait out the storm. I found a hole in the ground big enough for me to crawl into. It was dark and I imagined all types of creatures that might be lurking inside, but, I had to get out of the storm, or I would have been sucked into it, and cast to the sea. As my eyes adjusted to the darkness, I realized I could move about inside, it was rather large. I was fairly close to the mouth of the hole, and the wind was viciously pounding the rain into the opening. I was still getting wet. The tide was drifting into the opening and filling the space. There was about a foot of standing water. I thought that if it continued it would fill and I would be trapped. I was cold and shivering, from both fear and exhaustion. I ventured deeper into the hole, which I soon realized was a cave. The water level was receding, the further I progressed into the blackness. Finding a dry spot to rest, I sat down, with no strength left within me, curled up and fell asleep. I do not know how long I was sleeping, but awoke disorientated, confused, as if waking from a nightmare. I hysterically moved about the cave searching for something or someone. I was ragging with fever, and my mouth was so parched blisters had formed. I needed water, and soon. My head ached and the blood pounded in my ears. My clothing was all tattered and I had several deep gashes on my body. I ached all over. My eyes nearly shut closed, and my throat was raw. I needed to find water. I needed to find help, but where?

I thrashed about, colliding with the wall and it made me fall back and knocked what little breath I had out of me, but it made me stop moving. I laid there on my back, the storm roaring at the mouth of the cave. I looked up and saw that it was not black as a deep well. There was some kind of light ahead, yet I could see that it was still dark outside. Fear came to cover me like a shroud. Dove sono stato? Ero morto? Was I dead and this was hell. I touched my body it felt real. So real in fact, that I had pain everywhere. Was this a terrible nightmare? I was inconsolable. I sat there in the darkness and cried. After I could cry no more I determined that if I was not dead, which did not seem to be possible, that if I wanted to live, which I was not sure that I did, I would have to get out of there.

For her part, Lucia, now sitting raptly on the settee, her legs balled under her gown, waited in silence, her mind racing, her own mouth dry with expectation to learn about the cave and the mysterious light emanating from within. She must not betray herself by acting too nervous. She tried to set her face to a neutral expression but one of academic interest. Lucia knew she was such a terrible liar she could never hide her feelings, her face always gave her away. She would try to keep herself under control. She had to.

The Professor, in no hurry to finish his story, sat anchored to the chair. His eyes closed as if living the nightmare all over again, drew a long, solid puff from his cigar expelling the air with its pungent fragrance. Fixing his stare at the recumbent young woman before him, he smiled ever so slightly, and resumed his tale. His voice was low and strained with emotion. "When I collected my wits I looked about and saw that there was an opening in the rock from where the light was coming. My first thought was that I had stumbled into the shelter of a hermit. I had heard stories of how some men wandered off and never returned making their homes in caves. I was not afraid but I knew I needed to be cautious. I crawled over to the opening and saw that it was large enough for me to crawl through. I poked my head into the opening and was startled to see that it was bright as day. I quickly looked back over my shoulder to take a bearing on my location and to confirm that it was still dark outside. What kind of devil magic was this? Light in a cave in the middle of the sea surely this was some kind of mystical lair. I tried to be calm after all I had studied at the university and held considerable knowledge. I could not let tales of demon serpents and mermaids disrupt my mind. However, in the end there was no help for it. The sight before me captivated me. An enchantingly magnificent illumination filled the space and basked me in its warm glow. A feeling of serenity mesmerized me. I rationalized that the storm was still howling only a few feet from where I stood, yet, there was no sign of its presence within the safety of this place. It was a universe unto itself. Isolated and protected by the sea its secret safely hidden by nature. I felt like a child that was nestled inside its mother's womb, all fear cleansed from my mind. It was hauntingly quiet even the raging roar of an embittered sea could not disturb the beauty of the place. I truly thought that I had died and this was Heaven.

I saw that I could stand, the ceiling height was voluminous. A glow, so luminous, so tranquil, permeated the cavity of the space. It was not like daylight. There was no sun. It was like moonlight when you are on the water, its light reflected and glimmering off the water. Soft subtle weightless and buoyant light cascading effortlessly on all that it touched. Words could not adequately express its essence. I stood there transfixed by its beauty, caressed by its serenity, and prayed that if I were dead that this would be my Heaven. After a short while, the academic within me came to grips with the enormity of my situation. Here I was, stranded in the middle of the sea. Two of my compatriots were safe back home. They of course knew that we were still out to sea. Would they send help? Would they assume that we drowned in the storm? An overwhelming sense of dread came over me as I made my assessment of my present situation. My best friend was dead, swallowed by the sea, and here I stood alone in a cave that glowed with a mystical power. I had no boat, no food, no water, and no means of calling for help. How far was I from shore? What was I to do?

I looked around and saw that there were small mollusks attached to the rocks. I liked eating them at home so why not here. I thanked the Blessed Mother and all the Saints that I still had possession of my knife. I pried off one and dug out the savory little morsel of flesh. I had never eaten one raw, but I rationalized that it was much the same as eating a clam or oyster. It tasted good. I was hungry. I started a frenzy of gathering and shucking as many as I could find. Once I had my fill, I was thirsty. There was a little bubbling sound coming from the base of one of the walls. I gingerly began a thorough investigation of my surroundings. To my utter amazement there, fixed at the base of a wall was a bubbling little stream of water. It glowed. I was afraid but put my finger into the stream. It lit up. How strange and wondrous? When I removed the finger, it stopped glowing. I did it again but this time with my whole hand. When I removed my hand, it was wet and I brought it to my nose and sniffed. There was no odor of fetid purification or any other smell, so I tasted it. It was not salty. I thought to myself here I am dying of thirst but there is a source of water for me to drink. Logically, I knew that if I did not have water soon I would surely die. Why not? So, I made the sign of the cross, invoked Jesus and His Blessed Mother and cupped my hands to the source of the glowing liquid. I closed my eyes and licked the water. It was the most fabulous water I have ever drunk. Greedily, I knelt down and lapped up my fill wondering of course if my innards were now glowing. It did not matter at this point. Once I had my fill, I washed my face, and cleansed the small wounds that I had sustained during the storm. I was now fed, watered, and clean. It was time to formulate a plan of escape.

Going back through the opening in the rock, I waded against the shallow pool of standing water. As I neared the mouth of the cave, I could see that the storm had subsided and the sea was calm. I looked up to the sky, which was a cloudless blue. The smell of fresh sea air filled my nostrils and I renewed of mind and spirit. I came out and saw a small patch of grass, which slipped into the sea, covered with sandy silt. Crabs and starfish, and other little sea creatures were either lying or scrabbling along the miniature beach. It was the most picturesque sights I had ever seen. Life was good, I was alive, the storm had passed, and now I must make my way home. I found the highest spot on this little outcropping, and surveying the surrounding area, was shocked to see that I was but a few kilometers from the mainland. Assessing the distance, I was sure that I could swim to shore. I did."

Professor Fragoli stopped, hesitated, and then said with such emotion, that his voice was palpable "I have never, not once, shared this story with anyone. You may be wondering why. The finding of that cave, the sparing of my life, and the memory of my dead friend, were too personal to share with anyone. What I experienced was a gift bestowed upon me by God." Lucia, tears cascading down that alabaster skin, those blue eyes intense upon his face simply said, "I know." They gazed upon each other searching for solace, sharing a kindred feral knowledge of something so strange and exotic, each holding a mystical awareness within themselves of this secret, so precious a gift that they were unable to share it with others. Professor Fragoli was stunned and relieved all at once. "How? When? Where?" His eyes searched her face, and he waited, until she had collected herself before she answered.

Lucia felt it was strange that someone should know exactly how she felt. Professor Fragoli's confession was just the insight she needed to tell him about her own experience in the grotto. She let a few moments pass before she spoke. "I was out riding one day and came to the end of our property line. It cascades down to the water. It was very hot that day and so I decided to take a swim. I discovered a small cove and swam up to it only to find a grotto in the cliff face. I entered, the water being shallow and clear I found that I was actually walking on some kind of manmade tile. The grotto was deep and led to an anteroom with the same design on the floor. I also found stairs that had been carved from the rock wall that leads to the surface above."

The excitement of telling her own story was intriguing, her teacher sat enraptured by the tale. He, like Lucia, did not interrupt but anxiously waited for the details. Lucia was speaking rapidly from both nerves and eagerness. Professor Fragoli was puffing his cigar, chewing the end and watching her intently. Those expressive eyes, the color of the sea, mirrored her emotions. Lucia sat up straight on the settee, leaning forward, the teacher leaning inward, and her voice low as if she needed to whisper.

"The glow was such a magnificent shade of blue. It cast a blue tint on the surface of all the rocks, floor and of course the water, which reflected it back into a prism of many brilliant hues. What was the color of your cave?" The teacher was never disappointed with the depth of perception in Lucia's mind. He had not realized that the color he had experienced in his cave was a fabulous shade of emerald green.

"My cave glowed the color of the precious stone, emerald, but, not a strong, steady, intense color; it grew and lessened in color and shade. I am surprised that these caves can have different colors. Perhaps it has to do with the water temperature, rock formation and the level of phosphorous in the shale. It is the phosphorous, a chemical element, which occurs naturally, that, causes the glowing phenomena. Its name comes from the Greek *light bearer* and from the Latin *Lucifer.* This chemical element is essential to life. After my own encounter in the cave, I did an extensive study of the subject. So far, man has recorded five locations on Earth where these caves exist. In all my studies I did not find any mention of either my own location or where you just described, however, if I come to understand you correctly human beings have inhabited your cave. Yes?"

Lucia was so engrossed in what her teacher was saying she almost missed the question. He repeated it. "People, humans, have made your cave?" Shaken from her reverie, Lucia thought for a second then answered. "Yes. I believe it was here for centuries, or at least a very long time. But I did not tell you the rest of my story." Professor Fragoli looked bemused. "There is more?" Lucia smiled, pleased with herself. "When I was exploring the cave, there suddenly occurred a deafening rumble, and then a putrid smell of sulphur infused the air and I gagged. It was then instantly followed by a tremendous shower of hot mist, which sprang from a small hole in the rock face. As quickly as it came, that is as fast as it went away, leaving a hot fine vapor clinging to the air." She finished with a sigh and her shoulders finally relaxed.

Professor Fragoli with the telling of the final part of the story moved to the edge of his chair. "Are you saying that there was a natural spring, a sulphur spring, in the cave?" His tone was a little more intense than he meant it to be. Lucia looked astounded, as if she were being interrogated. She hesitated, and then jumped into the answer. "Yes. I believe it is, but of course, with no foreknowledge of such a thing, I cannot be certain." They sat there for just a few minutes, in silence, each formulating their own thoughts and conclusions on the subject.

At last, Professor Fragoli spoke softly to Lucia, not as her teacher, but as someone who has shared a similar life altering experience. "Perhaps, you and I could return to your cave and see it once more, and maybe find out who had dwelled there so long ago?" The exuberant Lucia, filled with dreams of adventure, jumped up off the settee and bounded over to the startled teacher. She threw her arms around his neck and kissed his cheek. "Yes. Oh, Yes. Quando possiamo andare?" She demanded to know when they might go. The teacher caught off guard laughed and said "Soon, very, soon. We must prepare, but we must do so in private. Not everyone will understand or appreciate this gift. Understand?" Lucia fully comprehended his meaning; she too felt that to bring others to this sacred place would be a violation of some holy trust. "Ti prometto che sarà presto. It will be soon," said her teacher.

CHAPTER NINE

THE EXPEDITION

Monteforte

It was agreed that Lucia and Professor Fragoli would go separately to the meeting place not to arouse suspicion. They were to meet in three days at the furthest point on the Monteforte estate. Lucia gave her teacher instructions "Professor you must ride your horse taking the footpath that follows the cliffs. Proceed with caution, for if it should rain the night before, it will be very dangerous. Your horse may be reluctant to climb down from the steep escarpment, but if you go around the edge of the property, just a little further, it gradually tapers down to the sea. I will bring some food and a change of clothing. We will have to swim to the grotto. Is this acceptable to you?" Lucia asked this as a courtesy, but knew her teacher would not miss this opportunity to experience the cave for anything.

Professor Fragoli, not used to taking instruction, gave a sly smile to his prized student. "Hai imparato bene mia piccola bellezza dai capelli rossi. Yes I understand what will be required. Is there anything that I should bring?" Lucia was slightly taken back by his familiarity in addressing her as a redheaded beauty, and lowered her eyes and said, "Yes, if you could bring some implement to dig out the steps, so we can see where they lead." The teacher, instinctively ran his fingers over his mustache when he was in deep thought, grinned then responded, "Ah, I almost forgot about that. Yes, I can come with some type of tool. It is set;

we meet at sunrise on Wednesday.I am very anxious."
Lucia could hardly contain her excitement "Until
Wednesday then."

Tuesday night Lucia tossed, turned, and slept
very little. When she did finally manage to fall asleep,
she had strange dreams of being trapped within a
watery grave. She woke with a start, and was soaked
in sweat, yet she shivered with chills. Unable to get back
to sleep, Lucia got dressed and went down to the
kitchens. It was early but already there was much
activity. Carlo, the baker, was kneading dough for the
daily bread, Loretta was in the hen house gathering
eggs, and Giorgio was overseeing the delegation of
chores for the rest of the staff. Upon seeing Lucia, he
dismissed the small group he had been talking to and
came over. "Mistress Lucia, good morning, is there
something I can do for you? It is very early are you
well?" Lucia gave a little chuckle at Giorgio's concern
but answered, "I'm fine. I could not sleep, so I decided
to come down for an early breakfast. Can you have
them prepare something simple for me? Oh, by the way,
I will be taking Apollo for a long run today, please
prepare a large basket, enough for two. I like to give
him treats when we ride for a long time. You
understand. I apologize for disrupting you so early."

Giorgio, like the rest of the staff, loved Lucia. He
knew that Mistress Sucretti had chosen her as the next
mistress of the manse yet that is not what drew him to
her. Lucia was kind, but unbending in her sense of
honor and loyalty. She possessed all the qualities that
a woman in her position would need to sustain her
control over such a vast empire. "Of course Mistress, I
will have them prepare your breakfast immediately, and
would you like it served on the veranda? The sun is just
over the cliffs, it will be lovely just now. We shall have
a basket for you to take with bread, cheese, salami,

apples and wine. Is that acceptable?" "Oh yes Giorgio, but, could you squeeze in a little dolci." Giorgio laughed heartily "That would have been the surprise. Ah, now you spoiled it." Lucia turned to leave then quickly remembering said to him "I will also need zollette di zucchero e due carote. Apollo, he's big and eats a lot, he loves his sugar and carrots." "Don't you worry that pretty head, Giorgio will see to everything. Ah, Mistress, be careful near the cliffs."

After eating her breakfast, Lucia went to the stables. The smell of hot manure and damp hay always made her relax. There was something about the sights, sounds, and smell of a stable that calmed her nerves. The grooms were busy shoveling shit and pitching hay, but all movement stopped when they saw Lucia. Giorgio had sent the basket ahead, and instructed Gandolfo to have Apollo ready for his mistress. Lucia was thrilled that all had been prepared. "Good morning Mistress Lucia you are up with the sun today. Apollo is already to go and very excited. Where are you going so early?" Lucia loved the old man because he loved horses and took exceptional care of Apollo.

"Apollo and I are going for a long run. With all the dolce I give him he needs the exercise." Gandolfo laughed heartily, "You spoil him Mistress." Lucia thanked the groom who brought the saddled Apollo to her. The horse was whinnying madly, and he prodded her pocket, where the stash of sugar was kept. Lucia hugged the big muscular neck, scratched his long nose, and dug in for his treat. Gandolfo cupped his hands and boosted her into her saddle. "Mistress it rained last night. If you are riding the cliffs be very careful." Lucia had not realized that it had rained; even in her restless state, she had not heard the rainfall. "Don't worry Gandolfo, I am aware and shall be mindful of where I ride. I will see you before supper. Have a good day." She started out of the stable and was called by one of the grooms, "Mistress you forgot your basket" he shouted and ran after her with the heavy bundle. "Oh thank you Piro." The young groom, he was about seventeen, looked with cow eyes at his mistress. He was in love, but there was no help for it. Handing up the basket he brushed her hand and sighed. Lucia was oblivious of his attentions, her mind focused on the day's mission. Off she cantered with a contented Apollo.

The ground, before reaching the cliff side path, was firm and Apollo galloped merrily. He loved to run and stretch his powerful legs. It was a pleasant day, not so hot, but it was still very early. Lucia loved to ride early in the morning, there was a certain peace that filled the air. As they were coming up on the cliff path, Lucia reined him up just a little, so he could test his own footing. Apollo had a keen sense and slowed himself down. The ground was slick, with a mixture of the morning dew from the mountains, and the rain that had fallen during the night. It was slippery, but the big animal found his footing. Apollo knew too well the dangers of the cliffs, having nearly plunged over them once. His ears twitched, his head moving from side to side, as if shrugging off an annoying insect. He stomped the ground, but with a gentle nudge in his side, he prodded on.

Now, Lucia's thought went to Professor Fragoli, and she feared for his safety along this path. She had warned him of the dangers, and hoped he had heeded her instructions of taking the longer route to the far side of the estate. It was early and she had time to worry. Slowly they trekked down to the scrubby sand patch that slipped into the sea at the outer perimeter of Monteforte. As she made her approach, to her amazement, Professor Fragoli was already there, sitting on a patch of grass smoking his cigar. He had on homespun clothing and just a linen shirt, breeches and no neck cloth or waistcoat; he looked much younger than he usually did. Seeing her, he immediately stood, removed his cap and bowed slightly. Coming to take the reins, and give her a hand off the massive stead. Apollo was apprehensive and made to bite the teacher, but Lucia clicked her tongue and patted his neck and he calmed down. Professor Fragoli had stepped back to avoid being bitten. "Good Moring Mistress Lucia, I see you bring your own bodyguard with you. He is a fine animal." " Ah, good morning Professor. I was worried for you with the path being so slick. This is my friend Apollo."

Lucia was now off her horse and went to hobble him near the professor's horse. Both animals were very excited to have a companion. Once again, Lucia dug into her pocket, and retrieved two lumps of sugar, one for each horse. She left the lunch basket tied to her saddle. Lucia was suddenly embarrassed at the thought of removing her gown so that she could swim.

"Professor I must apologize, but I must remove my gown, so that we can swim to the cave." Her teacher waved his hand, as if in dismissal of the awkwardness of this action, and said, "Of course, do not feel embarrassed, I understand. Your honor and privacy are safe with me." Quickly she stripped down to her shift, but this time had prepared herself by wearing pantaloons under her shift. Lucia gathered her wild mane of fiery curls, and twisted them into a tight bun at the back of her neck, which she secured with several small combs. Finally organized, she addressed her companion. "Shall we begin our adventure?" Her eyes, those penetrating orbs that were the color of an azure sea, were dancing with anticipation. For his part, the professor had busied himself while Lucia was making her preparations, trying not to watch as she stripped down to her shift.

"Avanti`!"

Professor Fragoli weighted down with a canvas sack, which Lucia assumed held some kind of pick or shovel. He had his dagger secured in his waist belt, and at the sight of it, Lucia ran over to her horse and fetched her own small dagger from the leather pouch she always carried on her saddle. Nervously, she waded into the water, which was calm and refreshing. Her teacher followed, but soon caught up with her, and in little time, they were within sight of the grotto. When they came to the mouth of the cave, the teacher stopped. "Are you sure you want to do this?" Lucia who knew that she had to continue simply responded, "I must." He did not answer, but closed his eyes for a moment, then nodded his head in agreement. Lucia made the sign of the cross and silently invoked the blessings of Saint Michael, Saint Lucia and the Blessed Mother. Cara madre tenerci al sicuro. With a deep breath, she led the way. Entering the cave was like being swallowed by a monstrous sea creature. Once her eyes adjusted to the darkness, she found her bearings. It seemed so familiar, yet so strange. The last time she was in this place she had been alone, now bolstered with the presence of someone who shared her secret, she did not feel the desperate fear and loneliness. Lucia did not look to see if the professor had followed her, she knew he was there. It took a few moments before their pupils had dilated sufficiently to let them focus in the diminished light.

It was just as she had remembered. The water was clear, and looking down at her feet, which were submerged in water up to her calves, she could clearly see the tiled pattern she so vividly remembered. Professor Fragoli was now beside her, and he crouched down to touch the floor. He gently touched his fingers to the tile tracing the pattern, his eyes following its course. "I cannot imagine who would have created such work." Lucia did not answer but proceeded deeper into the belly of the cave, and he silently came along.

Just now, they reached the opening in the rock wall. Lucia stepped aside and beckoned her teacher to come forward. "Look inside." The man ducked his head through the hole and gave out a slight gasp. He shivered but stayed mute. He kept still and just watched for a short while. Then, having found his composure, entreated his student "Lucia, shall I go first?" Lucia's mouth was dry with emotion; she coughed to clear her voice. "If you wish, I shall be close behind." She felt that it was important for him, as a man, as an older person, to go first. She understood his feeling of protection.

The professor was an agile, lean man and easily slipped through the opening. She handed over the canvas satchel, which she thought was heavy. He waited for her to make her passage through the hole. They stood there in rapt exhilaration. There was no need to speak. They were absorbing the sense of the place, its essence permeating their souls. With no further hesitation, the trance broken, they separated and walked around the enclosure. The illumination from the rocks was lighting their way. Again, like the first time she came, the tile floor was free of water save the slick film of algae that coated its surface.

Now, for the first time since he entered over the side the teacher spoke. His voice strained with emotion, his eyes watery with grief, "Lucia, this is too magnificent. Look at the work, the effort it must have taken to construct this place. I cannot thank you enough for sharing this with me." Lucia was beaming. She directed him to the spot where she had encountered the belching mist. As if by mental will, the thing started to rumble. At first, it was a low rumble, then building into a deafening roar. It gushed out a tremendous plume of hot, fetid smelling, mist. They each lurched back to avoid being scalded. The professor was intrigued; the scientist within him was coming to grips with the situation. "I did not encounter such a thing as this when I had my own experience. It is wondrous. There must be an underground spring that feeds into here. I must look closer." Lucia was frightened. "Be careful Professor." He nodded, but was already examining the wall from which the eruption had come.

His hands were intensely searching for the source of the spring. He reached down into the gap from whence the mist spewed, and to his shock, found a lever. He said nothing, but grasped the lever to pry it free. It was stuck, but he dug in his heels, and with all his strength grasped hold of it and pulled. It gave way, and he fell back on his haunches, losing his balance and landed on his ass. With an immediate retraction, it groaned, scraped, and slowly pushed back the rock wall.

Lucia was not paying attention to what her teacher was doing; she was looking for the steps, which she wanted to start digging. Hearing the curse and thud of her companion she turned instantly to see what had happened. "Professor, are you alright?" The answer was overridden by the exposure of a room that had appeared through the rock formation. "What?" she huffed. Her whole body was shaking. How was this possible that was a solid rock wall? Lucia looked with utter incredulity at her teacher who responded likewise. They were both in a state of bewilderment.

They peered through the aperture with wide eyes trying to absorb all they saw. Without preamble, Professor Fragoli entered the room. Lucia followed closely. Fear, was the first emotion that washed over them. It was a large room, it glowed with the brightness of an unearthly light, which bathe everything in a warm blue tint. The ceiling was twenty or more feet high. There were paintings, no not paintings, but mosaic designs, which decorated almost every inch from the ceiling to the floor. The detailing was so beautiful and intricate of composition. It was like walking into a church.

They stood silently in awe, absorbing all they saw, wondering, and imaging what they had discovered. There was granite tables and stone benches grouped to one side. Along the far wall were scrolls, books, and manuscripts, many of them thrown about in a pile as if the inhabitants had left in a hurry. On the tables were quills and gourds, used to hold ink, their bowls stained from the liquid. It smelled of old leather and dry parchment with the underlying stench of sulphur. What was this place? The scene before them, thinking it could have been a present day monastery anywhere in the world, fascinated them.

Professor Fragoli went to examine the manuscripts, of which there were hundreds, all rolled and neatly stacked upon stone shelves. Lucia was right by his side. He gently, reverently, picked one up, with the skill of a surgeon placed it on one of the tables, and unrolled it. His hand trembled with excitement. Lucia looking over his shoulder was dumb struck. "What language is this? I have never seen such writing. Have you?" The Professor was intensely examining the object that lay upon the table. With his finger, he traced the letters, each one meticulously inscribed, rendered by a learned hand. He was stroking the parchment with the touch of a mother on her newborn babe. Lovingly, he caressed the document, gazing with soft warm eyes at its content. Lucia was anxious to know what manner of language was this and broke the silence. "Professor, what is it?"

Without leaving his gaze from the parchment the teacher, his voice shallow said, "I believe these are ancient Byzantine manuscripts. For centuries past, the Greeks had come to Southern Italy to escape persecution and for their freedom. They brought with them the knowledge of Aristotle. You will remember that Aristotle was a famous philosopher and worshipped with the same fervor as a God. The Byzantine monks highly sought after for their ability to translate those ancient texts in what was then modern day Latin. One of the largest concentrations of Byzantine monks was here in Naples. I cannot be sure but I would wager that these were some of the lost ancient manuscripts." Professor Fragoli's enthusiasm was palpable, Lucia could feel it coursing through his body and spilling over to her own.

Lucia could hardly contain her excitement. "Do you mean we have discovered something ancient and very important?" He took in a gulp of air and exhaled slowly "If these are authentic, and, I cannot imagine they are not, they will be a significant scientific discovery. We must be careful not to tell anyone about this until we are sure. These manuscripts will be destroyed, if not cared for properly. They are priceless antiquities and must be treasured for their value to human development." Lucia was shaking at the thought that they held something so important in their possession, that it would change history. She did not speak. She could not imagine the ramifications of this discovery. "What shall we do?" The teacher, astounded by what he was looking at, hesitated then replied, "We must collect two or three samples and have them examined by experts on the subject of historical authenticity. Once they confirm what I believe to be the true nature of these documents, we will then approach the Department of Antiquities for permission to remove them and send them to a museum of our choosing. Do you agree?" Lucia was quiet. She was contemplating the course of their actions and the simple plan that her teacher had expressed. She took her time in answering but then came to a decision. "I agree that we must be sure that these are what we think they are. However, since this property lies on the estate of Monteforte it is the property of my family, and I will do nothing without my aunt's permission. If she agrees, once we have the documents examined, that they go to a museum, then, and only then, we will proceed. Agreed?"

The man stood there with his mouth open, stunned at the authority and sense of possession in his student's demeanor. He shook himself then realized that this young girl was now truly a woman. Lucia would be a woman who would command the vast empire that belonged to her family with fierce respect for what was her domain. He was impressed with the maturity she had just demonstrated. Bowing, he looked her straight in the eye and said, "I do apologize Mistress Lucia for presuming to make any plan without your express consent. I must admit that my enthusiasm at this find has clouded my judgment. I would never do anything to undermine Mistress Sucretti's lawful claim, this is after all, part of the family estate."

Lucia satisfied with his response continued. "Which of the manuscripts shall we take? In addition, more importantly, I think we should now try to dig out those steps. If they lead to where I think they do, we will prevent these precious documents from exposure to the sea water." Again, the teacher overwhelmed by the intelligence of this young woman, made a mental note never to underestimate her. "Let us see. I agree with your assessment of the situation to expose these ancient documents to the water, which might destroy them. We must be extremely careful of how we handle them, since for all these years they were preserved by the steam from the spring. The moisture from the mist has kept the papyrus lubricated, or they would have crumbled into dust."

Leaving the rolled manuscript on the table the professor joined Lucia in the outer chamber where she had first seen the steps. He removed a pick from the canvas bag he had carried into the cave. Carefully he started scratching at the imbedded earth. Little by little, clumps of sod were raining upon them. Lucia took the hoe from the bag, and began piling the debris to one side. It was hard work, and they had to proceed slowly, so as not to have the entire opening collapse upon them. They hacked away for what seemed hours, making painstaking progress. At last, they could see a small shaft of light above. Spurred on by the prospect of reaching their goal, they worked faster, a bit less mindful of a collapse. They now finished the job, and light rays cascaded down into the steep stairwell. At the top of the opening, the pick clanged hitting metal on metal. The professor, pleased with having succeeded in uncovering the mouth of the entrance, saw a heavy metal grate covered the opening, affixed with a rusted lock. He banged on the lock with all his might to pry it from its hinges, but to no avail, it would not budge.

"Lucia, we must go back the way we came and work the lock from the surface above. We have no leverage here in this narrow stairwell." They agreed that they could not affect the opening of the grate from their present position. "I feel guilty to expose this beautiful place to others who do not understand or appreciate its beauty. Is it wrong to desecrate this sacred place?" Lucia had tears rolling down her cheek. She was forlorn. "I understand how you feel my dear sweet Lucia. You are wise beyond your years, yet all great discoveries have under the right supervision, become knowledge for humanity. Sometimes possessing knowledge is both a treasure and a curse." "I just don't want to betray the beauty of this place. It feels so holy to me. However, I do understand our responsibility to history and to my family. We must proceed with caution. I know someone, a monk, who I will bring one of the manuscripts to and see what his opinion is. The other two I will entrust to your experience in the academic world."

Professor Fragoli now very aware that he was no longer in control, if he ever was, would abide by any decision Lucia made. Resigned to the fact that they could not release the grate from their present location, they decided to take three random manuscripts, secure the inner vault, and leave the way they came. "I have an idea," Lucia announced with some excitement. "I am sure I know where these steps begin. Let us wrap them carefully in the canvas bag and slip them through the grate, they will be on the outer side of this cave when we come around, that way we will be able to keep the grate secured until we are sure the manuscripts are ancient. What do you think Professor?"

Once again amazed at the clarity in Lucia's reasoning, and in full accord with the process, he acknowledged, "I think that is an excellent plan. Let us proceed." They chose two additional random manuscripts, together with the original they had first looked at. The professor, his shirt completely dry, removed it and wrapped the three precious documents within it, and then placed them carefully in the canvas bag. He then climbed the steep steps to the top of the grate, and slipped the bundle up through the slats. Perfecto!

When he came back down, he noticed that Lucia had gone back into the vault. He saw her kneeling in front of what he was sure was an ancient altar. In a stone niche` was a carved wooden cross so crude of design but powerful in its presence. Her head bowed in reverence as she prayed. He would not dare to disturb this moment for Lucia. He waited until she was done. Watching her walk up to the sacred spot, she placed her finger to the cross, and then leaned over to kiss it. Her hair had come down and the glow from the rocks shimmered on the vermillion tresses. Her alabaster skin reflected like fine porcelain. Lucia was so beautiful of body, mind, and soul. When he was sure she was done, he coughed politely to announce his presence. "Are you ready?" Lucia did not answer, but turned, imprinting the images on to her heart and soul, and then made for the opening. Climbing over the spring opening, she noticed that her teacher was shirtless. "What happened to your shirt?" Suddenly self-conscious, he stammered for a second then replied, "I used it to wrap the manuscripts before I placed them in the bag for protection." Lucia could not help but stare at his bare chest. Catching herself, she averted her eyes, "Oh that was very wise."

Professor Fragoli reached up under the spring's mouth and felt for the lever once again. Finding it secure in his hand, he pulled. It seemed easier to maneuver this time. Sure enough, it came to meet with the rest of the rock wall, blending seamlessly into the rock formation its entrance concealed from the world. Lucia let out her breath with a sense of relief that the sacred chamber was now once again safe and secluded. "I will leave these few tools for our next trip," announced the teacher. Lucia spent from emotional exhaustion just nodded.

Making their way out of the cave, they wadded into the shallow cove. The mild water felt refreshing on their skin, and Lucia was grateful for its washing of the fetid scent of the sulphur, which had given her a headache. As the sun dappled over her teacher's bare chest Lucia realized that he was very muscular, and a fine soft down of brown hair coated his chest. His abdomen was tight, and his homespun breaches were hanging so low that she could see the clutch of hair rising up from his belly button. He was a very attractive man. He caught her looking at him and he gave her a sly grin, she tried to look away but it was too late. The blush that was already on those beautiful cheeks grew in intensity. Lucia was embarrassed but her teacher was pleased that she had noticed his well-toned body.

They made their way back to the small sandy beach from whence they had embarked on their adventure. Both Apollo and the professor's horse grazed happily, but as soon as Apollo heard his mistress, he whinnied excitedly and stamped his feet. Emerging from the water, her shift clinging to her curvaceously supple body, her hair wild about her face and shoulders, the professor felt his blood rushing to all parts of his body, especially his lower extremities. He watched as the thin shift caressed her breasts, which were full and round and sat high with the nipples straining against the fabric. She had brought two linen towels. Lucia handed one to her teacher and with her own, she blotted the excess water from her face and body. She spread her towel on the tiny beach and reached to her saddle for the basket, which Giorgio had prepared for her earlier that morning.

"Come Professor. Let us have some refreshment. Sit here." The man felt he needed to chastise himself for the thoughts that were taking over his mind and body. Lucia's beauty was captivating, even to a man who was probably old enough, maybe even older, than her father. He felt awkward in his nakedness, and instead of sitting on the towel, he draped it over his shoulders. He bent his knees up to this chest to hide his physical yearnings. Lucia seemed aware of the situation, got up, and reached for her gown, which she had secured to her saddle. She pulled it on over her wet shift struggling to tie up the back laces. Seeing this little battle unfold, the teacher came behind her, and placing his hand over hers, took the laces and began tying them for her. He gathered her long wild curls and brushed them aside to have access to the loops. A man had never touched Lucia so familiarly, other than her father. She felt his breath on her neck but stood stone still. They both knew that one false move would be dangerous. When he finally reached the last loop, he pulled just a little tighter than Lucia would have liked, and let out a long breath. She turned "Thank you." Without any hesitation went back to the towel and sat down. She busied herself with taking out the linen sheet and placing the items from the basket upon it. Once the small buffet was laid, she asked the professor to open the bottle of wine. "Professor, would you please open the wine" as she handed it to him. Deftly, he withdrew his dagger from his belt and pried off the wax seal. There was only one glass "I'm sorry but Giorgio did not know that I would have a guest, there is but one glass." He smiled and said, "I will drink from the bottle."

They sat cordially for some time, sharing their meal, drinking their wine and reflecting on the events that had begun the day, but there was a tension hanging between them that was thick as fog. The teacher rationalized that he was too old and Lucia argued that she was too young, their thoughts preoccupying their minds. It was the teacher who broke the silence "Mistress Lucia, I want to tell you something, but I find that my words are not easy to speak." Lucia was going to interrupt him but he waved his hand to stop her, and she waited feeling awkward and uncomfortable. "I feel that certain feelings have passed between us. I know you sensed it also. I will not deny that I love you and could ravage you right now, right here. My body is trembling with the mere thought of touching you, but I will not. You are too perfect for such lust. I am an old man and you deserve a young prince. I cannot express my feelings of shame for what I might have impressed upon you. Can you forgive me?" Lucia knew the teacher had aroused her; it was her first foray into sexual arousal. She also knew that she would not give up her maidenhead for lust, when that day came it would be for love and love alone. Lucia met his eyes, her own azure blue windows to her soul now fully exposed, but yet, she met his straight on, with her voice deep and sultry "I did feel the attraction between us and I enjoyed it. It was the first time I had ever had such a desire but there will be no help for it. I will not give up my maidenhead for sexual pleasure, only for love." She could see that the usually arrogant academic, who was so sure of himself, was wounded and that hurt her. "Professor Fragoli, I respect you very much, and I am flattered to think that a man of your age and experience would have such feelings for me. I pray this does not change our plans, or more importantly, our respect for each other. I love you too, but I want to learn more from your mind than your body. I am not sure if I am saying the right words, but I hope so."

Imperceptibly the tension lifted. The teacher cocked his head and stared at his pupil. "I am not sure who has become the teacher and who the student. I have learned so much from you today. We will forget what might have been, and concentrate on our fantastic discovery. As soon as possible, without causing too much mischief, I will bring the manuscripts to two separate colleagues of mine. I will tell them that while on a trip to Greece I found them in an obscure book store, and if they could shed any light on their content and authenticity I would be most appreciative."

Lucia was so relieved that they had been forthright about their feelings. She did not want to compromise their relationship, but was thrilled at the experience. The teacher reached for her hand, which she slipped into his, and gently he kissed it. "You are so special; someday you will meet a man who will worship you."

After a little while, with Apollo getting anxious to leave, they decided that Professor Fragoli would go to Florence and Rome to seek out the two men he thought capable of judging the manuscripts. "I will not come back to Monteforte until I have the information we need. I shall make my excuses to Mistress Sucretti of having some pressing personal business, and with promises of returning shortly." Lucia had already risen from her linen towel and had packed all that was left into the basket was now anxious to leave.

The teacher, now standing very close to her, seemed suddenly a little shorter, but surely as handsome as before. He was still bare-chested and the sight left Lucia slightly dry mouthed. He was so close she could smell his manly sweat, which was glistening on his bare shoulders. She tried not to stare at him but could not help herself. Lucia grabbed hold of her pummel, and the teacher clasped his hands to boost her into the saddle. Her heart was racing and she had tiny droplets of sweat on her upper lip. His hand came to rest on her thigh and she shuddered. "I will see you in several months. Tell no one. Be careful." Lucia knew she must leave before she said or did something stupid. "Farewell Professor."

CHAPTER TEN

A BOOKBINDER

Milan

Dominic Fragoli had been many things in his thirty plus years, some of which he was definitely not proud of, but being a teacher had been one of the highlights of his life. Along the road of life, he had encountered a multitude of interesting and unsavory characters, who he considered acquaintances. One of those whom he had known from his youth was Antonio Sanfranco, a brilliant and learned man, who had a penchant for criminal dealings. Antonio and Dominic had grown up in the slums of Napoli. They were accomplished pickpockets, who realized early on that being intelligent and educated would be greater resources for stealing large sums of money, not simple coins. The professor knew the manuscripts in his possession where authentic and priceless. There were collectors and museums throughout the world that would pay a fortune for them. He thought about the lovely Lucia and felt a pang of sorrow. She was so vulnerable and trusting, he hated to deceive her, but she was young and would soon be the heiress of Monteforte. She would get over his betrayal and the theft of the manuscripts in time.

Dominic Fragoli arrived in Milan in the late evening. He went to an inn that he had stayed at many times. It was located in the heart of the city and offered not only clean rooms but other amenities as well. The proprietor remembered him, and gave him a familiar greeting. "Signore Fragoli, it is always a pleasure to have such an honored person such as yourself stay at our humble inn. Will you be here long Signore?" Dominic loved when people treated him like a gentleman of wealth and refinement, and on the outside he definitely would pass for both of those, but on the inside he was a ruthless thief. "It is good to be back Paolo. I am here on business for a day or two. Please bring my bags to my usual room." The young serving boy then escorted him to a room overlooking the square. He gave the boy a few coins and asked "What time do they serve breakfast?" The boy who could not have been more than ten said, "We start to serve at six o'clock in the morning. Will you be in need of anything else Signore Fragoli?" "Yes. Bring me a bottle of your best wine, some cheese, bread, and fresh olives. I would also require the company of a young woman someone young and pretty. Puoi fare velocemente?" The boy answered, "Ah, yes Signore Fragoli I will get everything you need very quickly." The boy turned on his heels and he heard him scurry down the stairs.

Dominic had not been with a woman in a long time, and just having spent some interesting time with Lucia, he felt his erection growing at the thought of her. He closed his eyes, remembering their encounter on the beach. The sight of her curvaceous young body caressed by her wet shift made him hard, and his hand went to his manhood. He was remembering the nipples of those full round breasts standing at attention, and the feel of her alabaster skin as he tied her corset. His hand was holding his rock hard erection, stroking the silken head with his thumb, when there came a loud rap at the door. Startled from his ministrations, he quickly put his swollen penis back in his breeches. "Come" was the chocked response. Standing there was the young boy straining under the weight of a loaded tray, and trailing behind him was a pretty young girl of perhaps fourteen or younger. She looked frightened.

"Signore, I have brought all that you have required. This is Carmela. If there is nothing else you require I will be leaving?" The teacher was watching the pretty Carmela, pushed into the room by the boy, who whispered in her ear and gave her a pinch on her arm. She grimaced but said nothing. "No, you have done well. Here is a little extra for getting it so quickly." The boy smiled broadly, and bowed with a deep formal foot. As the teacher was walking toward the door, the boy said softly "Signore, she is not so much experienced, you may have to beat her a little." The teacher replied "Ah, well thank you for the information. I will give her all the instruction she needs. Good night. Have someone call for me promptly by seven o'clock in the morning." "Very good Signore."

The teacher closed the door with a little more force than he would have wanted, and the pretty Carmela jumped. "Would you care to join me for some wine?" Dominic Fragoli could be quite charming when he desired. The girl just nodded her acceptance. When she reached for the proffered glass, her hand was shaking. The teacher rather enjoyed being the first to seduce a young woman. He liked them young and inexperienced; it gave him a certain power over them that he very much liked. "Come here Carmela let me see you better in the light." The girl did as she was told and came closer to where he was sitting; a candle cast a golden blush on her flawless olive skin. She had long black hair held in place by a bone comb. She was a classic Italian beauty with dark eyes shrouded by long thick lashes and a full mouth. She was petite and on the skinny side, but she presented herself very well.

"Take off your clothes." The girl was trembling so badly she could not get her fingers to undo her laces; he thought she was going to cry. "Here let me help you."

252

First, he undid her thick wavy hair tossing the comb aside. Gently, he started to unlace her bodice, kissing her neck and telling her "You are very lovely Carmela. I love your full mouth, and see how your tiny breasts respond to my touch. I am going to teach you something nice to do to men with that mouth. Do not be frightened, I will not hurt you if you do exactly what I say, and do what I want." Dominic enjoyed being the teacher. By now, the girl was completely naked and very embarrassed. He looked appraisingly at the child before him, and thought that she would become a beautiful woman. His hands were stroking her breasts and he pinched her taut little nipples. He slipped his finger between her legs, and she wiggled and squirmed until her baby clit was hard, and then she came panting in his hand. She made a nervous giggle. He commanded her to get on her knees as he stood in front of her, his sex inches from her pretty face. "Open your mouth very wide. I want you to take me into your mouth, as deep as you can, and move your head back and forth and rub your tongue over the head. Do it gently and do not bite. If you bite me, I will beat you very bad. Do you understand?" Carmela, paralyzed at the sight of his erection, but obediently did as she was told. Their evening proved most satisfactory for Dominic Fragoli who envisioned it was Lucia on her knees before him. After he had his way with the young Carmela, who was sore and crying, he sent her away to enjoy what few hours remained for his sleep.

The young serving boy roused the teacher from his sleep. "Signore, it is time to get up," announced the almost feminine voice from the hall. When he did not answer the boy gingerly came into the room. "Signore?" Dominic rolled over and opened one eye. "Oh yes. Is it seven o'clock already?" "Yes Signore Fragoli shall I have them start to prepare your breakfast?" The teacher who slept in the nude threw the covers off and got out of bed. The boy wide eyed at the sight of the naked man and marveled at the length of his cock. He saw him staring and stroked himself, the boy swallowed hard. "Signore, no wonder Carmela said she was in great pain. I have never seen such a size on a man before. Salute! Signore." The teacher laughed very heartily, "I have spoiled her for the next poor bastard with a little cock." The two stood there laughing, but the boy was not sure what he meant. "Go get my breakfast ready before I give you a feel of my big cock in your scrawny ass." The boy practically flew out the room and down the stairs.

When Dominic Fragoli came down to breakfast two of the older serving girls were staring at him, primarily his penis. Dominic was pleased as a peacock, that either the boy or Carmela had informed every one of the size of his manhood. He just laughed and winked at them and they blushed. A matronly older woman who reeked of fried onions and sweat served his breakfast. She had pushed up her breasts to seem more appealing. "Is there anything else I can get for you Signore? There is nothing I cannot do." She had her breasts practically falling out of her gown. Then there was a sharp thwack and the woman jumped from pain and surprise. "Get in the back" arose a deep growling voice from behind her. A look of horror plainly written all over her homely face, the man, a fat greasy looking older man with a meaty, dirty hand, pulled her by her braid with such force she almost feel over. "Can I get you anything else Signore?" growled the filthy, foul smelling cook. Dominic would not even dare to ask for water at this point. "No I am fine." The man huffed and as he was walking away, he was undoing his belt. A few moments later, he heard the muffled cries of a woman and the thwacking of a leather belt. The vision of that belt tanning that woman's ass gave him a hard cock. He shook his head to clear his thoughts and bring himself back to business.

Antonio Sanfranco was his business and he needed to get to him as soon as possible.

Dominic Fragoli thought, so far this has been an interesting and delightful beginning to what he hoped would be a very profitable trip. Dominic always enjoyed coming to Milan a place where he could mix business with pleasure. It was a city filled with academics and wealthy cultured people. Milan was a city where a man could satisfy all his tastes, no matter how perverse, but in the most discreet manner. He walked with a light step given his activities of the night before. He loved the taste of fresh young micia. He would have to stop thinking about that before everyone would notice his bulging breeches.

Antonio Sanfranco's bookstore was located two blocks behind the Basilica of Our Lady of Sorrows. The streets were narrow and paved with ancient bricks. Dominic a lover of history, marveled at the age of the bricks, as he made his way past all the little shops, and the masses of people that were lining the streets. Early morning in Milan was a busy time. People coming and going to their work, the Universita, the shops of every description, and several fine museums were all within walking distance. The delicious aromas wafting in the air from the panetteria he just passed made his mouth water. Unable to resist, Dominic stepped into the shop and was greeted by the most delicious smell of freshly baked goods. On impulse, he purchased a pie filled with goat cheese and topped with figs. He had the owner prepare him an espresso and then sat at a small table on the street. As soon as he bit into the delicate treat, he was rewarded with a most delectable taste. Dominic lingered at the table for a while, unsure of his feelings about seeing Antonio Sanfranco.

Unlike his home city of Naples, which was filthy and dangerous, Milan was a clean cosmopolitan city. Elegant shops lined the streets. It was a beautiful city. He was enjoying the stroll observing the many inhabitants. A young woman with three small children caught his attention. She was still rather young and waif thin. The children, two boys and a girl were clutched one to each arm, and the tiny girl was strapped to her chest. Dominic marveled at the ability of the skinny woman to contain such a brood of children. In addition to all that, the woman was pushing a small cart, with bags of what he guessed were items of food. He thought for a fleeting moment, that it would be nice to come home to the arms of a loving wife and family. Then one of the boys hit the other and they started to fight. The mother was trying to break it up, and then the little girl started to cry, until finally the mother hauled off and smacked both of the boys hard enough that he could hear the thwack across the street. It was at that precise moment Dominic put away any desire to be a father or husband.

Dominic knew he carried in his bag two priceless manuscripts they alone would be enough to secure a very leisurely life. He was never one to venture into something half way. An adventure once started would have to be finished. Dominic Fragoli was a man of insatiable greed. He wanted it all. Having grown up in poverty he was determined to end his life as a rich man. He patted the bag at his side.

Finally, he reached the shop of Antonio Sanfranco. An unassuming little storefront on a back street in the middle of Milan, the shingle over the door read simply, "Sanfranco Libris". By habit, his hand on the doorknob, Dominic scanned the street to see if anyone had followed him. He then smiled to himself, knowing that no one knew he was even there, or what priceless items he held in his possession. The only other person who knew was Lucia, he had warned her not to tell anyone, besides he had her so mesmerized by his suave manner that she would tell no one. Of that, Dominic Fragoli was sure. Lucia was just like every other woman he had ever known. Show them a little attention, stroke their egos with words of affection and flattery, and they will spread their legs very soon. He thought that the next time he went to Monteforte he would take Lucia's womanhood. The idea of it made him feel tingly all over.

It was already late morning by the time Dominic entered the tiny shop, the smell of aged parchment and dry leather came to his nostrils, and he drank it in. The store filled from floor to ceiling with shelves lined with antique books from all over the world in every language. There were tables stacked high with numerous volumes. It was old and dusty and yet Dominic Fragoli was elated to be there. There were several men, most of which looked surprisingly like himself. Dressed in a finely tailored waistcoat, breeches, and silk stockings, Dominic Fragoli looked every inch the academic. He had powdered his hair this morning but did not wear a wig. Sitting in a small niche toward the back of this organized chaos was Antonio Sanfranco. He had not seen him in ten years, but the man defied the laws of nature. He looked like he was in his twenties, when in fact he was in his mid-thirties. His raven black curly hair showed no sign of greying, and was not powdered but clubbed back with a leather thong. His deep rich olive skin was smooth and wrinkle free. Antonio's eyes were black and intense but with true intelligence behind them. Most women would agree that he was a handsome man, with sharp chiseled features in a lean muscular body. Antonio Sanfranco presented a very pleasing package. His youthful appearance enhanced by his enchanting smile that showed off straight white teeth. The only nod to his age was the use of spectacles with which to read. Dominic knew he was attractive, but now seeing his old friend, made him a little jealous of his own aging appearance.

Antonio seemed deeply engrossed in the stack of papers strewn across a battered desk. An elderly well-dressed man approached him with a question regarding a tome he held in his hand. Their two heads together, they examined the book carefully before the man was satisfied with the answer, and decided to purchase his selection. It was while he was wrapping up the purchase that Antonio happened to look up and saw his old friend. Their eyes connected and that familiar bond held immediate recognition. Antonio gave that infectious smile and a nod of graciousness. The elderly patron, package in hand, was starting to leave and Antonio came from around his overloaded desk to embrace Dominic with such warmth and affection. "Dear Friend, it has been too long." They kissed each other's cheeks and pounded one another's backs. "Yes Antonio it has been ten maybe more years since last we saw each other. The Gods of Old Age have been very generous to you. You look the same as the last time I saw you." "Ah, you were always a bad liar Dominic, but still it is good to see you again. What brings you to Milan?" "I am here on business. Your kind of business Antonio and I hope you will be able to assist me."

Antonio seemed genuinely happy to see his old friend. The two men reminisced for a while then Dominic sensed that Antonio's interest in his visit was piqued. "Antonio I have in my possession a manuscript that I would like you to look at and appraise." Antonio seemed mildly interested but had to interrupt their fraternal meanderings to attend to his patrons. "Dominic it is almost midday, why do we not go and have our supper and we can talk then? I know this wonderful café a short walk from here. They serve a superb vintage of wine and the serving girls are very attractive." "That sounds very good. I will just enjoy myself looking around until you are finished with your business. Don't hurry; this is like dolce for me." They both enjoyed good books even when they were poor boys in the slums of Napoli. Dominic was remembering one particular incident when Antonio and him broke into a book store, very much like the one he was now standing in, and they did not take the money in the box, which they surely could have used, but instead stole as many books as they could carry. He fought back the urge to laugh aloud.

Antonio having served the last patron was finally ready to close up his shop, and placed a placard in the grimy window, announcing its closure and reopening at eight o'clock in the evening. The two men, both dashingly attractive, swaggered animatedly to the café. Antonio was greeted by a perky but cubby serving girl whom he embraced with kisses on each cheek. The girl giggled and a light blush brushed her cheeks. As she turned to lead them to a table in the back under an arbor, he pinched her fat ass. She turned as if scorned then said "Antonio I know you desire me, but, sadly I am promised to a prince." They laughed with great mirth and Dominic assumed this was their usual banter. Once seated, Antonio took the liberty to order, which was fine with Dominic who had to admit he was hungry. "So tell me of this manuscript you have." Dominic was about to reach for his bag but the girl arrived with their wine, a loaf of bread and a plate of olives. "Rosa, forget that prince and marry me." "Ah, if only you were a prince surely I would wed you then. But for now I shall return with your supper." They toasted to their past and future. "Now to the present" said Dominic and he reached down to retrieve his bag. Carefully he spread out the manuscript. From the second he unrolled the ancient parchment he watched Antonio's eyes blaze into the manuscript, he had immediate recognition of what Dominic had surmised was truly something priceless.

"Where did you get this Dominic?" Antonio was so excited he was breathless. Dominic had seen this reaction in his friend many times in the past, and was not disappointed to see it again. Now for the first time since leaving the cave at Monteforte, did Dominic truly feel the magnitude of his discovery. "That is not important for now. Is it authentic? I believe it is, just by way of where it came from. I can get more, many, more, but first I must know what it is, and how much it is worth." "Just from looking at it I can see that we have an ancient Byzantine manuscript. From the form of language and writing, it probably dates back to the early sixth century, give, or take a century. It is very old, but remarkably in perfect condition. I have seen these manuscripts in a museum at the Vatican, and those were not in as good a condition by half. They are beyond priceless. Tell me where they come from?" Dominic was just about to say no, when Rosa, her fat ass jiggling, arrived with an arm full of steaming hot plates. It smelled so good Dominic's mouth was watering. "Let us eat first; there will be time for talk later." The food was superb just as Antonio said it would be. They ate until their stomachs would burst, but while the atmosphere was jovial, there was an underlying tension. Dominic could see that behind the laughing eyes there lurked a devious fiend. He did not for a moment underestimate or trust Antonio, but he was the means necessary for Dominic to sell the manuscripts.

"Ah, Rosa, Cara, it is time to say farewell. I regret that I am not the prince of your dreams, maybe someday you will give this peasant a chance." He grabbed the giggling serving girl in an amorous embrace and planted a kiss on her mouth. They said their goodbyes and strolled out to the rialto. The weather was cool and crisp at this time of the day, and most of the streets were empty while people were to their supper. "That was most enjoyable Antonio. I am stuffed like a pig. Let us go have a cognac in a quiet place where we can talk. Do you have some suggestion?" "Yes, it is not far from here." They walked with what Dominic perceived was a determined pace. By now, Antonio, now baited, was obsessed with what he had seen. Dominic knew from their past that once Antonio set his eyes on a prize there was nothing short of death or murder that would prevent him from seizing it.

They came to the end of a narrow street, which was more like a passageway. It seemed dark and isolated with a few beggars lying across doorways. From an upper window, a dark haired woman called down to them "Ah, Signore, would you like some company? I am lonely for a handsome man." Just at the sight of the buxom woman, Dominic could feel the blood rush to his groin. Antonio knew of his friend's penchant for sex and said, "Put that whore out of your mind you will come away with the pox before morning." Antonio shouted back "Not today Mistress, my wife is feeling lonely too." The whore cursed them both to hell. They laughed.

Pulling open the tavern door the odor of human sweat and stale ale came to Dominic's nose. After that delightful supper, the thought of sitting in that dark, fetid bar was overwhelming, but he followed Antonio's lead. He selected a table at the back of the room away from curious eyes and ears. He asked for two glasses of their finest cognac, which seemed to be a surprise to the serving boy. Dominic assumed their clientele did not require such refreshments. He also told the boy to bring two candles and two of their best cigars. They spoke of simple things in familiar conversation, and of what each had been doing in the decade of years that had passed between them. "How is your mother?" Dominic asked remembering Felisa Sanfranco as being a beautiful and intelligent woman. "Sadly, she is very ill, the doctor tells me it will be soon. I pray that God takes her quickly. She is in great pain and it breaks my heart to see her suffer. She has had a very interesting life as you know. It was only after I was born that life had become more comfortable for her financially. One of her clients took a special interest in me and my mother. While I have never met him my mother often spoke of him and his great generosity." Antonio made the sign of the cross and added "May God bring her peace." "I am sorry for her pain. I will always remember that my family had very little, but your mother would find a place for me at your table. She was like a second mother to me. Send her my best wishes." As quickly as the sorrow had seeped into Antonio's face, that is how fast it left.

Once the drinks, candle, and cigars arrived it was back to business for Antonio. There was little small talk after that. "Let me see the manuscript again." Dominic was reluctant to take it out in public. "Don't worry, none of these people can read, never mind know a priceless antiquity." Hesitantly, Dominic took out the ancient scroll, but not before, he removed a linen scarf from his coat and wiped the table. He carefully and deliberately made a display of opening the parchment. Antonio was anxious and moved in his seat. With expert care, he examined the parchment for quality. He sniffed at the vellum. Withdrawing a jeweler's loop from his pocket, he began a meticulous examination of the lettering. Dominic sat back sipping his cognac, which he thought was surprisingly good given the place they were sitting in. He distracted himself by making rings with his cigar. It had been a long time since he had smoked a good cigar, and realized that he truly enjoyed it. Dominic was in no rush and wanted Antonio to be completely contented with the contents of the manuscript, after all, the more valuable he determined it was worth, the more money Dominic would garner.

After what seemed a long time, Antonio, removed the loop from his eye, carefully replaced it to its case and put it back inside his coat. He rubbed his eyes with a linen scarf and wiped his face. Finally, he looked up into Dominic's face, and there was an odd expression on his own. Dominic was not sure exactly what was going on with his old friend, but he was wary for it. Not wanting to seem eager, Dominic met his glare, and continued making smoke rings. He was amused that Antonio was trying to be coy about the authenticity of the document that lay before them. Antonio raked his thick black curls into place, and his mouth started to turn up at the corners. "Well, old friend, you have finally found the pot of gold. This is truly an ancient manuscript. I will need more time to translate its content. Leave it with me for a few days while I decipher the translation. In the meantime, I will begin to send out discreet inquiries to the more educated of my patrons. This item will require a very specialized palette and one that belongs to a deep purse. They both gave a devious chuckle. "Now will you tell me where this came from and how many you have?" "Dear Antonio, my oldest friend, you know that I will not share that information with you just yet. Not that I distrust you, but only because it is poor form to show your cards before the pot is full. Yes?" Antonio's immediate reaction was one of wounded trust, but then in a few seconds, he was a shrewd card player himself, he recovered and nodded in agreement, his facial expression changed to a warm but guarded smile. "Of course old friend, I know you will tell me in due time. I assure you that I must find out soon so that I can make us a king's fortune."

Antonio knew he had just hooked his childhood friend with visions of wealth beyond their wildest imagining. Even as children, always Antonio was the implementer of their criminal schemes. Dominic did not have the foresight to understand the long-term value of wealth. Antonio's mother had been a prostitute with a clientele of very wealthy married men. Her discretion made her sought after by the more powerful men who did not want a mistress but needed to relieve their sexual cravings.

Felisa Sanfranco was not only beautiful but also intelligent and when not entertaining powerful men, she would be reading and educating herself to keep their interest piqued beyond sex. Felisa was versed in several languages including Latin. History and music were her favorite subjects. Felisa had taught herself to play the flute. Her clients were so used to the finer things in life that she needed to surround them with that familiarity. She had made many important connections, and kept all their secrets. Felisa finding herself with child had confronted the man who had impregnated her. At first, he was angry and threatened to kill her and her unborn child. She swore she did not want anything from him but wanted him to know he had fathered the babe. After the child came, the resemblance to the man was so uncanny; there was no need for the man to deny his son. While he would never leave his wife and children, the man, an honorable man, cared for both of them financially until his premature death.

With waist length black silken tresses that fell upon light olive skin and almond shaped amber colored eyes Felisa Sanfranco was exotic. She had a beautiful mouth and straight white teeth. She was of average height but carried soft voluptuous curves. Her breasts were round and firm with big dark nipples that beckoned to be sucked. Her tiny waist sat upon a full fat ass that men wanted to caress at the mere sight of it. Felisa Sanfranco was every man's erotic dream. Not pure and wholesome but dark and sensual. Her body coupled with her mind was the perfect courtesan package.

Growing up Antonio Sanfranco was exposed to these men of power and wealth. Taught by his mother and select tutors, but even as a child, the element of adventure and mischief could not be driven from the boy. Many a beating did Antonio receive for pick pocketing or stealing. His mother would say, "Antonio, why do you do these things, we have more than enough money to buy whatever it is you desire?" He could not confess to his mother it was the thrill of stealing that made him excited, not the item he stole. As he grew older, his adventures became more intellectual in nature and he found that the excitement found him by way of those who sought his expertise in specialized areas, primarily books, antiques, and manuscripts. He became rich, powerful, and necessary to the criminal world. For her part, Felisa Sanfranco thought her son was a trusted book purveyor, and that is exactly what Antonio wanted her to think.

It was growing late and Antonio knew that Dominic would not tell him the location of where the rest of the manuscripts were hidden. He would have to find a way to extort the information from him. In the meantime, he had a business to run and a dying mother to attend. Dominic would not last long with such a secret; they both knew it. Antonio on the other hand, was patient and would wait him out.

CHAPTER ELEVEN

THE VISITATION

Monteforte

Antoinetta and Lucia, two sisters, who had come to Monteforte as girls were evolving into captivating young woman with grace and poise and an outstanding education. During these years, Donato and Rafaela came to visit their daughters as often as they could. At first, they resented the fact that their girls could not be with them, but as time went on, they realized that they could never afford to give their daughters the opportunity that they were getting at Monteforte. Rafaela, always living with the history of what her Aunt Maria had done to her grandmother Lucia, and the bad blood between them, suppressed her own feelings in order to let her girls have every chance at a better future. Her aunt had offered that Donato and Rafaela come and live at Monteforte but they knew it was not for them. Donato was an independent man and would not be happy to be idle.

Rafaela had gained a reputation as a skilled dress designer and with money that her aunt sent to her she was able to establish a design shop in Florence.

For her part, Maria Sucretti had changed. On one particular visit, Maria Sucretti had asked her niece to join her in private to talk. Maria knew that she would have to make amends for her past sins against her sister-in-law Lucia to Rafaela. Lucia Rizzo was beloved by her family, and in order for there to be complete absolution Maria would have to repent the wicked deeds she had perpetrated against her.

Maria had thought long and hard about how this conversation would evolve. It was an overcast day at Monteforte. The sky was grey and the sea barked with anger, yet it was still warm. Maria invited Rafaela to join her for espresso on the terrace off her bedroom. It was quiet, away from the other visitors. From here, they could enjoy the view of the expansive garden. The wind off the sea was picking up and Maria thought that there might be a storm brewing. "Come Cara, sit here, and let us talk. Your visits are so infrequent. Tell me, how is your life these days?"

Rafaela was anxious to tell to her of all the good fortune they have had since the day Gaetano, the coach driver, had brought her and Donato that bag of gold coins, which her aunt had given them. Little did she know that Maria Sucretti, with contacts everywhere, knew exactly how successful her niece had become? Her designs were sought after by all the wealthy and affluent women in Italy, and she was sure would soon spread to France and Spain. Rafaela was very talented. Rafaela, who was very modest and not used to all the attention her designs were generating, answered "Because of you Zia Maria, my family has prospered. With the money, you had sent, so long ago, we were able to establish ourselves, and with hard work, have been successful. Thank you." Maria did not want to push Rafaela too hard and was satisfied with her answer.

Mistress Sucretti, now having set the stage for what was to come next, sat back in her chair. The wind had settled and it was unusually quiet. The birds, sensing an impending storm had sought their shelter in their nests. She closed her eyes absorbing the calm. With a determined will, she took up her cup and sipped the espresso, which was strong and fortified her spirit.

Placing the cup back to its plate she looked directly at Rafaela and spoke.

"Rafaela, I am truly sorry for all the things I have done. Your grandmother was a good woman, and my brother, while I loved him, became so ill with grief after the death of our parents that he could love no more. I thought I was trying to protect our family name and honor, but the truth of the matter was I was so jealous of your grandmother Lucia that I tried to destroy her. She had everything I did not. She was loving, caring, and a wonderful mother. Since I could not have my own children, I wanted to take hers. Lucia proved she was the better woman. I lost." Rafaela sat there watching her aunt intently. One of the most powerful people in all of Italy was confessing her sins. Rafaela dreamed of this moment but somehow the victory was not as satisfying as she had hoped. The woman before her was aged but still commanding, yet she had mellowed. Maria Sucretti was still beautiful, in the way that old women age with grace, but her eyes were no longer fierce, her mouth was soft at the edges and her demeanor was contrite.

Her aunt continued in a soft but commanding tone. "I have met with my avvocatto and have drawn up the necessary documents that upon my death Monteforte, and all its holdings, will be given to Lucia. I have made Lucia the primary beneficiary of my estate. While Antoinetta, and the boys, will receive a sizeable fortune, Lucia will wear the mantel of Mistress of Monteforte. Lei è il mio cuore. Lei è tua nonna. Lucia is strong of mind and heart. Lucia will be the heart of Monteforte. I have also made special provision for you and Donato."

Rafaela was about to protest this overwhelming news, but in one movement of her hand she raised her finger and stopped her. "This is not to be discussed with anyone. There are those in this part of Italy that would relish the thought of my death. While I have made many friends, I have also made many enemies. Becoming the Mistress of Monteforte is not just the whim of an eccentric old woman; many obligations that come with this gift. Many lives depend on the continued prosperity of Monteforte. I will groom Lucia to become the next Mistress of Monteforte. As for you, Donato, and your other children, I have made provisions for all of you. Antoinetta will be given a very handsome endowment enough to keep her in comfort for her whole life. The riches that these two girls have brought to my advanced years is beyond comprehension for someone like yourself. You are enriched by the love of your husband and children. You have all shared the best and worst that life has offered. For me, life, while on the surface seems like a fairytale, has been lonely and miserable. When someone lives in misery, he or she become miserable. I thought I would die here in this castle alone and unloved. I believe that my girls love me as much as I love them. I have given them the gift of hope and opportunity. I know they will use them wisely. The time has come to choose a husband for Antoinetta. There is a young man from a good family that I would like her to meet. They have been a close alliance with the House of Rizzo for generations. The present Lord Catalano is a friend of mine, and they are very wealthy in their own right. I have known his son, Tomaso, since he was born and he has grown into a fine young man. Ah, if all goes well with these arrangements, then with you and Donato's blessings the marriage contract will be completed. When, and if, Antoinetta finds this suitor to her liking, I will host a gala to announce both the marriage of Antoinetta, as well as to introduce the new Mistress of Monteforte. You must not tell the girls of what I am planning. The marriage of Antoinetta must be of her own will, I will just help her find a suitable husband. I will send word to you when everything is arranged."

With these last words, she made an almost indiscernible slump, and looking exhausted, rang her tiny bell, and instantly Giorgio appeared from nowhere. "Please bring my niece a bottle of our best wine and a platter of fruit and cheese. Prepare enough for her and her husband and bring it to the west terrace. Also, see if Antoinetta and Lucia would like to join them there. If so, make enough refreshments for all. Thank you." Giorgio, ever the faithful servant, bowed and went off on his mission.

"Zia Maria I am speechless. This is too much to absorb. I do not deserve this and neither do my girls. You have been more than kind all these years. You not only took in my children and treated them to everything I could only wish for them to have, but all these years you have silently sent gifts of money and opportunity to Donato and me. Do not think that I am not aware what you did for Genaro. His works of art have become famous throughout Europe thanks to the patron you secretly have become. Antonio, Andrea, and Francesco have all benefited from your generosity." Again, the old woman held up her finger to silence her. "I did what was right. You gave me the gift of your daughters and I have repaid you. As for Genaro, his talent has been the foundation of his own fame, not my patronage. I ask you, no, I beg you; never reveal what I have done. A gift is only good if it is truly free of obligation. Now go meet up with her husband and children and enjoy the afternoon. We shall meet up for supper. I am weary and must rest."

With her dismissal having been issued Rafaela got up, bent down to kiss her aunt who said, "There is much I must do before I leave this world. I have after these many decades found my mission. Andare e godere della bellezza di Monteforte. We shall have many things to discuss before you leave." Before she went off to meet, her husband Rafaela, still standing by her aunt said simply "Thank you for everything I am so happy that Giovanni Romano brought my girls to you. He is a good man and I see that you are both happy. È una benedizione per tutti." Rafaela was truly happy that her aunt had finally found happiness after all those years of being alone. With her instructions, Rafaela retreated to the west terrace where her husband Donato was waiting. The sky had cleared, and the sun found its way through the clouds, depositing brilliant rays of light upon the terrace. The birds, sensing that the danger of a storm had passed, once again came out to serenade all those who would listen. Maria sat there satisfied with what she had done, and relieved with the knowledge that her beloved Monteforte would remain in the possession of Lucia, the daughter she wished she had borne. The sun felt suddenly good upon her tired bones and its warmth comforted her.

As she sat there relishing the moment she felt the presence of someone nearby. She opened her eyes and Giovanni Romano was standing over her. He bent down and kissed her so gently on the lips. His hands cradled her face "Ah, Cara, stavo cercando te. Giorgio mi ha detto se qui. Sembri stanco. Stai bene?" "Yes my love I am fine. I am glad Giorgio told you where I was. I was just now talking with my niece Rafaela about some plans that I have made. You know that I have chosen Lucia to be my successor, and that I have in mind a special young man as a husband for Antoinetta. You also know that I have met with my avvocato to make all the necessary legal documents for the settling of my estate. What you do not know is that I have made provision that you will live out the rest of your life here at Monteforte, with all the rights and privileges you now have. That if you choose to leave Monteforte that a sum of one million lire is to be given to you." Giovanni Romano, who had been standing, now hearing this statement, came to sit beside Maria, his knees suddenly weak. "Cara I do not deserve this, I am nobody. What have I done for this generosity?" Maria her eyes filled with fire "What have you done? You have loved me and brought me the greatest happiness. You brought me Antoinetta and Lucia. You have loved me in ways I could never even have dreamed. That, my love, is what you have done. I can never repay you for all that you have bestowed upon me. I love you." Maria was fierce, not with anger, but with passion. Giovanni got up and picked her off the chair. "I love you so much Cara." He kissed her with such love and passion and their tears mixed with each other's. "Come let us go lie down" he pulled her to himself, and with a firm arm around her slim waist, half walked half carried her to her bed. Giovanni then lifted her onto the bed. "Shall I leave Cara? Do you want to sleep for a while?" Maria smiling coquettishly said, "No, please come and lay with me. Make love to me." Giovanni met her smile and wolfishly replied, "I thought you would never ask." They laughed happily and he joined her for a pleasant afternoon.

While the Mistress of Monteforte treasured her intimacy with Giovanni Romano was emotionally and mentally exhausted. After they had made love, she started to doze, her body spent with the afterglow of their sex. She was thinking that there would be much planning in the coming months. Every detail down to the most basic item must be without flaw. This will be the coming out party for her Lucia, the future Mistress of Monteforte.

CHAPTER TWELVE

THE PRICE OF LOVE

Monteforte

Lucia could hardly contain her desire to get the manuscript to Brother Vittorio, but first she would have to get back to the house undetected, or she would have to explain the condition of her present appearance. She was a mess. Her hair was so tangled she dreaded the thought of having to comb it through, and her gown had become soaked through from her dripping shift. She reeked of sweat and sea salt. What a mess! Surely, Sophia would ask her what she did this time.

Professor Fragoli, after Lucia had left to return home, had lingered for a while relaxing on the beach, the warmth of the sun upon his bare chest. He felt excited at the thought of Lucia's supple young body. As he laid there daydreaming of her, he became aroused, and had a full erection, which he promptly attended to. Lucia and Apollo had made their way back to the stables. Normally she would have taken her time and brushed Apollo herself, but under the circumstances, she had to escape any curious questions, and make her way quickly back to her room to wash and change. The stables were quiet, it was midday, the animals were fed and their stalls mucked out. She was thankful for the coolness of the stable for it was a hot day and her gown was plastered to her sticky body. She took in a deep breath relishing the scent of the place.

When Apollo came into the stable, he had aroused his fellows, and there went up a chorus of whinnying followed by stamping. Lucia knew it was only a matter of time before one of the grooms came to see the cause of the excitement. Sure enough as if on cue, Piro came hurriedly into the stable. Upon seeing Lucia, his eyes grew wide. "Mistress are you alright? What has happened to you?" Lucia took a deep breath and said, "Well we went for a long vigorous ride. Heated after all the riding, I decided to cool myself in the water. It was going fine, I was wading in up to my knees, when a big wave came and pulled me under. Here I am, wet as a fish and smelling just as bad." Piro with his big cow eyes clung to every word she was saying watching her mouth as she spoke. Lucia for the first time noticed that he was a handsome young man, a little older than she was; he had deep almond eyes and a nice smile. He stood just a few inches taller than Lucia, and she saw his strong chin. He smelled of horses, which she did not find objectionable. His arms were very muscular and he had a fine build. She always thought he reminded her of someone, and now for the first time it struck her that he reminded her of her brother Andrea.

Growing up Lucia, the youngest of the Banfi brood, had little interaction with Andrea. He was a highly intelligent person but lacked social skills. He liked being alone with his books and his numbers. Yet, the little time he did spend with her was always warm and interesting.

The groom collected himself and asked, "Are you hurt? Can I help you back to the house?" He reached for her arm than recoiled in a moment of realization of his position. Lucia did not want to cause Piro any undue anxiety and replied "Oh no I am fine, at least better than I look and smell." They laughed but she knew she needed to retreat as soon as was polite. "Piro, please give Apollo a good rub down and some extra water and hay. He worked very hard today. Thank you for your concern."

The young man, his mouth dry with arousal, just nodded and bowed deeply. Finally, he found his voice "Anything for you my Mistress. Don't worry yourself I shall take special care of Apollo." Again, he bowed deeply and forced himself to turn to begin his ministrations on the willing animal. Lucia addressed his back "Thank you Piro" then promptly left with a sigh of relief.

She made her way unseen back to her room. Stripped down to her soggy shift, which was stinking with a combination stench of sulphur, sweat and sea salt. She rang for Sophia who appeared after a few minutes. "Oh my God! What have you done now? Can I not leave you for a moment without finding you like a drowned cat?" Lucia was prepared, and rendered the same story she had just given to Piro. Sophia just looked at her and shook her head. "It would have been better if you had been born a boy. If Mistress Sucretti would see you now you would be in big trouble. There is no help for you...I will be back with hot water. Oh, my God, these clothes are filthy and they smell! What shall I do with you?" Lucia was smiling and came over to her maid and gently gave her a kiss on the cheek "But you still love me. Yes?" Sophia laughed and gave her a hug "Sì, ma ancora cattivo odore."

After several weeks when she thought she would not be missed, Lucia had decided she would venture to the Abbazia di Montecassino. It was an ancient and holy place. Many people came to the abbey to seek help for their health and other afflictions. It was famous as a sacred shrine that held healing powers. It was one of the first monasteries built in southern Italy by Saint Benedict. Lucia told Sophia to tell anyone who was looking for her that she was going for a long ride with

Apollo, and that she would be gone all day, but would try to be back before supper. Lucia rationalized that she was not really lying since it was a long ride. "Mistress you are going alone it is very dangerous? I will come with you." Lucia thought for a moment then realized that no one knew of her discovery except the professor. "I will manage, thank you for your concern."

Lucia had Piro saddle Apollo. The groom was curious as to where she was going so early in the morning. "It is very early, another long ride Mistress?" Lucia slightly annoyed that he was questioning her answered curtly "Yes." He would not relent "Where are you going today?" Piro was eyeing her intently his ears red as beets, he knew he should not ask her where she was going, but he just wanted to talk to her. "That is none of your concern." Wounded he lowered his head and brought Apollo around so that Lucia could mount him. She could not help but notice his broad back and muscular arms as he tended the horse. Piro was the only one besides herself that could manage the giant animal without being bit. Cupping his hands to boost her into the saddle he gave her, an extra strong lift and she nearly flipped over the horse. Apollo, startled by this unexpected move, lurched forward and Lucia landed on the ground. She was furious "You stupid fool. Did you try to flip me over the horse?" She could not stop herself seeing Piro's grinning expression and landed a sharp slap across his cheek. Just at that very second Gandolfo hearing the raucous of elevated voices came out of his office to see Lucia strike Piro. He came running over "What is going on here?" he snapped at Piro whom he now had by the scruff of the collar. The groom was visibly scared and knew that he was going to punished for what had happened.

Lucia grabbed Gandolfo's arm and he stopped instantly. "Mistress?"

"Gandolfo, this was a silly misunderstanding on my behalf. Piro was helping me mount Apollo but was just a little too strong with his push. Apollo got scared and moved and I fell." The old man looked from one to the other but he was truly not satisfied with that answer. "Why did you strike him Mistress?" Lucia only half lying said, "The truth is that I was embarrassed that I fell off Apollo and landed on my ass. Then I saw he was trying not to laugh but could not hide it."

Now the old man realized what was really going on. Piro was trying to show off how strong he was and failed. She fell off the horse and felt foolish. Such is the way of these young pups always trying to sniff each other's asses. Gandolfo accepted her explanation and released Piro with a push "Go get the rest of the horses their breakfast. Now." Piro with his face aflame bowed deeply and scurried off. "Gandolfo don't beat him. It was my fault." She searched his face, but knew there would be some corporal punishment inflicted on the young groom. "Do not let it cloud your mind. I need to keep order Mistress. That is my job."

He bent and cupped his callused hands to boost her up. He handed over the reins and with a tired grin said, "I'll go easy on the boy." Lucia just nodded but felt a terrible discomfort. She was now settled on Apollo and making her way out of the stable. As she was passing, she saw Piro down by the well, which she would have to pass. She cursed that she would have to see him but there was no help for it. His head bent low to his work, she pulled up beside the well and he raised his eyes to her face. "I'm sorry Piro for making trouble for you. Please forgive me." He smiled then came round the well and looked up "Thank you Mistress for what you did." Lucia choked "Will he beat you?" Piro looking brave said, "He will have to, because by now everyone will know what happened. Please do not concern yourself I have been beaten before."

"PIRO" came the roar from the stable. The groom just closed his eyes tightly and did not hesitate for a second but started running back toward Gandolfo and what would be his fate. Lucia watched and Gandolfo already had the leather belt in his hand. He caught her eye and waved her on. With a lump in her throat, she prodded Apollo to go, and as if to shut out the scene that was playing, out in the stable, she put him to full gallop.

She came to the main gate and the two guards, whose names she did not remember said, "Where are you going Mistress? Will one of the men be going with you?" Thinking to herself, she wanted to scream, "Will no one leave me alone." "No I am going alone. I will return tonight." There was a frantic look on their faces. "Alone, to return tonight, by yourself, this is no good! Mistress that is not possible. It is too dangerous, there are bandits everywhere, and you could get hurt." Lucia by this point was in no mood to put up with their nonsense. "Move aside and let me pass." Apollo was now so close to one of them that if he had the mind he could have knocked him over, the thought having crossed Lucia's mind. "But Mistress, please be reasonable, one of us will come with you, or we will get Nicko, or any one of the men to accompany you." Lucia, her cheeks now as red as her hair, quietly said "Move. Open the gate immediately." With heads bowed, they did what they were told. As an afterthought, she shouted, "Do not follow me, or tell anyone I am gone." She ventured to turn her head back to see their horrified faces. Pleased that she did not let them strong arm her into not going she now let Apollo have full rein and they had Monteforte long behind them in no time. It was a clear day and thankfully not so hot. She relaxed with the wind blowing into her face. It would have been perfect except her mind kept going back to poor Piro and his fate.

***

Whenever a servant was punished, it was generally something that all servants were forced to witness. It was a means of deterrent for those who might contemplate the same transgression. Gandolfo was usually the enforcer of these corporal punishments. By now, everyone on the estate already knew that Piro was going to be whipped. One of the older kitchen maids had brought a bucket of hot water, clean towels, and salve. These events did not happen often but when they did, it was a cause of much anxiety among the staff. A crowd of dour faced servants was now gathering at the stable.

Gandolfo who dreaded this aspect of his position was getting himself prepared. He loved Piro whom he had apprenticed since he was a small boy. He had great promise and was a highly skilled horseman. Gandolfo had already sized him up to assume his position once he either could no longer function adequately or died. It was a very responsible job and he had many people under his direct supervision. He was as powerful on the outside of the house as Giorgio was on the inside. He made the sign of the cross and asked Saint Michael to guide him in the ways of the just and to have mercy on his soul.

About an hour later, all was ready. Gandolfo had two of the other grooms throw a rope over one of the high beams. Piro came over to him with head bent. "Take off your shirt boy. It pains me to have to do this. You know it. But you have to get those thoughts out of your mind or they will destroy you." Now he lowered his voice so that only Piro could hear him. "Mistress Lucia cannot be for you. You are only a peasant. She will take Mistress Sucretti's place when she dies. Do you understand me? I know she is beautiful but that beauty, those thoughts, will have you dead." Piro just stood there with his torso exposed waiting for his fate.

Gandolfo instructed the two grooms that were nervously awaiting orders to tie Piro's hands to the length of rope that was hanging from the beam. They did, the one who was his close friend whispered, "I'm sorry Piro. I will pray for you." The young victim feigning courage smiled and nodded in appreciation. "Now pull the rope so that his arms are held tight above his head. Piro now stretched, with his broad back bare and unblemished, faced the silent crowd. He hung his head down between his arms bracing for the first blow.

It came 'whack' hard and fast. For one second he could not feel the pain but then the searing sting came. 'Whack', another blow and now his flesh was burning. He did not scream out like a little girl. He closed his eyes tightly, but as the lashes were coming hard and fast he felt that he would no longer be able to breathe. His arms were straining against the ropes and his mouth was dry from fear and pain. How many? He could no longer recall.

Suddenly, it stopped and Gandolfo came around to face him, sweat pouring down his tired face. He asked in a low, almost sorrowful voice, "Is she out of your mind yet?" Piro, who was always honest, answered in a voice so deep and horse that Gandolfo had to put his ear to the young servant's mouth to hear him, "Not yet my Lord." Gandolfo knew in his heart that there was no hope for it. "We will continue until you have a clear mind." "Yes my Lord." There was a gasp from those gathered and more than one of the little kitchen maids were crying. The males were wondering if Lucia was worth this punishment. Gandolfo was sure that more than a few felt like Piro, but kept their thoughts to themselves.

After what seemed forever, the pain had become secondary to the ache in his arms and the thirst in his throat. Once again, Gandolfo came around to face Piro who was now a wounded animal. "Is your mind clear boy?" Piro did not answer immediately he had neither, strength, or enough saliva to respond but just nodded. Gandolfo thanked the Blessed Mother that he did not have to inflict any more on this poor love struck boy.

"Cut him down. You two carry him carefully back to his bed. Maria tend his wounds; make sure they do not fester; and for God's sake bring him some good wine and plenty of it. Bring some for me also. Now, the rest of you, let this be a lesson, get back to work." Gandolfo went back to his private quarters, buried his face in his hands, and wept. He hurt the boy, but he hoped it would make him think twice next time he had dreams of Mistress Lucia. Of course, who could blame him, she was perfect in every way. There was no hope for it.

Piro was unconscious when they brought him back to his bed. They laid him on his stomach and Maria set to work. She prayed that he stayed that way while she washed and dressed his wounds. The tears were falling freely down her matronly face. She too loved Piro and now prayed that he would heal quickly of both mind and body. Maria carefully and gently washed his back with a mixture of olive oil and rosemary. She patted it dry and then applied a salve of congealed olive oil, boiled and mashed garlic, and rosemary. Working it into the wounds to soothe the burn and promote healing. Finally, she brushed on honey and laid thin linen strips as bandages. The honey would hold them in place.

Maria sat there for a long time wanting to be there when Piro awoke. She had one of the little kitchen girls bring some broth and fresh bread and a new jug of wine. He started to stir, she felt his cheek, and it was on fire. She got up and although it was warm in the sleeping quarters, she could see that he was shivering with fever and placed a thin blanket over him. She drew a rag from the bucket, wringing it out she wiped the sweat from his handsome young face.

He opened his eyes and tried to move but recoiled from the intense pain. She got a spoon and put some broth in his mouth. Little by little, she got half of the bowl into him. He begged her to stop. "Piro, sweet boy, do you want some wine to dull the pain?" He nodded trying to exert as little effort as possible. She filled a wooden cup half way with wine and placed it to his lips. He drank it down quickly. She refilled the cup knowing that he needed to dull the pain. Again, he polished it off. "You must take your time with the wine, or your stomach will heave it up." I will fill it again but go slowly. There was a deep polite cough from the back of the room. Standing in the doorway was Gandolfo looking like someone had beaten him. He motioned for Maria to leave. She got up, straightened her gown, and withdrew. As she was leaving, he grabbed her arm and whispered, "How is he doing? Did he eat? Did you give him the wine?" She knew the older man's feelings for the boy. "Yes he had some broth and I gave him some wine. I will stay with him for the rest of the day. He has a fever." The older man just nodded and choked back his own tears. She stepped outside.

Gandolfo came over to Piro and sat down beside him. The boy opened his eyes to see who had come. He was going to try to get up but Gandolfo put his hand on his arm. "Stay still. You do not have to work until you feel stronger. I want you to know how sorry I am that I had to do this to you. My worst fear is that it has not cured you of your desires. We all have desires son. Many years ago, I dreamt of Mistress Sucretti with the same passion as you now have for Lucia. There was no hope for it then and there is no hope for it now. Do us all a favor wipe it from your mind." Piro did not answer but Gandolfo saw the tears in the boy's eyes. Both their hearts were broken.

Gandolfo rose to leave and in a hoarse voice Piro said, "Thank you my Lord. I know you are a good man and I love you for it. I will do my best." Gandolfo, overtaken by emotion, kneeled down and kissed the boys cheek.
"Rest." Then he left.

CHAPTER THIRTEEN

THE ABBEY

Montecassino

Lucia followed the only road, if you could call it a road, which led to the abbey. It was mostly a path that had over time, been trampled by enough sheep and cows that it had worn itself into a serviceable road. Apollo was in his glory and rode with no hesitation. It was a long ride and she cursed herself for not having brought some small meal. A piece of bread and chunk of cheese would have been quite welcomed at this point. She abandoned that thought from her mind, and focused on getting to the abbey. She was pleased that she had gotten such an early start. With any luck, she could get to the abbey, see Brother Vittorio, and be back before supper.

It seemed like they reached the abbey in no time. Apollo was a strong animal and with his powerful legs, they rode hard, and now she had the abbey in view and she forgot all thoughts of Piro, hunger, or the trip back. Lucia just wanted to relinquish her prize to the monk for his assessment. When last she came to the abbey she had seen only the back, where the monks worked and the pilgrims came with their baskets of food, to sit about after their long journeys. Approaching the abbey from this direction Lucia thought she had the wrong place. At first, it looked like a Roman temple with pillars and columns. There were statues and remnants of what was once the site of an ancient structure.

The one story stone structure occupied a vast landscape. It looked like several buildings had grown together over many centuries. Lucia wondered about the age of the place, and made a mental note to ask the monk when she spoke with him. She was hot, tired, hungry, and thirsty, to say nothing of sad for Piro, which she told herself, she needed to put out of her head. Coming up to the front the first thing she noticed were the three massive bronze doors. They caught the light from the sun and the bronze glimmered in the morning sun. One of the lay brothers who helped work the fields and tend the animals spotted her. He did not wear a robe or sport a beard and tonsure but was dressed in worn sweat soaked homespun shirt and breaches. He let his hoe fall to the ground and came over to her. "Mistress, may I assist you?" Lucia had already dismounted and inquired, "I came to see Brother Vittorio. Is he here?" The lay brother replied "Yes Mistress. I will go and tell him that you are here then, I will take your fine horse and give him water and hay." "Oh thank you. Don't you want to know my name?" The lay brother smiled broadly exposing missing teeth. "I know your name; you are the Mistress Lucia of Monteforte. Yes?" Lucia's eyes grew wide with astonishment. "How did you know my name?" The little man with bright dancing eyes chuckled, "Why Mistress you are famous. How many other bella cappezzi rossi's are there around here?" Having said that and still laughing he opened the right door into the abbey and asked her to wait there for Brother Vittorio. "Ah, Mistress, he is no longer 'Brother Vittorio' now he is Abbot Vittorio." Lucia was surprised and pleased that he had been elevated in rank which she thought all the better for her new discovery.

Lucia struck dumb by the beauty of the abbey, wandered into the main nave of the chapel. It was huge with soaring ceilings decorated by frescos, mosaics, and paintings. In the middle of the floor was a gigantic octagonal Roman well, surrounded by stone columns and life size statues. She walked to one of the soaring windows and could see the surrounding mountains and sweeping views down to the sea. It was breathtaking. She was so absorbed in her thoughts she did not hear the monk approach. He coughed politely to announce himself.

"Ah, Brother Vittorio, I doubt you remember me but a few years ago my sister and I stopped here on our way to Monteforte and you were very gracious to us. My name is Lucia." The monk had changed since last she saw him. He was still tall as she had remembered, but now his beard was clipped close and trimmed, his robe once worn and frayed was new and clean. His overall appearance was of a man in his middle thirties in good health. His skin glowed like warm polished wood and his tonsure matched the rest of his skin color. The monk's eyes had the most dramatic change. They were a soft amber, and seemed to have become wiser. "Hello Mistress Lucia, of course I remember you and your sister. How have you been? From the looks of you I believe all has been well?" Lucia ruefully smiled and replied, "I am so impressed with this monastery. When last I came I did not see this portion, it is magnificent. I heard that you have been elevated to Abbot. Congratulations I am sure that you earned it." The monk bowed his head trying not to acknowledge that he had been raised in rank. He was a modest man she could see that.

"What brings you to our sacred abbey? Where is your party?" "I have come alone. There is something of such importance that I have not shared but with one other person." The Abbot, now concerned commented, "You came all this way by yourself, without escort?" She

286

just nodded, too anxious to waste time on the subject. He sensed her feelings and moved on to the nature of her visit.

Lucia had almost forgotten the manuscript, which she had laid down on the table in the foyer. "Abbot it is a long story, do you have a few moments to spare for me?" The monk intrigued by her announcement courteously bowed and said "Of course my dear. Shall we walk and talk at the same time." Lucia was thrilled to be there in this holy place she felt grounded by its sense of history. "Please Abbot tell me the history of this wonderful place." The monk looked pleased that she would want to know about the monastery.

"As you undoubtedly noticed, Montecassino is not your typical monastery. The Romans originally built it in 536 A.D. as the Temple of Diana. Diana as you may recall from history was the pagan Goddess of the Hunt. Over the centuries it was destroyed three times and rebuilt. The three massive doors in the front represent the Father, Son, and Holy Ghost. Some say they are for the Past, Present, and Future. The latest reconstruction was just twenty years ago. Come let me show you the Chapel of Relics. There are many of the original remnants from the Roman temple. Where we are standing, this octagonal well was the site of an ancient well, which we still draw our daily water from, which is said to have healing powers."

Lucia leaned over to look down into the fathomless well. "Abbot, it looks so deep, do you know how far down it goes?" The monk was now standing beside her, also peering down into its depths "The folklore says it goes to the center of the earth. Of course, no one has ever gone down to see. At least not by their own will. It is also said that as a sign of faith early Christians were thrown into the well to see if they could survive." Lucia shuddered at the thought of being thrown down into that dark hole.

"Come let me show you the relics." They walked in companionable silence, Lucia soaking in her surroundings in awe. When they reached a massive carved door, the monk started to speak once again, "this is the Chapel of Relics. It is a very holy place filled with the bones and other sacred items from various saints and martyrs. While we are in here we will not speak out of reverence for their holiness." Lucia nodded and quietly slipped in behind the monk, his brown robe absorbed in the dimness of the space. The air was still, compressed, and smelled of dust and decay. There were niches` in the walls with skeletal remains in various degrees of decomposition, all fully clothed in robes with gold or silver thread designs. Some wore miters designating their status as pope or bishop and were encased in glass casks. Smaller niches` housed chalices and monstrance's of pure gold encrusted with precious stones, and others held books and other artifacts. It was a large space with a center altar. Candles burned at the foot of full size statues of various saints. A groin-vaulted alcove that enshrined a life size statue of Saint Benedict held a plaque that gave information about the saint, who had claimed Montecassino from the ruins of the original pagan Roman Temple to Diana. It was sad, frightening, and mystical all in one. When the monk pressed her arm to leave, she was happy for it.

When they had closed the heavy door behind them, she was relieved to be out in the bright atmosphere of the nave. "Mistress may I offer you some refreshment, a bite of food, and then we will speak of your reason for coming here today." Lucia who was starving graciously agreed, and they went to sit outside by an arbor. In moments, a young friar came with arms laden down with a heavy tray. The young man, perhaps in his teens, struggled under the weight of his burden, but wore a smile on his homely face. Being too young to grow the customary beard, his face was smooth and hairless save for the angry scar that ran across his cheek. The abbot spoke kindly to the young man "Ah, thank you Brother Peter. This is Mistress Lucia her family is a great support to our abbey. I will be occupied for the rest of the afternoon, if anyone comes, tell them they must wait." The young friar continued smiling as he unloaded the items from the tray. Lucia could see there was fresh baked bread, a slab of cheese, figs and a bowl of olives. There were also two cups and a decanter of wine. When he had completed his work, he bowed deeply, and left in silence, his brown clad silhouette scurrying back to the abbey and disappeared.

It was still a beautiful day, and the abbot and his guest, sat and filled themselves from the repast that had been brought. Lucia declined a second cup of wine, and enjoyed her simple lunch in this special place, with memories of her first day at Monteforte. "Much has changed with you since you first stopped here." Lucia's eyes lowered "Yes Abbot I have learned many things in those years. One of which is the reason for my visit." The monk sensing that she was anxious to tell her story got up and said, "Shall we retreat to the library. It is cool there and we can speak of your needs." Lucia was grateful to follow. "Abbot, I must stop first to pick up my package, which I left in the great hall entrance." He smiled "Do not concern yourself, the lay brother you met on the way in already brought it to the library." Lucia smiled, nodded, and thanked God for the administrations of good servants, religious or not.

They reached the library after a long walk through the various hallways and chapels. Montecassino was huge, with many extensions that added to the original structure over the centuries. The room reminded her of her library at Monteforte only it was bigger and religiously decorated. The wood beamed coffered ceiling rose to a height of twenty or more feet. Stained glass windows carried prisms of jewel-toned brilliance around the room and depicted scenes of martyred saints, Blessed Maria and Jesus; it was like walking into a church that had books. It was wonderful. The room smelled of candlewax, polish and leather bound parchment. Lucia drank it all in and was grateful for it.

In a stone-carved alcove was a large wooden desk that was intricately carved, a pair of standing candleholders stood on either end to cast a good amount of light, since it was so bright, no candles were lit. Sitting in the middle of the desk was her package. There was an ornately carved high back armchair behind the writing desk and two small chairs in front. The abbot walked around and sat behind the desk, and offered one of the chairs in front to Lucia. She sat waiting a moment to speak. "There must be hundreds, if not thousands of books and manuscripts here." The Abbot, who was so proud of the facility, looked appraisingly around the cavernous room. "This Abazzia was once considered one of the foremost centers for learning. Even today, our highly trained brothers, labor painstakingly over ancient manuscripts for translation. Many people come here to find knowledge."

"And you my dear, why have you come?" Lucia tried to restrain her excitement but blurted out "I have discovered an ancient place, and the package that sits before you is just one piece of the mystery. I was hoping that you could tell me what it is and how old it is?" The monk smiled broadly and reaching for the package asked "May I open it?" "Of course, Abbot, please do so." There was a small gilded dagger on the desk, the monk took it up, and carefully cut the bindings that Lucia had tied around a piece of canvas to protect the manuscript. Again, carefully, almost reverently he unrolled the parchment. He placed square pieces of polished marble as weights on all four corners to keep it flat. He stood up to get the full impact of the document that was lay before him. Lucia studied his face, his thoughts now consumed by the knowledge that was before him. His hand gently touched the parchment, a finger tracing the strange markings. His reaction was much the same as Professor Fragoli. Lucia waited her anxiety and excitement building. A soft golden glow filtered from the stained glass windows and basked the monk in its light.

Slowly, Abbot Vittorio sat down. His mind was somewhere else; his eyes were wandering as if searching for some clue as to the content of the document. He turned to look at Lucia "Where did you find this?" Lucia recounted the story of how she came to find the hidden cave. She also told him about Professor Fragoli. Moreover, how he was taking two additional manuscripts, one to Rome, and one to Florence, for authentication. The monk sat quietly listening with great interest to her story. He asked only, those questions that needed to clarify a point. When Lucia had finished she sat back in her chair "That is what brings me here today to see you. Can you help me?" The monk also sat back in the chair, now stroking his beard, the amber eyes twinkling with anticipation.

"Mistress Lucia you have brought me something that is so ancient and important I am not sure even where to begin to describe its content and historical significance. I am ashamed, but I do not possess the absolute knowledge to comprehend its true secret, but there are brothers here who do hold such knowledge. You say there are many of these manuscripts all at the same source?" "Yes. The cave I told you about is located at the farthest point of the Monteforte estate. It is well hidden, and only myself and my tutor, have knowledge of its existence." Lucia was thrilled, because she knew that the place she had found was holy and sacred. "How shall we proceed?" she asked in a nervous voice. The Abbot, with narrowed eyes asked, "First, do you trust this professor? Now, before you answer you must be sure, because what you have discovered is priceless. There are those who would pay a king's ransom to possess them. Do you understand?" Lucia nodded. "Does he know that you were coming here for us to examine the manuscript?" "No I decided after praying to the Blessed Mother that this would be a good place to start. I wanted my own answers." The monk silently agreed with this decision. "That was very wise of you Mistress."

Lucia did understand why the monk asked of her and hesitated. "I know him from my years at Monteforte, but do not know anything more other than the stories he has shared with Antoinetta and me. As I had told you, the only reason why I confided in him was that he had shared the same experience as a young man. I believe him to be an honorable man." The monk sat there deep in thought stroking his beard. "You will need to leave this with me and I will have Brother Angelo look at it and perhaps, with much guidance from Our Lord, we will be able to translate it. You were wise Mistress not to share this with anyone else." Lucia was in deep thought, and she could never hide her feelings, the monk seeing it written all over her face asked "What troubles you Mistress?" She took a long, deep breath and slowly released it responding, "I have not told my aunt, Mistress Sucretti, of this discovery. Is it a betrayal to her?" The monk came around the desk and sat in the chair beside her. He reached for her hand and she give it to him. "Mistress, it can only be a betrayal if you know what you have, and then take what belongs to the family, and cheat her out of it. The only caution I have for you is to watch for the professor. Temptation can corrupt even an honorable man. It will take several weeks, if not months, for Brother Angelo and me to decipher this ancient language. I can tell you for sure it is Greek but what it says, and how old it is, I cannot say. I would, once we get it translated, like to see the sacred place that you have described. I know that Byzantine monks and scholars came to this area and had a monastery near Monteforte, but then an earthquake descended on this very location, and they all perished and the monastery was destroyed. I will gather more information."

"Dear Abbot, I would be so honored to bring you to this wondrous place. It is beyond all description. It feels like Montecassino." The monk looked excited, but he was a learned and patient man, and knew from experience that what may seem like a treasure on the surface many times turns out to be a curse. "Come my dear Mistress, let us go to the chapel and pray for the guidance and knowledge of Jesus, that he may show us the way." Lucia was happy for the suggestion. They spent a while in silent prayer each to their own thoughts and petitions to Jesus and His Blessed Mother. Lucia prayed for strength in making good decisions, and asked the Lord, if what she had found was truly good for everyone. She thanked the Lord for her Aunt Maria, her sister and brothers and especially her parents, her Uncle Giovanni and for Abbot Vittorio. "Lord Jesus, make me a better person and fill me with the knowledge to make good choices. Watch over all my family and those I care about, also Lord watch over Apollo."

With their prayers offered up for spiritual and physical guidance then with a silent nod, they retreated to the main reception hall. The monk took both Lucia's hands into his own looking into those eyes and said "Mistress Lucia, you are a wise and beautiful woman, guard herself against those who would destroy those gifts that Jesus has given you. You have been given this knowledge for a purpose, of that I am sure. The test will be what you will do with it, and that is something we will pray for together. When my work is complete, I will bring you the news of what we have discovered. On that trip to Monteforte, I will ask you to show me this sacred place and then we, along with Mistress Sucretti, will decide the best path to take. Agreed?" Lucia searched his face, which was ruggedly handsome, looked into his deep amber colored eyes, and knew she could trust this man with her life. "Yes Abbot I agree. I have been praying for help from the Blessed Mother ever since I first came upon the place. She led me to you, your work will give us the answers we seek. Thank you for your gracious hospitality, it is getting late and it is a long ride, would you have them bring Apollo around." The monk for the first time seemed upset. "You came here alone? I thought you had one of your male servants waiting for you. It is very dangerous for you to travel alone. I will send one of the brothers to escort you." Lucia was annoyed that no one thought her capable of traveling by herself; and bowed deeply to the monk, but responded "That will not be necessary, Apollo runs like the wind, and we will be back in a few hours. It will still be light by the time we reach home. I thank you for your concern. I will be anxious until I see you again. Thank you and pray for me."

As if by magic, Apollo appeared in the front courtyard. He looked well fed and rested. The abbot walked her out and nodded to the brother that had originally taken the horse. He went away with her thanks and she stood there with the monk. He took her face into his hands and gave her a kiss on each cheek.

"Be safe Lucia and may Jesus and all the saints protect you." He made the sign of the cross on her forehead and then bent and cupped his hands to boost her into her saddle. "May Jesus hold you in his hands until we meet again." Lucia was filled with a feeling of hope, or was it maturity; she was not sure exactly which, but whatever it was she felt good. Waving farewell, she gave Apollo a little kick in the ribs and off they went. It was a good day.

CHAPTER FOURTEEN

THE ENCOUNTER

Montecassino

Lucia was dreamily riding along enjoying the scenery loosely holding Apollo's reins. It was still warm even though she could see that the sun was coming closer to the mountaintop. She was thinking about Abbot Vittorio and the abbey and what a beautiful place Montecassino was. She would go back now and then just to renew her spirit. Her mind was drifting lazily as Apollo trekked over that old path with the clean citrus scent of lemons wafting on the breeze. It had already been a long day with so much drama. Lucia's heart was heavy with thoughts of the scene from this morning, and she prayed that Piro was not badly hurt. Her long ride to the abbey, meeting with Abbot Vittorio and the heat of the day made Lucia struggle to keep her eyes open, she was starting to doze.

She did not even see the man who suddenly appeared from nowhere, and he gave her and Apollo a start. The big animal was clearly agitated and swung his massive head from side to side, ears twitching and feet stomping. Lucia had all to do to calm him down. "That's a good boy. It is all right. Stay still now." He steadied but was not pleased with this intrusion. Lucia was furious "What are you doing scaring us like that? Where did you come from?" The man was dressed all in black with a slouch black hat that half covered his face. She peered at him but could only see the long black beard. His voice was deep and menacing "Ah, what have we here, a bella cappezzi rossi, and her beautiful horse? Am I dreaming?" He came closer. Lucia could now see those eyes. They were intense black orbs that looked at her with a lecherous smirk on his vile face. "Traveling alone Mistress? Surely someone who is obviously as wealthy as you would have servants with her." Lucia trying to control her fear snapped back "Don't worry yourself they are not far behind" although she feigned courage, her voice betrayed her. As if slapped into reality the voices of all those she had spoken to this day came back to haunt her. She should not have been traveling alone. Soon the sun would be setting and she would be alone and it would be dark.

Apollo was growing more agitated and was stamping nervously he sensed the evil intent of the stranger. "Why don't you come off that great animal and we can talk. I won't hurt you." Lucia was now getting frantic her mind going to a plan of escape. The man was blocking her path. "I told you my servants, who had to stop at the Abrazzia di Montecassino, will be coming shortly." The man threw back his head in hearty laughter. "You are a poor liar my beauty. I have been watching you since you left the abbey. You are quite alone of that I am sure." With every word, he was stealing closer to her. She was sweating; her hands were wet on the reins. Her mind was racing. Lucia in that split second knew she would have to defend herself against this intruder or die.

"I am very wealthy; if you do not harm me I will give you a substantial reward." Again the man laughed. "Ah, don't worry Mistress; I know exactly who you are. A beauty such as you will fetch a fortune from the gypsies. Between you and that horse, I will be set for life. Of course, first I will have to sample the goods. Lucia knew what would happen if she was kidnapped and sold to the gypsies. Dread and fear were so real and so present she could smell her own fear. She thought of the dagger she always carried on her saddle. Trying to delay the man who was tall and sturdily built, she moved to grab the bag "I have some gold in my bag, let me get it out and I will give it to you." She made to untie the bag, it was almost done when the man lunged toward her.

Apollo turned instantly and bit the man on the shoulder. "You bastard if you were not going to fetch me a lot of money I would kill you and sell the meat." He reeled his powerful arm back and punched Apollo with all his might in the snout. The animal was dazed but recovered rearing up on his hind legs. The man lost no momentum and reached for Lucia. She lost her grip on the reins and had no purchase to stay atop the horse. He threw her to the ground with a thud. He slapped Apollo hard on the hind end and the horse took off at a full gallop. Now, without her horse, and thrown to the ground, Lucia was truly scared.

The man who smelled of decaying teeth and foul body odor fell upon her. He put his filthy mouth on hers and she bit his lip. He slapped her face so hard she felt the sting and her eye started to water. He grabbed her by the hair, which had come undone in the struggle. Lucia tried to roll over to dislodge the big man. He was too heavy to push off. "You are a wild young bitch. Ah, a temper to match that fire red hair. Well I can take care of that. A little while with me and my strap and your ass will be mine. Maybe I will hold on to you for a while before I sell you to the gypsies. I am sure you are a virgin. Yes?" With a big dirty hand, he took hold of the bodice of her riding gown and pulled it until it torn in half. "Nice big tits. You have skin like alabaster. You are big as a man, but I am sure that your clit is sweet as honey. I'll let you know in a few minutes." He put his foul mouth on her breast and sucked her nipple. "NO" she screamed. "You can yell all you like rossi, there is no one to hear you."

Lucia was horrified, she closed her eyes and started to kick, and punch and scratch her assailant with every ounce of strength she could muster. She managed to throw him off her and she rolled on to her hands and knees. She spotted the leather pouch with the dagger, which she had managed to untie just before Apollo reared up. She knew she needed to reach it.
He held her with an iron grip on her ankle and pulled her back. "I'm going to take a strap to that big pearly white ass. I will tame you bitch. You will be begging me to stop." The man was angry. Lucia was sure he had not noticed the bag on the ground that was just under a small bush. She kicked him in the head with her free leg. "Whore! I may just kill you and be done with it." He was scrambling to his feet. He was fast. He was standing over her and gave her a swift kick in her ribs. Lucia screamed in pain gasping for breath. He grabbed her by the hair and yanked her head off the ground. He put his face next to hers. "You will behave. Do not make me kill you. Do as I say if you want to live." Lucia who had succeeded in retrieving the dagger hid it in her pocket. She knew that she was no match for him one on one, but would wait for the right moment when he was off guard. "Are you going to behave?" he roared. With her head throbbing from him pulling her hair, Lucia lowered her eyes and in the most contrite look, she said, "I will be good."

The man smiled broadly showing rotted teeth. "That's a good girl. But I think you need a little more persuasion." He straddled her while she was still on her stomach and removed his belt. He swept up her gown and moaned upon seeing her bare bottom. "Oh God, that is a beautiful sight. I am going to have some fun with that big round ass. First I have to teach you a lesson to make you understand that I am your master, and you will be my love slave." On the last word, Lucia jumped from the sting of the leather meeting her bare skin. He swung the belt over his head in an arching motion and came down hard again. Several more times and Lucia was raw and bleeding. He was laughing and telling her "Who is the master now bitch?" Lucia was becoming weak from pain. She told herself she must not lose focus but keep her head clear.

She knew he was enjoying himself and was distracted with inflicting pain on his victim. Lucia moved her hand to her pocket and slowly took out the dagger. She hid it in the folds of her gown. Finally, he was done. "Now that you have been schooled in the proper way to behave, I will show you what a real man does to a disobedient woman. Roll on to your back bitch." She struggled to maneuver her body the pain in her side stole her breath away. Lucia could see the scratch lines that ran down his ugly cheeks. She obeyed. He threw up her hem and his eyes grew wide at the sight of her womanhood. He was breathing rapidly. He threw off his shirt the stench of an unclean body made the bile rise to her throat. He tried to kiss her but she turned her head. "Still you don't obey your master." His drew back his arm and hurled a slap across her mouth cutting her lip. Lucia could taste the iron of her own blood. He swung again and got the other side of her face catching her nose, which instantly started to bleed. He took her breasts one in each hand and squeezed them so hard she cried out.

Lucia prayed to the Blessed Mother that she would find the courage and strength to stop this animal before he defiled her. She did not want to lose her virginity to this evil man. Pretending to be semi-conscious, she just laid there not moving. She did not see but knew he was undoing his breeches. He clutched her groin stroking the patch of red hair and slipped a wet finger inside her clit. He was groaning with anticipated pleasure. He moved the finger in and out trying to rouse her. She continued to feign unconsciousness. "Damn you whore; I want you awake to know what I am doing to you." He shook her shoulder and roughly slapped her face to rouse her.

She had her hand on the hilt of the dagger. Lucia knew she had but one chance to save herself, just one chance. She would have to time her attack precisely. He was sitting on top of her, his penis exposed and rock hard against her belly, his foul breath puffing rapidly in her face. Lucia, her eyes closed, prayed silently 'Jesus forgive me.'

In one split second, Lucia with the dagger drawn tight against her body thrust the blade deep into the chest of her attacker. His eyes drew wide with shock. At first Lucia held her breath thinking, she had not hurt him. She was sure she had aimed for his heart. The blade having slid into the flesh with all the strength she had. He looked at his chest, which was running with blood. His head moved slowly from side to side. He opened his mouth "Whore!" Both his hands grabbed for the hilt of the dagger but he was already too weak. He started to fall as if in slow motion to one side with his hands still on the dagger, his eyes rolling to the back of his head. Blood seeping through the wound where the dagger stuck out of his chest and pooling around them, the smell of it strong and rank.

Lucia tried to crawl out from under his limp body but could not generate the energy needed to do so. She could draw no breath from the ache in her side where he had kicked in her ribs. Her head ached and she was gagging on her own blood. Panic filled her mind. She lay there with the thought that surely she would die and no one would find her. She cursed her own arrogance at all those who had warned her of the dangers. Why had she not heeded their warning? This was surely a punishment from God for her pride. The face of her assailant after she plunged the blade into his heart would haunt her all the days of her life. The last thing she remembered was praying "Forgive me Father" then the darkness came.

CHAPTER FIFTEEN

THE RESCUE

Montecassino

It was nearly dark by the time Apollo reached the entrance gate of Monteforte. The guards seeing the horse knew something was terribly wrong. They also knew that they should have told someone that Mistress Lucia had left early in the morning, and now her horse returned without its owner. Fear of reprisal for not telling someone of her departure was overshadowed by what might have happened to the young mistress.

Gaspar, the younger guard, grabbed Apollo's reins but the big animal would not let him mount. He pulled the animal through the gate. He could plainly see that he was agitated. Apollo knowing he was home took off at full gallop toward the stables. He was wicking and sorting loudly as he approached the stables. His fear and agitation was spreading throughout the stable and all the horses started to stamp in their stalls. A couple of young grooms hearing the commotion came to see what was going on, thinking a wolf might have gotten in the stable and was causing the animals to become frightened. They saw it was Apollo and cursed Mistress Lucia, whom they were upset with from the punishment Piro had received because of her earlier in the day, and thought she had just left the horse and had not seen him to his stall.

Gandolfo came out of his room just as Gaspar, breathing hard to catch his breath came running up to the stables. "What is going on here?" shouted Gandolfo. Gaspar bent with his hands on his knees said, "Mistress Lucia left early this morning, and now the horse returns without her. Something is wrong." Gandolfo in the midst of all the anxiety of the day had lost track that Apollo was missing. Always Piro took charge of the big animal. He was the only one who the horse would obey. Even now Gandolfo tried to reach for the reins and Apollo, his lips pulled back showing a snarling set of big yellow teeth, ready to bite the first person to come near. Gandolfo knew that the horse would lead them to Lucia wherever she was and that the only one who could manage the huge animal was Piro.

In a low sad voice he said to one of the grooms, go get Piro. "But my Lord he is injured." The old man was tired both physically and emotionally, and now he was scared for his young mistress. "Get him now," he almost whispered. The boy hurried off. A few moments later, he appeared with Piro holding on to his shoulder, the young man weak with pain and fever. "Piro, I am sorry, but you are the only one who can take control of this horse. Mistress Lucia is missing and I think Apollo can take us to her. Do you think you can find the strength to ride him so he can lead us to her?" "Yes my Lord." Gandolfo knew Piro would do anything for Lucia, but he feared he was too weak. "Maybe this was a mistake you are too weak with fever I will send someone else." Piro would hear none of it "I am able my Lord. I will find my Mistress."

Gandolfo, while Piro was getting ready to ride, walked up to the mansion and found Giorgio in his room. He explained the situation. Giorgio was furious. "How did she leave the estate without notification to anyone? I will personally kill those who are responsible if any harm has come to Lucia. I will go tell Master Giovanni.

Wait here until I return." Giorgio stormed off to tell Giovanni Romano what happened.

Quietly, Giorgio found his master in the library. He and Mistress Sucretti were reading. The servant coughed politely. "Yes Giorgio." He bowed and asked if he might speak with Master Giovanni privately. Maria Sucretti looking concerned asked, "Giorgio is everything all right?" He did not respond. Giovanni Romano was on his feet and walking out into the hall with the servant. "Master, this morning Mistress Lucia went riding, as you know she has missed supper, and just now Apollo has returned without her. I fear that something might have happened. The groom Piro is the only one who Apollo will let ride him, he will take the animal in search of her."

Giovanni Romano his eyes filled with fear did not answer immediately but stood silent. "Get the wagon ready. Put blankets and towels in it. I am going to follow Piro until we find her. There will be a little time before it is completely dark." Giorgio said "My Lord I will come with you." Giovanni said forcefully "No. You are to stay with Mistress Sucretti. I will take Gandolfo with me. I need you here in case she comes back on her own. Now go and get the wagon ready." By now, Maria Sucretti was in the doorway of the library. "Giovanni, what is wrong?" Giovanni took both her hands in his, and kissed each one, then answered attempting to calm his own voice. "Lucia, she left early this morning and has not returned. Apollo has come back without her. She would never leave her horse. I am going with Gandolfo. The groom Piro is the only one who can manage the horse. Apollo will take us to her. If we find her and she is hurt, I will bring her to the nearest farm and stay the night. Try not to worry but pray for her safety. Giorgio will stay with you here. I will find her. I promise. I love you." Tears were streaming down Maria's face. "Dear God watch over her. Giovanni find her and bring her home to me." Giovanni said, "You must tell Antoinetta, it would not be right if she finds out tomorrow. It is her sister. I must go now."

Giovanni met Gandolfo and they went off to the stable where the wagon was stocked and waiting for them. They also took torches and covered lamps. Gandolfo helped Piro onto Apollo, his skin was hot to the touch, but he protested that he was fit to ride. Maria got hold of Gandolfo's arm and whispered "that boy is sick with fever watch that he does not fall from that beast. Be sure to give him water, I have put two sacks in the wagon. God be with all of you. I will pray for Lucia's homecoming."

They took off following the big horse who was clearly agitated. He did not hesitate and did not need prompting but took off with a gallop. The wagon had difficulty keeping pace. Gandolfo silently prayed that Piro would find the strength to finish this mission. He was an honorable, love struck, man.

Piro was sweating a cold sweat, even though it was a warm evening. His mouth was dry from the fever and his head throbbed. He was talking softly to Apollo just as he always did. "Apollo take me to Lucia. You know the way I will let you lead me. Please Apollo find her." The young man his heart pounding his back burning prayed, "Dear Lord Jesus help me find Lucia. You know I love her, even though our love can never be. Hail Maria, full of grace, the Lord is with Thee..." he prayed every prayer he had ever learned; it was the only thing left within him. He was getting weaker and felt as if he would fall off the horse, so he wrapped the reins around his waist, and then wrapped it around the pummel of the saddle.

The sun was so low in the sky it was kissing the sea. There would be maybe an hour until it would be too dark to see anymore. The big animal ran sure-footed on the rocky path. Piro could hear the clang of the harness from the wagon back in the distance. This path was difficult for a horse in the daylight, but a wagon in the dark was impossible. It was comforting to know that if he failed to fulfill the mission there were others who would find his beloved mistress.

Apollo was starting to slow down twitching his ears and shaking his head from side to side. Then suddenly he stopped, stomping his hooves and going in a circle. It was almost dark but Piro could make out a hump silhouetted nearby in a copse of shrubbery. He gingerly dismounted the horse, but held on to the reins to steady himself. His head was spinning, and he had to swallow hard to keep the bile from reaching his mouth. He took a deep lung full of air and let is out slowly to steady himself; with his sleeve he wiped the sweat from his brow. When he felt the world stop moving, he started to approach the mound that looked out of place. As he came closer, he saw what his heart would not reconcile. A man lay half-naked curled on top of Lucia. The man, covered in blood with a dagger sticking out of his chest. Both bodies soaked in the putrid scent of decaying flesh. His eyes fell upon the exposed genitalia of his beloved mistress. Her breasts exposed and bruised. Lucia's beautiful face, beaten, bruised and covered in blood, carnage the likes of which he had never seen. He knelt down with his face in his hands and sobbed thinking she was dead.

The wagon pulled up once they saw Apollo who was still moving about aimlessly in a state of nervous confusion. They called out to Piro who cried back his location. The two older men arrived on the scene and gasped. While Gandolfo pulled the dead man from her body Giovanni Romano covered her discretely to save her decency. He came over to her head and cradled it lovingly in his arms. He was crying. She felt warm to his touch so he felt for a pulse. It was so weak he almost missed it but sure enough, there was a slight throbbing in her neck. "Dear Mother of God she is alive! Gandolfo get a blanket." Piro who was sobbing so badly he did not understand what Giovanni Romano had said. "Piro she is alive we must get her help. Where is the closest place to here?" The young man shaking from shock and fever tried with all his might to clear his head. "Tell me quickly." Gandolfo by now was back with the blankets, which they wrapped Lucia in. Her body was bloody and limp. "The Abrazzia di Montecassino is not far we will go there."

"Gandolfo can you get the wagon in here?" asked Giovanni in a frantic voice. "There is no room for the wagon my Lord I will carry her." Piro said in as steady a voice as he could "I will carry her." Gandolfo, who had told Giovanni Romano what had happened earlier that day, knew that the boy was running on sheer nerves. He was sick with fever, and was now heartbroken. The two older men looked at each other but knew better than to argue with him. Piro with his last ounce of strength scooped Lucia into his arms and carried her on unsteady legs back to the wagon. He laid her carefully in the wagon, covered her with the blanket, and then fainted. Giovanni and Gandolfo who were standing beside the wagon lifted him into the wagon laid him on his stomach next to Lucia; they then tied Apollo to the rig and headed to the abbey.

The trek to the abbey was easier since the road was well worn from the pilgrims. It was now dark and even with their lanterns it was a slow procession. Once they reached the abbey, Gandolfo got down from the wagon and pounded on the door. They waited and after a few minutes they heard the heavy metal bolt slide back from its lock. The monk who answered the door just opened it a crack. "Who goes there?" "I am Gandolfo, I am with Mistress Lucia of Monteforte, she was attacked and is badly injured. We need help." "Dear Mother of God. Come. Come. I will get Abbot Vittorio." The young monk ran off to get the abbot. Gandolfo and Giovanni Romano came into the great hall to wait. The abbot came running down a long hallway.

"Where is she? I told her not to go alone, but she would not hear of it. I have sent for Brother Ronaldo he is in charge of our infirmary, he will tend to her wounds." Giovanni Romano told him of the injuries of Piro and that he would need medical care as well. "Of course, whatever is needed, I will arrange for the two of you to have a bed for the night. Leave the wagon and horse, one of our brothers will tend to them."

Brother Ronaldo a small man so slender of built his robe hung as if from a scarecrow. His quick eyes and wiry frame suggested that he was a man of action. Together with Gandolfo, Giovanni Romano and two brothers they managed to carry Lucia and Piro to the infirmary for treatment, each was assigned a bed. "My Lords please do not concern yourselves, for now, Abbot Vittorio has made provision for your rest. With the help of Brother Franco, we will start to treat their wounds. Good night."

CHAPTER SIXTEEN

MY SISTER

Monteforte

Maria Sucretti remained in the library for a time. She was scared and her heart was heavy. She knew that no one was to blame for Lucia's actions. She was as bullheaded as any young buck. Her fearlessness and determination would make her the best candidate for Mistress of Monteforte. Maria smiled to herself thinking that Lucia was just like her namesake. She looked at the painting on the wall of Lucia Rizzo, her sister-in-law, and prayed for her young niece. "Jesus keep her safe."

Giovanni Romano was right. Maria would have to tell Antoinetta that Lucia was missing. She would not want her to hear from anyone else. Maria steadied herself, rose from her chair, and proceeded to Antoinetta's room. It was now already dark but Maria could see that there was a soft glow of light coming from under the door. She stared at the heavy wooden door thinking of just how to tell Antoinetta that her sister was missing. There had been much discussion at supper regarding Lucia's absence, but it was not odd for her to miss the evening meal. She was often out riding Apollo coming in well past supper.

Maria knocked gently on the door. "Come" was the honey voiced response. She opened the door to find Antoinetta sitting at her desk writing. "Yes Marianna, what is it?" Maria smiled "It is I my dear." Antoinetta dropped the quill and turned quickly to address her

310

aunt. "Zia, what a nice surprise, please come in. Please come and sit down. I was just writing a letter to Mama." Her niece motioned to the settee under the window. Now upon seeing her in the light concern written all over her face Antoinetta asked, "What is wrong Zia. Are you ill?" Maria patted the cushion next to her and her niece came to sit by her side. "My dear niece Gandolfo came to get your uncle. Apollo has returned without Lucia. They fear that something has happened to her."

Maria watched as Antoinetta absorbed the information. Her eyes grew wide. "Where is she? Is she hurt?" There was panic in her usually calm, soft voice. Anticipating these questions Maria held up her hand to quiet the girl. "I know as much as you. Giovanni went with Gandolfo and Piro to find her. They are quite certain that Apollo will be able to lead them to her. If she is hurt, they will find the nearest farm and bring her there for the night. Giovanni has promised to send word first thing in the morning. That is all I know."

Antoinetta ever the older sister with pain in her voice said, "She is a pigheaded fool. Why does she do these things? I have begged her not to go too far. She never listens. If something should happen to her I would never forgive myself." The tears started to well up in those beautiful cognac colored eyes. Maria grabbed her petite shoulders and drew her to her chest. She stroked the long luxurious tresses and softly whispered in her deep commanding voice. "Sweet Antoinetta you are so different from your sister. Someday, maybe soon, you will meet a good young man and settle down to a wonderful life with many babies. I know this is what you want and I am happy for it. Lucia is a wild spirit who, at least for now, lives to seek knowledge and be free. Sometimes I wonder that she should have been born a man. We cannot fault her, but just love her for who she is. Let us just pray for her safety. Whatever has been done we cannot undo. We shall know come the morning what is going on. For now all we can do is ask for divine intervention."

Both Maria and Antoinetta sat there for a long time finding comfort and strength in each other's arms. Silently they prayed for Lucia. She was the driving force in so many lives. Her presence lit up a room. Her beauty was stunning. She had to be safe. She just had to be. Morning would take forever to come.

After a while, Antoinetta still sobbing for her sister dozed off to sleep from exhaustion. Maria was bone tired and every muscle in her body was in pain. She did not want to move to disturb her niece, but the pain was overwhelming. Carefully she maneuvered herself off the settee, and lifted Antoinetta's slender body onto the cushion. She slid out of the room, closing the door as silently as she could, and went to her own room. She met Giorgio on her way. He was carrying a tray with two glasses. "Mistress I thought you and Mistress Antoinetta might need a drink to settle your nerves."

Maria was now at her own bedchamber. "Yes, bring it in. Antoinetta cried herself to sleep poor child. She is worried sick for her sister as am I, as I am sure we all are, but I could use a drink. Please come in and join me. I don't want to be alone."

Giorgio came in and set the tray on the table near the settee. Maria sat down with what seemed the weight of the world on her shoulders. Tears of anxiety cascaded down her handsome face and she did nothing to hide them. Giorgio handed her one of the glasses, which she took. "Sit down Giorgio and join me." He did. They sat there for a few moments the servant waiting for her to regain herself. "Mistress I will find out who is responsible for this and they will be punished." Maria was weary but knew that no one could have stopped her. "Giorgio, my dear and faithful friend, do not punish anyone. There was no way to stop her. She has a mind of her own. That will be both her blessing and her curse when she takes control of Monteforte. You know that I have designated her as my successor. She is strong of mind and body. There has been enough sorrow today. I have heard of the beating Piro was given this morning. I am sorry because he is a good young man."

Giorgio sat at the edge of the settee with his glass in his hand, his head bowed in resignation. "I know your intentions Mistress and I believe you, as always, you have made a wise decision in choosing Lucia as your successor. It will be our honor to serve her, as we have served you, with love and respect. I agree that the beating of young Piro was unfortunate, but the poor young stud is in love with Mistress Lucia, and there is no help for it. He must learn his place in life, and if that requires a beating, then so be it. I will pray for both of them. Can I get anything else for you Mistress?"

Maria said "No. This will do. Let us drink to the health and safety of Lucia and all those who are not in the safety of Monteforte this evening." They both raised their glass and drank. "Thank you Giorgio. Good evening. If you hear anything, I do not care what time it is come to me. I am sure I will not sleep until someone arrives with news in the morning." With that Giorgio, having drained his glass, stood and bowed deeply. He reached for her hand and she gave it to him, and he kissed both hands saying, "All we can do is pray."

Maria finally settled her weary body to her bed. She could not find peace, and in the dark called upon the Virgin Maria, Jesus and all the saints to make things right. Her thoughts traveled over the day's events, and she could not help but shed a tear for the young man Piro, whom she had known since his mother gave birth to him at Monteforte. His father had died several years later in a hunting accident and his mother, heartbroken for him, died shortly thereafter. Piro, a ward of the estate, and as such was taken under the wing of Gandolfo. Under his tutelage had now become a fine horseman. When Gandolfo can no longer maintain his position, it will fall to Piro. Maria sadly knew that he was in love with Lucia, but she was sure that all the young men on the estate loved her. Why would they not? She was kind and generous; there was nothing the servants would not do for her. She will be the perfect Mistress of Monteforte. Dear God watch over her.

Maria prayed that morning would come soon and bring with it news of Lucia.

CHAPTER SEVENTEEN

THE INFIRMARY

Montecassino

When Brother Ronaldo unwrapped the blanket from Lucia's body, he gasped at the sight of her. He remembered seeing her earlier that day. She was hard to miss, strolling comfortably around the abbey with Abbot Vittorio, her beauty and stature could not be missed.

Carefully, with a sharp dagger, he cut away her tattered gown, only to find her bruised and battered from head to toe. For all his years in medicine he had seen many naked women but none as perfectly proportioned as Lucia. Her height with those long slender legs so perfectly shaped, the full hips with her rounded ass, and the large breasts with that tiny waist. Michelangelo as a match to his famous statue of David could have sculpted her. His hands quivered as he examined her body. He prayed hard trying to keep his libido locked in his mind. It had been another lifetime since he had been with a woman, and never one like Lucia. His heart was heavy at the thought that a lustful beast had defiled such beauty; he could not help the tears that fell from his eyes.

Brother Ronaldo had come to find his religious calling later in life. He had been formally trained as a physician in Rome. After years of practicing the healing arts, he felt that he needed more. He found the answer to what he was seeking in joining the order of Saint Benedict. Here he could still practice his medicine since the infirmary was open to all those in need, and still find solace in a religious life. Ronaldo was a highly skilled physician and much sought after.

After a moment's composure, the doctor within Brother Ronaldo took over. He went over her young supple body starting at the head a patch of hair had been torn out from pulling. He could see clearly by the purple and yellow bruises that she had sustained multiple blows to her face. There were no broken bones to the eye sockets although they were badly swollen. He thought that her nose might be broken but there was too much swelling to be sure. There were bruises on her cheek and a gash on her upper lip. He opened her mouth and all her teeth were in place.

Ronaldo gently moved her head from side to side and was grateful that her neck and spine seemed to be unharmed. He moved on to her torso. His eyes drifted over her body ravenously devouring her skin the color of unfired porcelain. His hands trembled as he traveled over the declivity of her tight flat abdomen. Her breasts had taken quite a beating from the purple and blue marks, and there was a bite mark on the one nipple. There was a long scrap probably made by a rock or branch he could see the dirt that had embedded in the wound. So far, her injuries were nothing that would not heal. Lucia was still unconscious and he was grateful for that. She would be embarrassed to be examined so intimately by a man, even a monk, even a physician.
Then he saw the boot imprint on her ribs and the protruding bones. They would have to be set then, wrapped back into place. The monk, his body on fire with desire, bit his lip so hard it started to bleed. He prayed for the weakness of his flesh, and that his erection would go away before his assistant returned.

Coming to her genitalia, he smiled at the crimson patch, a true cappezzio rossi.

There seemed to be no bruising to the pelvic area. He made the sign of the cross, took in a deep breath, and spread her legs. There had been no vaginal penetration. That bastard had not taken her virginity. He silently thanked God for this gift. All the rest would be just a matter of time to heal but no permanent damage.

He rolled her on her side to check her back and groaned when he saw the beating she had sustained to that lovely ass. Lucia's backside was raw, and angry lashes crisscrossed her bottom. Moving down her legs there was nothing but a couple of bruises. He saw that her left ankle, which was swollen, had been severely bruised, and had deep purple and blue marks but appeared not to be broken.

By now his assistant Brother Franco was back from tending the young man that they brought who was also injured. "How is the boy? Have you seen to his needs?" The young monk, perhaps as old as Piro, could not take his eyes off the naked Lucia. Brother Ronaldo felt for the young monk, and knew that if he would someday be a skilled physician, he would need to deal with the temptations of the flesh. "Franco did you do as I said." The young monk did not remove his eyes from her body but answered "Yes Brother Ronaldo I did. Will Mistress Lucia live?"

Before he answered that she was just badly bruised more than anything that was life threatening the older monk knew he needed to talk plainly with Franco. He pulled him from the table that Lucia's body was lying upon, so that he could capture the young man's attention without the distraction of this beautiful creature. Gently, he took the monk by the shoulder and they stepped away with their backs turned on the body. "Listen to me Franco. I see within you the makings of a good doctor. While Mistress Lucia is truly beautiful she is a patient that is injured and in need of our trust and knowledge. You are a healthy young man with desires.

To see this body so sensual and strong is hard. I understand how you feel. However, you must put your mind to the needs of this poor woman that some evil man has beaten nearly to death. Do you understand?"

Brother Franco, his head so low Brother Ronaldo could see his tonsure, picked up his head and the tears were rolling down his face. He was ashamed of his lustful thoughts; he would seek his own punishment for his weak flesh. The older monk felt sorry for the young man who probably had never experienced sex and probably never would. It was sad. Brother Franco, wiped his nose on his sleeve, straightened up, and said, "I am so ashamed of myself. I am weak. I will make a good confession later today. I am sorry for what I've done." The older man turned the boy to look him straight in the eyes. "Do not punish yourself so severely you are but made of flesh and sexual desire is healthy and normal. It is what we do and how we act upon those desires that make us the men we are. The poor woman lies here beaten and wounded because some animal, disguised as a human man, had evil desires for her. You are not that man, but you are still a man. If you wish to be a good physician, you must see past your lust and only see that someone needs your help. Understand?"

Brother Franco did understand, and the older monk could see that he was now ready to help his patient. "Where shall we begin? There is so much damage." Ronaldo smiled and said a prayer of thanksgiving for not only his young assistant but for himself. "Bring lots of hot water, soap, towels, and leeches. Bring lots of leeches."

Together they worked, washing Lucia from head to foot. Once she was thoroughly washed her ribs were wrapped tightly to push them back into place. They put salve on the raw areas of her buttocks. Brother Franco found a simple shift of homespun linen, pulled it over her body, and plaited her hair. Brother Ronaldo had placed leeches on her face to take down the swelling. The two monks, finally finished with their ministrations, felt satisfied that she could now rest, and hoped she would sleep for many more hours.

Brother Ronaldo took the first shift to stay with Lucia. It was only hours until first prayers. He sent the younger monk to bed to get some rest. He sat there, in the silence of the night, haunted by his desire and ashamed that he had succumbed to his lust. He removed his robe, taking a leather strap, fell to his knees, and mortified his flesh until the desire left his mind and body. He prayed for forgiveness.

Piro stirred on the pallet they had laid him on. The fever was still ragging but he remembered what happened. His head was pounding and his mouth was dry. The thoughts of seeing Lucia were so disturbing to him that he wept. She had been so injured that he was sure she would never heal. He wished that he had killed her attacker. He fell back into a restless sleep filled with terrible dreams.

Morning came early at the abbey, with bells tolling their beckoning wail. Giovanni Romano had cried himself to sleep. He had during his life seen and done many evil things, but the sight of his dear Lucia so damaged, was a terrible blow to his heart. Lying there in his barren cell brought him back to memories of his own daughter Rosalie and his wife Natalie. How he had loved them. He was not there when they fell prey to the plague. They had died alone, and now, his precious Lucia had been alone, to face that monster. He cursed himself for his failings. He rolled off the pallet they had prepared for him and fell to his knees, and begged God for forgiveness for all the wicked things he had done. Giovanni Romano thanked God for his life now with Maria, and his girls Lucia and Antoinetta. He prayed for strength to do better. He would stay at the abbey until he could take Lucia home. "Please Lord Jesus, make her whole again."

Brother Vittorio came with a soft knock on the cell door to get Giovanni Romano. "Good morning Signore` Romano. I would take you to see Mistress Lucia now if you wish." Giovanni who had been up for hours was dressed and ready to go. "Yes Abbot I am most anxious to see her." They silently made their way to the infirmary. When they came into the room, Giovanni gasped at the sight of the leeches covering her face. "What is this?" he demanded in a horrified voice. Brother Franco who had been watching over Lucia did not hear them enter, and rose so quickly from his chair he almost fell over. "Ah, good morning do not fear my Lord, they are harmless leeches. When Brother Ronaldo returns from morning prayers, which will be very soon, he will remove them." Giovanni looked in disgust at the bugs that had now swollen to twice their normal size. Abbot Vittorio placed his big hand on the older man's shoulder "Brother Ronaldo is a highly skilled physician. Wait here for his return; I will look in on our young man." Giovanni just nodded. Brother Franco motioned to the vacated chair and Giovanni accepted. He reached for Lucia's hand, which was cold, and a chill ran up his spine.

The abbot came to the adjoining room of the infirmary and entered to find Piro on his knees praying. He came over to the young man "How are you today Piro? I am Abbot Vittorio. You were unconscious when they brought you in last night. Come sit down." He put his arms under Piro's shoulders and lifted him easily on to the pallet. He could see the wet cheeks but did not comment. The groom had made a swift attempt to wipe his face dry. "I am fine. How is my Mistress?" The Abbot knew that he was still harboring a fever, but again did not want to embarrass the young man. "She will heal over time. Her wounds are on the outside but she will probably hold scars on the inside for much longer." Piro his face in his hands sobbing said "Abbot can you hear my confession?" The monk bowed his head and simply replied, "Yes my son."

Again, Piro fighting his fever and the burning wounds on his back, came to his knees and making the sign of the cross began. "Bless me father for I have sinned. I am so ashamed that I have had lustful thoughts of my mistress. I cannot put my desire for her out of my head. I know it is wrong, and I have prayed for forgiveness. As you can see even the whipping I got did not help. Then, when I saw her, when I saw that animal upon her naked body I wanted to kill him with my bare hands. I don't know what to do."

The monk, his eyes closed, listened with a heavy heart, knowing the young man before him had sustained more punishment than most men could take. "Listen to me my son. You have done nothing wrong. I do not believe that your desire is purely physical. I believe that you love your mistress. You love her because she is good and caring. To have seen her abused and damaged in such a way would cause any man to want to protect her. All men, even I as a religious, have thoughts and desires. It is only when we act on those desires that it becomes a sin. You know that through prayer all things are possible. Keep your mind pure and your body will follow. It is not easy; the flesh is weak to the temptations of the body. I believe you have suffered enough, and for your penance say ten Aves." He placed his hand on Piro's head to make the sign of the cross and could feel him burning with fever.

"Now come and take your rest. We must break that fever or you will be good for no woman. I will send

Brother Ronaldo around to look at you and one of the brothers will bring you some breakfast. Rest my son you are weary. I will pray for you." Piro flopped down on his stomach and began his penance. "Ave Maria piena di grazia ...

While Giovanni Romano sat, waiting for Brother Ronaldo to come speak with him of Lucia's condition Gandolfo came quietly to the door of the infirmary. He too was shocked at the sight of the leeches all over her face. Giovanni seeing his tired eyes grow wide said the doctor put them there. "Gandolfo, take the wagon and return to Monteforte. Mistress Sucretti must be sick with worry that we did not return. Tell her Lucia is alive but injured and cannot be moved. I will stay with her until I can take her home. She is not to worry that her injuries are not life threatening. Tell her Piro is being treated also until his fever breaks. We will all come home together. In three days come back with the wagon to get us. Thank you Gandolfo, but leave right after you have taken your breakfast. Leave Apollo here, I think seeing him will make Lucia happy." The old Master of the Stables, tired and heartbroken, came over to his Mistress and placed a gentle kiss upon her burning head. He did not mask the tears falling from his eyes. "As you wish Master, I shall pray for her full recovery." Giovanni grabbed him and the two men, both of whom had lived long lives, and who had seen so much, wept for this beloved young woman.

Gandolfo's return to Monteforte was met with apprehensive anxiety. As soon as he had washed himself, he went up to the main house. There Giorgio greeted him. He told the story as he had lived it. Giorgio was shocked but relieved that his young mistress was not mortally wounded. "When will they come home?" Gandolfo replied, "Master Giovanni has instructed that I come in three days with the wagon to bring them back." Giorgio acknowledged that with a thoughtful nod. "Gandolfo, Mistress Sucretti is on the terrace of her bedchamber. She is up and dressed. Go to her and tell her only part of the story you just told me. There is no need to distress her more than she already is. When Master Giovanni comes home, if he chooses, he can tell her all the details. For now, she only will need to know that Lucia is alive and not badly wounded. Understand?" Gandolfo understood perfectly what Giorgio was doing and agreed. He knew that he should come with the news, so that Mistress Sucretti would feel more confident with the story.

Gandolfo made his way to her bedchamber, seeing the door open he entered. There, on the terrace was Mistress Sucretti and Antoinetta, talking softly with each other. He made his way through the luxurious room and politely coughed to interrupt their conversation. "Oh Gandolfo you are back. What news do you bring of my sister? Is she hurt? Where is she? Can I see her? Did you bring her home?" The rush of questions overwhelmed the man. Maria Sucretti grabbed her niece's arm to prevent the barrage of questions. Gandolfo smiled and bowed thankfully to the older woman. "Mistress Lucia is injured but mostly bruises and some broken ribs. We took her to Abrazzia di Montecassino, which was closest to where we found her. They have a full infirmary and Brother Ronaldo is a highly skilled physician. He assured Master Giovanni that Mistress Lucia will heal very nicely."

"When will she be able to come home?" "Master Giovanni has requested that I come to get them in three days. That will give the monk time to tend her." Antoinetta jumped up and ran to give Gandolfo a kiss; she was rushing from the terrace "Zia, I must go tell Sophia who has been weeping for two days now. I will come back later."

Maria smiled and motioned for Gandolfo to come closer. "What happened to her Gandolfo?" The man lowered his head and spoke in a deep voice. "We are not totally sure. When we found her, she was unconscious and a man lay at her side with her own dagger in his chest. He was dead." "Did he violate her?" Gandolfo told her what the monk said, "There was no penetration to her womanhood." Maria visibly was relieved.

"What of Piro?" Gandolfo stood a little taller, and with pride in his voice, answered. "He found her, and then carried her to the wagon. Then he fainted from fever. The monks are treating his wounds and his fever. They will both heal. At least their bodies will."

CHAPTER EIGHTEEN

AN ANIMAL IS BURIED

Montecassino

He was hungry and angry for having lost the last meal to a pack of hunting wolves. The massive head snorted and sniffed from side to side. He was roaming the woods in search of his next meal. It had been several days since last he had eaten. His keen sense of smell picked up a scent that seemed promising. Grunting and snorting he followed his instincts with caution. He already had suffered a nasty gash at the hands of his enemies.

It was not long before the scent became stronger. The rancid odor of dead meat was like perfume to his highly sensitive nose. The coarse bristling fur on his body prickled at the smell. He hurried along on those sturdy little legs that supported that big body. He was all in a huff as he neared the source of his delight. He was in a full run, his tiny hooves making great strides. As he came closer, he began to salivate.

Circling his prey, not sure, if this animal was dead or badly wounded, he proceeded with caution. He was now snorting furiously coming closer with each circle. Finally, when the creature made no sound and did not move to defend itself he approached. It was now full darkness, the only glimmer of light coming from a crescent moon, which cast an ominous shadow over the still figure. The wind from the sea carried the iron stench of blood, its aroma driving the wild animal to its victim. The big animal was now crazed with desire and hunger.

He threw all caution aside and fell upon the body. He was at first hesitant this was a strange animal like none he had ever killed or eaten. He smelled odd.

Sniffing the source of where the blood was the animal with his razor sharp teeth gnawed at the wound. A metal object obstructed the hole. He was angry. He growled at the inert body his sharp yellow fangs biting deep into the soft tissue of the man's belly. He shook his head violently, trying to dislodge his prize, and was rewarded with a succulent morsel of meat.

He continued making progress finding the taste different but satisfactory. He burrowed his long snout into the deep recess of the belly, and found the liver and entrails. He ate until he could take no more. With a trail of intestines dangling from his mouth the big animal found himself a comfortable place to rest for the night.

He would be back in the morning for breakfast.

***

After speaking with Brother Ronaldo, they decided that Abbot Vittorio and Giovanni Romano would go and bury the attacker. They would bring one of the lay brothers with them for help.

It was still morning by the time the trio reached the place where Lucia's body was found. Dismounting their horses, they gathered their shovels and picks they had taken a blanket to act as shroud for the man's body. They could smell the stink of decaying flesh before they could see him.

The odor of dead meat together with the blood had attracted the wild animals that roamed the mountain. The wound where Lucia's dagger had entered her assailant's body was teaming with maggots. Birds had gouged out his eyes, leaving the sockets empty and black. His tongue lay engorged and swollen outside of his mouth, the top lip pulled back in an eternal growl showing blacken decayed teeth. A trail of guts drifted off into the thick brush.

The lay brother they had taken with them was the same one that had tended to Apollo on the day Lucia arrived at the abbey. "Boars must have gotten to him Abbot, had been wolves they would have taken him back to their den, they hunt in packs. The boars usually roam alone. I see this one did quite a bit of damage." The monk acknowledged his agreement as to what his lay brother assessed to be true.

Abbot Vittorio clearly not used to seeing this carnage looked like he was going to be sick. The boar had done severe damage to the remains. There were ragged teeth marks where the guts and genitalia had been. The entrails splayed across the lower portion of the body, and there were chunks of meat missing from the exposed torso. It was a horrific sight. The monk made the sign of the cross and closed his eyes, fighting against the bile in his throat.

Secretly, Giovanni Romano was pleased that this man had come to this end for what he had done to Lucia, and God only knew how many other innocent people he had harmed. He prayed for forgiveness, but in his heart, he could not truly make his contrition. Lucia would mend on the outside, but he knew she would have changed on the inside. It reminded him of his beloved Natalie, who, after having sustained that beating from Salvatore Sucretti, was never the same. Violence and humiliation alter a person. He prayed for his sweet Lucia.

Giovanni Romano said nothing but came to the body and removed the dagger from the man's chest. It came out with a whoosh. He wiped the blade and hilt on the shirt that lay near a brush. He would return this to Lucia. She would want it. It saved her life of that he was sure. The other two men did not say anything but they understood what he had done and why he had done it.

They laid out the blanket and carefully picked up the corpse. The smell mixed with the heat of the day was overwhelming. The body was then wrapped in the blanket and they marked out a place to bury the body. "We will bury him here where he died," said the abbot "I cannot bring him to our abbey for burial in the monastery's cemetery. I know he was not in a state of grace when he died." There was pain and sorrow in the monk's voice, but he could not disguise his disgust for the man that lay before him.

The ground was hard and dry and the lay brother who was used to tending the fields began picking at the dirt. It was a long difficult process. The ground was filled with rocks, and it took a long time to dig the grave deep enough so that the marauding animals would not be able to dig him up. Even though they searched, they could not find any trace of how the man got to this place. There were no shoe marks from a horse or mule. Where did he come from? It was a mystery as to his identity. All three labored hard to finish off the grave. When it was done they laid the man in the hole. Abbot Vittorio took out a vile of holy water and sprinkled it on top of the body. "May Our Lord Jesus Christ show you more mercy than you gave to others. May your soul, and the souls of all the faithfully departed, through the mercy of God, rest in peace. Amen." He made the sign of the cross over the inert lump of human flesh then they proceeded to fill in the grave.

There were no words passed from the three men as they completed their task. Once the grave was covered the lay brother asked his superior "Abbot, will we mark this grave?" The monk thought for a moment then replied "Let us gather as many large stones as we can find, and we will lay them in the sign of the cross. We cannot place a name, we do not have one, and if someone comes to seek this man, we can direct them to this site. They all agreed that was the best solution. It was already noon by the time they had finished, the sun was blazing high in the sky; they were hot, thirsty, and hungry. They found a shade tree nearby and the lay brother took the bags that hung from his horse. Inside the bag was fresh bread, a slab of cheese and some olives. From another bag, he produced a skin of wine. They sat there in the welcomed shade for a while refreshing themselves from their labors. They spoke very little, each man affected by what they had seen and done.

After a while, the lay brother announced to his abbot "I need to return to the abbey, there is much work to prepare for tomorrow's harvest. I will leave the two of you to rest. I will see you back at the abbey." With that, he was off. Giovanni Romano spoke "That is a fine man. Is there some way to reward him for all his trouble?" The monk just smiled and said, "He is a man with a past. He came to be at our monastery while escaping from the law. I spoke on his behalf to the Magistrate and they agreed that he would not go to prison as long as he stayed at the monastery. That was ten years ago. Now he is one of us and I am happy for it." Giovanni Romano who also had a past understood the gift of being safe from the law. He just nodded.

"Abbot, I have done many things in my life that have not pleased the Lord. I have prayed for his mercy and forgiveness and until now, I felt confident that He forgave me my sins. I cannot find mercy for the man we just buried. He would have damaged my sweet Lucia, killed her, or worst, sold her for her body. How can I forgive such a person?" The monk seeing the distress in the old man said, "Giovanni, the families of those you have injured in your past feel the same way you do toward the man who attacked Lucia. Yet, you have confessed your sins to Our Lord, begged his forgiveness and felt sure that He gave it to you. Are you; are we, any of us, so different from the man in the grave? Yes, we may not have raped or killed, but we have injured others in our life. We can only receive mercy if we give it. In time, when you see that the girl has recovered you will feel differently. For now, the pain is too great, you are reminded of this hatred every time you look at that damaged face, but Brother Ronaldo assures me that it is only superficial and will heal without any permanent scars. Giovanni you are a good man do not carry hatred in your heart. Let us say a prayer together for the courage to forgive this man and in so doing we will be forgiven."

The monk dropped to his knees, made the sign of the cross, and Giovanni Romano followed his lead. "Lord Jesus, give us the strength of will to find forgiveness for others as you have found love and mercy for us. We pray for our beloved Lucia that she too will find peace with what she has done, and that she will be able to forgive this man. Amen."

"Time is the greatest healer of all wounds."

CHAPTER NINETEEN

SHE AWAKES

Montecassino

It was early evening before Lucia finally awoke. Earlier Brother Ronaldo had removed the leeches. What remarkable little creatures they were. They had done a fine job of sucking all the blood from around her swollen eyes. There were of course the bruises, but the swelling had gone down significantly. Already she was starting to regain her usual beauty. Her head throbbed from where the man had yanked out her hair and banged her head to the ground. She opened one eye at a time and her gaze fell upon the smiling face of Giovanni Romano. Her lip still badly bruised had a scab that formed on the cut. She smiled back. "Padrino, where am I?" Giovanni fought so hard to hold back the tears that were welling up in his eyes "You are safe my bella cappezzi rossi. You are at the abbey. Do you remember anything?" Lucia closed her eyes at the question. Tears started to fall down her bruised cheeks. "Yes, I remember it all. I killed a man. He was going to sell me to the gypsies, but first he was going to do terrible things to me. I had to protect myself. I am so sorry."

Giovanni Romano scooped Lucia into his arms and kissed her head. "My darling child, do not fear you did what was necessary. I spoke with Abbot Vittorio and he says God will forgive you. You will make your confession and then you will feel better. I also spoke with Brother Ronaldo, he is the doctor who has been caring for you, and he says that the only damage that will require some time to heal are your ribs which were broken. Everything else is just bruises. I have seen you with worst when you fell off Apollo last year. Remember?" He was stroking her head and spoke in a low soothing voice. Lucia was sobbing, but at the mention of her horse and the reminder of the day she feel off him, she smiled through her tears. "Where is Apollo? The last I saw him was when that beast of a man punched him so hard in the nose then slapped him hard on his rump. He was running at full speed. Is he hurt?"

Giovanni just smiled. Here she lay all beaten, bruised, and worried for her dear horse. She was amazing. "Apollo is our hero. After he left you, he found his way back home and Gandolfo came to get me. We did not know how we were going to find you out here in the dark. No one knew where you had gone." His voice grew harder, "and we shall speak more on that when you are better." Giovanni, again softly, continued, "The only one who could ride him was Piro. Of course, you know what had happened to him earlier that day. The poor boy was injured and with fever, but he was the only answer to locating you. So he rode Apollo, who led us to where you were, then Piro carried you to the wagon and then he collapsed. Brother Ronaldo is also treating him for his injuries and the fever. He is in the room next to us" Lucia was dumbstruck by this story.

"Oh Dear God, I am so sorry for all this trouble. I just wanted to come here by myself, but if I had not been so pigheaded, none of this mess would have happened. Poor Piro will he ever forgive me? Can I see him?" Giovanni Romano knew that he needed to speak frankly to his niece regarding the young man and his feelings for her.

"Lucia my darling, you must not encourage any feelings between yourself and Piro. It is his feelings for you that have caused him to be whipped. I know you are concerned, but a young man can mistake concern for something else. Do you understand what I am trying to tell you?" Lucia for the first time realized what Giovanni was trying to say. She was embarrassed to think that she was the cause of his being beaten. She stupidly thought it was because he had tried to throw her off the horse, and she might have gotten hurt. She was so sorry to have given him any wrong impressions. She would have to apologize. Giovanni Romano saw the look on her face, and inwardly felt the young man's pain. Lucia did not have feelings for him, but sadly, Piro was in love with her. "Lucia, did you understand what I said?" She roused herself from her thoughts and nodded. "Yes Padrino, I understand, and I am sorry for it. When can we leave to go home?" Giovanni ever the patient man said, "Tomorrow Gandolfo will come with the wagon to take us home. The doctor says you cannot ride Apollo for a while until your ribs mend."

As they were talking, Brother Ronaldo came into the room. He looked tired. When he saw that his patient was awake, his mood brightened. "Ah, I see our young mistress is awake. How are you my dear? He came over to examine her face, head, and torso. She gasped when he prodded her side. "I am sorry. It will take a few weeks for the ribs to mend back together, but, other than a few purple marks, and you will be as good as new." The monk had a jovial personality and it lifted Lucia's spirits. "There is no infection and no fever. Your backside will be sore for a little while, but I suspect you might have gotten some of that for coming here all by yourself." Giovanni Romano raised the eyebrow on his good side, and nodded, trying to look menacing. Lucia trying to act contrite pouted her lips.

"Ah, Mistress Lucia, I see that you are back to yourself. A few bruises but you will mend." came the baritone voice of Abbot Vittorio. He came to her bedside and kissed her forehead. "Thank God you are safe here with us and not so damaged." Lucia grabbed for his hand and asked if she might speak with him alone. Her uncle and the doctor nodded and left the room. "Oh Abbot, I am truly sorry for what I have done. I am sure by now you know that I killed that man who attacked me. He did terrible things to me and I am ashamed for it. I had no choice, he was going to rape me, and then sell me to the gypsies. Abbot, will God forgive me?" The monk sat in the chair by her bed and kissed her hand. "Do not concern yourself my child. God sees and hears all that we do and say. You did not kill for pleasure, or money, but out of survival. It is up to God now to see to the man's punishment. I am very pleased that you are not terribly damaged. As for the gypsies, this was probably a terrible loss for them; I think you might have made a good gypsy girl." For a second Lucia looked stunned, then started to laugh, but had to check herself because of the pain in her ribs. He was rising to leave with her hand still clutched in his; she said, "Did you tell Master Giovanni why I had come to the monastery yesterday?" The monk looked at her "No I did not. We are not certain what may, or may not be with those manuscripts, and until we are sure, we should not speak of their existence. Do you agree?" Lucia was pleased that Abbot Vittorio felt the same way she did. "I agree."

They were still talking when a soft rap came from the hall. It was Piro looking worn and ragged. "Piro, come see your mistress." He came into the infirmary and upon seeing her gasped. "Oh dear Mistress Lucia, I am so sorry. I wished it were I that would have killed that animal. Brother Ronaldo said that you will heal in no time, I am so happy to hear it." Lucia slightly wounded by his reaction to her looks recovered herself and asked, "How are you doing? Master Giovanni told me that you rode Apollo to find me, and then carried me to the wagon, even though you were injured and fevered." The young man, his head bowed, said in a voice so soft and low she could barely hear him "I would do anything for you my mistress." The monk hearing that said a silent prayer for the young man, he would need it.

CHAPTER TWENTY

THE HOMECOMING

Monteforte

As he had been instructed after three days Gandolfo returned to the abbey to bring his trio home. When he saw his mistress he was pleasantly surprised "Ah, Mistress Lucia you look wonderful. The bruises are healing so well. The last time I saw you your face was covered in black ugly fat worms. It was horrible." Lucia her eyes bright once again replied, "I am glad that I was unconscious for that part, but Brother Ronaldo assures me the leeches work miracles. Are we going home Gandolfo?"

"I am waiting to see Master Giovanni and the doctor. If they say you can travel I have the wagon ready to go. Mistress Sucretti and your sister are very anxious to see you. They have sent a clean gown for you." As if on command the Abbot, her Padrino and the doctor all came into the infirmary. "There is my beautiful patient. How are you today?" asked the jovial monk. "I am fine. My ribs hurt a little but otherwise I will do." Giovanni Romano acknowledged Gandolfo "You have everything ready for us to travel?" Gandolfo nodded and bowed deeply.

"Well then Cara, it is time to go home. See if you can walk?" said Giovanni Romano. Lucia swung her legs over the bed she had been lying in for the past few days, and to her surprise, the room started to sway. The color

336

drained from her face, and Brother Ronaldo jumped to catch her before she fell. "You must go slowly. The blood needs to get to your head. Sit up first. Then we will try to stand." Lucia obeyed. She got herself steady with a few deep breaths. Slowly the color returned to her cheeks. "Can you all leave?" The men looked at each other in a unified question. "Why?" ask her Padrino. "I need to get dressed. Zia sent a clean gown for me." Brother Ronaldo shooed the others from the infirmary. "I will help her." Together with the monk's help, Lucia put on the clean gown. "I will leave the bodice loose for now. Do not remove the wrapping around your ribs for two more weeks they need to mend together. Promise me Lucia that you will not remove the wrappings?" The monk tried to look stern, but there was a smile on his face. "I promise Brother Ronaldo. Thank you for everything you did for me." The monk took her face in his hands and kissed each cheek. "I will keep you in my prayers." She was now ready to go home.

***

Gandolfo with his big hand around her waist helped Lucia to the grand entry hall. There waiting for them was Abbot Vittorio. Lucia detached herself from Gandolfo and took the monk's outstretched hand. "Thank you, and everyone here, for all your love and care. I will never forget what you have done for me. I will see you soon." The abbot in a kind voice said "May the peace of Our Lord Jesus Christ be with you always Lucia." He then made the sign of the cross on her forehead and bent to kiss her cheeks. Holding her arm securely in his powerful hand, he escorted her out to the waiting wagon. Gandolfo had made a pallet of sorts for her to rest upon. He and Giovanni Romano lifted her onto the wagon and she rested comfortably.

Lucia heard Apollo's excited whickering. Piro was riding him and they came close to the wagon. Lucia straining to reach her horse, but quickly drew back from the pain, was very happy to see her. Piro looked triumphant astride the huge animal. "Good morning my mistress, you look beautiful." The second the words left his mouth, the groom wanted to slap himself. The other men just smiled and shook their heads. There was no hope for it. Lucia's face flushed but she graciously responded "Thank you Piro for taking such good care of Apollo." The young man just bowed his head and turned the horse toward the front of the wagon. "Well shall we leave?" Everyone nodded their assent. "Abbot Vittorio, it is with great appreciation that I say farewell. Thank you for all your care to my beloved Lucia and the boy." Giovanni stepped closer, gathered the monk in a manly embrace, and spoke in his ear. "Pray for my wretched soul." The monk embraced him back and replied, "I already have, and will continue to do so. Peace, be with you Giovanni."

Lucia, although happy to be on her way home, was sad to leave the peace of the monastery. There was something magical about the place. She waved until she could no longer see the abbey, which had drifted off behind the horizon. It was a warm day and the constant rocking of the wagon lulled her to sleep. She dreamt of a meadow filled with roses and lemon trees their scent filling her nostrils, and of deep green grass caressing her softly in a bed of nature. She had no pain and her mind was at peace. This was the first time in three days that her mind was not haunted by what had happened to her in the woods. It was only when the wagon and its rocking motion had stopped that she opened her eyes to find herself at her beloved Monteforte. She was still in the midst surrounding peaceful sleep when she heard the excited cries of Antoinetta and Sophia.

"Oh my dear sister, look at that beautiful face. That animal I would have killed him myself." Tears of both sorrow and joy rolled down the dark olive face of her sister Antoinetta, two sisters who were worlds apart in both body and mind. Gandolfo had come around with Giovanni Romano to help Lucia out of the wagon. Sophia coming hesitantly, not wanting to hurt her mistress "I missed you Mistress. I prayed for you. Thank the Blessed Virgin you are home safe." The young maid was also crying tears of joy at Lucia's homecoming. Piro came around with Apollo. He dismounted and brought the horse to his mistress. "My dear faithful friend, thank you for bringing me help." Lucia was stroking the horse lovingly and kissed him. The horse whinnied and bobbed his head at her touch. Piro was grinning like a fool.

Now, as they were coming to the mansion, standing there tall, proud, and elegant was Maria Sucretti. Lucia escorted by Gandolfo and Giovanni Romano came to stand before her. "I am so sorry Zia for all the trouble I have caused." Her aunt put her finger to the girl's mouth. "You are, who you are, we shall never change that. I am just grateful to Jesus and all the saints that you are not damaged. I love you and would have died if something terrible would have befallen you." It was now that those amber colored eyes brought forth tears. She carefully and gently embraced her beloved niece. "I love you Lucia." Lucia with her own tears whispered "I love you too Zia."

Regaining herself, Maria Sucretti addressed the maid. "Sophia, Gandolfo, and Master Giovanni will bring Lucia to her room. Undress her, bathe her, and put her to bed. If she should get up let me, know. I will have Giorgio bring refreshments. Do not leave her. Understood?" The young maid with dancing eyes bowed deeply "Yes Mistress." Softly she said to Antoinetta "go with them see if you can help. I know you want to talk to your sister." She also nodded and bowed slightly to her aunt.

Standing in the shadows of the grand foyer was Giorgio. A look of sad concern etched on his handsome face upon seeing her. He made a footed bow "Mistress Lucia it is wonderful to see you. We all prayed for your safe return. If it would not trouble you, some of the staff would like to stop by your room later to give their best wishes." Lucia was overwhelmed by the gesture. "Of course, just give me some time to bathe and rest. Sophia will tell you. Thank you Giorgio it is good to be home." Lucia leaned forward and gave him a kiss on the cheek. The servant bowed deeply and a flush came to his face.

Lucia was weary, but she did not know why, because she had slept on the trip home. Sophia saw the tiredness in her mistress's face. "Come Mistress, let us get you washed and changed, so you can rest." Lucia did not protest. "Brother Ronaldo said I cannot remove the wrappings around my ribs for three weeks." Sophia, who was filling a basin with warm water, just nodded and helped Lucia from her gown. She gasped at the sight of her bruised and battered body. Sophia cried as she gently washed her mistress's back and saw the raw marks on her bottom. When she turned around, she gasped at the deep purple marks around Lucia's breasts. "My dear sweet mistress I am so sorry for all this pain you have endured." Brother Ronaldo had sent her home with a clay pot filled with healing salve. "Sophia can you put some of the salve on my wounds?" She did not have to ask but that was why they all loved her.

Lucia was grateful that Antoinetta decided to go to the kitchen to instruct the cook what to make for her sister. She did not want to face Antoinetta and let her see all this damage. There would be too many questions, and she did not want to relive that terrifying experience again. It was bad enough that that beast haunted her dreams. She knew, over time, they would ask, and she would have to tell them what happened, but for now, she just wanted some peace.

Sophia was gentle with her machinations. When she was done, she lifted the shift over Lucia's head and helped her to her luxurious bed. Carefully, Sophia combed through the mass of strawberry curls, trying to coax the comb through the labyrinth of tangles. She spotted the bald patch and lump the size of a robin's egg, and just about the same color, on the back of Lucia's head. She bit her tongue not to say anything, but cursed the demon who caused all this pain to her beloved mistress. With exceptional care, Sophia was able to work through the mess, and plaited Lucia's long thick hair. She perfumed her body, and rubbed scented olive oil on her face, hands, and legs. Lucia felt renewed.

Just as they had finished, Antoinetta burst through the door with an entourage of kitchen staff carrying trays of food. "You my dear sister look drawn. You will eat a good meal. You need to keep up your strength." Antoinetta, ever the older sibling, had the staff, who all bowed, set out a veritable feast. Lucia was hardly hungry, but knew better than to object, she knew it made Antoinetta feel better to be doing something for her. With their task completed the four young kitchen maids came over to her bedside, bowed deeply, and one by one they kissed her hand. The oldest of the group Olivia said, "Dear Mistress, when we heard what happened, the entire house cried. We all went to the chapel to pray for your safe return. We thank the Blessed Virgin that you are home with us. We love you." The four maids curtsied and practically flew out of the room. Antoinetta, as if to confirm the veracity of what they just said, came over to Lucia, and with her honey-toned voice said, "We all prayed for you. I do not know what I would have done if you died. Thank God you are here with me now." The two sisters embraced, kissing each other with love and gratitude.

Antoinetta turned to Sophia, who shared in their moment, and asked her to get two glasses and some cognac. She left to go retrieve the liquor. They were finally alone; Antoinetta came close to her sister's side and asked gingerly "Did he rape you?" Lucia had anticipated the question; she was just surprised at its timing and directness; that was not usually her sister's character. "No, I killed him before he did." Antoinetta's petite frame sank in relief at the knowledge. "When you need to talk about it, I will be ready to listen." Lucia was relieved that Antoinetta had resumed her normal diplomatic demeanor. She left her side and busied herself preparing a plate for Lucia, who was oddly enough now hungry.

Mistress Sucretti came to Lucia's room after supper. "How are you this evening my dear niece? I did not come earlier because I knew you needed time to settle your mind." Lucia loved her aunt, respected, and admired her wisdom. She did not hover, but was always present. "I am better now that I am home. I am so sorry Zia for the worry and pain I have caused. Please forgive me." Lucia choked back her tears. "This is not your fault." Lucia saw that her aunt wanted to say something, "Zia what troubles you? If you are worried that my attacker took my virginity I assure you he did not." Maria Sucretti smiled but replied, "That is not my worry. I know you defended yourself and of that I am proud."
The older woman drew a chair toward the bed. She sat down as if weary. "Lucia there is something I wish to tell you. No, actually there is something I wish to ask you." Lucia was surprised, having thought that she already addressed everyone's burning question regarding her safeguarded womanhood, but just waited for her aunt to bring forth her question.

Without preamble, her aunt straightened her spine and placed her hands in her lap. She looked directly at Lucia. "I want you to be my successor. In other words, upon my death, or when I so choose, I want you to become the Mistress of Monteforte. Do you agree to that?" Lucia was stunned and speechless. She closed her eyes for a moment thinking she had dozed off and was dreaming. When she reopened her eyes, she knew it was real. "Zia, what are you saying? Only you can be Mistress of Monteforte. I am nobody. Are you ill?"

Maria Sucretti knew her niece probably better than the girl knew herself. She took a deep breath. "I do not mean that this will happen tomorrow, but I am getting old. I have no children, no apparent heirs, at least none that I would entrust with the honor and responsibility of taking over my estate. From the day I first saw you, and how you loved being here, and then how you have grown in wisdom and intelligence, I knew I had made the right choice. I have already spoken to your mother and father they have agreed. I know it was very presumptuous of me, but I have instructed my avvocato to draw up all the necessary legal documents. When I tell them to do so, it will be official." Lucia, with her mouth open, could hardly absorb all that her aunt was saying. It was so much to take in.

"Before you answer me with your decision, I want you to know that I love you as if you were my own daughter. You possess every quality a true leader should have. The staff loves you and would do anything for you." The older woman looked tired and was making her way to leave when Lucia reached for her arm, "Zia, I am not sure that I am worthy of this profound honor, but, I trust you and respect your judgment. If you think, I can do this, than with the deepest appreciation I will accept. Just please pray that I am half the woman you are." Maria Sucretti did not even attempt to conceal her happiness at Lucia's acceptance, and did not wipe the tears from her wise old eyes. "Thank you my darling Lucia. You have made an old woman happy. Starting tomorrow we will begin your training as Mistress of Monteforte." They embraced and kissed each other. Maria was getting herself ready to leave but Lucia held her back.

"Zia, there is something I wish to talk to you about. It is regarding Piro." Maria sat herself back in the chair and hoped Lucia was going to make a wise decision. "You have heard that on the day I went to the abbey Gandolfo whipped him?" Maria answered, "I have." Lucia seemed slightly embarrassed but continued speaking "I believe he is in love with me. I have feelings for him as well, but not like that. He is a good person, but he will not be able to control his feelings, and I fear it will be his undoing."

Maria was grateful that her young ward understood that their relationship would be difficult. "What would you have me do?" Maria asked hoping that she would make a wise decision.

Lucia, with her head low upon her chest, answered, "Although it would pain me to see him gone, I would ask that you send him to France or Spain to be educated. He is bright and I believe he would do well. After he sees what life is like outside of Monteforte, if he desires, he can return. I know Gandolfo has chosen Piro to be his successor. What do you think?" Maria was amazed at the wisdom of her niece and of her thoughtfulness. "I think that is a wonderful idea. I will speak to him in a few days from now, and then make all the arrangements to send him to stay with my friend and business associate, the Marquis de Fauntil, who has a grand estate in Provence. I am happy you have come to such a wise decision. Let us hope Piro agrees with this proposition." Lucia was also happy that her aunt agreed. "I hope so." "Zia, there is one more thing. Can you tell Antoinetta of your decision? I am not sure she will be so happy."

Maria Sucretti took pause to construct her answer. "Antoinetta is not like you Lucia. She wants a different, more stable life. She wants a husband and children. Again, I have spoken to your parents, and we have agreed that I shall introduce her to a fine young man, whom I believe would make a wonderful husband for our Antoinetta. At first she might be a little jealous, but once she meets the young man I have in mind, I am sure she will lose all interest in being the Mistress of Monteforte. Do not concern yourself; I will take care of everything. Rest Bella. Tomorrow we begin."

BOOK THREE

CHAPTER ONE

A MISTRESS IN TRAINING

Monteforte

Lucia was happy to be home in her own bed, sadly, found no comfort in her sleep, which was too deep, her mind surrounded by the events of the days past. She rose early as she always did, but cursed that she could not take Apollo for his usual run. She would send word to Piro to take him out. She thought about Piro and found herself flushed at the notion of him. He was an attractive young man, tall and muscular, with good straight teeth and fierce dark eyes. It pained her to think that he had taken such a beating because of his feelings for her. She found him attractive in a sexual way, but could never find sustenance in a long-term relationship with someone she could not discuss literature or history. She felt bad that she had asked her aunt to send him away, on the pretense it was for his sake, when it was really for her sake. If he became educated, their relationship could have a chance.

She slowly got out of bed to make her morning toilet. She ventured into her bathroom quietly, not to disturb Sophia, who slept in the small adjoining room. She removed her shift, and for the first time, truly looked into the full-length looking glass. The sight of her bruised and battered body shocked her. The purple bruises were starting to turn a rich shade of yellow. Her full breasts hurt at the touch, and the bruises, like those on her face, were a deep golden yellow. The wrapping around her ribs was driving her mad. She wanted to rip the bindings from her body. She turned so that she could see the angry red welt marks on her ass. Lucia's whole body started to tremble, not with fear, but with anger. She chided herself for letting that prick do this to her. The next time, if there were ever a next time, she would strike first. She would need to be strong of body and mind, if she would be the Mistress of Monteforte.

Lucia stared at herself in the full-length mirror, gleaming with an inner pride, knowing she was capable, and excited to be the heir to the Monteforte fortune, with all the gifts and responsibilities that came with it. Lucia Banfi Mistress of Monteforte, it sounded very good to her ears.

***

Lucia slept haunted by strange dreams. She dreamt of the man who attacked her. Who was the man, and how did she not see him? Where had he come from? In her dreams, she forced herself to try to see the surrounding landscape, just before he stepped out from the brush, but she could not remember. She tried to recall a horse or a mule; surely, Apollo would have sensed another animal and alerted her. Even though it was a dream, she would swear that she could still smell the foul odor of his breath, and the stench of his unclean body.

Then her dreams brought her to her conversation with her aunt about becoming the next mistress of Monteforte. It was so strange, because in this dream she met a man who was trying to take Monteforte away from her, claiming he was the rightful heir. The man, she could not see his face, was menacing and cunning, a worthy opponent for such a prize. They would fight, but not hand to hand, the man would plot against her in the most devious ways. She tossed, turned, and was fighting all night with invisible foes. These dreams came to her every night. She prayed that God would let them pass from her mind.

When she finally awoke, it was still dark, for morning had not yet arrived. She laid there soaked in her own sweat in a midst of fear and anger. A cold chill ran up her spine, and she tasted blood in her mouth. Lucia was still tired, but was afraid to close her eyes, for the memories of the dreams she had just had.
Who were these men and why did they want to harm her?

***

Maria Sucretti was at breakfast on the west terrace. It was a crisp clear day with a nice breeze off the sea. A thin midst covered the mountain like a veil of sheer gauze. Lucia took in a deep breath and let it out slowly to clear her mind of her restless night. She stretched her arms over her head then reached down to her toes. Her body was stiff and her muscles tight from not using them. She missed her long morning rides with Apollo. She promised herself she would go see him later today, and bring him sugar and carrots.

"Good morning Bella. I see you are feeling better. Exercise is good for the body and the soul." Maria Sucretti was still as fit and slender as a young woman was, if not for the white streaks that laced her beautiful dark auburn hair, she would still look very young.

"Ah good morning Zia, you look well rested this morning. Where is Zio Giovanni and Antoinetta?" Maria, with a look of concern on her handsome face, answered,

"Giovanni went hunting with Gandolfo and Giorgio. Some of the men had told them that they had found slaughtered sheep, and that there were wild boars roaming the mountain killing our sheep. So they are out there hunting them before they kill off all the sheep. I pray they are careful those animals are very dangerous. As for Antoinetta, I have spoken to her about my decision and she is very happy for it. She is down in the kitchen with Marcello making a special breakfast for us." Lucia was relieved that her aunt had told Antoinetta of her decision; she would see for herself her sister's reaction when she arrived from the kitchen. Antoinetta was a master at disguising her feelings.

A short while later Antoinetta arrived on the terrace, leading a small group of maids who were carrying trays laden with an assortment of food. Upon seeing Lucia, she ran over to embrace her. "Sister, I am so happy for you. Zia has told me of her plans for you. It is wonderful, and I know you will make an excellent Mistress for Monteforte. In honor of this news, I have helped prepare a small feast. I hope you both enjoy it." At the end of the procession of young kitchen maids came the rotund Marcello, in his entire splendor as head chef, his white coat shinning in the bright sun. His head covered with a linen cap. He made a deep, formal bow to Mistress Sucretti and her two ladies. The little maids scurried around him, obeying each command, as they set forth the sumptuous feast.

He came over to Mistress Sucretti, "Good morning my Mistress, I hope you enjoy what Mistress Antoinetta and I have prepared for you and Mistress Lucia. These are some of the latest dishes from France. One of our purveyors has brought word of them to me. I have tested them to be sure, and they are most savory." Maria Sucretti smiled and gently patted the chef's big belly "I see that you are very diligent in testing all our food." The big man laughed heartily as did everyone, even the little kitchen maids, and then promptly, covered their giggles. "Come Mistress, you must sample everything. He extended his meaty hand to her." Antoinetta was very excited "Lucia, try this one it is my favorite thus far." Lucia was hungry, and it all looked and smelled so good. Marcello had the maids dishing out portions to the three women. "Mistress" he said in his throaty voice "Mistress Antoinetta is a fine chef. She understands the art of food preparation and has a good palette. Lucky the man she marries, he will never grow skinny." Again, Maria could not resist "Let us hope she does not test all her dishes such as you do Marcello, or she will never find a husband." It was good fun and the chef, his belly jiggling with laughter, just bowed deeply. "Oh Antoinetta this is delicious. What is it?" Antoinetta beaming with pride announced, "Marcello says these are called 'crepes'." "I don't care what they are called, they are so light, and the filling is wonderful. Zia you must try these, here take a bite of mine." Maria was delighted that her niece had become so proficient in the kitchen; it was an excellent skill to possess. "Mistress Lucia, you must come spend some time with us in the kitchen. There is much you will need to know," bellowed Marcello in his friendly way. "Yes Marcello, but, I fear, much like you, I will want to sample every dish." They all laughed. Marcello and his staff excused themselves with wishes for the trio to have a pleasant repast.

"Zia, I am so full, that I am afraid the wrappings around my ribs, will soon burst. I need to get some exercise, or I will look like Marcello, even without learning how to cook. Do you think I could take Apollo for a leisurely ride?" Her aunt looked at her with a cautious eye "If you do, make sure you do not stray too far, and go very slow. Maybe take one of the grooms with you." Antoinetta was not so sure "Lucia do you really think that is advisable?" Lucia looked hopelessly at them "It is already almost two weeks since Brother

Ronaldo wrapped my ribs. I do feel better. I will go easy, I promise." They both sighed knowing there was no hope for it.

Antoinetta had excused herself to go and tell Marcello how they all ate like pigs, and that everything was delicious. Lucia, excited at the prospect of riding her horse, was getting ready to leave, when her aunt grabbed her arm. "Lucia I would like to speak with you for one moment now that we are alone." Lucia sat back down next to her aunt. "I had spoken to Gandolfo about your suggestion for Piro's future, since it is he who is responsible for the young man. He was very grateful that you understand the situation. I then called for Piro to come and speak with me. He received it better than I would have thought. I think he too needs to find himself. The thought of travel and education is an enticing treat for a young man such as himself. He is bright and will do well I am sure." Lucia was so happy for Piro, yet in her heart, she was sad that he would be leaving. "I too am happy for him Zia. He will make us all proud I am sure."

"Now go, enjoy your ride, and take your farewell of Piro. He will be leaving in the morning." Lucia got up with great enthusiasm, kissed her aunt, and left in a flurry of swirling petticoats. Maria Sucretti thought to herself that, at least for the moment, one problem was solved, but knowing her niece, and how men were attracted to her, there would be many more Piro's before it was done.

***

Lucia found herself in the stables, breathing in the rich, familiar scent of manure and hay, and it calmed her. There was something about being with the horses, which always made her happy. Maybe it was because they represented freedom for her. She could ride them and escape the confines of the estate. Yet, now for the first time, there hung an ominous dread deep within her, that she never experienced before, a cold chill went up her spine, and she shook it off. Gandolfo spotted her first. "Ah, my dear Mistress Lucia, you are looking like your old self, soon you will be here early again in the morning to take Apollo for his rides. He missed you. Piro has been doing a good job but it is not the same." He was smiling but there was sadness in his eyes. "Mistress Sucretti has spoken to me about Piro, and she has spoken to him as well. I suppose you know that he leaves tomorrow. I will miss the boy. He is bright and very good with the horses." Lucia approached him and reached for his hand, which he gave. "Gandolfo we will all miss Piro, but if he stays here he will suffer. We will all suffer. He is being given a great opportunity to better himself, to become educated at one of the finest institutions in all of France. When he has done, and seen all that he desires, he can come home to Monteforte. There will always be a place for him here. Do not worry he will do well."

Gandolfo listened to the young woman before him and was amazed at the clarity of her vision. "I also have great faith in Piro whom I love like a son. This is a great gift, and I believe he understands its value. I am so grateful to you and Mistress Sucretti for this. I am without words as to how wise you have become. Mistress has told me of her plans for you, and I believe she has chosen wisely. It will be my honor to serve you until I die." With that, Gandolfo went down on bended knee and kissed her hand. A deep crimson flush rose on Lucia's face. When he arose, Lucia said, "It is I, who have been honored by all of you. My aunt has bestowed a great gift upon me. I hope and pray that I am worthy of the trust she has placed in me. I will depend on people like you dear Gandolfo, to guide me when I lose my way. Thank you for all your hard work." She then leaned forward and placed a gentle kiss on his cheek. There were tears in both their eyes. "I will get Apollo and Piro. I am sure they will both be happy to see you." Lucia watched as Gandolfo strode off to fetch both her horse and his groom. He knew she loved them both. She was just quietly gazing about the stables, enjoying the sights and sounds of an active stable when Piro arrived, looking strong and healthy once again, with Apollo at his side. The moment Apollo saw her he became excited, whickering, and stomping. When he came close, he nudged her side looking for his favorite treats. She obliged and reached into her pocket and produced a chunk of sugar. "I think you only love me for the treats I bring you."

Looking over at Piro who was smiling but held sadness in his eyes, she said, "Piro are you well? Has your back healed?" The young man inclined his head and spoke softly "I am fine Mistress, do not concern yourself. You have endured the most pain and suffering. I have prayed for you. You look as beautiful as always, but how do you really feel?" Lucia was a little embarrassed at the intimacy of this conversation, but sensed that Piro was a little more confident than usual, since he would be leaving in the morning. "I am almost healed. They will cut away the bindings from my ribs in two days. I will be so grateful for it. I am sad that you will be leaving, but we both know that it is best for everyone, especially you, if you put some distance between yourself and Monteforte. My aunt has told me of the place you are going, and I must admit, I am feeling some little jealousy. To travel to such a city as Paris, and to study under some of the most intellectual minds, would be so exciting. Are you happy at the thought?"

"Would I lie and say that the thought of going to Paris is not the dream of every man here? No, I cannot. Would I stay if my place here would be such that I could be with you? Yes, then, I would not go. I will miss you, and will work to become a man that maybe, someday, you would possibly consider worthy of you." Lucia was about to speak but he stopped her. Seeing the bright rose flush on her face he said, "I am sorry if I have embarrassed you my Mistress. My heart speaks these words. When I found you lying there so damaged, my only thought was, if only I had been there, I would have killed that animal with my bare hands."

The tears came quickly to her eyes as she looked upon his handsome face. For some reason he seemed older, taller, more attractive than she had ever remembered. Why hadn't she seen this Piro before? She knew that no matter what she thought, it could not alter the situation. If he did not leave something would happen, and most probably, he would die for it. She could not risk that he would suffer because of her.

"Will you ride with me for a little way? My aunt does not wish that I would go alone." He nodded and went to get a horse. She watched him with his broad shoulders and tight ass saunter toward one of the stalls. In a few minutes, they were riding toward the cliffs, sea breezes cooling the air. They rode in silence for a long while. When they came near the edge of the cliff, Lucia suggested they rest for a few minutes, for her ribs were hurting. Piro jumped down and hobbled both Apollo and his own horse. Carefully, he helped her down from the big animal. She was happy to rest and sat down on a patch of grass. "Please, come, sit down." Piro had thought wisely to bring a skin of water, which he offered to her. Lucia drank deeply, thankful for the cooling liquid. He drank after her, and then joined her on the grass. They sat there awkwardly in silence. They had never been alone before, and this familiarity, was foreign to both of them.

Lucia could not control herself she asked hesitantly "Were you the first one to find me?" Piro, with his head lowered, did not meet her eyes "Yes." Her voice choked, she said, "Did you see all that he did to me?" "Yes." She was angry "Why don't you talk to me?" Piro, his face flushed, turned to look at her directly "Because I cannot face you without shame." "Whose shame is it, mine, or yours?" He commanded himself to face her "It is my shame. I could not take my eyes from your naked body. I wanted you so bad. My desire could not see your pain. I am a beast for such lust. That is why I must leave here. I want you so bad, that I will die, or be killed, for my desire."

Lucia was crying, and with deep emotion in her voice said, "I am the one who has been shamed. You have all seen my body. The body I have vowed to give only to the man I love. That animal took that honor from me. I curse him to hell." Piro grabbed her hands in his and she did not resist. "You have done nothing wrong. You are still a virgin. It was like seeing a beautiful angel. Your skin is like marble. Every part of you is perfect. Any man would desire you. I make you a vow. I will work hard and learn many things, and someday I will return to Monteforte, and ask you to marry me."

He came close to kiss her then pulled away. "Why did you pull away from me?" Piro straightened his broad shoulders "because now I am not worthy of you, but upon my return, I will kiss you. Pray for me Lucia."

They left and made their way in silence back to the stables. When he helped her down his face brushed hers, and Lucia's skin was tingling with arousal. "Will I see you before you leave?" Piro already had Apollo's reins in his hands "No, I will leave at daybreak. I do not want to see you. I cannot see you. It is too hard." Lucia had tears falling down her face, she grabbed for his hand. "I wish you good fortune. I know you will become a great man. I will pray for you." Piro fell to his knee, still holding her hand, "it was my honor to have served you my mistress. I will return for you" then he kissed her hand and moved to take Apollo to his stall.

From the far corner of the barn, Gandolfo cloaked in the shadows, was witness to the scene that had just unfolded, and his heart was heavy. This boy had become a man before his very eyes. His heart was broken for this young couple. Gandolfo thought that it would be thoughts of Lucia that would drive Piro to success.

CHAPTER TWO

PREPARATIONS

Monteforte

The preparations for the society event of the century were underway. Maria Sucretti gathered together all of her lawyers and business managers to complete the invitation list. The engraver was summoned and an array of the finest silk paper stock, was spread across her desk. She chose a soft ivory colored parchment, which would be hand written in gold ink. The engraving would painstakingly be done by hand. Each specially sealed with the Crest of Monteforte.

When she was satisfied with both the list, and the content of each precious envelope, she summoned Nicko and instructed him to gather two others, whom he trusted, to make a proper appearance, and hand deliver, each invitation. The cast of characters was impressive and far-reaching. Maria Sucretti had cast her net and was trawling for the biggest fish in Europe.

It was done. In six months, the most prestigious families in all Italy and Europe would converge upon Monteforte. The Mistress of Monteforte had summoned them and they would accept. Within two weeks of the first delivery, the responses were coming in. Dukes, Earls, Marquis, Barons, and merchants of such wealth, and importance, that their names topped all of Italian high society, as well as across the continent. In total, three hundred elite would converge upon Monteforte.

The level of activity in and around the castle was never ending. It seemed that artisans of every area of interest convened to renovate and restore the musty old façade. An entire compliment of gardeners, under the supervision of Giovanni Romano, were sent from Rome, to redesign the extensive gardens. Painters, plasterers, and artists had converged upon the sleepy fortress. To pay homage to her nephew Genaro, Maria had sent solicitors to broker several of his works for the party. Food purveyors from around Europe came with their wares, bringing the finest meats and cheeses, the freshest seafood and vegetables, were selected with care. Table linens, glassware, and cutlery retrieved from the family vault, washed, and polished. No detail was overlooked.

Antoinetta and Lucia were overhauled as well. Designers from the most famous couture houses in France were brought in to design the latest Parisian fashions. Rafaela, who was personally designing Maria Sucretti's gown, would oversee the designs and fabrication. The sisters were young women now. So much had happened in the years since their arrival at Monteforte. They had grown physically and mentally, and their keen sense of intelligence had blossomed into confident and sophisticated women. They had been exposed to the best Europe could offer.

Antoinetta, ever the older, more sullen sister, had evolved into a stunning Italian beauty. Her well defined features with dark eyes playing against tawny sun kissed skin. Her petite frame was delicate and toned, the raven black hair curling and framing the classic Roman face. Antoinetta knew she was beautiful in the traditional style of southern Italy, and carried herself with dignity and reserve. She was shrewd and slow to respond, always contemplating her answer. She would be a great diplomat. Antoinetta was cautious and moody. Maria Sucretti loved her niece, but knew she had chosen wisely in making Lucia the next Mistress of Monteforte.

Lucia, now sixteen, was breathtakingly beautiful. She was tall, and in her bare feet stood five feet nine inches. She was strong and athletic, well proportioned, and stood proud and defiant. Her skin was alabaster with an undertone of peach. The freckles that sprinkled her nose and checks gave her a Nordic appearance. Her eyes were the color of the Mediterranean Sea. The blue was so pure and clear, and the fire within, was ever present. Her tresses were the color of strawberries dipped in gold. Lucia's head was a mass of curls and ringlets that were enthroned atop a magnificent face and cascaded down her back. Her high cheekbones were kissed with a perpetual splash of peach blush. Lucia's mouth, with its sculptured cupid's bow, which accented her full sensual lips, made it seem like she was always pouting. Lucia was the polar opposite of her sister Antoinetta, not only in outward appearance, but also in mood and temperament.

Lucia was not cautious but spontaneous and reactive. She was a hunter of knowledge and adventure. She wanted more and more information. Her tutors could barely keep up with her thirst for learning. She would debate history or religion with some of the most learned professors in Italy. Because of her demand for the latest works on various subjects, the library at Monteforte was bulging at the seams. It became so important that local educators, even the clergy, asked for permission to lend some of the more current publications. Her quest included many of the rarest and obscure manuscripts. Lucia drank in every aspect of life. She would venture down to the kitchens of Monteforte and learn to prepare many different kinds of dishes. Lucia loved to eat, and approached cooking as if she did all her studies, with intense desire to excel. Before long, even her culinary abilities were outstanding.

Maria Sucretti watched her young wards mature, two sisters, two different worlds, and each lovely and special, but, with different appetites. Antoinetta, mild and mellow, would be the perfect wife and mother, while, Lucia was a fierce competitor and ever-in motion. As she was getting older, Maria could not sleep, and would take to getting up during the early morning hours. With the sky, still dark grey she would sit upon her veranda and all too often would see the light coming from Lucia's room. What was she doing at that hour? Lucia read voraciously. Her mind could not get enough information to satisfy itself. Then, as the sun would rise over the cliffs, Lucia would venture out to ride like the wild wolves on the back of her beloved Apollo, along the paths that led to the sea. She was a powerful woman. Lucia's long golden red hair floated in the wind like flames licking the breeze. Her athletic form gracing the sand like an Arabian stallion cantering along the seashore. Lucia was so beautiful. It was during those early hours that Maria Sucretti knew it would be Lucia who would reign over her beloved Monteforte. Therefore, before she died, she must share the many secrets of this magical place with her niece, but for now, she would watch and pray. The world was ever changing and there was much turmoil in Italy as in all of Europe and beyond. Her sources were keeping Mistress Sucretti informed as to the state of the current undertow brewing. Maria Sucretti was scared and cautious.

Mistress Sucretti with fingers in the pockets of every known political entity kept well informed. She would guaranty the safety of her domain before her death to ensure that her family was protected from any upheaval. Maria had cultivated an atmosphere at Monteforte, which had been the epicenter of civility amongst the wild Neapolitans for generations. She must maintain that order for her girls.

It was time to let the world know who the new Mistress of Monteforte would be. First, the marriage of Antoinetta had to be arranged. Maria had summoned several of her closest advisors to find a suitable husband for her niece. After much deliberation, Maria Sucretti made her decision. His name was Tomaso Catalano, the only son and heir apparent; he was twenty-one years old and was formally educated. He was tall and ruggedly handsome and most importantly he was the son and heir of the Catalano Olive Oil fortune. Catalano Olive Oil was exported throughout the world. It was used in some of the finest restaurants and wealthy homes all over the world.

Maria Sucretti personally knew the Catalano family for two generations and they were business partners in the oil export end of the Catalano Olive Oil Company. Their estate was not far from Monteforte and the patriarch was Carlo Catalano. They were a good family with roots dating back centuries. They worked the land and developed their product into a world-class commodity. Tomaso was perfect for Antoinetta. Of course, now the task of bringing these two together was at hand.

Mistress Sucretti sent a hand written note to Lord and Lady Catalano to invite them to lunch at Monteforte to introduce them to Antoinetta. Zia Maria had much to do before their arrival. The Catalano's would certainly be looking for a substantial dowry for Antoinetta. Maria Sucretti called her personal banker to arrange the transfer of one million lire into an account in the name of Antoinetta Banfi. She then called her lawyer, and instructed him to establish a trust in Antoinetta's name for her villa in Roma, which was estimated to be worth two million lire.

Maria Sucretti knew that for now, the hook had been baited and the Catalano's would be attracted to the worm. For their part, the Catalano's would insure that Antoinetta would be well cared for as wife to the next heir of the Catalano fortune. The only unknown in this arrangement was Antoinetta's reaction to Tomaso. A private dinner party would be arranged at Casa de Catalano next month and the two would be introduced. Tomaso would be told of the situation, but Mistress Sucretti thought it best not to let Antoinetta in on their little conspiracy. Women, by their nature, always like to believe that it is 'love at first sight' and Zia Maria would not want that illusion to escape her niece. After Antoinetta was successfully engaged to Tomaso, she would then put her full thrust into settling Lucia into her new role as Mistress of Monteforte.

***

Carlo and Lydia Catalano arrived at Monteforte with all the fanfare of visiting dignitaries. When their coach pulled up to the estate Giorgio and a retinue of footmen, grooms, and maids greeted them. They were a handsome couple, both from old world wealthy families that had been united by an arranged marriage. Giorgio ceremoniously escorted them to the west terrace. It was a magnificent day and the sea breezes made the temperature very comfortable.

"My Lord, Mistress will be joining you shortly. May I bring you some refreshment until her arrival? Lady Catalano, what shall be your pleasure?" Giorgio, who had been groomed from birth to be the maître de casa enjoyed entertaining visitors. "No thank you. We shall wait for your Mistress." Giorgio made a deep formal bow and retreated from the terrace. In a few moments Maria Sucretti, the elegant mistress of the manse, made her appearance on the arm of Giovanni Romano on her right and on her left Antoinetta.

Carlo Catalano immediately rose from his chair to greet Maria and guest. "Ah, Mistress Sucretti, how lovely to see you; you are looking as beautiful as ever." Carlo, who Maria had known most of her life, was a big flirt, but very charming; he seized her hand and kissed it, then kissed both cheeks. "Dear Carlo, you never change, as charming as ever. Lydia, my dear, so happy to see you, it has been far too long. You are lovely as always." Lydia Catalano remained seated, and flushed slightly in acknowledgement, all the while keeping her eyes on Antoinetta. "Carlo I do not believe you've met my husband, Lord Giovanni Romano. Giovanni may I introduce Lord Carlo and Lady Lydia Catalano." Giovanni Romano, tall and slender, was dressed in a splendidly tailored waistcoat in a rich dark brown. He wore his eye patch to match his waistcoat. He bowed grandly to the couple "My Lord, Lady Catalano, the pleasure is mine." Maria was very proud of him. She loved him deeply.

Who is this stunning creature?" bellowed Carlo Catalano. Maria stepped slightly to one side to bring the diminutive Antoinetta to the foreground. "This is our lovely niece Antoinetta Banfi. Antoinetta may I present Lord and Lady Catalano." Carlo made a very grand bow, eyeing her up and down appraisingly, and then kissed her hand. Antoinetta curtsied deeply and batted her eyelashes. "It is my pleasure to meet both of you. My aunt has spoken very highly of the two of you." " If it pleases your aunt, we would be delighted if you would join us for lunch." Maria Sucretti nodded to her niece "Cara would you like to join us for lunch?" Antoinetta replied, "I would love to join you. Thank you."

Marcello, always the showman, presented the lunch selections himself, served by a small army of little kitchen maids. It was an outstanding presentation of delicious food, much of which was grown on the estate. Lord Catalano's hearty appetite was very appreciative of the vast variety of dishes. Maria could see that Lady Catalano was more interested in her soon to be daughter-in-law. Antoinetta had that morning helped Marcello prepare the now famous 'crepes' for dessert.

In his robust baritone, Marcello announced that the dessert was a specialty of Mistress Antoinetta. The Catalano's had never tasted such a treat. "Oh my dear this is superb. You must tell me how you make this. I would love for my chef to have the knowledge." Antoinetta was beaming as was apparent by the deep rose flush on her cheeks. Marcello who was informed secretly by Mistress Sucretti that these were Antoinetta's potential in-laws chimed in "The little mistress is an accomplished chef. She understands how to prepare food and can run the mansion kitchen. Of course, that is if I would let her." The big man laughed heartily and winked at his young mistress.

"Mistress Antoinetta, you can come to Casa Catalano and take charge of our kitchen," said Carlo with a nod to his wife. "Tell me of your interests, besides cooking?" Antoinetta acting appropriately demur informed them of her interests in literature, music and the arts. Maria Sucretti was watching them like the magistrate officiating at an inquisition. She was sure they were impressed with her niece. To get her to leave so that Maria could speak freely with her guests she said "Cara, why don't you go write down the formula for your famous crepes. I am sure Lady Catalano would like that. You would like that Lydia?" Lady Catalano, no fool as to Maria's motives, agreed wholeheartedly "I would love that, but I still want you to come and show my chef how to do it." Antoinetta was smiling, and rising, excused herself to go off and write down the ingredients for her guests.

Carlo Catalano watched the little sparrow disappear then turned to his wife and Maria Sucretti. "What a lovely young woman. She is not only stunningly beautiful but intelligent and charming as well. Don't you agree Lydia?" Lady Catalano, herself quite handsome, smiled serenely and said, "I believe she would make a wonderful match for our Tomaso. He is quite eager to meet her." Maria, ever the businesswoman, detailed the substance of Antoinetta's dowry. Without acting overly pleased, they both nodded appreciatively. "I have considered many possible suitors for my beloved niece and your son ranked very high in the process." She turned facing Carlo directly "Carlo we have known each other since we were babies. Our families have been united in business for generations, I trust and respect that your son, like his parents, will be an honorable husband for my niece."

Lydia Catalano responded. "I will tell you that Carlo and I strongly approve of Mistress Antoinetta, but, it is ultimately our son's decision. In addition, as I understand, she is not aware that we are desirous of matching the two of them. Let us hope that all parties find this arrangement satisfactory." Carlo picked up his glass from the table and holding it up said "To Tomaso and Antoinetta, with God's blessing." The four matchmakers drank heartily.

CHAPTER THREE

CASA CATALANO

Sorrento

Nicko pulled up to the main entrance of Monteforte with the big black carriage. Gandolfo had one of the stable grooms braid the horses' manes with brightly colored ribbons, they were excited and anxiously waiting for their passengers to step out, even they sensed the importance of this meeting. With much ceremony, Giorgio pushed open the two massive ornately carved cypress doors of Monteforte, to make way for Mistress Maria Sucretti flanked on either side by her niece and Giovanni Romano. The Lady Antoinetta, her stunning good looks and flowing black tresses were punctuated by a specially tailored evening gown in emerald green. Antoinetta's sultry olive skin glistened under the glow of emerald and diamond jewelry, taken directly from the Sucretti vault. To her right was the debonair Giovanni Romano, tall, dignified and handsome. Mistress Sucretti, even at her advanced age, her beauty was timeless. The woman carried herself with the dignity and confidence, someone in her place in life must possess. Maria Sucretti held her straight posture and regal air. The three were shockingly elegant, emerging through the arched doorway, with Monteforte the perfect backdrop to this striking trio.

Immediately Nicko ran to assist Mistress Sucretti to the carriage. Mistress very rarely ventured beyond the walls of Monteforte, the outside world came to her, so this must truly be a special occasion. Maria Sucretti graciously accepted her servants arm as he proudly escorted his mistress to the carriage with Antoinetta and Giovanni Romano following close by. Nicko was informed of the destination a few days earlier by Giorgio and of the nature of the expedition. He could feel the concentration of his passengers who spoke very little for the entire trip.

Nicko eased the impressive big black carriage up to the Catalano estate. While it was not as massive as Monteforte, it was still imposing. The moment they pulled into the villa courtyard several servants descended upon them. Nicko pressed his way to open the door and assist his passengers. Nicko proffered Mistress Sucretti his arm for support, but she declined, it was Giovanni's arm she wanted. Standing straight to her full height, Maria Sucretti set her face into a mask of poised confidence. She never looked back, but knew that her Antoinetta was trailing right behind her; carrying herself in the manner she had been taught. The servants scurried around the carriage to retrieve the numerous boxes that Mistress Sucretti would give to her hosts, while others raced to announce the arrival of Mistress Maria Sucretti of Monteforte to the Lord and Lady of Casa Catalano. It was very akin to introducing the Queen of England, with the exception that Maria Sucretti had more power than her English counterpart did.

Casa Catalano was designed in the style of classic Roman architecture, being built atop a hill, with vistas of all the surrounding acreage of the owner's empire. The Catalano family had held the villa for many generations. The villa was as sturdy and unmovable as its inhabitants. Maria Sucretti smiled inwardly at her wise choice, for these were people who were worthy of her beloved Antoinetta. Together their combined wealth and power could control much, maybe all of Italy and beyond.

Carlo, Lydia, and Tomaso Catalano greeted them. All splendidly attired for the occasion. "Dear Mistress Maria and Master Giovanni how nice to see you so soon. Mistress Antoinetta we are delighted you could join us. May I introduce our son Tomaso?" Maria thought to herself 'what a handsome young man. These two will make beautiful babies. Now if only Antoinetta finds him suitable.' Tomaso Catalano was magnificently sculptured. Fine boned with a strong angular chin and high cheekbones. His thick black hair clubbed back and held simply with a leather thong. He wore no powder or wig. Maria guessed judging by Giovanni Romano that he was at least six feet and two inches of all muscle. His broad shoulders filled his perfectly tailored waistcoat to perfection. He wore a thin mustache that highlighted his full mouth. When he saw Antoinetta, a warm glow lit his face. He smiled broadly, exposing straight white teeth.

Tomaso bowed a deep-footed greeting to Mistress Sucretti and Master Giovanni. "Welcome to Casa Catalano. For years, my father has spoken of you Mistress Sucretti and your keen sense of business. Master Giovanni it is an honor to meet you." He then turned his complete attention and charm, just like his father, thought Maria, to Antoinetta. "Mistress Antoinetta, if I may be so bold, you are breathtakingly beautiful. I am charmed to meet you." He swooped down to the petite Antoinetta, who was coquettishly poised, with eyes lowered and a deep rose blush on that gorgeous face. "Thank you Master Catalano. I am looking forward to our acquaintance." He reached for her hand and kissed it deeply. She curtsied. He then offered his arm, which she took graciously, as they proceeded ahead of the smiling quartet.

Observing the faces of the trailing foursome, Giovanni Romano was not sure who was more delighted that there was a physical attraction between Tomaso and Antoinetta, his wife or the young man's parents, either way it would be a good match. For his part, Giovanni Romano could not have been happier. He had prayed that his two girls would be settled, now, at least one of them would have a good husband. He knew he would have to work twice as hard at his prayers for Lucia to settle down.

Dinner, as would have been expected, was fabulous. When it came time for dessert Lydia Catalano announced that her chef, armed with the recipe given to him by Mistress Antoinetta, had prepared crepes. "Now Mistress Antoinetta, we shall see if they are as good as the ones you made. Tomaso, you must try these, they are delicious, and at least they were when Antoinetta made them." The young man's eyes had never left Antoinetta. Their heads were together throughout dinner, smiling and talking with ease to one another. "I can't wait."

The Catalano's chef brought out a huge tray of the French delicacies; his mistress sampled one and nodded her approval. The man, who looked nothing like Marcello, sighed with relief. "Vincenzo, these are very good, but, sadly, they are not as good as Mistress Antoinetta's." The chef, by either forewarned design, or not, bowed deeply in a wounded display of sorrow. "I apologize Mistress Catalano; perhaps the beautiful Mistress Antoinetta could teach me herself how they are made." Carlo Catalano who had been relatively quiet for most of the evening now chimed in "Well Vincenzo, she may not come for you, but, she might come for Tomaso." They all laughed, even Antoinetta, who was now brightly flushed. "I would be very happy to come back and show you how it is done, but, alas, we don't know if Tomaso even likes them." Maria, for the first time, saw a different side of her niece, and she thought to herself that she played that card perfectly. The next move was Tomaso's.

Vincenzo brought the tray over to his young master and offered a sample. Tomaso selected one and took a hearty bite. He was savoring the taste, playing to the enraptured audience as if sampling a fine vintage, his eyes closed. "What say you son?" Carlo was an impatient man, and for his trouble received a pinch from his wife, who gave him the dead fish eye. "I will need several to be sure, but, these are delicious. Now Mama you say that Antoinetta's are more superior, then surely to be fair to Vincenzo, we must have her back to demonstrate her skills." They all laughed once again including Antoinetta. Tomaso had played his hand perfectly as well.

Tomaso invited Antoinetta for a stroll in the garden after dinner. The older members of the group retired to the salon, where the men smoked and the women chatted. In hushed tones, it was generally agreed, that this fledging relationship seemed very promising. It was Lydia Catalano who spoke "They make a handsome couple don't you agree Maria?" "I believe there is a fire growing even as we speak. They are both beautiful and would make a grand match." Carlo who seemed absorbed in his conversation with Giovanni Romano broke off and approached Maria Sucretti. "Mistress, if your niece finds that she would like to marry Tomaso, we shall conclude all the necessary documents as soon as possible. I was thinking that since we have received your kind invitation recently, that would be the perfect time to announce their engagement. Do you agree?" Little did he know that is exactly what Maria had planned in addition to introducing Lucia to all of Europe's high society. "Yes I very much agree. Lydia?" Carlo's wife reached for Maria's hand "Maria our son is precious to us and his happiness is the most important thing. If it pleases him, as well as her, then we should move forward. It would be a good union for all concerned." Giovanni Romano, who had been quietly observing all the maneuvering of the players, now ventured, "They must be happy first, and everything will fall into place." Maria, who lived for forty years without the man she loved, felt the weight of his statement and understood. "You are so right Giovanni." They all nodded in agreement. Giovanni held up his glass and said, "To love." The foursome clinked their glasses, and drank with fervor.

Quite some time had passed before Antoinetta and Tomaso returned to the house. They were smiling and talked endlessly. He was making grand gestures and she was baiting him with doe eyes. It was done, of that Maria Sucretti was sure.

Nicko pulled up with the big black carriage, and after their farewell's Maria and Giovanni took their seats waiting for Antoinetta. Tomaso held the petite beauty like a songbird on his arm and walked her to the carriage. Nicko smartly moved aside and let the big man settle her to the coach. "I shall come for you tomorrow. Yes?" Antoinetta, her eyes lowered, mouth pouting answered "Yes. I look forward to see you." He was still holding her hand and kissed both hands. "Until tomorrow!" Tomaso closed the carriage door. As the carriage wound its way down the long path, she kept looking back to see that Tomaso was still standing there, until the carriage had disappeared from the mansion.

It was an animated ride back to Monteforte. Antoinetta could not stop talking about how nice the Catalano's are especially Tomaso. Maria ventured to ask, "So, where are you going tomorrow with Tomaso?" She giggled, "We are going riding." Maria was shocked "Riding, but, you hate horses." "Zia, I like them now." Giovanni Romano just shook his head and laughed. "Wait until Lucia hears that you are going horseback riding" said her aunt with much sarcasm in her voice. "You should have let Gandolfo teach you to ride."

Antoinetta acting coy replied, "Now Tomaso can teach me everything I need to know." Giovanni Romano who was sitting across from Antoinetta reached for her hands "Cara, just remember your place, sometimes when we are young and in love we make regrettable choices. If you truly find Tomaso to your liking, I am sure he will act in an honorable fashion." Both Maria and Antoinetta were stunned at the directness of Giovanni Romano; however, Maria was happy that he said it.

When they reached Monteforte, Maria whispered to Giovanni that she was going to walk Antoinetta to her room for a private discussion. He understood, gave his wife a kiss and said "Cara, hurry to our bed, I desire you." Maria's womb jumped to attention, the pangs of desire stirred with her. "Don't concern yourself I am ready." He just smiled. Maria was a willing and capable bed partner. As she turned to leave, he grabbed her ass with a firm squeeze.

Maria walked arm in arm with her niece to Antoinetta's room. Marianna was there getting her mistress' nightshift ready and turning down the big luxurious bed. Maria asked Marianna to get Antoinetta a glass of cognac, which she used as an excuse to be alone with her niece. "Antoinetta come sit with me for a moment. Let us talk about this evening." Maria could see that Antoinetta was flushed with excitement, and would probably not sleep tonight in anticipation of seeing Tomaso the next day.

"Oh Zia I had such a wonderful time, Lord and Lady Catalano are such lovely people." Maria could not control herself "What of Tomaso?"

At this question, Antoinetta lowered her head. Maria seized her niece's chin and raised it so that she could look directly into her eyes. "You like Tomaso?" "I know this may seem foolish but I think I love him. He is perfect in every way. He is handsome, which anyone can plainly see, but, we all know that is not enough."

Maria thought to herself 'that was a wise statement' and just remained quiet. "Zia, when I was speaking to him it was like we had known each other all our lives. He sounds like my father and brothers, like Zio Giovanni, and all the special men that have touched my life. I am so excited to meet him here tomorrow. I want to find him outside the safety of his home and see how he will act toward me then."

Maria was truly proud of her niece. "Antoinetta, I am so pleased that you find him not only physically attractive, but that you are comfortable with his personality. Outward appearance, can only last so long, then it is the mind that must comfort you. I do not want to embarrass you, but I must say, do not get carried away with your infatuation. If this is a good match, which I believe it is, he will want to touch you in ways that until now you have not been exposed to. Make sure he understands that you will make him wait for his prize. Understand?" "Zia, I will not let any man take my womanhood until our union is blessed before God. You, and my parents, have taught me to respect myself. I will not disgrace myself or any of you, I promise. Nevertheless, Zia I do think I am in love. Am I crazy?" Maria Sucretti drew her petite niece into her arms, planted kisses on her head and cheeks "No Cara, I do not think you are crazy. I am very happy for both of you because I think our handsome Lord Tomaso feels the same way. Please do not break your neck tomorrow."

CHAPTER FOUR

THE RIDING LESSON

Monteforte

Antoinetta slept very little with thoughts of her new relationship with Tomaso Catalano. She crept out of bed at first light so as not to alert Marianna that she was up and quietly walked to Lucia's room. She did not knock but silently opened the door and slipped in closing the door behind her. Coming to Lucia's bed, she looked at her beautiful sister sleeping and thought 'Thank God Tomaso saw me first; surely he would have chosen Lucia over me.' Antoinetta quickly put that thought out of her head and stroked her sister's hair. It felt like thick raw silk, with the sun just over the rise of the mountain, a glint of sunlight dappled across her hair and face. She was truly beautiful.

Lucia stirred "Good morning Bella" said Antoinetta. Lucia opened one azure blue eye, rolled on her back and said "Good morning. Are you all right? You are never up at this hour." Antoinetta quipped, "Yes I am fine. I need your help." Lucia was still groggy with sleep "Help with what?" Her sister now all animated told her of the meeting with Tomaso Catalano. Lucia was aware of their dinner engagement but did not know how it was going to play out.

"Oh Antoinetta I am so happy for you but what can I do for you?" Antoinetta was embarrassed to tell her sister, whom she had been ridiculing all her life about horses, that she needed some pointers on riding.

"Well, now don't get angry at me, but he is coming here today to take me riding?" Lucia bolted straight up in her bed her luxurious mane of strawberry curls wild around her face said "What! Did you not tell him you hate horses and cannot ride?" Antoinetta, her head in her chest, whispered "No." Her sister threw her long elegant legs over the side of the bed and said "Antoinetta this is not a joke, you could get hurt." For her part, Antoinetta said, "I know. That is why I have come to you so early. I need you to teach me to ride before Tomaso comes."

By now Lucia, who towered over her diminutive sibling, was on her feet pacing in front of the bed. "That is impossible. Are you insane?" "Please Bella, help me, I do not want to seem like a fool." Lucia looked at her pleading face "No, it is I who am a fool, because, as you well know, it is I who is going to get dressed and take you down to the stables. Yes?" Antoinetta jumped up and threw her arms around her sister's neck. "Yes. Thank you my sweet sister. I will owe you many favors for this. Can we hurry?" Lucia was already at her wardrobe getting her riding gown out. With all the noise, Sophia came bounding into the room. "Mistress is everything all right?" Lucia clearly flustered replied "No. This silly sister of mine NOW wants me to teach her to ride a horse." Sophia looked shocked "But Mistress Antoinetta you hate horses."

Antoinetta who was already dressed and prancing around the room answered "Yes Sophia I do hate horses, but, Lord Tomaso Catalano loves them, and so now I must love them too." The young maid looked dazed "Oh, I understand, I think." All three started to giggle with excitement.

Making haste the two sisters made their way to the stables, which were now a bustling mass of servants mucking out stalls and feeding the horses. Gandolfo spotted them. "Ah, to what do I owe the honor of both my lovely Mistress' this early in the morning?" Lucia approached Gandolfo as if consorting with a peer, and announced in a grand manner "Good morning Gandolfo, I know you will find this amazing, but, Mistress Antoinetta, the one who hates horses, wants us to teach her to ride before the morning is done." Gandolfo, his bushy brows meeting to form a quizzical frown, said "Why?" Lucia teasing just smirked, "She is in love, and there is no help for it. Lord Tomaso Catalano, her new beau, is coming to take her riding, and she forgot to inform Lord Catalano of her fear and hatred for horses."

Gandolfo, feet spread apart, hands on his hips, stood there laughing heartily. "Ah, now I understand. However, Mistress Antoinetta, one cannot learn to manage a horse in just a few short hours. It is too dangerous." Lucia was smiling broadly "I told her as much Gandolfo, but, she will hear none of it. So we must get to work immediately."

The seasoned servant knew he had no choice but to comply with the request. Lucia looked at him and said, "Please have them bring up Apollo and one of the gentler mares, perhaps Venus?" Lucia had named all the horses in the stable with mythical names. "Yes. I think Venus is a good choice" Gandolfo left to ready both animals. Lucia was enjoying herself, for once she felt superior to her older sister. "It smells so awful in here how can you stand it?" Lucia breathe in deeply the rich aroma of hot fresh manure and damp hay, which were perfume to her senses. "You will get used to the smell." Antoinetta wanted to vomit, thinking to herself, "I will never get used to that putrid odor."

Gandolfo returned with the massive Apollo who was whickering at the sight of Lucia. One of the young grooms had Venus in tow. Venus was one of the older mares. Her chestnut coat was shiny and her mane was streaked with golden hair. Lucia was fond Venus and had learned to ride on her years earlier. By this time, a small audience of grooms had appeared to watch the events that were taking place. It would have been hilarious to see this exhibition had it not been so important to Antoinetta. She sat there paralyzed by fear, looking like a little porcelain doll atop this massive animal. She was soaked with sweat and there were ringlets forming around her petrified face. She was gripping the reins so hard her knuckles were white with strain. Lucia had all to do to control herself from laughing.

"Gandolfo you must help me. Tomaso will be arriving soon and I have not moved from this spot." "Mistress, why don't you just tell Lord Catalano that you despise horses and riding?" Antoinetta was beside herself "how can I do that he loves horses, he breeds horses, he rides horses, for all I know he could be a horse." Everyone started to laugh and for the first time Antoinetta realized there was an audience watching this fiasco evolving. She shouted "Don't you all have something to do. Go, go, do something." She was shooing them away. Lucia was laughing so hard she nearly fell off Apollo. Gandolfo taking pity on his young mistress barked, "You heard Mistress Antoinetta, go to your work."

Apollo had just about enough of this nonsense, and decided that he was going for a run. Without any forewarning, he started to gallop at full speed, almost dislodging Lucia, but she quickly recovered reining him up short. "Now, there is a perfect example of what to do when your horse acts on his own. Mistress Lucia knew exactly how to rein in her horse. You must be firm but gentle to the animal. If you tighten the rein on the right, he will turn right. If you want to go left, tighten up on the left. If you want him to stop, pull in both reins together. Speak to your horse. Pat your horse and tell him when he has been good. Scold him when he had been bad. They are extremely intelligent animals and respond very well to humans. Now, let us take a ride around the fence. Yes?" Antoinetta nodded, but truly did not feel any connection or warmth toward the horse. Gandolfo came over to Venus and spoke gently to her, then prodded her to walk around the paddock. Venus was a good-natured horse. "Keep your back straight and her head up. Ease up on the reins." Gandolfo was jogging along with Venus. Antoinetta was starting to look a little more at ease. For some reason Apollo was trying to spur Venus into a run. Lucia chided him for being a bad boy and the horse settled down.

"Antoinetta you may not know how to ride, but, you look very good sitting up there. Perhaps we can make up some reasonable excuse why you cannot go riding today." "Lucia that is impossible. What would prevent us from riding? No, I will just have to learn, and, quickly." Lucia was shaking her head and wanted to scream 'who is the idiot now' but decided that her sister was suffering enough. This exhibition of horsemanship went on for another hour. For her part, Antoinetta managed to sit the horse without killing herself and toward the end almost enjoyed herself.

Gandolfo helped her dismount and commented, "I do believe you will be fine. Just do not get too confident, the horse will sense that you think you know how to ride, and may go off faster than you wish. Hold back the reins, but do not injure the horse. Keep your back straight and your head up, and you will look like a fine lady who has been riding all her life." Antoinetta looked bedraggled "I must go and freshen up before Tomaso arrives." Lucia was bored and wanted to run with Apollo "I am going for a run I will see you when I return. Good luck sister, do not kill yourself, or hurt the horse. Yes?" Antoinetta pouted off to freshen up before Tomaso came. 'Dear God please don't make him ask me to go riding' she silently prayed.

CHAPTER FIVE

THE PROPOSAL

Monteforte

Tomaso arrived late in the morning astride a magnificent Arabian stallion; both animal and rider were handsome. Tomaso with his large frame sat the horse so beautifully his straight broad back and head held high were a picture of form and breeding. He wore a rich blue riding coat, over his breeches, his stocking legs showed off his well-developed calves. He wore no wig and no powder, his jet-black waves held back with a leather thong. Tomaso was confident and sensually attractive.

Dismounting, he handed the reins to one of the grooms who came to take Tomaso's horse "shall I brush and water him my Lord?" Tomaso was patting his horse "Yes thank you I just gave him a good workout." Once the animal was led off to the stables Tomaso, arms filled with packages, was greeted by Giorgio. "Good day Lord Catalano, I am Giorgio the maître di casa. Mistress Antoinetta has instructed that you wait for her on the west terrace." With a deep bow, Giorgio led the way to the west terrace where refreshments were waiting. "My Lord would you care for some wine, while you await Mistress Antoinetta?" Tomaso with a broad smile replied, "That would be wonderful I am very dry. This is such a magnificent place have you been here long Giorgio?" Giorgio was pouring the wine "Monteforte is the most splendid place to live. I am so fortunate that I was born here on the estate, as were my parents and grandparents. When I was young Mistress Sucretti sent me abroad to be educated, and now I enjoy my position here. It is an honor to serve Mistress Sucretti and Master Giovanni as well as the young mistresses'. Will there be anything else my Lord?" Tomaso just shook his head no, and drank deeply from the glass of fine vintage wine. He was sitting there just enjoying the vista from the terrace to the sea; a whisper of a breeze scented the air with the aroma of lemons.

Out of the corner of his eye, Tomaso caught the stunning vision of Antoinetta, now freshly changed, her hair neatly combed, and a healthy flush on her lovely face.

"Oh there you are sweet Antoinetta; you are a vision of beauty. Please come and join me. Shall I pour you a glass of wine; it is of such an excellent vintage?" When she approached, he took her face in both his hands, looked in those deep sultry eyes, and kissed each cheek. "I did not sleep last night with the thought of seeing you today. Come sit let us talk." Antoinetta was flushed from the top of head to her toes. She wanted to giggle but just batted her thick long lashes. "I too did not sleep in anticipation of seeing you Tomaso."

"Antoinetta, I am embarrassed, but, you will think I am mad, but, I don't care, I am going to tell you anyway. I am in love with you. From the moment, I saw you your beauty smote me. Then when I spoke with you and could see that you are a woman of great intelligence and wit, my heart and mind was made up. Will you marry me?" Antoinetta was stunned, her mind went blank, her heart was pounding, and her voice went mute. "Oh, my little song bird, do you not feel my love. Have I offended you into disgust? I am so very sorry for my brazen outburst. Please forgive me."

Antoinetta, finally gathered her wits about her and responded "Tomaso I thought I was also mad, for I feel the same way about you. I told my aunt last night when we came home that I thought I was in love with you. Is such a thing even possible? Can two people fall in love so quickly? My mother said that is how she fell in love with my father, on first sight. Do you believe in fate?"

Tomaso was now standing and scooped the petite Antoinetta into his arms. "Yes Cara, I believe in God's will and destiny. I love you. Marry me. If you say no I will die." Antoinetta with tears cascading down her sun kissed cheeks as "Yes. Yes. I will marry you." Tomaso, a giant of a man picked her off her feet and twirled her in the air. "You have made me so happy." He got down on bended knee, reached into his coat pocket, and pulled out a sparkling ruby and diamond ring the likes of which Antoinetta had never before seen. "Please accept this ring as a token of my love and my vow of marriage. When shall we tell our families?" Antoinetta's head was dizzy with excitement. "Sunday. We shall have both families here at Monteforte to announce our wedding. Do you agree?" Tomaso still holding her tightly kissed her on the mouth. It was a deep sensual kiss, his tongue exploring her mouth. She was shocked but could not pull away. "We shall make the formal announcement at your Aunt's gala in two weeks. Most of those present will come to the wedding." Tomaso kissed her again, this time longer, and his tongue probed her mouth flicking in and out. Antoinetta's heart was racing so fast she was sure he could feel it. His large hand caressed her back and stroked her hair. Antoinetta's knees were getting weak and she felt tingling in her womb. Tomaso moved from her mouth to her neck and nibbled on her ear lobe. His hands were roaming her torso getting very close to her breasts.

Then, just as suddenly as if struck by lightning, Antoinetta pulled back. With all her strength, she slapped Tomaso hard across the face. They were both in shock. Her hand stung from the impact, she was trembling. She pushed Tomaso to arm's length. He was panting and Antoinetta could see by the bulge in his breeches that he was aroused. "I am so ashamed Cara. I did not mean to act so forward. Please forgive me. It is only that your beauty mixed with my love is driving my desires."

"Tomaso I will not dishonor myself or my family. If you want me, and I pray you do, we will wait for our union to be blessed before Our Lord Jesus Christ in the sacrament of marriage before we bed. I am a virgin, and will remain that way until our wedding night. I hope you understand." Tomaso his face a deep crimson took her hands in his and fell to his knees "I am humiliated by my actions you must think I am a lustful beast. I do not know what I was thinking. If your uncle had seen that, he would have me whipped or killed. Will you still marry me?"

Antoinetta was upset, happy, scared, confused, and aroused. She was crying, but not sure why she was crying. Tomaso took a linen scarf from his coat and dabbed at her wet face and eyes. "What have I done? Will you forgive me?" He was truly sorry for his actions and fearful that she would reject him. Tomaso knew of the arrangements that had been made between Maria Sucretti and his parents, yet, he also knew that while they would delight in this union for so many reasons he, in his heart, was truly in love with Antoinetta. She was clearly upset and for what should have been, a breathtaking moment turned into a dishonorable proposition. Tomaso was so very ashamed of himself. He was not sure what came over him. He had been with women, many women, and had never acted so brazenly.

"Tomaso yes I will marry you, but we must keep our desires honorable. Let us forget that this unfortunate thing happened. Shall we take a walk in the garden my Zio Giovanni has been designing it for weeks now. Let us go and see it. Shall we?" "Yes I think that would be a splendid idea," said the wounded Tomaso. They walked down to the spectacular gardens hand in hand but moodily silent. Tomaso was happy for the distraction to his otherwise poor behavior. There were a dozen men working like drone bees with Giovanni Romano overseeing the work.

"Hello Zio" called Antoinetta happy to see him. "Ah Cara, I see you have brought a friend. Hello Tomaso." Giovanni Romano was covered in dirt and grime his hands were encrusted with soil. "Lord Giovanni, I see you are hard at work. It looks like the gardens at Versailles, perhaps even better. Don't you agree Antoinetta?" Antoinetta with her chin on her chest said, "I don't know, I have never been to Versailles, nor France or anywhere other than here." Tomaso was wide eyed "You have never traveled? Oh, but of course, a young mistress such as yourself would never travel alone, how stupid of me. Well, we shall have to find a remedy for that. Yes?" Antoinetta's eyes flashed with excitement. "Yes."

Giovanni Romano could feel the vibrating tension between them. Fortunately, for Tomaso he thought it was their joy at being together, thankfully he was not aware of what had just transpired on the terrace above where he was now standing. The same thoughts were running wild through Tomaso's head.

"What a lovely day for a walk. You two go on and enjoy this beautiful day I have work to do. Tomaso, will you stay for supper?" Tomaso put on a sad frown "That would have been wonderful, but sadly I am expected at the shipyard in Naples this evening. We are receiving a large delivery of specially made casks for our new harvest of olive oil. We have them custom made in Madrid. The same company has made them for our family for generations, it will be my loss I assure you. I believe Antoinetta has graciously invited me and my parents to come on Sunday. I hope that will be acceptable to Mistress and yourself?"

"I am sure there is nothing that would be more pleasing to my wife. She adores your mother, and your father always makes her laugh. Until Sunday." Tomaso gave a deep bow "My Lord do not work too hard." Giovanni waved them off and set back to his work. He was grinning as he watched the two stroll off toward the stables.

When they reached the stables, Tomaso turned to look directly at Antoinetta. "I pray that my poor behavior has not tainted your feelings for me. I beg your forgiveness and vow that I would never do anything without your permission. Your beauty, and my feelings for you, are driving me mad with desire. Will you forgive me?"

Antoinetta was wounded and angry, but thrilled at the thought of his lust for her. "I forgive you Tomaso. I too feel the heat of desire, but we must for the sake of our marriage and our families, keep that fire within ourselves until it is right. You agree don't you?" Tomaso looked relieved. "Yes my darling Antoinetta. I will dream until our wedding night of the passion that we will share. I must leave you now but you have made me a very happy man. Until Sunday." He bent down to give her a kiss but just lightly brushed her mouth. Antoinetta pulled him firmly toward her and offered up her mouth, which he took gently but firmly. "Fino a domenica il mio amore."

The fate of Tomaso Catalano and Antoinetta Banfi was now sealed. After the appropriate time for engagement, the wedding would be announced at the gala at Monteforte. The guest list would be a collaboration between the two most powerful families in the region. For their part, Antoinetta and Tomaso, seemed genuinely happy which pleased Zia Maria, who had been a prisoner of an arranged marriage to the dead Salvatore Sucretti. Right this moment life was good.

Lucia knew that something was brewing with her sister, she had never seen Antoinetta so excited. "What is going on with you?" asked Lucia who had just come in from her daily ride on Apollo. "Lucia, dear Mother of God, you stink." Annoyed, Lucia replied, "Well already we forgot about horses and riding. Please Lucia, please Gandolfo, please, teach me to ride. Tomaso loves horses, he breeds horses, for all I know he may be a horse. Were those not your own words just one week ago?" Lucia was mocking her sister and doing so with great joy. "Lucia, I swear, if you don't go and wash up this very minute I will beat you."

The whole house was buzzing with anticipation of the arrival of the Catalano's. Everyone from Maria Sucretti down to the youngest kitchen maid knew that Antoinetta and Tomaso were going to announce their engagement tonight.

"Lucia, Bella, go get ready for dinner, Tomaso and his parents will be arriving shortly. Your sister is very excited. Wear something nice." "Zia I don't know who is more excited my sister or Marcello, he has prepared a feast". With that said; Lucia, still flushed from her ride, came over and planted a kiss on her sister's cheek then one on her aunt. "Lucia, Antoinetta is right you do stink!"

Lucia retreated to her room where Sophia had her bath already waiting and a lovely gown laid upon the bed. "Thank you Sophia. I will call you when I am done bathing, perhaps you could do something with this wild hair of mine, and the salt water makes it curl into tight knots." Sophia laughed, "Do you have any idea how many woman, myself included, would kill for your beautiful red hair?" She was getting ready to leave and remembered "Oh Mistress a messenger came while you were riding with a letter which I left on your desk. I will be back in a little while. Mistress Maria says you better hurry." " Tutto bene, tutto bene, mi danno pochi minuti." Lucia thought to herself; just give me a minute by myself. She was truly happy for Antoinetta and understood what the union between Monteforte and Catalano would mean for all their futures. She also knew that she would soon be dragged into a never-ending array of wedding plans. For now, she was hot, tired and wanted her own solitude. She stepped out of her riding gown and wrinkled her nose. She threw up her arm and sniffed her armpit; it was the pungent odor of fried onions. Lucia, disgusted by her own body odor, suddenly laughed at herself. 'Lucia Banfi you stink'.

The arrival of the Catalano's was nothing short of the anticipation of waiting for the minstrels to perform. You knew what they were, and what they would do, but it was fun to wait for it to actually happen. Lord and Lady Catalano were floating on air, and their son was smiling like a fool. "Lord and Lady Catalano, may I introduce my niece Lucia Banfi" Maria Sucretti was beaming. Lucia looked stunning. Carlo Catalano said, "I would never have taken you and Antoinetta for sisters. However, two women that are more beautiful I have never seen. I am enchanted to finally meet you Mistress Lucia." Carlo kissed her hand but his eyes ate her up. Lucia curtsied deeply a deep blush kissed her cheeks. "Lady Catalano, how nice to meet you, my sister has been saying very nice things about you." Lydia Catalano was a stunningly attractive woman "Oh my dear Lucia what beautiful hair. You are quite stunning. I wish I had more sons." Lucia smiled and bowed.

Tomaso who was just behind his parents came over to Lucia. "Finally I have the honor of meeting the beautiful sister. Antoinetta speaks of you endlessly. I hope we become good friends." Lucia gave Tomaso a dazzling smile "I hope to call you brother." Tomaso gave her a kiss on either cheek and whispered into her ear "Soon, very soon, sister." Lucia liked him already. They would make a good match. Antoinetta was so serious, and she could sense the playful side of Tomaso, they would be a good balance for each other.

"Where is Mistress Antoinetta?" bellowed Tomaso. From the end of the long hallway, with the soft glow of candlelight illuminating her silhouette stood the petite Antoinetta. Tomaso, without further acknowledgment took off down the hall to meet up with her. He swept her off her feet in an embrace, twirling her in a circle.

Giorgio and a small army of servants, much to the delight of Zia Maria who was her charming self, very deliciously presented dinner, which Marcello had slaved over for two days. Tomaso enchanted Antoinetta, for their eyes never left each other. It was during the second course that Tomaso could no longer contain his excitement stood, reached for his glass with one hand, and holding Antoinetta's hand in the other, announced "Dear family I, Tomaso Catalano, have asked the beautiful Antoinetta Banfi, to be my bride. And she has accepted." It was something we all knew, but once it was spoken aloud the reality of it hit everyone, including the soon to be bride and groom. "Please join us in a toast for good wishes."

Everyone rose. It was Giovanni Romano who said "Antoinetta and Tomaso, si può sempre trovare il vostro equilibrio. Maggio nostro Signore Gesù Cristo benedica entrambi e porterà molti bambini. Salute." Maria Sucretti thought 'yes Dear Lord make these two special people find love and happiness and make lots of babies.' They all clinked their glasses in well wishes. Maria Sucretti now spoke "We shall announce this beautiful union at the gala that I will be hosting in two weeks. "

Is that acceptable to you Lord and Lady Catalano?"
Carlo Catalano stood, his chest puffed out like the proud
papa, "Yes. The whole world will share in our
happiness."

Lucia ran to her sister and hugged and kissed her
"I am so very happy for you sister." Antoinetta with
tears flowing freely from her eyes said, "I wish that
Mama and Papa could have been here." Lucia felt her
pain but knew that her parents would certainly have
approved. "Do not concern yourself they respect your
judgment in all things. They will be here for the gala."
She then turned to Tomaso, "I now have five brothers
to love. I know you will be good to my sister. I see the
love you hold for her in your eyes." She reached out to
take both of their hands "I wish you both all the love
and joy in the world. I want to be an aunt right away.
Yes?" Antoinetta was blushing so deeply her cheeks
were on fire. "Lucia you are embarrassing me. Be good.
I love you."

Everyone in turn came to give the happy couple
their kisses and well wishes. Lucia watched and was
only slightly envious of their love for each other. Lucia
had many eligible suitors, but could not find someone
who shared her gusto for life, and certainly, an Italian
man would never let her be as independent as she so
desired. Lucia had already accepted that she either
would be alone for the rest of her life or would take a
lover, but not a husband. For the beautiful redheaded
Lucia, life would prove to present many challenges, her
love life being the most complex of all. She thought
that, for once, she would like to be like Antoinetta, just
another woman who could love and be loved by just
another man. Se la maledizione della sua nascita era
vera lei mai essere Benedetto in amore o matrimonio.
Lucia did not believe in curses or old wife's tales, but if
what they said were true, she would never find
happiness or love in marriage. The concept of being a

subservient wife and mother was very abhorrent to her, yet in her heart, she wished that she could be ordinary. Yet that was not meant to be her destiny...

CHAPTER SIX

NEWS

Monteforte

Lucia was tired, and after dessert excused herself. She knew this was just the beginning of many more dinners, wedding planning, and gown fittings. She was already exhausted and it had just started, but she was happy for them. As she was getting ready to settle down for the night with a special book that she had sent from Rome and only arrived the day before, she noticed the letter on her desk. Quickly she undressed, washed and with Sophia's help undid her hair, which the maid had coiffed into a very continental fashion. "Sophia, how did you learn to make such an elaborate hair design?" The maid was smiling "when the merchants come to give their reports to Mistress Sucretti they bring me drawings of the latest fashions from France, this was one of the designs I saw. I am pleased that you like it." "Mistress." Lucia looked up from her book "Yes. Sophia."

"When Mistress Antoinetta marries will she leave Monteforte?" Lucia put down the book "I don't know. It is customary for the bride to make her home with her husband's family." "Why do you ask?" Sophia her chin upon her chest "You will be lonely without your sister." Lucia came over to Sophia and gave her a hug "Yes, but I have you." The maid smiled and kissed Lucia on both cheeks. "Good night Mistress." "Good night Sophia."

Anxious to start her much anticipated book, but too curious not to open the letter she received, Lucia decided the letter could be disposed of quickly, and she could then enjoy her book. Lucia was examining the letter, which had a familiar seal, but she did not immediately recognize it. Carefully she broke the seal and began reading.

Dear Mistress Lucia,

I have some disturbing news. I have been told by one of my colleagues that the manuscript is worthless. Yes, it is old but of no value. I am still waiting to hear from my other associate to get his evaluation of their worth.

Please do not despair we have all the time we need to make sure of the antiquity of the manuscripts.

Once I have received word from my friend I will come to Monteforte and we will discuss our next step.

For now, I pray that you are well and I look forward to our next meeting.

Affectionately,

Dominic Fragoli, Professor

Lucia could not believe what she was reading; she read the letter three times. Surely, he was mistaken. How could this be? She folded the letter and placed it inside her book. She sat there, the desire to read the new book was gone. Lucia needed to speak with Abbot Vittorio, he was the only one she trusted, but how was she to go there without arousing suspicion. She must think of a plausible excuse to visit the abbey. This time she would take someone with her.

She was so tired but could not sleep. The weight of the letter she received hung like a yoke around her. Lucia knew, she could feel, that this was a sacred place and those manuscripts were there, preserved for so many years, for a purpose. Blowing out the candle, she sat there in the dark, the grey smoke from the wick smoldering its ghostly vapor lingered in the air surrounding her. Her mind was wandering to the cave. Eventually she dozed off to a restless sleep in which she was being hunted by someone. She kept looking over her shoulder but could not see their face. She felt their presence but could not stop them. Who was trying to harm her? Why? Lucia fought her invisible foe throughout the night and awoke tired and anxious. She must get to the abbey.

Lucia awoke tired and angry with herself for letting her emotions get the better of her. As mistress, she would have to deal with every issue with a logical head. She willed herself to rationally think of a reason to go to the abbey. That is it she thought, and mentally patted herself on the back. I will go with the excuse of inviting Abbot Vittorio and Brother Ronaldo to the gala. Lucia was proud of herself and decided today would be as good a day as any. She would ask Gandolfo to ride with her to the abbey.

At breakfast, Lucia announced that she was taking Gandolfo and riding to Montecassino to invite Abbot Vittorio and Brother Ronaldo to the gala. "Zia that is the least I can do since they took such good care of me. Don't you agree?" Maria Sucretti did think that would be a nice gesture on their behalf. "Lucia you needn't go yourself I can send a messenger to deliver two invitations." "No Zia, I feel that it must be personal or surely they will decline. Besides, I have not taken

Apollo for a lengthy ride in such a long time. He loves it when we go far."

Antoinetta caught the tail end of the conversation and whined "But Zia we were going to choose dress designs for the wedding today. Lucia you cannot go. Zia make her stay." Lucia was annoyed "Why do you insist on making me pick gown designs, you reject everything I pick. Antoinetta, I promise, no matter how hideous the design is I will wear it without an argument. Just please, do not make me sit through that again, but, I further promise if you make me stay I will make you miserable."

"Antoinetta, Cara, I think Lucia is right. You do reject all her suggestions. If she is promising to wear whatever you choose, let her go and I will help you make a good selection." With her head down and lips, pouting Antoinetta reluctantly agreed. "Yes go on then, but I warn you that I shall pick the most awful dress for you just for spite."

"Zia, I don't think Antoinetta should get married? She is nothing but a spoiled brat. I wonder if Tomaso realizes he will be marrying a child." Lucia who had risen from the breakfast table ducked just in time to avoid being pelted by a handful of grapes that Antoinetta had aimed at her. "You may be right Lucia. Antoinetta what has gotten into you?" demanded Maria Sucretti with a broad smile on her face. All three were laughing when Giovanni Romano walked over to the table. "Good morning ladies." The handsome man made a gallant bow to his three favorite people. "There seems to be much merriment this morning. May I share in the fun?"

"Zio Giovanni, my dear sister would rather go riding on that dreadful beast to Montecassino, than to stay here and help me select gowns for the wedding. Isn't that selfish?" Giovanni knew he had just stepped on a hornet's nest but there was no hope for it. "Lucia, why are you going to the abbey?" The look of concern was written all over Giovanni's face. "I would like to personally invite Abbot Vittorio and Brother Ronaldo to the gala. I know if I send a messenger they will decline, but if I go personally, they might accept. After all they did for me; I feel it is only proper to show my gratitude."

"Ah well that sounds like a good idea, but, you will take someone with you. Yes?" Lucia knew better than to argue, and, secretly, she was frightened to travel by herself. "Yes, Zio Giovanni, I will ask Gandolfo." "Lucia if Gandolfo is busy I will gladly go with you. I am sure your aunt will be busy with Antoinetta all day."

"Well I guess it is all settled," pouted Antoinetta. "Lucia gets to go and do whatever she wants regardless of my feelings." With that, Antoinetta picked herself out of her chair and stormed off inside the house. "Thank you Zia and Zio Giovanni I should rather shoot myself in the foot than waste a whole day looking at gown designs. I will be home for supper. Let me get going." Lucia quickly kissed both her aunt and uncle and headed toward the stables. She felt her pocket to be sure she had the letter from Professor Fragoli.

"Gandolfo, may I ask a favor of you?" "Of course my mistress how can I assist you?" "I wish to go to the abbey and invite the Abbot and Brother Ronaldo to the gala, and I wish to do it in person. Is it possible for you to accompany me on my journey to the abbey?" Gandolfo seemed pleased that Lucia had asked him to go with her. "But of course I will go. Give me a few moments to give everyone the day's instruction and I will be ready shortly. Will we take horses or the carriage?" " Oh, thank you Gandolfo. Let us take the horses. Apollo is anxious to go on a long ride."

A few moments later Gandolfo and two grooms appeared with Apollo and Venus all saddled and ready to go. "I had Maria put some bread and cheese and a skin of wine together for us." "Wonderful. Shall we get started, it is already late morning?"

"I am surprised that you are taking Venus on our trip," Lucia said to Gandolfo who chuckled. "Well to be truthful, after what Venus had to endure last week with Mistress Antoinetta I thought it only fair to give her a treat." They both laughed heartily.

CHAPTER SEVEN

THE INVITATION

Montecassino Abbey

It was such a pleasant day for a long ride and Apollo and Venus were enjoying themselves. Gandolfo was a good traveling companion who rode well and spoke little.

Lucia was enjoying herself, the abbey was a higher elevation than Monteforte, and the air was thinner and crisper. They passed through many lemon groves and the fragrant scent of citrus, with its clean fresh perfume, made Lucia feel renewed.

After a while, she turned to asked Gandolfo "Have you heard from Piro? Is he settled in his new place?" Gandolfo, who looked like he was also enjoying the ride, replied, "Yes Mistress, he writes that he has been placed in a good position at the estate of the Marquis de Fauntil, who is an old friend of Mistress Sucretti. The Marquis is a powerful man in France, and as such has been able to secure Piro a seat at the Universita de Paris. From what Piro tells me, it is very difficult to establish a position there. He is concerned that he might not be able to keep up with the other students, most of which come from wealthy families. The Marquis, who appears to be a kind and wise man, has engaged the services of a tutor for Piro to get him through the initial months of learning the language, and to acquaint himself with his surroundings. He tells me he is happy but misses everyone here at Monteforte. He sends his special regards to you Mistress."

Lucia shifted slightly in her saddle, suddenly uncomfortable about hearing of Piro's adventures. "I am happy for him Gandolfo. This is a wonderful opportunity and I pray he does well. I know he will work hard. He promised me he would." Gandolfo, his eyes looking down, "Yes my dear Mistress, he has very lofty goals that he has set for himself. I just hope he can achieve them. I pray for his success and his well-being." Gandolfo just nodded and did not say any more. Lucia fell silent until they reached the abbey. She was excited and apprehensive to share her letter with Abbot Vittorio. She thought what if Professor Fragoli said were true? How is it possible for that place to be there and these manuscripts are not ancient?

Gandolfo had dismounted and entered the abbey to find someone to announce their arrival. Within a few moments, he returned with the lay brother that had helped Lucia on her first trip to Montecassino. Lucia was as happy to see him, as he was to see her. "Mistress Lucia, it is so wonderful to see you once again. I see that you are as beautiful as ever. I am sure that Abbot Vittorio and Brother Ronaldo will be so excited to know you are here."

Lucia, her cheeks flushed at his apparent enthusiastic reception, said "Oh thank you so much. I am truly happy to be back. Can you tell them of our arrival? We shall wait in the great hall. Thank you again." Lucia with the aid of Gandolfo had dismounted "I will help him with the horses Mistress. When you are ready to leave they will come and get me." Gandolfo and the lay brother took away the two horses. Lucia stepped into the great hall.

It was dark and cool inside the great abbey, its thick stone walls held back the heat from the sun. Lucia drank in the scent of candlewax and incense. The cool air washed over her body, the dim light calming her senses. She closed her eyes and felt her body relax, encased in the safety of this holy place. She wanted to run to the chapel and prostrate herself before the altar asking Jesus to guide her, to give her strength and make her a wise woman; her thoughts were interrupted by the sound of soft footfalls on the stone floor. It had only been a couple of months, but she felt like she had left the abbey so long ago. Her life had changed so dramatically in that short time.

"My dear Lucia I am truly happy to see you. Come; let me gaze upon that beautiful face. I see that you are fully recovered at least on the outside. How are you?" asked the soft deep baritone of Abbot Vittorio who had embraced her in his muscular arms. "I am healing on the outside but inside is much slower to mend. Much has happened in the short time since last I saw you. I am sorry if I have interrupted your schedule. Do you have some time for me?" The monk, taller than her, bent his head and kissed her forehead with great gentleness "I shall make whatever time you need. Let us go to the library and talk, or do I need to take you to the chapel?" Lucia wanted to go to the chapel to renew her spirit before they spoke of the contents of the letter. "Abbot, take me to the chapel, I wish to renew myself and make my confession."

The monk solemnly nodded his head, placed his hands inside his robe, and led the way to the chapel. It was even darker than the great hall. The smell of incense was strong, almost overwhelming, and the air was cold. Lucia shivered. The monk indicated the confessional box and they both stepped into their respective places. Lucia was sweating in spite of the fact that she was cold. Her eyes now adjusted to the dark she heard the velvet curtain slide open by the monk. "Bless me father for I have sinned" as Lucia made the sign of the cross. "I cannot find it in my heart to forgive the man who attacked me. I have begged the Lord Jesus to give me a gentle heart, but He has not sent it to me. The man haunts my dreams, and I find no pleasure in my sleep. I have cursed his soul for what he did to me. Yet I am sorry for having killed him, because I know I should be. I am very confused. Help me."

"Lucia, it was not so long ago that this outrage happened to you. Our Lord knows you did nothing wrong. It is not a sin to protect yourself from harm. That man violated you. Of course, now, you cannot forgive him. In time, you will come to understand that everything in life has a reason. Even the evil things that happen have a reason. It is only what we do with that evil that makes us sin. God had sent that man as a test of your faith and courage. You have passed the test. Do not let the devil fill your heart and your dreams with cursed thoughts. You did nothing wrong and Our Lord Jesus forgives you. I want you to say one rosary every night before you go to sleep as a protection against evil dreams. You will see that before long you will no longer dream of your attacker. May the blessings of Our Lord Jesus Christ be upon you. Your sins are forgiven. Let the peace of Christ, all the angels and saints descend upon you. Io ti assolvo dai vostri peccati. Nel nome del padre, figlio e Spirito Santo. Amen."

Lucia felt clean and refreshed, she knew that she would sleep well tonight. She blessed herself and exited the confessional. Abbot Vittorio wearing his hood over his head was on his knees facing the altar. Lucia fell to her knees and prayed for God's blessings. After a few minutes, they both arose and left the chapel. They were heading toward the library when Lucia grabbed the monk's sleeve. "Thank you." The monk, now with his hood removed from his head, said nothing, but patted the hand that was planted on his arm, and with a warm smile silently reassured her that all as well.

When they reached the library the monk indicated the alcove where he sat behind the carved desk and she took the chair right in front. "Now that we have visited the chapel shall we speak of how you are progressing?" Lucia took in a deep breath reached in her pocket and extracted the letter from Professor Fragoli. She handed it to the monk without explanation. He accepted it and carefully opened it. He read it with interest. When he was finished, he folded it and handed it back to Lucia. She wanted to burst out 'what is he saying' but held her tongue.

The monk sat back in his chair, his eyes closed, and pondered his response. "Lucia, do you remember when I had told you, 'Do you trust this man?' and you told me that you did. I believe that there is something wrong with this letter. Brother Angelo and I have been working on the manuscript that you left with me. We have determined it to be authentic and dating back hundreds of years. It is Byzantine Greek and ancient. So why, unless the person who was reading it was unqualified, which given his supposed status as an expert is unlikely, did the professor write this letter, which is clearly untrue, to you?"

Speechless, Lucia just sat there looking at the monk whose eyes were still shut tight. She waited for him to open his eyes. The monk leaned forward, opened his eyes, and faced her. His eyes were intense and his expression was suddenly guarded. Lucia felt a fear pass over her. "Abbot I am not sure what you mean?" The normally soft lines around the monk's mouth were now taut and his voice was edged with a repressed anger. "I am trying to tell you that this professor is either very ignorant, or he is trying to trick you into believing these manuscripts are worthless. Brother Angelo, who is an expert in these matters, assures me that placed in the wrong hands these priceless antiquities would garner a fortune. Lucia you are young and innocent to the ways of the world. There are those, who for the sake of riches, like the man who attacked you, would do anything for personal gain. They would murder, rape, steal, and betray. I cannot say with any certainty that the professor is trying to deceive you, but I must caution you to be wary of him. Do you understand?"

Sadly, Lucia did understand. "Abbot I do understand, but what course am I to take. He knows of the secret cave and all its contents." When she first read the letter she felt betrayed, but she did not want to believe that Professor Fragoli would do this to her. Why would he do this? Money? Fame? How did he expect to get away with it, after all she knew of the existence of the cave, its contents and now the monk knew as well? Abbot Vittorio was thinking, his eyes closed in deep contemplation. He opened his eyes, which were now burning with decision. "Lucia, there are two steps we must take. I will accompany you back to Monteforte and we shall retrieve all the manuscripts, which we will bring back here. Second, we must enlist the aid of your uncle Giovanni Romano to help us find out more about this professor, because if I know anything about human nature, and if he is trying to persuade you that the manuscripts are worthless, he will return one way or another to steal them. When I am at Monteforte you and I will talk privately to your uncle who I believe knows a great many people who can help us."

For the first time since reading the letter, Lucia felt relieved. She could confide with someone else. Giovanni Romano would know what to do, he always did. In a matter of minutes, a solid plan was formulated. Abbot Vittorio and Brother Angelo would come back to Monteforte with Lucia and Gandolfo on the pretense of counseling Antoinetta on her upcoming nuptials. They would create a rouse by substituting the original ancient manuscripts with reproductions of similar content. Brother Angelo had dozens of such copies. Once the bait was set, they would let the professor make the next move. In the meantime, Giovanni Romano would gather more information on the good professor. It was a good plan, now, if it could only work.

Lucia was left to find Gandolfo and tell him of our returning guests. A light midday meal was being prepared for them. Just as the meal arrived so did Abbot Vittorio and Brother Angelo. They all knew not to speak in the presence of Gandolfo. It was a hearty meal and all shared pleasant conversation. "Gandolfo will you see that the horses are ready. I want to return to Monteforte before dark." Without any hesitation, Gandolfo got up and headed toward the stables.

It was the abbot who spoke in a low tone "I have shared our story with Brother Angelo and he agrees that something is very wrong. As we planned, he has packed a sack filled with worthless manuscripts. Our journey will last two days. Upon our return, here to the abbey we will place the originals in our secret vault. There will only be the three of us who knows the truth." Brother Angelo quietly said, "I must agree with the Abbot, anyone who possesses knowledge of ancient manuscripts would have known these to be original and priceless. We must be wary of this man and his associates."

It was dusk by the time they arrived at Monteforte; just in time for dinner. Zia Maria and Zio Giovanni were delighted to have guests, especially the beloved monks. Giorgio scurried off to have two guest rooms prepared. While the monks were led off to wash, the dirt off from the long ride Lucia approached her aunt and uncle. "I hope you don't mind the intrusion, when I told the Abbot of Antoinetta's upcoming wedding he was very excited to talk with her. Brother Angelo, whose duty at the abbey is to maintain its famous library and all its contents, had heard of our extensive library and since the monks must travel in pairs Abbot Vittorio invited him to join us."

Maria Sucretti was delighted to have them, as was Giovanni Romano. "Bella, they are welcome to Monteforte any time you wish. For that matter, you may invite anyone you wish. This is your home now." "Thank you Zia you are always so gracious."

After washing for dinner, the monks appeared at the heels of Giorgio. "Dear Mistress and Master, it is so kind of you to receive us on such short notice. We hope we have not inconvenienced you." Abbot Vittorio bowed deeply to his hosts. Giovanni Romano came over to the monk and gave him a hearty manly embrace "We are so happy to see you Abbot and welcome Brother Angelo." Conversation flowed freely and soon Giorgio announced that dinner was being served.

Antoinetta's appearance prompted Abbot Vittorio to rise from his seat and greet the soon-to-be bride. "You must be the bride. I can see the blush of love all over you. I have known Lord Tomaso since I first came to Montecassino and his family. They, like your family, are most generous to the causes of our abbey. May I make myself and Monetcassino available for any of your needs Mistress Antoinetta?"

Antoinetta was happily taken off guard by the straightforwardness of the monk. She curtsied and said, "That is most generous of you Abbot. I shall extend that invitation to Lord Tomaso." Everyone was now seated and dinner was served. The monks, who generally dine on a simple, meager fare, were shocked at the quantity and variety of food being presented. They ate with hearty appetites. Brother Angelo confessed, "Dear Abbot, I will have to do penance for the sin of gluttony. I have eaten so much I am sure God will make my stomach ache. But sadly, I must admit I would do it again." Everyone laughed.

After dinner, cognac was served on the terrace. It was a warm evening but a steady breeze cooled the air. "Zio Giovanni while Giorgio prepares the dessert, why don't you join Abbot Vittorio and Brother Angelo and I in the library. They are most anxious to see our vast collection." Giovanni Romano was too wise not to know when he was being baited. "Yes, of course, come see our collection. It is mostly the work of Lucia."

"Zia, Antoinetta, we shall not be too long. Have Giorgio come for us when dessert is ready." Maria Sucretti nodded she knew Lucia was so proud of that library.

Antoinetta came to sit by her aunt "Zia, do you think that Zio Luigi would marry Tomaso and me at Montecassino. We would then come back here for the wedding reception." "Cara, I think that is a splendid idea and I am sure that Abbot Vittorio would be delighted to have a Bishop celebrate a wedding at the abbey.

First, you must ask Tomaso, then we shall ask Luigi, then we ask the Abbot for permission to have the wedding performed there. I think that would be lovely. Let us see what Lucia thinks." "Ah, Lucia, the one who does not want to participate in any of the planning of my wedding, and we must ask her opinion. I am so angry at her." "Antoinetta you know Lucia has no head for these details. Why, I was not good enough to help you with the designs today?" Maria Sucretti put on a wounded face. "No Zia, you were wonderful, and yes, I suppose you are right. If it was left up to Lucia we would be wearing riding gowns and coming down the aisle riding horses." They laughed and all was forgiven.

The conversation on the terrace was light and jovial, while an air of solemnity emanated from the library. Once inside, Lucia closed the door behind them, and asked everyone to be seated. She sat next to Giovanni Romano and took his hand. He held hers gently stroking it, yet his eyes never left her face.

"What is it Cara?" "Zio Giovanni I must first begin by telling you a story that happened a long time ago. When I first came to Monteforte, I was discovering new things and places to play and hide from Antoinetta. I came upon an opening in the cliff wall that was hidden by overgrown vegetation. I was being called by Antoinetta and Sophia because they thought something happened to me. I vowed that someday I would come back to that secret opening and discover if it held any treasures, but sadly, I had forgotten about its existence. Then not so very long ago I was out riding along the beach with Apollo, it was a very hot day, so I decided to take a swim to cool myself. To my surprise, I came upon a hidden cove. I swam to the mouth of the cove only to find that it was shallow and led into a cave." At this point Lucia paused in the telling of her story to see the faces of her audience. The two monks, having no knowledge of this part of her story, were listening with great interest.

Lucia continued, "I ventured into the darkness of the cave. Then to my amazement, and at first horror, as I was threading through knee-deep water, my legs started to glow. I wanted to scream out in fear, but suddenly realized that I was not afraid. Actually, I felt safe and calm and thought there was a holy presence surrounding me. I dunked my faced into the water and could clearly see from the illumination by the strange glow that the floor upon which I was standing was not sea silt but mosaic tile. I was shocked that such a thing would exist in the middle of the sea. I continued to advance into the recesses of the cave. As I advanced deeper the water receded, and the pattern displayed on the floor became more visible. The height of the cave was enormous and covered in beautiful designs with mosaic and gold inlaid from ceiling to floor. It was bright as if lit by a hundred candles."

The three men sat in rapt attention, no one asked any questions, no one moved, but sat waiting for her to finish her story. Lucia drew a deep breath and went on "I found myself standing in the middle of a large room. I wanted to be frightened because I knew this was something strange but I did not find the need to be scared. Then, from one side of the room, I felt the floor rumbling, it grew louder and in one second, a thunderous roar exploded from the floor and vomited a great wall of steam. The mist of which was so hot it almost scorched my skin. For the first time I felt fear. I jumped back from where the wall had spewed forth its venom and fell into a depression on the other side. When I had recovered from the initial shock, I found myself looking up into a stairwell. A stairwell that went nowhere, or, at least I did not think it led anywhere. I found a large clamshell and used it as a shovel, and was carefully picking my way through layers of earth until I finally saw the first glimmer of sunlight. Making a hole large, enough to peek through I knew exactly where the stairwell led. I needed to get out of there before the next onslaught of the wall erupted, so I left the way I came with the promise to return to discover more about this secret and enchanting place." Lucia was excited and getting exhausted from telling her story, but she knew she could not rest now.

The young Brother Angelo asked "Mistress what were the designs on the mosaic?" Lucia smiled broadly and said, "I didn't realize it until this last trip to the Abbey, but, the design that is inlaid in the Chapel of Relics, which, Abbot Vittorio told me, was the oldest portion of the Abbey, the one with the two greyhounds in flight, is the same design as on the cave floor. I was paralyzed with wonder when I realized that both the Abbey and the cave share the same design.

Giovanni Romano, still holding Lucia's hand, said "Go on with your story Cara, I am most interested."

"After I left that day I vowed myself to secrecy. This would me my sanctuary, my secret place. One afternoon, after I had received a lesson from Professor Fragoli, is when everything changed. The professor was sitting here relaxing, smoking his cigar, when I casually asked him about the most exotic place he had ever been. The professor often told Antoinetta and me of his many travels to the Pyramids and Jerusalem and even Africa. He told me the story of how when he was a very young man he had gone fishing with two of his friends, and out of nowhere a great storm came up out of the sea. It washed them up into this cave. He suddenly realized that it was not dark inside. A strange and beautiful emerald glow was all over him and everything it touched. At first, he thought he should be frightened, but like me, felt a warm calming embrace envelope him. It was then that I told him of my own experience in the cave. For two people to share such a profound experience was not merely coincidence but destiny. Several days after that shared story we met at the beach where I first went swimming. We swam to the cove and entered the cave. It was just as I had remembered, but this time I felt more secure with having someone to share this beautiful experience. The professor walked around the room examining every wall, then, as before, the far wall started to rumble, roar, and spit forth the hot fetid steam. Once it subsided, the professor knelt down and tried to find the source of the steam, when he found a lever. He grasped hold of the lever and with all his strength; he was able to pull it back. It screeched and cried but finally it gave way and opened. That was when to our total amazement we discovered the inner chamber of the cave." At this point, they all looked at each other. The Abbot now addressed Lucia directly. "Lucia is that where you found the manuscripts?" "Yes Abbot it is. They were stacked high on shelves and tables. It very much looked like the abbey where the monks translate and copy the ancient manuscripts at Montecassino."

"Please continue." Lucia was grateful for the opportunity to finish her story. "We then discovered the manuscripts and it was Professor Fragoli who believed that they were priceless antiquities. He suggested we take two to be studied by two different colleagues of his, one in Rome, and one in Florence. I took one for myself. I brought that one to you Abbot.

After we secured the manuscripts, the professor resealed the inner chamber by reaching down and closing the lever. I was concerned that the manuscripts would be ruined if we swam back with them. I had told the professor to bring a shovel or pick so that we could clear the debris from the stairwell, which he did. We worked for hours trying to move the layers of earth from the opening. Finally, we cleared the stairs, but to our agitation were prevented from climbing out because at the top of the stairs was an iron gate that had been secured with a heavy lock. However, since I knew where it led, we decided to pass the manuscripts through the opening and tossed them to the ground on the other side, which we retrieved later. We parted with the promise that in a few weeks Professor Fragoli would be in contact with me regarding the manuscripts. The last I heard from him was the letter I brought to you Abbot."

Lucia produced the letter and showed it to Giovanni Romano who read it with great interest. A man of few words, Giovanni absorbed the content of the letter, and then just refolded it and handed it back to Lucia. After a few moments, he asked, "Lucia, why did you not tell me and your aunt of this discovery sooner?" Lucia had dreaded that question which she knew would eventually be asked. "I didn't want to concern either of you until I was positive of their worth. I knew that Zia would be angry with me for venturing to such a place by myself, now, especially after what has happened. I am sorry." At this point Abbot Vittorio joined in "Master Romano, I am partially to blame for this situation as well. I had advised Lucia that it was not betrayal at this point not to include you and Mistress Sucretti in this find since at that time we were not certain if it was necessary. I hope you are not offended." Giovanni Romano, a look of deep concern on his face answered, "I am concerned because Lucia, who is good and pure of heart, and does not understand the ways of evil, that she did not inform us of her discovery. My concern lies with the man, Professor Fragoli, who knew the value of these manuscripts, and who might try to contact those in the criminal world who could sell them for him, because in so doing she has placed herself in extreme danger. It is not the knowledge of the worth of the manuscripts that concerns me, Lucia has more than she can spend in ten life times, I know it was not to conceal from us these priceless antiquities, but for the independence that she felt its knowledge gave her. That knowledge could now cost her life. I, sadly, have lived in that world, and know ruthless men who would stop at nothing to possess such a prize as these manuscripts." Giovanni Romano was clearly upset and Lucia, tears rolling freely down that beautiful face, grabbed his hands and looked into his face. "I am so sorry for all the trouble I have caused for you and my aunt. You must think I am a terrible person."

Giovanni Romano took her hands and placed them first to his lips and kissed them, then held them to his heart. "Cara, you could never be a burden for us. We love you so much. We are worried for your safety. Being the Mistress of Monteforte is not just a pretty title, it is a way of life that can be dangerous at times. You face many difficult challenges. I will find out as much as I can about Professor Fragoli, and whom he has contacted in the underworld; for now, we will keep this among the four of us, until I know who we are dealing with. Understood?"

Lucia, with those eyes the color of the sea, fell into his arms, and kissed his cheeks. "I love you all, and will do all that I am able to be the woman I need to be to all those who are part of Monteforte. Please help me do better and be better. Pray for me." He embraced her with all the love he had, and felt the tears run down his own face. The monks sat there in uncomfortable silence, knowing they were part of a very personal moment. Lucia asked, "What will we do now?" "I shall take a trip to Naples and find some of my old contacts, and see if I can dig up any information, not only the professor, but any of his known associates. For now, you and the good brothers, will say nothing, and go about your plan to replace the existing manuscripts, before someone comes to take them. I am thinking since there is no access by land, other than the guards at the gate, they may come by sea. Therefore, I will have two men guard the beach by the cove, and I will tell them that we received word that there have been pirates marauding the coast. Do we all agree to that plan?" Giovanni Romano directed the question to all of them. "I think it is a good plan but dangerous for you Master Giovanni. Can you not send one of the servants in your place?" "Unfortunately that is not possible, since the people I need to speak with are very wary of outsiders. Who knows, perhaps even I will come away with no news, since it has been over twenty years since last I was involved in such activity. I am confident that some of the old timers will still be around and will grant me access to their knowledge. I will be prepared to pay a heavy toll for this information, but in the end, it may save Lucia's life."

Satisfied with the outcome of their short, but intense meeting, the four agreed on strict silence. Lucia asked the monks "Tomorrow, at dawn, we will meet at the stables, and ride to the location of the land opening to the cave. Yes?" The two just nodded their acceptance. Giovanni Romano stood and said, "Now, let us go and be jovial, for Mistress Maria is very wise and will suspect that there is something brewing."

As they were about to leave the room the abbot held back until Brother Angelo and Lucia were strolling down the hall. "Giovanni, I feel partially to blame for all this mess. While I am more than aware of ruthless men, I did not realize how serious this could be. If anything happens to Lucia, I will not forgive myself. Tell me of what I must do to protect her." "Abbot, this is not your fault, or even Lucia's, it is the fault of evil, greedy men. We have not even begun to experience the lengths to which they will go to achieve their prize. Be vigilant, it will not take someone too long to surmise that she would come to you for assistance. Lucia is now a marked woman, and if they do not find the manuscripts, they will try to make her tell them where they are. I am truly fearful for her life." "Then we will be very careful, and as you say vigilant."

The two embraced and Giovanni asked Abbot Vittorio to pray for him. They left to join the others. When they entered the room there was an animated conversation between Brother Angelo and Antoinetta as to the vast collection in the library. The monk played his role very well and apparently had absorbed some of the flavor of the library which he shared with Maria Sucretti and her niece Antoinetta. Giovanni was relieved not to have to tell Maria what was really going on, at least, not just yet. A feeling of both excitement and dread filled Giovanni Romano, at the thought of venturing into the haunts of his past life. He would use the excuse of going in search of some exotic flower for his masterpiece garden, and he would do that tomorrow. He needed to find the source of this problem before it got out of hand.

CHAPTER EIGHT

THE DECEPTION

Monteforte

Before retiring for the night, they agreed that Giovanni Romano, accompanied by Nicko, would head to Naples to seek out information on Professor Fragoli. Lucia, Brother Angelo, and Abbot Vittorio would leave at daybreak for the cave.

As she lay in her bed, Lucia's mind could not help but wonder what problems lie ahead of her. She would never have thought that Professor Fragoli would betray her, but she had been wrong about so many things. She chastised herself for being too trusting and not more discerning when it came to people's character. After a long while, she fell asleep and lapsed into a frightful night of disturbing dreams.

She awoke with a start, and was soaked in sweat, even though it was cool in her room. The dream that woke her was still fresh on her mind. In the dream she could see a man, tall and handsome, she knew this man, or, had some connection to him, but could not determine from the dream who he was. There was an attraction to him but one of underlying fear. She could not distinguish his face clearly in her dream he was shrouded in fog. Lucia had an ominous sense of dread that surrounded this man, and knew that at some point she would have to confront him in a battle, the outcome of which was not clear. She hated these dreams and always woke with a feeling of agitation and fear.

It was nearly time to leave for the cave. She got up made her toilet and dressed silently, then make her way to the kitchen. There she found the two monks sitting to a simple breakfast. "Good morning Mistress you seem anxious to get started," said Abbot Vittorio who was finishing what must have been a slab of bacon and a hunk of bread with cheese. "Yes I am very excited for our adventure. I will have a little breakfast then we will get started." Since the household was beginning to stir, there was no further conversation regarding the cave and its contents. Giorgio seeing the trio asked about their early start. "I wanted to take the Abbot and Brother Angelo down to the cliffs to see the sea. Brother Angelo is not from this part of Italy and we were talking about it last night. Oh, by the way, Giorgio could you please make up a lunch basket for us to take with us. Send it down to the stables. Thank you. If my aunt or sister are looking for me tell them I'm out riding with the good monks." Giorgio bowed deeply and made hast to prepare them a basket. As always, Lucia filled her pocket with sugar and carrots for Apollo.

Once they made their way to the stables, Gandolfo helped the grooms ready two horses and Apollo. "Gandolfo I need to take a pick and shovel with us. Brother Angelo was told to look for is a certain plant that grows down by the cliffs, which Brother Ronaldo would be interested in for medicinal purposes. Can you get that and strap it to one of the horses?" "Yes certainly Mistress. You all will be very careful. It has rained now overnight and you know how slippery the cliffs can get." "Thank you Gandolfo, you are always so kind to worry about me. We will be careful I promise."

They left the stables just as the sun was coming up over the mountaintop. It was a bright, clear, day and their spirits were lifted. Lucia, having had some forethought as to how to hide the fake manuscripts, had told Brother Angelo to take the bundle that he was carrying when they first arrived at Monteforte, and store it on the far side of the herb garden. When they reached there, he jumped down and retrieved the package.

In a short while, they had reached the spot where the grate covered the entrance to the secret stairwell. It was well hidden by thick scrub bushes. The trio dismounted, hobbled their horses, and made their way to the grate, which was still as Lucia had left it. It was the abbot, a solid muscular man, who took the pick and heaved it high over his head in an arcing motion. "Clang!" The pick found its mark and it came down hard on the rusted lock. Nothing happened. Again, the monk, with great determination, heaved it high over his head and with an intense grimace on his face brought the pick down with all his might. "Clang" This time the lock broke apart.

Brother Angelo knelt down and began scraping the encrusted earth from around the steel grate. Slowly, the earth was giving way. After a while, he had made a clean job of it and the grate, with its hinges screeching from the exertion, gave way. They entered carefully, trying to dislodge clumps of earth that had fallen during their excavation. Lucia went first, when her foot finally set upon the mosaic floor she let her breath out. The sheer excitement of being in that sacred place once again was a joy.

The monks, mouths agape, stood there in the middle of the antechamber in utter amazement. Abbot Vittorio, his eyes wide "Lucia this is exactly as you had said and more. The illumination is astounding." Brother Angelo was speechless and filled with wonder. Then, as if on demand, the cave started to rumble and roar, and seconds later, the hot malodorous steam erupted from the far wall. The monks jumped back in utter surprise. Lucia was giggling to their embarrassment. "This is the steam of which you spoke." "Yes, and the lever to open the inner chamber lies just under that opening in the rock wall. Come, we must hurry, before it erupts again." It was the abbot who followed her lead, and just as she had instructed, the iron lever was just within his reach, and he pulled with all his strength until it creaked and moaned as it opened, revealing a spectacular sight. "Hurry, cross over, before the steam comes again." They did as Lucia said and leapt into the cavernous inner chamber.

The two monks stood speechless just looking around. The volume of the ceiling height with the attention to detail and intricacy of design astounded them.

The Abbot knelt down and made the sign of the cross, his fellow monk followed as did Lucia. They bent their heads in prayer and adoration. The abbot completing his prayers prostrated himself and kissed the floor. Brother Angelo followed his example Lucia did not.

The three stood up and reveled in a silent stupor. "Lucia this is beyond all imagining. It must be thousands of years old, and I cannot help but think that it holds some connection to our Abbey. I am in such awe of its splendor. How this came to be in this place is a mystery I will spend the rest of my life trying to unravel." Brother Angelo seemed to be floating across the floor, looking, touching, and experiencing all that he could. "Abbot this is a sacred place. I can see that it is ancient but preserved with such miraculous care." He went over to the wall of manuscripts, and randomly picked one up and laid it across the battered wooden table. "These are just as if they had been written yesterday, and, yet, I know that they hundreds of years old.

The reaction of the two monks filled Lucia was great joy and pride. "You see, I told you it was beyond all reasoning. Here look over at this place." In a niche carved into the rock wall was an altar. A primitive statue, the remnants of which were still visible which had been placed in a spot for veneration. "Brother Angelo did you bring some parchment and quill?" "Yes Abbot I did." "Excellent. Now I would like you to draw the details of some of these mosaic depictions, so that we might have a record of what is in here to study their origin." "I can help. I know how to draw." "Very good Lucia, you help Brother Angelo with his recording, I will continue to explore and see what else we can find. I cannot believe that it is so bright in here."

The abbot explored every inch of the chamber, while his fellow monk and Lucia made careful renderings of what they saw. There was something missing, but he could not find what his mind told him was wrong. "Where did this chamber lead?" he asked himself. They worked diligently in silence for hours. Finally, the abbot said, "let us change out the manuscripts for those we have here. They did as he had said and decided that there was no more to learn from the chamber at this time. When they emerged from the stairwell laden down with priceless manuscripts, and many detailed drawings, they needed to rest.

Brother Angelo was animated, talking to his superior, while Lucia set forth the modest lunch Giorgio had sent with them. "What do we do next?" Abbot Vittorio, a mouth filled with bread and cheese, waited until he had finished chewing, and then answered, "We wait. First, we must hear from your Uncle Giovanni to make sure, if the Professor has in fact set a dangerous triangle in motion. While we patiently await further instruction from your Uncle, Brother Angelo and I, will carefully go over each of the manuscripts in search of any clues that may inform us of the original creation of this sacred place." It was the young monk who spoke "Mistress Lucia, I cannot even begin to express how grateful I am that you have included us in this discovery. Not only for the knowledge, will we gather but also for the beauty and splendor of this place. I am convinced that within these ancient writings will be the secret of how it came to be. Monteforte holds many secrets yet to be revealed, of that I am sure." "Yes Lucia, Brother Angelo, has so eloquently stated my own feelings. We shall labor, day and night, in an effort to reveal what is held in these manuscripts. It is a great and honored trust that you have placed in us, and we will not disappoint you."

"Dear Abbot and Brother Angelo, if these ancient documents are nearly as valuable as you say, I will, I vow, take a large portion of the money and share it with your Abbey for those who are less fortunate. They will serve to bring not only knowledge, but also comfort to those in need. Thank you both for all your help, and I pray that none of us must face any danger from this discovery." They rested, speculating about what the manuscripts might contain, and who created them. The Abbot, speaking his thoughts said, "The most intriguing issue lies in the fact that there are so many similarities between the Abbey and this secret place. We must find out what the connection is." It was getting late and they packed up and headed for the manse.

After supper Maria Sucretti asked the two monks if would be staying for the gala. "That is most gracious of you Mistress Sucretti, but Brother Angelo and I must be getting back to the Abbey. We will be honored to attend the gala, and as you instructed, I will extend that invitation to Brother Ronaldo. We will leave just after breakfast tomorrow. Please accept our humble thanks for your generous hospitality, and know that you and your family are remembered in our daily prayers. Now, if you would excuse Brother Angelo and I for an early retire." The Abbot came over to Maria Sucretti who was seated at the far end of the dining table and kissed her hand with a deep-footed bow. "Mia signora, buona sera e maggio si dorme nella cura di Dio." The younger monk stood to the side, head bowed, waiting for his superior. "Grazie caro Vittorio Abate. Voi e i vostri fratelli sono sempre benvenuti qui a Monteforte. Buona notte". Antoinetta, who had been enjoying the monks' company also reinforced her aunt's sentiments, "Yes Abbot, please come any time you wish, and I will certainly speak with Lord Tomaso about having our wedding at Montecassino." "It would be our honor to officiate at such a blessed event Mistress Antoinetta. I look forward to seeing Lord Tomaso again. Good night and God bless the two of you." Lucia had been sitting silent, then suddenly rose, and said "Abbot I will walk with you for a moment. I have a question regarding the Abbey. Zia Maria, Antoinetta, I will say good night as well." She went over to her aunt then her sister giving both of them kisses.

Lucia walked down the great hall with the two monks. "Abbot, I cannot help but have mixed emotions regarding the cave. I love it because I know in my heart it is a sacred place, but I cannot lose the feeling that there is some kind of evil that lies within. Do you feel the same?" Strangely enough, the abbot did feel a sense of ominous danger, "I too feel there is something about that place that holds an evil spirit, but, I also believe that there is a holiness that will prevail. We must be cautious and pray for God's guidance." He stopped, turned and took her hands, "Lucia, promise me that you will be careful. Non fare nulla di stupido. Sono così preziosi che non vorremmo alcun danno di venire da voi. Mi prometti." "Abbot, I promise I will be careful and will not do anything foolish. Please let me know as soon as you and Brother Angelo translate the manuscripts." "Lucia, kneel down." She did as he said. He placed both his hands upon her thick strawberry head and closed his eyes. Invoking the blessings of Jesus, he said, "Dear Lord Jesus, watch over Lucia, and all those she loves.

Give her the blessings of your wisdom that she may know those who would harm her. Keep her safe against evil spirits. Nel nome del padre, figlio e Spirito Santo. Amen." He then gave her his hands, lifted her off her knees, and kissed her on each cheek. "Do not look for us in the morning, instead make your daily prayers, I will come back soon with our findings. Caro buona notte Lucia." Brother Angelo came over and kissed each cheek. "Good night Mistress Lucia. This has been wonderful. I am so excited to start working on these manuscripts. We shall see you soon. God bless you."

When she reached their room, she bid them safe journey and went to her own bedchamber. She was so excited but anxious for Giovanni Romano and Nicko who were in Naples trying to find out information on Professor Fragoli. She would find it hard to get to sleep tonight.

CHAPTER NINE

OLD HAUNTS

Naples

Giovanni Romano and Nicko found rooms in a nicely appointed inn in the center of the city. Giovanni had instructed Nicko that he would be busy all the next day and that they would meet up for a late supper. Nicko, whose sister lived in the outskirts of the city, would be happy to see him. "Do not worry Lord Giovanni my sister will be happy to see me for a few hours. She always complains that I never come to visit. I will meet you back here tomorrow evening at seven o'clock. Yes?" "That is good that you will see your family. Here is some extra money; I know she has several children, buy them some treats. Yes, seven o'clock will be fine. Nicko, if for some reason I am late, do not come looking for me. I am going in search of some old contacts and they are not friendly people. Understand?" "Lord Giovanni is it safe what you are doing?" "I hope so Nicko, but there is something I must find out to protect Lucia. Buona notte Nicko fino a domani sera."

Giovanni Romano did not go to bed, but instead took a carriage to the far end of the city where he was dropped off at the rialto that ran along the docks. It was the roughest part of Napoli. Small groups of men, young and old, stood around smoking and talking. They all eyed him as he passed. Giovanni kept his head down and wore an old coat and breeches. His black hat was pulled down low to cover his face and deliberately had not shaved. His overall appearance was surprisingly akin to those lurking on the street. Giovanni Romano knew where he was headed which was a dark side street, no more than an alley, he ventured down to the middle of a row of dilapidated buildings, praying that his memory was correct. A million thoughts ran through his head and his mouth was suddenly dry. His steps were steady but slow; willing his mind to remember which building was the one he was seeking. Very little had changed in the years since he had been the bodyguard and enforcer for Salvatore Sucretti at least, that infused his confidence.

He found the one he was looking for and hoped he was in the right place. There was no light coming from within but he knocked once, then two more in rapid succession. Miraculously the door opened.

Standing in front of him was a gnarly old man. "What do you want?" he asked in an agitated voice. The stench came from the open door that immediately brought Giovanni Romano back twenty years, the smell of stale cigars and male sweat. "I want to see "Signore Zingaro, tell him Giovanni the Roman is here." The old man did not respond further but slammed the door in his face. He stood there waiting in the dark a bead of sweat ran down his back. He wondered if the man he knew as Gaetano Zingaro was still alive, after all he would be at least seventy-five years old. It felt like an eternity, but was in reality only a few moments, before the door reopened and a huge bulk overshadowed the doorway. "Come." Giovanni Romano followed the massive form that was leading him into the inner recesses of the building. They came to a door, which the large man opened with a key. "Go in. Someone will come for you." Giovanni nodded and stepped inside the hall, the door closed with a thud and he heard the lock engage. He was locked inside. The sweat that had started outside on the street was running rampart down his back. He stood there in a dimly lit hallway, waiting to be presented to a memory from his past. Whom would he find, and more importantly, what would they do to him?

He did not have to wonder for long. A few moments later, a neatly dressed young man came to escort him to someone. Another short hallway, which ended with yet another door, this one was unlocked. He followed the young man into a beautifully appointed salon. The interior spoke of wealth and opulence, which was in such contrast to the outer chamber that Giovanni taken off guard and gasped slightly in response. "Signore, my master will be with you shortly. I was told to offer you some refreshment. Please be seated and take your rest. Wine?" Giovanni sat in one of the upholstered chairs that fronted an enormous ornate desk. "Wine will be fine." The young servant went to a carved antique sideboard and filled a glass from a crystal decanter. He presented the glass, bowed and retreated from the room.

Giovanni Romano sat there resting from the ordeal of traveling all day. The wine and the comfortable surroundings put him at ease. This was the place he remembered; he only hoped the man named Gaetano Zingaro was still alive. Giovanni heard the shuffling of feet and a grinding sound. A door concealed on the far side of the room opened, and there, sitting in a chair with wheels, was an older version of the man Giovanni the Roman remembered. Pushing the chair was a beautiful middle-aged woman.

Giovanni stood immediately upon seeing them. The man was old and frail, but the eyes were sharp and fierce. "Ah, Giovanni the Roman, it has been a long, long, time my friend. The years have not been kind to me, I am but a sick, old, man. What brings you to me after all this time?" Giovanni bent down and kissed the old man on both cheeks. "Caporegime Zingaro, it is an honor to see you after so long. Thank you for seeing me." "Come and sit we will talk. Magdalena bring me some wine and a cigar. Giovanni would you like a cigar?" Giovanni said "No. I do not smoke any more. My lungs were going bad." "Ah, it is too late for me. I will smoke and drink until they put my body in the ground." The woman, her dark skin highlighted by silver hair, her eyes cast down and hooded by thick black lashes, shook her head but did not speak. Dutifully, she went about getting him the wine from the same decanter, and then opened a silver and gold cask that sat upon the sideboard and took out a cigar. She snipped the tip, licked the body of the cigar, and went to the lit candle and proceeded to puff on it until the tip was glowing red and smoke filled her mouth. Letting out the smoke, she brought both the glass and the cigar to her master. She said not one word, bowed and left the room. The old man watched her as she quietly disappeared. "That one is my third wife, beautiful, but she cannot speak; when she was a child she was captured by gypsies and they cut out her tongue. She is the best wife I ever had, she doesn't speak." The old man laughed at his own sick joke.

"Let us drink to old friendships. Salute." They both drank deeply and Giovanni enjoyed the fine vintage, his mouth being so dry. He was at ease now and would feel free to seek the information he needed. "So, what brings you to me after so long?" Giovanni Romano put down the glass and looked directly into the wizened face. "Caporegime Zingaro, I need formation for the protection of my family. I know that you are aware of everything that goes on in your world. I apologize for coming to you after so long with no gift to present, but I will show my appreciation for your assistance." "Giovanni, I heard that after the murder of Caporegime Sucretti you left Monteforte and disappeared, only now to return after twenty years. I also heard that you have taken up a relationship with Mistress Sucretti. Is this all true?" "Yes Caporegime it is true." "Unless I am mistaken the good widow has her own small army of armed men at her disposal. Yes?"

It was now time for Giovanni to divulge at least some of the story, or he would not be able to enlist the aid of the head of the underworld. "All that you say is true. It is also known that Mistress Sucretti is growing old. She has appointed her niece, Lucia Banfi, to be her heir and next Mistress of Monteforte, as you know that is a heavy burden for a young woman. Already someone has tried to kill her. The person who set her up was a former tutor, Professor Dominic Fragoli. He stole a sacred manuscript from Monteforte, which Lucia had promised to give to the Abbazia de Montecassino. The monks say that whoever possesses it will be cursed. I need to know where this man is, and whom he has brought the manuscript to. It would have to be someone highly regarded for his knowledge of antique books and manuscripts. Can you help me?"

Giovanni Romano sat back, watched, and waited, for the old man's response. Caporegime Zingaro was a very shrewd man; it was that trait that had kept him head of the underworld for decades. The old man enjoyed his cigar, and took his time digesting what he had just heard. "Giovanni that is quite a story you have told. I have not heard of this professor or any news of this man. The man you seek, who only the wealthiest collectors go to, is Antonio Sanfranco, and he has a small shop in Milan. I know this man, and have engaged his services many times over the years. What would you have me do?"

Now, for the first time since Lucia had told him of the manuscripts and the cave, Giovanni felt that he could help protect her. "Caporegime Zingaro, would it be possible to make some discreet inquiries of this man Sanfranco, and of the professor Dominic Fragoli. I believe the two will be connected. See if he is working with Fragoli, and perhaps you can tell him you know of an interested collector for the manuscript. I will take care of the rest." " Giovanni, old friend, I can do as you ask because I am grateful that you killed that bastard Sucretti. His murder, which as I am sure you had surmised, I attempted on several occasions, which you stopped, was a great help to my early career. I am sure that you know that for yourself. I will do this favor for you. I will seek nothing in repayment this time. La prossima volta venite a me sarete disposti a pagare per il mio aiuto. Capito?" Giovanni Romano had spent the better part of his life in Caporegime Zingaro's world, and understood perfectly that the old man, who thought he had killed Salvatore Sucretti, which at this time he was not about to reveal it was the old dead servant Fernando who killed him, was giving him a gift. He also knew that the next time, which he silently prayed would never come, but if it did, Zingaro would exact a heavy toll for his help. Giovanni the Roman understood the rules and was a man of honor.

"That is most generous of you Caporegime Zingaro. I do understand. I thank you for your help. I need to be most discreet for the Mistress Sucretti is not aware of the danger to her niece, and I wish to insure that she never finds out. I will deal with this man in my own way. Above all, I must protect the Mistress Lucia."

"I too understand. I will get you the information as soon as possible. Are you staying in Naples or are you going back to Monteforte?" " I can stay but a day or two under a pretense of buying some supplies so as not to arouse the Mistress' curiosity. If I have not heard back from you in two days I will head back home." It was done." The contract between two old criminals was sealed; each would uphold their end of the agreement. Giovanni stood to leave, and came over to the old man and knelt by his chair, took his hands and kissed each in turn. Caporegime Zingaro placed a wizened hand upon Giovanni's head in acknowledgement of his homage. "Be safe old friend, I will find what you need; I want you to know that the Mistress Lucia is safe under my protection." "Dear Caporegime, you don't know how much that means to me. I will await your contact. God bless you." Giovanni rose and waited for the young servant to escort him out. Both the servant and Magdalena appeared through the secret door. The last words from the old man were "Essere attento Giovanni, Napoli e quelli che vivono qui non possie Caporegimeo l'onore abbiamo condiviso una volta." Giovanni would heed the advice of the old man who held that cripple finger on the pulse of the underworld. There was no honor among the new breed of criminals.

CHAPTER TEN

EXTRACTING THE TRUTH

Milan

Dominic Fragoli was delighted when two days into his stay in Milan he received a note from Antonio Sanfranco.

Dominic,

Please join me for a late supper at my home this evening. There are many things we need to discuss. I have some ideas as to how we will sell the manuscript. Eight o'clock. I will send my carriage for you. Bring the manuscript I need to translate something from it at the request of an interested collector.

Until tonight

He felt the adrenaline rush to his head. He was smiling to himself, thinking that he was so far superior to Antonio. He knew that his childhood friend could not resist the lure of the manuscript, which Dominic had dangled in front of him. Like a hungry fish, he had been hooked, and now all Dominic had to do was haul him in.

Dominic spent the day exploring Milan. He made some purchases, which were to be delivered to his hotel. One thing he bought was a very good bottle of wine to bring to his host this evening. He had spent the afternoon lazily strolling the strata's of Milan, and came

427

to the Museo Delle Belle Arti. He entered and spent several hours enjoying the many fine works of art. One painting captured his attention, which depicted Godiva upon her white horse. Her beautiful naked body astride the galloping horse; her long red tresses carried by the wind, her shapely legs hugging the magnificent animal. It was so erotic he instantly felt himself growing within his breeches. It reminded him of the beautiful Lucia riding her horse. He was sad at the thought of what had become of the precocious beauty.

He thought back to his discovery with Lucia in the cave. He knew that to accomplish his mission of securing all the ancient manuscripts for himself, he would have to eliminate Lucia. She was the only obstacle standing in his way of achieving a life of wealth beyond his wildest dreams. Clearly, his memory replayed the meeting with a man called Ruffino. He had gone to a bar in the lowest part of Naples, and asked some questions about how one would find a person who could accomplish the resolution of a delicate matter. While he thought himself cunning, those at the tavern knew he was looking for an assassin. He returned to the tavern late that evening, and approached by a seedy looking man who introduced himself as Ruffino. He was a foul looking and smelling man. "Signore I hear you are looking for a very dependable person to handle a difficult matter. Am I correct?" "Yes you are correct. I need a young woman killed as soon as possible. Can you do it?" The man was salivating at the thought, his beady eyes the color of coal looked right into Dominic Fragoli's eyes and reached his soul. "Who is this woman, and how will I find her?" Ever the practical man Dominic asked, "What is your price for such a job?" The man for the first time smiled broadly, in thus doing displayed a full set of decayed teeth, and when he leaned toward Dominic and spoke, the putrid odor of disease spewed from his mouth. "I will require more details about my prey, the more difficult the task, the more money."

Dominic was reluctant to tell him whom the intended target was, but decided that he needed to trust this man if he wanted the job accomplished. The professor took a deep breath and looked around, cautious not to be heard. Dominic would have changed his mind except that it was too late. He knew that the only way of getting to the manuscripts was to kill Lucia. "Have you ever heard of Casa Monteforte?" he asked the man. "Of course, who has not heard of this place?" "Ah, good, then you will go there and the new young mistress will be your prey." "Signore, have you lost your mind? A woman so wealthy that she has her own small army of men to protect her owns Monteforte. Surely, you must be mistaken." Dominic would have laughed at this sorry excuse of a human being but patiently, as if speaking with a child, explained "It is not the older Mistress Sucretti that I wish killed; it is her heir, the young Lucia Banfi." "How will I get to her, I am sure she is protected?" "Now that is easy, she is a wild one, and ventures out of the estate daily. She rides for hours on a huge white horse." "How will I know it is her?" "Again that will be simple. Look for a beautiful young red haired woman, with skin like marble and eyes the color of the sea." At this, the assassin smirked. "What will you have me do with her Signore?" "Do with her as you please, but make sure she disappears from the face of the earth. Kill her." "Since this is a difficult job you have given me, and a very dangerous one, I must ask for ten thousand lire." Dominic, who feigned to act wounded at the exorbitant charge, lowered his head, shaking it from side to side, then, finally looking up annoyed, said "That is a great deal of money. I will need until tomorrow to acquire it. Are you sure that you can fulfill my request?" "Signore you can rest assured that I am the man for the job. I am so confident that I will only require half of the money now, and the rest when it is done. Fair?" Dominic was so excited he almost laughed aloud. "I believe we have a contract Signore Ruffino."

The man left and Dominic lingered at the table finishing his drink. He was very pleased with the bargain he had just struck. He would have paid ten times that amount to get rid of Lucia. She was the only link to the fortune that was hiding in a cave on the estate of Monteforte. He would bet his life that she would not tell anyone of the contents or whereabouts of the sacred place.

Dominic made his way back to the hotel and waiting there were his few purchases. He washed and changed his clothes in preparation for his evening with his childhood friend. Promptly at seven forty-five, a finely dressed footman pulled up to the hotel. It was a rather elegant carriage, and Dominic climbed in and settled himself on the brocade seat, was impressed. He clutched the bottle of wine and thought to himself that perhaps he should have bought an even better vintage, but shrugged it off. The ride was pleasant and took no time at all. The carriage pulled up a long winding path, which was completely sheltered from the busy street. The footman came around, opened the door for Dominic, and escorted him to the front door of a stuccoed Italianate villa. Lanterns lit the path and front approach. Instantly the door opened and a wigged servant greeted him. "Signore Fragoli, my master welcomes you to Casa Sanfranco, please come with me, and my Master will find you in the salon."

Now Dominic was truly impressed, thinking the business of dealing in stolen antiquities was very profitable. He was lead into a stunning salon, replete with coffered ceilings adorned with cypress beams and walls covered in murals depicting hunting scenes. The furniture was upholstered of fine leather, as were the other furnishings that were scattered throughout the large room, which was elegant in a masculine way. Antonio always had a good eye for decoration. Heads of various and exotic animals graced the walls. This was a room that spoke of the exploits of its owner. Dominic would someday have such a home, and would design such a room. Antonio, who strode confidently in, interrupted his thoughts. He was impeccably dressed, and had clutched to his arm, a stunningly beautiful woman. They were smiling pleasantly and came into the room.

 Disengaging his prize, Antonio came to Dominic and gave him a manly hug. "I am so glad you could join us this evening, I hope it will be one you never forget. Ah, forgive my manners, may I introduce my assistant, Serafina." The tall, slender woman, her raven black hair left loose reached to her hips, the dark complexion with tawny blush was as smooth as polished stone. Her eyes burned into his, they were the color of emeralds. She cocked her head slightly to one side in acknowledgement of the introduction, ran her tongue over full sensual lips, and then gave a smile, which showed gleaming white straight teeth. Dominic felt the blood rushing to his lower extremities. He reached for her hand, kissed it, and said, "I am delighted to meet you, Serafina."

Antonio smiled, assured that the irresistible Serafina had already dug her claws into his friend. "Let us retire to dinner shall we?" At that, Serafina entwined both men, one on each arm, and proceeded to the dining room. A sumptuous table was set with fine linen and cut crystal. The houseman served an equally delicious meal. Light conversation between the two men ensued throughout the meal, which had each course accompanied by a different wine. Serafina sat next to Antonio and never uttered a sound, but was feeding him bits and morsels of food. Once, as she was eating a piece of meat it fell between her two full breasts, and she looked to Antonio to assist her in retrieving it. He pulled her bodice down just above the nipple, and reached in to get it, then teased her with it, and finally eating it himself. Dominic was engrossed in this little exhibition of sensual foreplay.

After dinner, Antonio whispered something in Serafina's ear and she excused herself. "Shall we have espresso and cigars in my private study?" By this time, Dominic who had already drunk five or six glasses of wine was more than ready for espresso.

Antonio went over to a burl wood cabinet and removed an ornately carved wood box from a glass shelf. He slowly opened it, and the room filled with the sweet, pungent smell of tobacco. He brought the box over to his friend and Dominic selected a cigar. There was a clipper and lit tapper on a small table next to his chair. He licked the fine wrapper and slowly held the tip over the burning candle until it glowed red.

Dominic enjoyed a good cigar and sat back inhaling its aromatic smoke. Antonio was gathering two glasses from another cabinet, and a decanter filled with a dark rich liquor was poured into each glass. Antonio brought over both glasses and placed one on the table by Dominic and one at his own table. They sat in companionable silence each enjoying their cigar. Antonio broke the silence "Dominic, I would like to propose a toast." Dominic picked up the glass and sniffed the rich, woodsy aroma of the blood red liquid "To old friends; and sharing secrets. Salute!" Dominic did not even pay attention to the toast but drank deeply of the rich liquor. It had an odd but pleasant taste.

A moment later from out of nowhere appeared Serafina. She was dressed in an extraordinary costume. Her upper torso was naked except for a sheer veil that was lightly draped around her. She wore a low-slung skirt of many layers in brilliant colors.

Antonio beckoned her to come closer. She obeyed. "Remove the veil," he demanded. She obeyed. Dominic could not believe what his eyes told him. To his complete astonishment, Serafina's nipples were pierced through, and a golden chain was strung between her two breasts. She also sported a ruby in her navel. Dominic then realized she was a gypsy. Slowly, erotically, she started to dance around him, undulating, and gyrating her hips. She came so close to him that he could smell her exotic perfume, and was wiggling her full heavy breasts in his face. Dominic was sweating, and his cock was hard as stone and begged for escape from the confines of his tight breeches.

Antonio could see that the girl captivated his old friend. Dominic had drained the liquor from his glass and Antonio had refilled it, while never touching his own. He snapped his fingers and Serafina came to Antonio's chair. She bent over and offered her breasts to him. He took the chain and pulled, stretching the long, dark nipples. He then placed one in his mouth and began a rhythmic sucking Serafina began to moan with delight. "Serafina, go to Dominic, please him." She obeyed. She came to him just as she had done with Antonio. Dominic had watched what his friend had done and did the same. This time, the gypsy girl fell to her knees before him, and began undoing the laces on his silk breeches, which were by now so strained they would surely tear.

Serafina unleashed the generous cock and looked wide-eyed at its length and girth. She moaned. "Suck it" Dominic demanded. She obeyed. When he was almost at his peak of explosion Antonio snapped his fingers and the girl stood, lifted her skirts and straddled Dominic. She gasped as he entered her, her hot womb taking him inch by inch until he filled her. She began a steady tattoo of moving up and down as she was impaled on the big erection. Dominic took her breast in his mouth and playfully bit on the skewered nipple while kneading the other.

Antonio was himself aroused at the sight of his friend and Serafina. He came over and the girl undid the laces on his breeches and took his own rather generous cock in her mouth. The threesome, were all engaged in each other's pleasures. This continued for a few minutes then suddenly stopped. "Dominic, Serafina knows many ways to please a man, will you let her pleasure you?" The gypsy girl had mesmerized Dominic who was nearing his climax. "Dominic, do not resist her, and do exactly as she wants, it will be an experience you will die for."

Dominic was insane with desire. His sexual dreams were coming true. He even liked the idea that Antonio was not only watching but also participating. He had never had sex with another man or in the company of another man. It was exciting. "Stand up and remove all your clothes." Dominic obeyed. "Come here and sit in this chair." He went. The chair, which he thought was oddly but sturdily constructed, had a collar made of leather attached at the top and leather manacles on the arm rests, and at the foot of the chair. It felt strange, but then everything about this evening was strange. He felt his head throbbing and his mouth of dry. He told himself not to drink any more liquor. He wanted a clear head to enjoy this wonderful experience. Serafina had also removed all her clothes. Dominic was pleased to see that she had shaved her mound. He could clearly see her attributes. Serafina, with Antonio's help, buckled the leather manacles around both his wrists and both his ankles to the chair. Dominic had seen such things in Spain, and the thought of surrender was very erotic. Next Antonio helped the girl to stand on the chair; both legs spread wide apart, her sex at Dominic's mouth. He stretched his neck, which was held tight by the leather collar to let his tongue slip into her clit. Antonio came around Serafina and from behind, spread her lips for his friend, the taste of her was delicious, and she smelled musky. He worked hard licking and slurping at her. Serafina was moving her hips and grinding her mound in his face. She came, and left his face wet with her juices. Dominic pleaded with them to let him come. "Do not let go of your seed Dominic. The best is still to come." "I cannot stand it much longer, I feel like I am about to burst."

Serafina came down from the chair. Dominic was straining against his restraints. He saw that she was going to put a hood over his head and tried to resist. "Do not resist Dominic," said Antonio who was sitting close by. "The deprivation of sight enhances the libido" there was an almost hypnotic tone to Antonio's deep voice. Dominic was so far gone in his sexual fantasy he would do anything to have the lovely gypsy girl. Serafina came so close her lips brushed his face, her tits bounced off his hairy chest, while she placed a black silk hood over Dominic's head, and tied it tight with a silk cord. He waited. He felt a tickling sensation around his testicles, which were now tight with his desire. He felt a searing pain as something sharp was inserted into each ripe testicle. He screamed with pain. "Oh Dominic is a bad boy, listen to him scream like a little girl. Serafina let us teach the good professor what happens to bad boys." Dominic was sweating profusely and suddenly became frightened by the blackness. He felt a panic of claustrophobia that he had never experienced before. Tears were running down his hot sweaty face. Even the stink of his own breath made him nauseous. Another scream pierced the silence as hot wax was poured over his cock. "Antonio, this is not funny anymore. Untie me right now. I don't like this type of sex." Silence. Dominic was starting to panic. "Antonio, please, don't do this."

This time Dominic felt the searing pain of a hot object inserted into his navel, another ear piercing scream, and with it an attempt to overturn the chair to escape, which was futile since it was bolted to the floor. "Why are you doing this, Antonio please don't hurt me. What do you want of me?" Silence. "Please tell me what you want. I will do anything." Dominic was on the verge of hysteria. The pain was causing him to become disorientated. He choked and gagged on his own vomit.

Antonio came over to Dominic's ear and whispered "Tell me where you got the manuscript and I will let you free." Dominic did not answer. Serafina grabbed Dominic's cock in a steel grip and slowly pushed a long sharp steel pin down from the tip, Dominic was going into shock, his body was shaking, and he was vomiting inside the hood. She quickly removed the object. "Dominic" came the soft, almost kind voice of Antonio, "this can stop, if only you tell me where the manuscript came from. I will continue my ministrations until either you die or you tell me the truth. I will know if you are lying. How will I know, you ask yourself? I have mixed a magical potion in your drink, which makes a man tell the truth. If you try to lie, you will become violently ill."

By now Dominic was desperate and was trying to force his mind to make up some clever story. "Let us try again, shall we? Dominic, where did you get the manuscript?" Silence. This time Antonio took a razor sharp dagger and Serafina grabbed hold of one of Dominic's nipples, "No! Please don't do this," he pleaded as Antonio sliced it off. Dominic slumped over in the chair. His head hung on his wet chest. They were prepared for this, and had a silver bucket filled with cold water, which they poured over the bleeding inert form of Dominic Fragoli. He was roused from his unconscious state by the shock of the cold water.

"Dominic you know that I am a patient man. You also know that I always get what I want. Now, for the sake of our childhood friendship, I am going to give you every opportunity to save yourself and tell me the truth. Remember if you lie you will experience terrible pain." "Do you understand what I have said?" Dominic who was now in a mental stupor of pain nodded his understanding. "Good. I do not like to hurt people, especially my friends. Shall we try again? Where did you get the manuscript?"

This time Dominic did not hesitate but answered, "Remove the hood, I can hardly breathe, and I will tell you what you want to know." Antonio nodded his assent and Serafina, her naked body touching Dominic's, as she made an unhurried ritual of untying the silk cord. She deliberately rubbed her sex against his hand as she lifted the vomit soaked hood. Dominic was a mess. Fragments of digested food, which clung to his neatly trimmed beard, marred his usually pristine appearance, his hair was wet with sweat, his cheeks streaked with tears, his eyes wild with fear and pain. A gleaming mirror hung on the wall just in front of the chair. He looked at himself and stared to cry. "Why Antonio, why have you done this to me?" Antonio quietly spoke to his old friend as if cooing to an injured child, "I have not done anything to you. You have forced my hand by not giving me the information I seek. I told you what would happen if you did not tell me, yet, you choose to disobey."

Suddenly, Antonio's mood changed, he could see that Serafina seemed nervous and tense. "Go get the whip." She hesitated for a mere second and scurried off to a locked cabinet and opened the door, retrieved a long whip with sharp talons on each lash. "Serafina let us show my old friend what happens when I am disobeyed. Yes?" The gypsy girl for the first time looked scared, but dutifully leaned over the exquisitely carved desk. Her bare bottom exposed for all to see. Thwack. The lashes of the long whip hit her flesh and instantly left welts. She did not move. Her head bent in supplication. Thwack. Thwack. Thwack. The sound was deafening. Then he stopped. Antonio was soaked with sweat, tears running down his face, the girl was silently weeping from pain. He took a linen scarf from his coat, dipped it in some kind of oil, and gently tended her open wounds.

"You see what you made me do. I did not want to hurt her, but you Dominic gave me no choice. I will ask but once more, then, you shall understand the pain you just made me inflict on his beautiful creature." He grabbed her hair in his hand and twisted it hard and taut so that her contorted face was looking at him. "I'm sorry my love. Forgive me?" She closed her eyes and nodded her assent. "Go my love, and tend to your wounds. I will be there shortly to satisfy your every desire." Serafina, never having said a word throughout the entire evening, left, her back and buttocks raw and bleeding and never turned to look at Dominic. He was astounded.

"We shall try once more. Please Dominic, you know I always win, do not make me hurt you anymore. Tell me how you came to be in possession of the manuscript and where they came from." Antonio, all the color drained from his face, his eyes were blood shot and wild with rage, Dominic knew that if he did not tell him what he wanted surely he would die. "You win Antonio," Dominic rasped in a low breathless voice. "I was the tutor for the two nieces of Maria Sucretti, Mistress of Monteforte. The younger one, Lucia, found them hidden in a secret cave. She brought me there. I have convinced her not to tell anyone until I discovered if they are truly authentic antiquities. She will do as I have instructed, she trusts me." Antonio had relaxed slightly. The whip still held so tightly in his hand that the knuckles were white.

Dominic's eyes never left the whip.

438

"Are there more?" Dominic hesitated for a split second and saw Antonio moving to raise the whip. "Yes, there are many, many, more." "Where is this cave?" Dominic told him the whole story. He thought that if he took Antonio into his confidence and showed him that he was not lying he would let him go free. "That is an interesting story Dominic. What were your plans for the manuscripts?" "I was going to ask you to be my partner, since you were the one with all the clients who wish to own such priceless works. There are enough to make us rich as kings. Please Antonio I have told you the truth. Let me free. We can be rich beyond our wildest dreams. Together, just like when we were boys." Antonio for the first time put down the whip, carefully laying it across the big desk. Dominic began to relax thinking he had finally struck an amicable bargain. He would kill Antonio once he had secured all the money from various collectors. "Untie me Antonio, let us seal our partnership." Antonio's face had once again changed back to his jovial demeanor. "Yes, of course, old friend. Partners." Antonio came around the back of the chair, withdrew the dagger from his waistband, and pulled Dominic's head back as far as it would go. He showed him the dagger and said "Dominic you were always a greedy, ignorant, fool. I never really liked you. You were a pig with women, and a coward with men. I will give you one last gift. I shall put you out of your misery." With that said, Antonio calmly and efficiently slit his friend's throat from ear to ear with great precision, and then kissed him on the mouth. "Good bye old friend, may you burn in hell." Antonio was spent mentally and physically. He would now have to dispose of the body. He thought, thank God for my beloved staff, they are loyal as well as resourceful. He removed his own blood splattered clothing and walked naked out of the room. From a secret door emerged the houseman who would clean up Antonio's mess.

CHAPTER ELEVEN

A MOTHER'S CONFESSION

Milan

Antonio Sanfranco was at his bookstore when a harried young boy named Armando came rushing in. "Signore it is your Mama. The doctor told me to get you right away, the end, it is close." "Thank you Armando, I shall come quickly, go tell them I am on my way." Antonio loved his mother very much and hated to see her suffering, he knew in his heart that this was probably the end. Felisa Sanfranco had withered away to a mere shell of her former beauty. For years, the rich and famous men of Italy had sought after her, not only for her body, but also for her formidable mind. Antonio carefully but quickly straightens the papers on his desk, he called back to his assistant Furio "I must leave; my mother has taken a turn for the worse. Do not disturb these papers on my desk. I do not know how long I shall be away. When you are done, lock up and go home. Thank you Furio." The young man, who was very studious looking, came to his master "Signore Sanfranco, I will keep your mother in my prayers. Dio richieda la sua casa al cielo." "Yes Furio. I also pray that God takes her to Heaven." He left the store with thoughts of his beloved mother. His stride was fast paced and steady. He put his head down and focused on getting to his mother's side before she died. It was already late afternoon and Antonio was annoyed that they had not sent for him earlier, but, he rationalized this scene had played out many times before, and each time his mother had rallied back to life.

440

Felisa Sanfranco's small, but exquisitely appointed apartment, was in the center of the city. It occupied two stories and from her upper bedchamber, a large floor to ceiling window overlooked the Basilica of Our Lady of Sorrow. It was a beautiful and serene view. Over the years that Felisa lived in the house she would daily look out that window into the gardens of the Basilica and find her peace. The drapes were open to let in the remaining sun into the room. Felisa always liked a sunny room. A beam of sunlight was cascading over her bed and warming her cold, tired body. She had agonized with herself all night regarding the information she would impart to her son, but in the end, she knew it was the right thing to do.

Antonio, out of breath, tried to compose himself before greeting his mother. The doctor met him. "Antonio it is time. There is nothing more I can do for her. She has been asking for you. I must warn you, that she is delirious from pain and may say things that seem strange, this is quite normal under the circumstances. I have given her an elixir to make her rest. I will be here in the salon taking a short rest. I have been here since last night." Antonio, who knew the good doctor since he was a child, embraced him with great affection. "Thank you. She always loved you. You know that." The doctor, a blush on his cheek, nodded and made his way to the downstairs salon.

Antonio waited outside her door, willing himself to calm down; his mind was racing as to all the things he wanted to say to her. His heart was pounding in his chest and his head ached. He drew himself to his full six feet and raked his hand through his thick short curly hair. He entered quietly so as not to disturb her. He thought she was sleeping her eyes were closed. She opened her eyes as he drew near. "Ah, it is my sweet boy. Antonio I must talk to you and you must listen and not speak until I am finished. Come to me." He did as she asked. He took her fragile hand, now just a thin layer of flesh covering her bones, in his own. It was cold, damp, and the color of a grey stormy sky. Her voice of frail but her eyes were clear and sharp.

"My beloved son, there are many secrets that I have not shared with you over these many years. I had taken an oath never to reveal what I am about to share with you, but, you have the right to know who you truly are." Felisa Sanfranco was laboring to speak her breath was thick with the odor of death. "I have done many things in my life that I am not proud of, but, you, my dear boy, are the best accomplishment I have ever achieved." She closed her eyes and continued in a soft, velvety voice as if she were dreaming. "When you were born I knew who had fathered you, but, out of fear I did not tell him. For a few years I did not see the man, he did not come to me as he had in the past, but, then, one day he came to see me. I had decided I would not tell him that he had fathered a son. He spent two days with me and on the last day, you came with your nurse to see me. The man, your father, was with me. When he saw you, his mouth hung open in astonishment. I had not realized even myself how incredibly similar you were in appearance to the man until I saw you together. He recognized it immediately. After a few pleasantries the nurse took you to play." Felisa was smiling at this remembrance. A thousand thoughts were traveling through Antonio's head. He, as a child, had begged his mother to divulge who his father was, but as he got older and came to know the nature of her profession, he understood that his paternity could have come from any number of men. He wanted to ask so many things but did not want to interrupt her thoughts. He was not sure if she was speaking under the influence of the drug the doctor had given her, but he felt confident she was in her right mind. Antonio kept his silence.

"He was angry with me. Why did you not tell me he demanded? I told him that I did not want him to think I was trying to exhort money from him. He had nothing to fear from me. I would not tell his wife that he had fathered a son with me. I was just so happy to finally have a child. The man, your father, was wealthy beyond even my own reckoning. He had promised that from that day forward he would care for you and me in the way a son of his should live. I had put no confidence in his promises; many men had made such promises to me, until one day his avvocato came to see me.

He brought many papers for me to sign. The man told me that an account in the Bank of Milan was set for you and there was a formidable amount of money for your future and your education. As for me, he also established an account, with a generous amount of money to be distributed on an annual basis. There were two provisos that I must agree to, one, that I must not tell you his identity, and second, that I would give up my profession. The second one was easy, especially given the money he had allotted for my care, was very agreeable." Antonio thought it all sounded plausible. After that, their lives had changed dramatically, and no more men came to visit his mother. "In addition, the house we are now in was a gift from your father to be handed down to you upon my death."

Felisa was truly struggling to catch her breath, her skeletal chest rising with great force, the strain of which was etched on her face which was so thin the skin was stretched to the point of tearing. Those eyes, sunk far into her skull were the only measure of life still within her.

"Dear Antonio, my beloved son, I cannot go to my grave without telling you who this wonderful man was.

Your father was Mateo Rizzo, heir of Monteforte." Felisa closed her eyes, gasping for breath, and with all the strength she could gather she squeezed her son's hand. "The documents which attest to your birth are hidden in a secret drawer in my wardrobe. Take the papers and do what you will with them. My obligation to Mateo, who died shortly after this agreement was made dies with me as well. You have the right to know who you are. I love you and have tried all my life to do what was best for you. I struggled even until today to give you this information."

Antonio could not comprehend this shocking news, and coupled with the eminent death of his mother, was all too much for him to absorb. Felisa started to cough, the racking of her lungs brought up blood. Antonio put all other thoughts aside and tried to comfort his mother. Finally, she stopped coughing and just flopped down into her pillows. Her skin was glistening with sweat but when he stroked her cheek, she felt cold and clammy. "I love you Antonio." The tears were rolling down her face and Antonio was crying. "Rest Mamma, try to get a little sleep, I will stay here until you awaken." He kissed her forehead and wiped the tears from her eyes. He knew she would never awake, but he also knew that he could not leave her until she drew her last and final breath. Antonio, who suffered from severe headaches, closed his own eyes in an attempt to stave off the debilitating pain. His heart was broken, for he truly loved his mother. He had never had anyone else in his life to love but her, and now he felt the burden of that loss so profoundly it felt like something was crushing his chest. Desperate for relief from the throbbing pain in his head he tried to fall asleep.

Antonio slept for an hour or so then woke with a start. The headache had subsided to a dull ache. He looked over to his mother who looked peaceful, but he knew that she was dead. He fell to his knees, laid his head by her side, and wept. His were the tears of the small boy he had always been in his mother's eyes. The one and only person who ever meant anything to him was now gone. Antonio Sanfranco was all alone in this world.

CHAPTER TWELVE

THE GALA

Monteforte

It was like being summoned by the Queen; the Lords of every region of Italy, France, Spain, and even America converged upon Monteforte at the invitation of Mistress Maria Sucretti. The preparation for this gathering was nothing short of monumental. Food was brought from all over the country, the finest wines, liquors, and an army of servants, grooms, footmen and entertainers were at the greatest gathering in decades. The grounds of Monteforte had been worked on and designed by Giovanni Romano and were a breathtaking display of botanical beauty. The castle had been meticulously restored to its original beauty. Guest rooms were prepared with the finest lines, the stables were ready to accommodate horses and grooms and carriages. Maria knew that she must host many people for several days and relied upon Giorgio, Marcello, and Gandolfo to be fully ready and stocked.

Genaro had arrived with a number of his most significant works of art. In his company had been his friend Giancarlo Marzoni an up and coming composer and accomplished musician. Giancarlo was establishing the Neapolitan School as the foremost opera house in the world. The handsome composer was in such stark contrast to his friend Genaro, who had the good looks of the Banfi men, tall, slender, and muscular, but his appearance was that of a distracted artist. He was not fashionably stylish, but his good humor and gentle demeanor were his most attractive attributes.

Giancarlo Marzoni on the other hand was a natural performer. His height, which was over six feet, was an attention getter in itself. Having come from a wealthy family, he was raised and educated in high society. He was strikingly handsome and was the product of an Austrian mother and Italian father. Blonde wavy hair, that he wore in a simple queue and fastened with a silk ribbon, accented his deep rich olive complexion. His eyes were a combination of blue and green with flecks of gold. Lucia had never seen such enchanting eyes. He had a long aristocratic Italian nose and high cheekbones. The broadness of his shoulders was enhanced by the indentation of his slim waist. He had a kind and humorous mouth and good white teeth. Giancarlo Marzoni was a handsome man and he knew it.

Upon seeing Genaro for the first time in several years, Lucia ran to him and embraced him with such love and affection. "Oh dear brother, I am so happy to see you. It has been far too long, but I have treasured all the letters you have sent from your many adventures across the continent. We must find time during your stay to sit and talk, I am fascinated by your exploits." Genaro pulled his baby sister from himself and holding her at arm's length was dumbfounded. "You cannot be my baby sister, where have you hidden little Lucia, I demand you produce her this instant?" Lucia giggled like a little girl and twirled around. "It is I dear brother all grown up."

"Lucia you are magnificent. You were always a beautiful little girl but now you have evolved into a breathtaking woman. I must paint your portrait. I must also congratulate you as the new heir of Monteforte. That is a very important responsibility for someone so young, but Zia Maria assures me that you are well suited to the task. I think so as well. Come here let me kiss that beautiful face." Lucia almost as tall as her brother came to him and he embraced her with great affection.

There was a subtle cough from behind Lucia, and she turned those penetrating azure blue eyes toward Giancarlo. "Lucia please let me introduce my friend Lord Giancarlo Marzoni." The dashing young composer gave a deep-footed bow and reached for Lucia's hand, which he kissed and held for a moment longer than necessary. "Giancarlo may I introduce my baby sister Lucia, Mistress of Monteforte." "Genaro why did you not tell me you had such an enchanting sister?" "Mistress Lucia, I am so honored to make your acquaintance."

The handsome and gallant young man smote Lucia. Trying desperately to seem aloof Lucia replied "Lord Marzoni it has been my pleasure to hear one of your opera's when last you performed in Naples. I enjoyed it immensely. I hear that you have received considerable acclaim for your work throughout Europe." Giancarlo was impressed with her poise and candor. "Well, coming from you my Mistress, that is the best compliment I have yet to receive. May I play a piece for you this evening?" Lucia her eyes hooded by thick strawberry lashes smiled demurely and cocked her head in replying, "I would be most offended if you did not." Just as the conversation was becoming more interesting the threesome was interrupted by Antoinetta who looked like a porcelain doll on the arm of her fiancé Lord Catalano.

"Ah there is my handsome talented brother. Genaro I have missed you." The petite beauty stood on her tiptoes to kiss her brother. "Genaro I want to introduce you to my fiancée Lord Tomaso Catalano." Genaro looked at the young bridegroom appraisingly and then acknowledged, "It is my pleasure to meet you sir. I have heard many good things of you from my sister's letters. I am happy for the two of you and I look forward to your wedding. May I introduce my friend Lord Giancarlo Marzoni."

Tomaso bowed deeply to the introduction and said "Lord Marzoni it is a great honor to meet you. I have enjoyed your opera's. I trust you have planned something for this evening's festivities?" "Ah, that is a secret Lord Catalano, but perhaps if the young Mistress Lucia would coax me, I could be encouraged to play something." Lucia's cheeks were a lovely shade of crimson but she responded "Perhaps you could entertain us this evening Lord Marzoni?" Giancarlo who seemed mesmerized by the redheaded temptress coyly replied "Perhaps." They all laughed heartily.

Genaro spoke "I am very confused. Two little girls came to Monteforte some years ago. Have you seen them?" The two sisters, who stood next to each other, were as different as night is to day, but equally as magnificent. "Now I see before me two of the most beautiful women in all of Italy, gentlemen do you not agree?" Tomaso raised his eyebrows and said, "I most surely agree Lord Banfi." Giancarlo waited a moment, stroking his chin as if in deep thought, and finally said "I am not so sure Genaro." The sisters looked wounded. Then he said with such a serious face "I am sorry, but I must regretfully disagree, I believe you to be wrong Genaro, I think they are the two most beautiful women in all of Europe." Well that brought such laughter that tears were coming from their eyes.

Lucia who was laughing was eyeing this new arrival with great interest. She had heard and seen his performance and knew he was a brilliant composer and musician, and now to find out that he also possessed a wonderful sense of humor, was even more interesting.

She would have to find time to talk privately with Lord Marzoni. She caught his eye and would swear that he was thinking the same thoughts as her own.

***

Carriages were arriving with the elite of European society. Their maids and valets, were laden down with boxes and casks, as offerings to the great Maria Sucretti, Mistress of Monteforte, accompanied Lords, with their Ladies.

At precisely seven o'clock Giorgio, clad in his best uniform, rang a bell and opened the doors of the salon and Mistress Maria Sucretti, and her heir apparent, Mistress Lucia Banfi, stood framed by the intricate woodwork of the entry, as if they were set on canvas. The elder woman, her age adding to the grace and elegance of her station, stood tall despite her years; while the Lucia's stunning, athletic form and energetic radiance captivated every man in the room. There was a communal sigh upon seeing these two women. It was not just their beauty or poise; their deportment set them apart from just their physical attributes.

The music stopped playing, and a hushed silence descended over the gathering. "My Lords and Ladies, may I present, the Mistress of Monteforte, Maria Sucretti, and Mistress Lucia Banfi" came the resounding baritone of Giorgio. There immediately arose a deafening roar from the crowd accompanied by enthusiastic clapping. Following right behind was Giovanni Romano, Antoinetta and Tomaso, Rafaela and Donato, and at the end of the procession Lord and Lady Catalano.

Lucia's waist length tresses artfully woven into interlocking braids entwined with strings of pearls, which hung at the sides of that gorgeous face, with the remaining locks cascading down her shoulders and back. Her gown, which she had designed with the help of her mother and aunt, was royal blue in color and the cut of her garment clung lovingly to every voluptuous curve of her athletic form. She wore only diamond earrings, a gift from her aunt, and a religious medal that Giovanni Romano had given her when she was a small child. Lucia always wore that medal in recognition and love for the man who was her protector. The setting sun reflected off her alabaster skin like light reflecting off polished marble. All eyes were on Lucia and she felt the heat from the roots of her head to her toes.

Lucia sought out her father to escort her to her place at the main dining table. With his wife Rafaela on his left and his daughter Lucia on his right, no man could have been prouder. Donato was dressed in a perfectly tailored waistcoat in a rich tapestry of reds, blues, and emeralds, his thick grey hair pulled into a neat queue, he still maintained his muscular form, and he was a handsome man. Rafaela was resplendent in an ivory silk gown embellished with pearls and semi-precious stones. The bodice encrusted with gold lace that outlined her full round breasts. The ivory caressed her deep olive skin. She wore her grandmother Lucia's cameo broach and ring, once seated; Lucia was joined by her Zia Maria and Zio Giovanni. "Lucia, I am so proud of you. There is not one person who is not envious of you in this room, and yet you carry yourself with pride and confidence," said Giovanni Romano. "Oh my dear niece I too am overwhelmed with love and pride. I have made the right choice and will announce it this evening." Maria Sucretti had tears in her eyes and Giovanni leaned over and gave her a supportive kiss she smiled lovingly at him.

The evening was spectacular in every way imaginable. Marcello and his staff had prepared an assortment of food the likes of which were never seen, and when he made an appearance to oversee the servers Lucia went over to him "Marcello, I cannot thank you and your staff enough for the fabulous taste and presentation of all this food. How were you even able to make so many different selections?" Marcello was beaming and bowed deeply, then took both her hands and kissed each one. "For you my young Mistress I would do anything. I am happy you have enjoyed the fruits of our labors. I have prepared something special just for you in honor of his momentous occasion, but that will be for later. For now I must return back to my kitchen or God only knows what will happen." Lucia kissed him and said, "Thank you Marcello and please thank everyone."

Lucia was strolling throughout the ballroom, stopped by so many of the guests who introduced themselves. The men were especially eager to make her acquaintance with comments such as "So beautiful, so tall, who are you and where did you come from? Are you married? Why are you not married?" Many of the women asked "What lovely hair. Who is your designer? How old are you? Oh my, you are very tall. Are you married? Why are you not married?" This onslaught went on for hours to the point that Lucia wanted to run away. Finally, she sought refuge in the garden. There among the whimsical animals and figures that her uncle Giovanni Romano had designed did she find comfort. It was cool, but most of all, it was quiet. She could hear the music and endless chatter drifting down to where she was, but thankfully, she was alone. Lucia walked around the topiary shrubs admiring the careful attention to detail that had been used in sculpting each individual form. It was akin to a living work of art, and reminded

452

herself to thank and compliment her dear uncle for the outstanding job he did in creating such a wonderful place. She found a stone bench and sat down. The aroma of citrus wafted on the breeze, it was clean and fresh, and filled her head with thoughts of riding her beloved Apollo. She closed her eyes and drank in the smell of rich earth and flowers.

Lucia was just enjoying a relaxing moment, when she was interrupted by the presence of someone standing over her. She was startled for a second then recovered herself. "I beg your pardon, Mistress Lucia; I did not mean to startle you. Please forgive me" came a low, velvety voice. "I too have come down to enjoy the cooling breezes from the sea. I cannot help but to admire this truly magnificent garden. It surpasses even the one at Versailles. Don't you agree?" Lucia was caught off guard "Yes it is beautiful. My uncle Lord Giovanni Romano created it. Sadly, I cannot compare it to Versailles since I have yet to travel to France. My Lord, I ask your indulgence for my ignorance, but I am embarrassed to say I do not know your name." Lucia was wondering who this man was, but, for that matter she did not know any but a select few of the hundreds of invited guests. The man made a formal court bow and answered, "It is I who have rudely invaded your privacy my Lady. Please let me introduce myself. I am Lord Antonio Sanfranco of Milan."

The man was tall and slender with broad shoulders. He did not wear a wig or powder, and his dark, curly hair was cut short and he sported a trimmed mustache. He was dark of skin and very handsome. He had an air of importance, or self-confidence, Lucia was not sure what it was but she felt as if she knew this stranger. There was a sense of foreboding about this man, but she could not decide if she was scared or curious. He was wealthy she could surmise by the cut of his clothing which complemented his natural good looks. When he spoke, he exuded an underlying intelligence.

Lucia was now standing next to the man and was feeling somewhat uneasy when Giorgio came rushing over to them. "Mistress I am sorry to interrupt but your presence is requested in the ballroom. Please may I escort you back?" Very happy to leave the stranger's company Lucia replied "Oh yes Giorgio, I was just getting some fresh air. Lord Sanfranco if you will excuse me, perhaps we will speak again." Antonio once again gave her a formal bow and replied "Mistress Lucia be assured that our paths will cross in the near future. I look forward to seeing you again. Good evening my Lady." Lucia latched on to Giorgio's proffered arm, and they headed back to the ballroom. "Giorgio did you know that man?" "No Mistress I cannot say that I recall ever seeing him before, but, then there are so many people from all over the world here, it would be difficult to know all of them. What was it?" Lucia felt odd and absent-mindedly replied, "When time permits, I would like you to check the guest list for a Lord Antonio Sanfranco of Milan." Giorgio made a mental note to recheck the list but was sure he did not recall such a name. "Ah, here we are, wait Mistress." From his perfectly tailored uniform Giorgio retrieved a linen scarf and "May I Mistress?" Lucia stood still while he wiped the shine from her beautiful face. "Now there you go. All ready to face your guests. Bella!" Lucia blushed and gave him a kiss and her thanks.

The moment she walked back into the ballroom all eyes once again descended upon Lucia. She was leisurely walking across the ballroom when she looked up and saw the face of the man she had just met in the garden, his dark eyes staring down at her. A cold shiver ran down her back. It was unsettling. Lucia now realized why the man who called himself Antonio Sanfranco looked familiar. She was looking at a life size portrait of her grandfather Mateo Rizzo, and was stunned to think that the man she had just met in the garden looked amazingly like him. Lucia was in a panic. She was scanning the ballroom for him, looking in every corner of the room. She spotted Giorgio and ran to him. Giorgio seeing the expression on her face immediately asked, "Mistress what troubles you? Are you feeling ill?" She said in a whispered but excited voice "Giorgio, where did the man I was speaking to in the garden go?" Her servant seemed confused "I do not know Mistress. I came with you back to the house. Why do you ask?" Lucia hesitated to say what she was thinking then went on "Giorgio did the man look familiar to you?" The servant thought for a moment then replied "Yes, but I thought it was my imagination." "Who did he look like?" Now it was Giorgio's turn to pause, almost embarrassed he replied "Master Mateo Rizzo." Lucia felt a slight relief knowing that someone other than herself had thought the same thing. "We must find him. I think he means to harm me." "I will get two of my staff and we shall search the castle for him. Do not fear Mistress." Giorgio squeezed her hand in reassurance. "Now go and have some fun this is your special night."

Lucia thought to herself how foolish she was acting, many people resemble someone you know, but as hard as she tried to rationalize the presence of this, man she could not get the feeling of foreboding out of her mind.

From across the   room she saw Abbot Vittorio, Brother Ronaldo, and Brother Angelo, immediately her spirits were lifted. She practically ran to them. "Abbot, Brothers, how good to see the three of you. I hope you are enjoying yourselves?" Abbot Vittorio grabbed her two hands and kissed each one, while the two brothers bowed deeply. Brother Ronaldo the physician who said,

"My dear Mistress Lucia you are breathtaking." He came over to examine her beautiful face. "Ah I see my little leeches did a miraculous job of healing your face. Are you feeling well?" Lucia who was glowing red from embarrassment said, "Yes Doctor those nasty little creatures are now my friends." They all laughed. The abbot spoke next "I too must echo the sentiments of my Brother. You look every inch the Mistress of Monteforte. I have been, and will continue, to pray for your health and safety." The young Brother Angelo was too flustered to speak; he was just looking at Lucia in a stupor. Brother Ronaldo sensing that his superior wished to speak with her said "Brother Angelo shall we partake of this delicious food. Tomorrow we can do penance for our gluttony?" The young monk, never taking his eyes off Lucia, just nodded and followed blindly.

"If I didn't know you were an angel Mistress I would swear that you have cast a spell on every man who gazes upon your beautiful face." Lucia cast her eyes down and made a pout with her full lips. "I am sorry, I did not mean to offend you, it was actually meant to be a compliment. Please forgive me." Lucia picked her head up and smiled broadly. "Do you have any news for me Abbot?" "Yes. Brother Angelo and I have been working day and night to unravel the mystery of the manuscripts. We are beginning to put together an explanation of how they came to be where you found them. It will be quite an interesting story when it is done. For now, do not concern yourself with such matters. You must have fun; this is a very special evening for you. I will come to see you when all is complete." The abbot bowed deeply and then made the sign of the cross on Lucia's forehead. "You are an angel Lucia." He then left her and joined his fellows are the table.

Giorgio was coming toward her when her brother Antonio suddenly spun around her. "Sister where have you been, I have been searching for you all evening? I wish to congratulate by baby sister on being named Mistress of Monteforte. Now you can lavish your poor old brother with riches." "Ah, before I will give you even one coin you must catch for me the biggest fish in the sea." They were laughing and Antonio, who had assumed his father's role, was a big burly man, swept her in his arms, and twirled her around. "I love you Lucia and I am very proud of you. I pray God keeps you safe. Come; let us join Mama and Papa and our family, to celebrate this wonderful evening." For the first time during the night, Lucia relaxed and was happy.

After a while, Lucia put her mind to rest and started to enjoy herself. About midway through the evening, it was announced that Lord Giancarlo Marzoni would perform one of his musical pieces. The dashing young composer, whose figure stood out in the gathered crowd, announced, "I have just this evening decided to name this new piece for the beautiful Mistress Lucia Banfi. It shall be known as *La Bella Rosa*." The crowd roared their approval. Lucia stood up and bowed graciously to Lord Marzoni. The composer sat to his work, which was resplendent in its sound. Lucia was very touched. The handsome and talented young man aroused her. Upon finishing his musical tribute, he stood to an overwhelmingly enthusiastic applause. He retrieved a rose from one of the floral arrangements and making his way through an exuberant mass of admirers brought the rose to Lucia, handed it to her and bowed deeply. She flushed.

"Mistress I hope you enjoyed that?" Lucia graciously accepted the rose said "Lord Marzoni you have done me a great honor. Thank you it was splendid." Everyone at the table came over to

congratulate the young composer on his talent. "Bravo Giancarlo" said Genaro with a hardy pounding of his friend's back. Giancarlo's eyes never left Lucia and she was happy for it. "Mistress may I have this dance?"
Lucia loved to dance and was very willing to do so "Yes Lord Marzoni." The handsome young composer was as delft at dancing as he was at the harpsichord. The two of them made an attractive couple gliding across the ballroom. After a short while, all the other dancers left the floor and watched as Lucia and Giancarlo, two elegant young people, gave a stunning performance of the art of movement. When the music stopped the crowd once again roared their approval. The coupled bowed.

Maria and Giovanni were watching and smiling. "Cara, they certainly make a fine couple, don't you agree?" Maria who liked the young composer replied "Physically they are perfect, but my heart tells me that our young composer is, at least for now, much too in love with himself. I would not want to see my Bella Lucia hurt." Giovanni thought about what his wife had said and responded, "You, as always may be right. Look at him he is an entertainer, perhaps more a man who would put his fame before Lucia." He reached for her hand and kissed it "You are so wise. I love you Cara." Maria blushed and squeezed his hand. Maria stood and said to Giovanni "It is time for me to make my intentions known. I will take Lucia to the center of the room and then I shall tell the world who the new Mistress of Monteforte will be." Giovanni stood as well and embraced his wife with great passion "Cara, are you truly ready for this?" "Yes my beloved husband I am." "Then so be it." Maria walked over to her niece and said, "It is time Bella." Lucia felt her heart drop but she was ready. This was her destiny, of that she was sure. She turned to Giancarlo "Lord Marzoni, would you excuse me there is some business to attend." The gallant composer bowed deeply and kissed her hand.

Maria Sucretti and Lucia Banfi strode elegantly toward the center of the ballroom. Giovanni Romano had gone before them to inform the musicians that they were to stop playing.

The music stopped and the crowd had settled down to a hush. All eyes focused on the center of the room. These two women, who were decades apart in age, but so similar in statue and mind, their beauty and poise commanded respect and attention.

Standing tall and sophisticated, the elder beauty cleared her throat, and in a resounding voice said, "I would like to thank all of you for coming to Monteforte. I know that many of you have journeyed from long distances to be here this evening. It is my honor to have you as our guests, as our friends and as our allies." At that, moment a uniformed serving boy brought over two crystal glasses on a tray for Maria and Lucia. Each of them took their glass. A small army of uniformed staff with Giorgio at the head had assembled. Maria holding her glass high in the air announced "Lords, Ladies, family and friends, it is with great love and pride, that I would like to introduce my niece, Mistress Lucia Banfi, who will become the new Mistress of Monteforte". The motion in the room stood still as if the earth had stopped rotating. Maria grabbed Lucia's hand. Lucia was both honored and embarrassed, but knew she could not convey her insecurity to this group. All eyes were upon her. With a deep breath, Lucia stood erect to her full height her head raised. Maria Sucretti watching her niece with the pride of a mother lioness, seeing her cub leave the pride for the first time. Maria stood back with regal elegance and deferred to Lucia, the transition of power witnessed by the most affluent members of society. They all bowed their acceptance. Lucia knew that this would be the defining moment in her life. She would either become all that being the Mistress of Monteforte meant, or, she would be viewed as just a pretty face with no sustenance. Inspiration comes in many ways, and in that flash of a second she felt the presence of her grandmother Lucia, her namesake, and she breathed in her essence and became the woman she was destined to be. She was Mistress Lucia of Monteforte.

She turned toward Maria Sucretti, "Zia Maria, it is because of your love and support that I am able to accept this wonderful honor." She then turned to the audience and spoke "When I came with my sister, Antoinetta, after the devastation years ago of the eruption of Vesuvius, I was but a frightened child. It was my family, especially my Aunt and Uncle who gave me the opportunity to become the woman I am today." Lucia reached out to Giovanni Romano bringing him to her side. "My parents, Donato and Rafaela Banfi and my brothers and sister have been a great support in my life and I thank them from the bottom of my heart."

"I would like to thank all of you who have come here to help me celebrate this most important day. I am humbled by your presence and bid you to enjoy all that Monteforte has to offer. I would, at this time, like to ask my sister Mistress Antoinetta and Lord Tomaso Catalano to come join me." Lucia waited while her sister and her future husband came into the circle. Once they arrived, she interlocked her arms around each of them and said, "I am so happy to announce the upcoming marriage of Mistress Antoinetta Banfi to Lord Tomaso Catalano. Please let us raise a glass to their love and good health." The crowd was yelling "Salute! Bona fortuna!" Lucia kissed both of them and then they left.

"There is one more thing I must do. I would ask my uncle Monsignor Luigi Rizzo to come join me." The priest clad in his finest vestment came to join her. "Dear Zio, you have been my spiritual star, and on this most important day I ask that you give me your blessing." The crowd had become very silent. "Kneel down my beloved niece. May the blessing of Our Lord Jesus Christ, His Beloved Mother, and all the Saints bring you the wisdom to fulfill the responsibility of being the Mistress of Monteforte. May you rule with justice and honor. Nel nome del padre, figlio e Spirito Santo." The big man bent down and lifted his beloved niece to her feet, kissed her with great affection on both cheeks and made the sign of the cross on her forehead. In his deep, bellowing voice he announced "Lucia Banfi the new Mistress of Monteforte!" there rose such a roar of approval from those gathered that the room felt like it shook. Cheers of "Bona Salute" went up throughout the room.

"Lucia this is a special day for me as well" he whispered in her ear "I have been named Bishop of Naples, but I cannot announce it until the Pope makes it official, so I too share in your happiness. I love you my bella cappezzi rossi." He hugged her so tight in his massive arms. "Dear Zio I am so proud of you."

The massive Marcello led a procession of uniformed serving boys and kitchen maids. The music resumed. On a bier carried by six servers was a cake nearly full size of Lucia seated upon her beloved Apollo. It was a breathtaking edible sculpture. Two torchbearers led the way and two brought up the rear. The procession paraded around the ballroom for all to see this incredible work of art. It was perfect down to the slightest detail. Lucia was speechless. A table was carried over and the bearers processed to it and ceremoniously laid down their burden.

The crowd was shouting and clapping, the music was joyous. Marcello came to Lucia "My Mistress I hope you are pleased." "Marcello I am without words at the work and detail of this magnificent sculpture. How did you do this?" Marcello was glowing with pride "That will be a secret I will share with you another time." Lucia could not believe how lifelike it was. "Marcello can we eat it?" "Yes of course you can." Lucia went over to him and threw her arms around him "Oh Marcello I am the luckiest girl in the world. I have so many people who care for me. Thank you so much." The big man bent to one knee and said, "It will be my honor to serve you for the rest of my life." He then kissed her hands. All the servers and kitchen maids came scurrying around Lucia to kiss her and congratulate her. Tears were cascading down her face. "Thank you all she shouted." The crowd was in a frenzy of cheers and shouts.

Giorgio came to her side "Mistress we all love you, and will be honored to serve you in the manner that we have served Mistress Sucretti." "Thank you Giorgio. I love all of you as well. You are not my servants but my family." "Mistress may I have them serve the cake?" "Yes, but first we must allow people to come and see it. It is a work of art. Don't you agree?" "Ah, yes it is, poor Marcello, and his staff have labored for days to creature it." Even as they were speaking, people were coming over to admire it.

Lucia went over to her Aunt Maria and gathered her wise face in her hands and looked into her eyes. "Dear Zia, there are no words to express how I feel right this moment. It is not the fact that you have given me such wealth and power; it is that you have given of yourself. You have given those who have loved and served you for generations. How will I ever be able to repay your generosity?" Maria's eyes filled with tears "Bella, there is no payment more substantial than your love, which you have given to me unconditionally. Before you came I was dead, alone and miserable. Now, I am alive, happy and filled with love and hope. My only regret is that I wish you had come into my life sooner. Lucia I love you as if you were my own daughter. Be careful my beloved child, now that you have wealth and power beyond your imagination, there are those, even family, who would try to take it from you. Be wary. Be strong. Be just."

Her family and many of the invited guests, all showering her with well wishes, suddenly surrounded Lucia. Antoinetta came to her side "Dear Sister I am so proud of you. I love you and wish you all good things." "Antoinetta I too am so happy for you and Tomaso, he will be a wonderful husband. The worse part of you getting married is that you will leave me and Monteforte and for that I am sad." "I will miss Monteforte, but we are not too far away and we will come often. You can ride Apollo to Casa Catalano." "Will you ride to Monteforte?" with that the two sisters laughed.

Giancarlo Marzoni came to stand at her side. "Mistress Lucia this is a great honor for you. I am very happy for your good fortune. I do believe that you will be a formidable ruler." Lucia was smiling at his formality "Lord Marzoni will you promise me something?" The young composer seemed anxious "Of course Mistress. What is it you seek from me?" "Whenever you are in Naples will you come to visit me? I find your company most enjoyable?" For the first time Lucia saw a blush color his cheeks "It would be my honor as well as my pleasure. I am fascinated to discover the private Lucia Banfi, not the public Mistress of Monteforte." "Ah, Lord Marzoni, we are one in the same." Giovanni Romano, with the thoughts implanted by his wife, was watching Lucia and the composer. They certainly made an attractive couple, but he was certain that Maria Sucretti, who understood human nature, better than anyone he ever knew, was right about the young composer. For now, Lord Marzoni was living life to the fullest and basking in his fame and fortune. Giovanni caught the look of fear and anguish in Lucia's face and followed her gaze. He stood there himself in shock.

Lucia was enjoying her little tete-et-tete with the handsome composer, when she was unexpectedly distracted by something. Her attention was drawn to the second story, which overlooked the grand ballroom, and to her terror, there stood the man from the garden, Antonio Sanfranco, under the life size portrait of her grandfather Mateo Rizzo. The likeness was so profound; it appeared as if the portrait had come alive. Lucia was not the only one who noticed. Giovanni Romano saw the intruder and was about to run after him when he disappeared into air as if by magic.

Lucia, those eyes that could penetrate stone, darted to her uncle and he nodded, that he too had seen the intruder. He approached her as if not to create attention. "Yes I saw him. We will talk tomorrow. For now, I will have Giorgio, and his staff, search the castle and alert those on the grounds. Tonight you will bolt your bedchamber door as well as your balcony doors. Sophia will stay in your room, and I will have someone stand outside in the hall. Let us not make a fuss to alert the others, but we must be cautious. For now you will continue to play your part, and I will be on the watch." Lucia listened, did not speak, and only nodded her agreement. Giovanni Romano cradled her face and kissed each cheek "Non ti preoccupare Bella. Vi proteggerà. Ti amo." Now for the first time she spoke "I am frightened Zio, but knowing you are here and will protect me I am already calm. I love you too."

Thankfully, no one saw the scene that had just played out between herself, Antonio Sanfranco and Giovanni Romano. Lucia watched as her uncle, taking long strides, but acting composed, made his way to

Giorgio. Seconds later, she sensed more than saw that an undercurrent of people were watching and searching.

"Mistress, I am wounded you have not heard a word I have said." Lucia her thoughts interrupted came back to her guest. "Lord Marzoni, I do apologize, there is much excitement this evening. When will you and my brother return to Florence?" The young composer smiling broadly replied "Not for two more days? Perhaps you could find some time to see me tomorrow?" Lucia was coloring with anticipation "That would be very nice. Let us meet tomorrow at dawn at the stables. I ride every morning, do you ride?" "Yes of course." "I will see you then Lord Marzoni, but, for now I must see to my other guests."

Not used to being brushed aside by women, Giancarlo Marzoni felt affronted by Lucia. He thought to himself that this woman would be quite the challenge. He smiled to himself and added 'I always love a challenge'. He watched her admiringly as she left in a swirl of skirts, her long torso accented by a tiny waist and full hips. The strawberry mane caressed her back like a shawl thick as silken yarn. He felt a twinge of desire rush to his lower parts. This one would not be easy and secretly he liked that.

Even though the hour was late, the whole castle was abuzz with a pitched frenzy. Lucia knew that for the next few days there would be no rest from the onslaught of visitors. There was a room that had been prepared that was stacked to the rafters with boxes, casks and cases of every gift imaginable. She dreaded the time and energy it would require to send notes of profound gratitude for some useless object or ill tasting wine. That she thought to herself would be an excellent job for poor Sophia.

As Lucia made her rounds throughout the grand ballroom, she constantly kept a watch for her garden intruder. Who was he; and why was he here? She saw that Giorgio had strategically placed serving boys at all corners of the room including the second story. They blended into the fabric of the castle and did not seem out of place. She also knew that both Giorgio and Giovanni Romano were watching her every movement. Lucia at that very moment decided she would not hide and cower from anyone but would learn to protect herself. She would become the hunter not the prey.

AFTERWORD

The journey of Lucia, The Mistress of Monteforte, continues in The Ruby Heiress as we follow Lucia, the beautiful and sensual young heiress to a vast empire, who struggles to maintain her independence in a world dominated by men. Soon to be released will be book three of the trilogy Lucia and the Gypsy's Prophecy.

Write me at MistressLucia@yahoo.com.